AND SO IT BEGINS...

"Our job right now is to keep you safe. The search for Ethwyn and the other Therengians will have to wait. I'm sure the Gods will understand."

She turned to face him, his arms still around her. "Do you really think the Gods take an interest in such things?"

"I suppose I do," he remarked. "Can't you say the same thing for your Saints?"

"An interesting thought," she responded, "and one to which I've not given much reflection. I've never considered myself to be very religious. I suppose that's common for mages."

"So you consider us meeting a chance encounter?" he asked.

"I'd say fortuitous," she confessed, "why? Are you suggesting your Gods brought us together?"

"I'm not saying anything, I'm just glad that we met, whatever the circumstances."

"Me too," she said, "but maybe it's time we moved on?"

"To where?" he asked. "We're already at the edge of the known world, where else can we go?"

"I don't know," she replied, "likely nowhere is safe for long. I'm not sure what to do."

He moved his face closer to hers, kissing her tenderly. At that precise moment, his stomach growled, and she burst into laughter.

"It appears it's time to eat," she said.

He blushed, "So it is!"

"Come along then," she urged, "let's get some clothes on and see what's for breakfast.

ALSO BY PAUL J BENNETT

A Plague in Zeiderbruch

EMBERS
THE FROZEN FLAME: BOOK TWO

PAUL J BENNETT

First Edition: January 2020

ePub ISBN: 978-1-989315-59-0
Mobi ISBN: 978-1-989315-60-6
Apple Books ISBN: 978-1-989315-61-3
Smashwords ISBN: 978-1-989315-62-0
Print ISBN: 978-1-989315-63-7

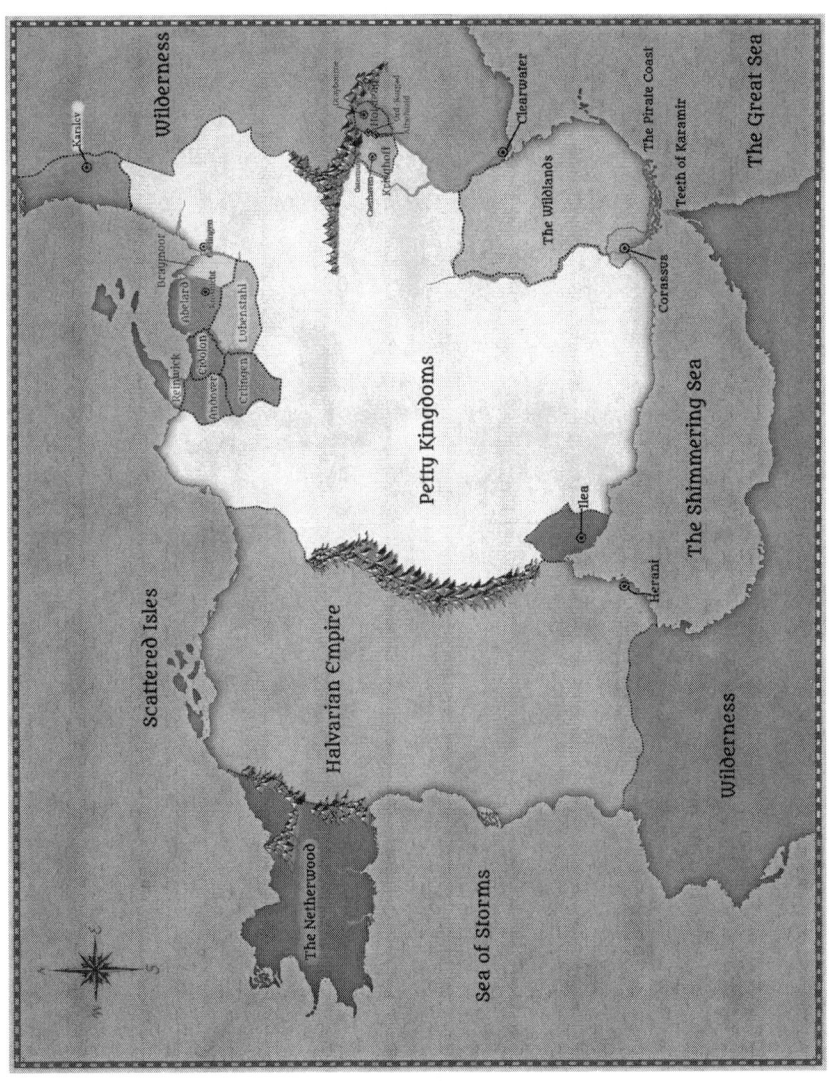

The World of Eiddenwerthe

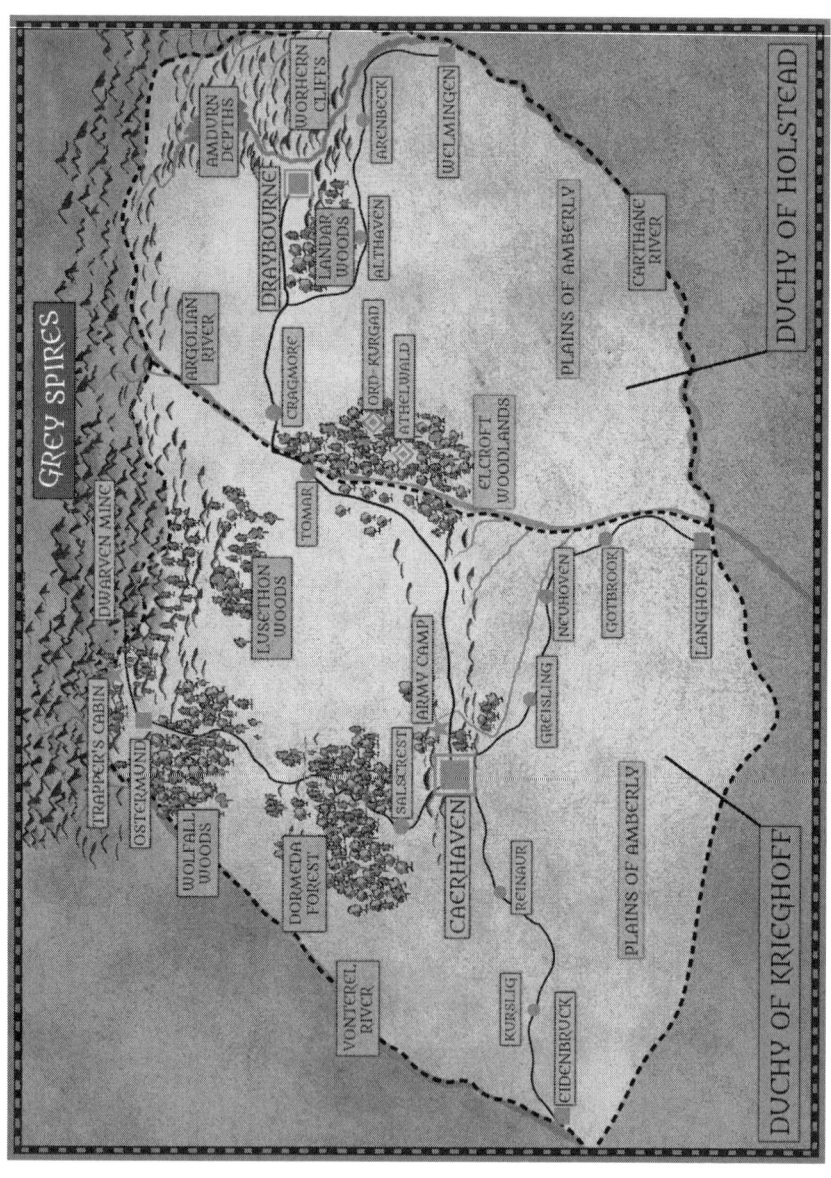

The Duchies of Krieghoff And Holstead

MORNING

Winter 1104 SR*
(Saints Reckoning)

Athgar opened his eyes to see the sleeping form of Natalia beside him, her bare leg laying across him, poking out from beneath the blanket. In the cold morning air, his breath frosted, and he looked over at the fireplace to see nothing but embers, their expected glow all but extinguished.

Calling on his inner spark, he pointed, and moments later, a small fire burst to life, its flames desperately trying to ignite the burned remains. It wouldn't last long, he knew, probably only long enough for him to rise from his bed and place more logs to fuel it, but to do that, he must first extricate himself from Natalia's limbs. He gently lifted her leg, deftly rolling out from beneath her and paused, making sure he hadn't disturbed her slumber.

Athgar stood, pulling a cloak from the back of a nearby chair and wrapped it around his shoulders. The chill was starting to wane, the magical flames driving it from the room, but he knew it wouldn't last. He moved to the fireplace, placing more logs, and waited, entranced by the fire as it slowly danced its way across the wood. The heat warmed him as he crouched, deep in thought. As a wielder of fire, he had learned to control this destructive force of nature, and yet the Orcs had taught him the importance of respecting it. As the flames grew, his mind wandered to more recent events.

After their encounter with the Fire Mage in the great port of Corassus, they knew they couldn't remain there. Thanks to Brother Cyric, they had been given horses, but their lack of riding skills and the cold weather had worn them both out. They had left the city with no clear destination but had finally found refuge here, in Ostermund, a little village in the foothills of the Grey Spires Mountains. It was far removed from the great cities of the Petty Kingdoms, and, he hoped, beyond the reach of Natalia's family.

"Athgar," Natalia called out, "what are you doing?"

He turned his attention back to her. "I'm just warming the place up," he explained. "The fire had burned down, and it was getting chilly."

"Come back to bed," she urged, "and I'll keep you warm."

He smiled as he moved towards the bed where she had rolled onto her back, her dark hair framing her pale face as she looked up at him.

"Well," she said, "what are you waiting for?"

"Can't a fellow admire his mate?" he asked, his face breaking into a grin.

"Is that what I am?" she said in mock seriousness. "Athgar's mate?"

"Oh, you're much more than that," he explained.

"Then come to bed and show me," she invited.

Athgar threw off his robe and climbed into the bed, pulling the covers around them as he snuggled up closer to her, and then she suddenly called out in protest.

"Your feet are cold!" she declared, shrieking in laughter.

"Then let's warm them up together!"

Some time later, Natalia awoke to the room still lit by the fire, filled with its warmth. She lay on her side, with Athgar snuggled up behind her. Deftly removing his arm, she climbed out from beneath his embrace to stand beside the bed and gaze down at him, taking in his youthful appearance. He was brown-haired, like most Therengians, with the patchy beard typical of a twenty-year-old, and she longed to look into his grey eyes, the mark of his race. She could stare into them for hours, she decided, content just to be with him.

Tearing her gaze away from the bed, she moved instead to the window, where the glass was frosted over, evidence of the winter that had descended upon them. Scraping away the frost, she gazed out upon the vista before her. Off in the distance, she could make out the peaks of the Grey Spires, not the biggest mountain range on the Continent, but undoubtedly impressive to one that had never seen such terrain up close.

Natalia longed to stay here, in Athgar's embrace, and spend a lifetime together in peace, but she knew it was not to be. Ever since her escape from the Volstrum, she had become a wanted woman, destined to be forever on the run from the family. They weren't her real family, of course, for she had been born a mere peasant girl, but when her magical potential had manifested early, she had been whisked away to be trained as a Water Mage and inducted into the Stormwind-Sartellian family. Once she completed her training, she had become the first-ever low-born to be inducted into the family as a battle mage, but then they had made known their intentions; she was to be bred with a Fire Mage to produce a powerful offspring.

Looking back down at the bed, she suddenly became keenly aware of the strange twist of fate that had led her to Athgar, or more accurately, he to her. She had balked at the thought of a forced coupling with an unknown Fire Mage, and yet here she was, doing the very thing she had fled from.

Athgar shifted slightly in his sleep, bringing a smile to her lips. He was no ordinary Fire Mage, she knew, for the Orcs had taught him a disciplined way of controlling his powers, rather than the full-strength magic expected of a Volstrum graduate.

Natalia turned her attention back to the window, staring off at the distant peaks to the north. Somewhere, beyond those mountains, lay Karslev, and the Volstrum. Was there any place that was free from their influence? She involuntarily shivered.

"Nervous?" Athgar's reassuring voice broke through her thoughts. He had risen from the bed, and she saw his reflection in the glass as he walked up and placed his arms around her.

"Not with you here," she replied. "You make me feel safe."

"Then what is it?"

"How long will we have to be on the run?" she asked.

"It depends," he responded. "How long will the family keep looking for you?"

"They'll never give up!" she admitted.

"Then we'll keep running forever," he promised. "We'll do whatever it takes to keep you safe."

"I can't ask that of you," she said. "You deserve a chance to live, to raise a family."

"Nonsense," he argued, "I am living. It's you that brought joy to my life. We'll see this through to the end, even if we have to destroy the entire family ourselves. In any case, we're safe here."

"How can you say that?" she asked.

"We've been here for almost two weeks with no sign of the family," he explained.

"But what of your own people?" she asked. "And you still have to find your sister, Ethwyn. I'm only getting in the way."

"No," he insisted, "you're not. If they've survived this long, they're still alive, and they'll likely remain that way. Our job right now is to keep you safe. The search for Ethwyn and the other Therengians will have to wait. I'm sure the Gods will understand."

She turned to face him, his arms still around her. "Do you really think the Gods take an interest in such things?"

"I suppose I do," he remarked. "Can't you say the same thing for your Saints?"

"An interesting thought," she responded, "and one to which I've not given much reflection. I've never considered myself to be very religious. I suppose that's common for mages."

"So you consider us meeting a chance encounter?" he asked.

"I'd say fortuitous," she confessed, "why? Are you suggesting your Gods brought us together?"

"I'm not saying anything, I'm just glad that we met, whatever the circumstances."

"Me too," she said, "but maybe it's time we moved on?"

"To where?" he asked. "We're already at the edge of the known world, where else can we go?"

"I don't know," she replied, "likely nowhere is safe for long. I'm not sure what to do."

He moved his face closer to hers, kissing her tenderly. At that precise moment, his stomach growled, and she burst into laughter.

"It appears it's time to eat," she said.

He blushed, "So it is!"

"Come along then," she urged, "let's get some clothes on and see what's for breakfast.

BREAKFAST

Winter 1104 SR

They made their way down the stairs and into the common room. The Owl was a busy place, even at this early hour, and they found themselves waiting for a private table rather than sitting with strangers.

Flames crackled from the fireplace, filling the area with its warmth. Even from where they were standing, they could feel the heat, bolstered, no doubt, from the warm bodies packed into the place. Natalia was soon sweating, though Athgar, probably due to his ability with fire, showed no such discomfort.

"Well?" said Athgar. "What do you think?"

"Of what?" she answered. "This isn't the first time we've come down for breakfast."

"Yes, but is it worth waiting for? Or should we go somewhere else?"

As if in answer to his question, the door opened, and a gust of cold swept through the room as a lone visitor entered, closing the door behind him.

Natalia shivered, then looked at Athgar. "I think we should wait," she said.

He laughed, "I thought Water Mages liked the cold?"

"We like water, not necessarily the cold," she replied.

"But you cast shards of ice, and you can make a wall of ice. Aren't those cold-based spells?"

"They are," she admitted, "but do you like sitting in a fire?"

He grinned, obviously enjoying the discussion. "No, I suppose I see your point."

They fell into a comfortable silence while Natalia scanned the room, searching for someone who might be leaving. When she returned her attention to Athgar, it was to see him staring at her, a smile playing upon his lips.

"Like what you see?" she asked.

"I do," he quickly answered, "but I was just admiring your hair. It makes you look so different."

She smiled, a common enough action these days. When she had fled the Volstrum, a scant three months ago, she had been ill-prepared for her journey. Her hair had been elaborately coiffed, her clothes worthy of the finest of courts, and her shoes the most stylish imaginable. Now, her hair was shoulder-length, her dress plain, and her feet were snuggled into warm boots. How far she had come in such a short time, she thought. The family would barely recognize her, or so she hoped.

Raised voices drew her attention. It appeared the inn's new visitor was taking exception to his treatment.

"It seems there's trouble," said Natalia.

Athgar looked at the bar. The innkeeper, a kindly fellow by the name of Lethrum Barnard, was throwing his arms up in exasperation.

"I don't care," he was saying, "I cannot give you room and board without payment. I'm not running a charity here, I've expenses to pay."

"And I told you," the stranger insisted, "it will only be a matter of a few days until my shipment comes in."

"It appears," said Natalia, "that the Dwarf is in distress."

"Dwarf?" Athgar noted. "What makes you say he's a Dwarf?"

"Look at his physique," she noted. "He has the broad shoulders typical of his race, far more so than Humans, and his head is larger in proportion to his body."

"I've never met a Dwarf," said Athgar. "What are they like?"

"I've not met any either," confessed Natalia, "but they are rumoured to be a stubborn race."

"What makes you say that?" he asked.

"We learned about them at the Volstrum," she said. "Their Earth Mages can be very powerful, and they're highly valued at sieges for their knowledge of stone crafting."

"That doesn't tell me much about them as a race," he said. "Surely, not every Dwarf has magic?"

"No," she admitted, "likely the percentage of casters is low, much as it is amongst Humans."

"I suppose that would make sense," said Athgar.

"This fellow seems to be in some type of trouble," she added. "Do you think we should help him?"

"Why should we help a perfect stranger?" he asked.

"Because it's the right thing to do," she retorted. "Wouldn't it have been nice if someone had helped you in Draybourne? Perhaps you wouldn't have lost all your possessions?"

"I suppose," he mumbled.

"You need to learn to trust people, Athgar. Not everyone is out to get us, you know."

"Who says I don't trust people, I trusted Brother Cyric didn't I?"

"You did," she said, "and that worked out for the best. Sometimes you just need to have a little more faith in others."

"I have faith in you," he insisted.

"Of course you do," she said, "but the real question is whether or not you're willing to put your trust in someone you don't know."

"Let's find out, shall we?"

Natalia smiled, "Does that mean you agree?"

"Yes, all right," he said, "let's help the Dwarf."

"I'm glad you said that. What changed your mind?"

"It's you," he confessed, "you bring out the best in me."

"Or worst," she suggested. "I suppose it depends on your point of view."

The Dwarf's voice was growing louder, causing more than a few of the patrons to start taking an interest in the discussion.

Athgar moved closer, getting the innkeeper's attention. "May we be of assistance?" he asked.

"Master Athgar," said Lethrum, "would you be so kind as to show this... interloper out the door?"

"What seems to be the problem?" said Natalia.

"This Dwarf-"

"Belgast," the Dwarf insisted, "the name is Belgast Ridgehand."

"This Belgast," Lethrum continued, "expects me to put him up with a room when he has no funds at his disposal."

"Is this true?" asked Athgar.

"In a manner of speaking," Belgast answered. "I have plenty coming, you see, but I find myself temporarily bereft."

"What funds?" enquired Natalia, her interest piqued.

"My business associates are running an iron mine in the Grey Spires," the Dwarf explained. "They mine the ore, smelting it down into ingots, then ship it here by wagon. There's one due any day now."

"But surely you'd still have to sell the ingots," said Natalia.

"I already have customers lined up for them," Belgast answered. "Smiths mostly."

Athgar looked at the innkeeper, but the old man simply shrugged his shoulders.

It was Natalia that offered a solution. "What if we lent him enough for a couple of days?" she asked.

"Are you sure?" said Athgar. "We hardly know him."

She turned to the Dwarf, "Well, Belgast? What say we loan you what you need? You can pay us back when your shipment comes in?"

The Dwarf bowed deeply. "I would be most thankful," he said.

"Then it's settled," said Athgar, turning to the innkeeper. "Give Belgast a room, and we'll pay for it. Do you want the crowns right now?"

"That's not necessary," said Lethrum. "You can pay when you settle your own room. How many days would you like?"

Natalia looked at the Dwarf.

"Three days should be sufficient," offered Belgast. "It's due in anytime now."

"Then three days it is," said Natalia.

The innkeeper looked relieved. "Very well. I'll have someone prepare a room for you, Master Dwarf. In the meantime, I'm afraid you'll have to wait. Might I suggest you take a seat?"

"Why don't you join us," offered Athgar, "we were just about to have breakfast."

"Yes," added Natalia, "I think a table has just opened up. Won't you join us?"

"I believe I will," said Belgast, "and once again, thank you for your assistance."

Natalia led them through the crowd, sitting as a server cleared away the previous guests' plates.

"This looks nice," said Athgar, "and close to the fire, too."

"Perhaps a little too close," noted Natalia. "I'll be sweating through the entire meal."

"Nonsense," said Athgar. He looked at the fire, raising his hand slightly as he did. Words of power issued from his mouth, barely audible in the crowded room, and then the flames shrunk, the heat noticeably less. "How's that?" he asked.

"You're a flame wielder?" said Belgast.

"A master of flame, actually," corrected Natalia.

"Impressive," noted the Dwarf. "I've never met a Human mage before."

"And now you've met two," said Athgar. "Natalia, here, is a Water Mage."

"A strange combination," said Belgast. "How did you two meet, if you don't mind my asking?"

"We met in Draybourne," said Athgar.

"Yes," Natalia agreed. "I thought he was attacking me, and I knocked him down with an ice spell."

"I was, in fact, trying to help her," the Therengian quickly added.

"Draybourne? Where's that?" asked the Dwarf.

"It's in the Duchy of Holstead," said Athgar.

"Isn't that on the border of Krieghoff?" asked Belgast.

"It is," said Natalia. "Have you been there?"

The Dwarf let out a laugh, a rumbling noise that sounded like he was choking. "I should say so," he said at last. "In fact, you're there now."

"I don't understand," said Athgar.

Belgast looked at him in surprise. "Ostermund is in Krieghoff," he explained. "Did you not know that?"

"No," Athgar confessed. He turned to Natalia.

"Don't look at me," she said, "all I know is we're in the middle of nowhere. If what the Dwarf says is true-"

"It is," insisted Belgast.

"Then we're close to where we first met," she said.

"Close being subjective," said the Dwarf. "Caerhaven lies to our south, but it's still some distance away. Likely a week or more by road."

"If that's true," offered Natalia, "then we are within two weeks from Ord-Kurgad." She saw Belgast's look of confusion. "That's the Orc village where Athgar learned his magic."

"You were raised by Orcs?" asked the Dwarf.

"No," insisted Athgar, "I was raised in a place called Athelwald. It's located on the border of Holstead. When my village was burned to the ground, I was taken in by the Orcs. They're the ones that taught me to wield fire."

"Remarkable," said Belgast. "I've never heard of a Human being taken in by Orcs before."

"I'm the only one that I know of," Athgar replied. "Tell me, do your people get along with the Orcs?"

"I assume, when you say 'your people', you're referring to Dwarves?"

"I am," said Athgar, "though I apologize if I've caused offense."

"My people are much like Humans," explained Belgast, "each with their own beliefs and follies. I can only speak for myself when I say that I have nothing against the Orcs. The truth is, I've had very little interaction with them. Dwarves are very pragmatic people, seldom living in areas where the green folk dwell, but I know we've traded with them in the past. How is your own race when it comes to them?"

"My people have always traded with them," offered Athgar. "How about you, Natalia?"

"We learned about them at the academy," she replied, "but until we met one in Corassus, I'd never seen one in person."

"So you went to an academy?" said Belgast. "I assume you mean a school of the arcane arts? I hear they're quite common."

"Not as common as you might think," said Natalia, "but yes, that's where I learned to control water in all its forms."

"I had no idea there were others," said Athgar.

"Why not?" asked Belgast. "Surely you didn't think mages trained themselves?"

"There are such things as wild mages," protested Natalia.

"Yes," agreed the Dwarf, "but they're notoriously unreliable."

"What's your background?" asked Natalia. "You mentioned you had some business associates. How did you get involved with them?"

"They're my distant cousins," he said. "I hail from Kragen-Tor, have you heard of it?"

"I'm afraid not," noted Natalia, "but the name reminds me of Kargen, an Orc friend of Athgar's."

"No doubt," said Belgast. "Dwarves and Orcs share similar words in their languages."

"Why is that?" said Athgar.

"We're both ancient races," explained the Dwarf. "It is said that when the first races were created, they all spoke the common tongue of our Ancestors."

"You seem well educated for a merchant," noted Natalia.

"That's because I wasn't always a merchant," noted Belgast. "I was raised as a scholar in the court of King Haglarith."

"I take it, he's the King of Kragen-Tor?" asked Athgar.

"He was," admitted Belgast, "but he died some five years ago. My position was no longer needed under his successor, and so I struck out on my own. As it turns out, my cousins had a business venture in mind."

"Bringing you here?" said Natalia.

"Yes," the Dwarf admitted. "Of course, it took some time to find the ore, and then even more to get everything up and running. While they were busy digging it out, I was lining up customers. I've always been good at negotiation, it's one of my strong suits."

"Except when it comes to innkeepers," observed Athgar.

"Well, yes, I must admit to failing there. Thank the Gods you came to my assistance, or I'd be out in the cold, freezing my toes off."

"So this is the first shipment," Natalia enquired, "the one you're waiting for?"

"Yes," Belgast replied. "I received word two weeks ago that they'd found what they were looking for. They assured me they'd have the ore here by month's end."

"That was two days ago," mused Athgar.

"So it was," said Belgast, "but it was only an estimate. Still, they promised to ship what they had by that date. I can't imagine what caused the delay."

"Hopefully, it's on its way even as we speak," noted Natalia.

A serving girl appeared, depositing three tankards on their table and then taking their orders.

"What's this?" asked the Dwarf, sniffing experimentally.

"It's a local delicacy," answered Athgar. "They call it iceberry wine."

"Never heard of it," noted Belgast.

"It's quite nice," said Natalia, "and a little sweet."

"Is it strong?"

"No," she countered, "you could drink it all day with no sign of intoxication."

"Then what's the point?" said the Dwarf, wrinkling his nose.

"It's pleasing to the palate," offered Natalia.

Athgar took a deep draft, then lowered his own tankard as he licked his lips, "Delicious."

The Dwarf eyed him suspiciously while Natalia delicately sipped her own drink. Belgast was in an apparent state of indecision. On the one hand, he distrusted the strange brew, but on the other, he was parched. Finally, succumbing to his thirst, he lifted the tankard and drank deeply. Athgar watched Belgast drain half the cup, then set it down, wiping his mouth with his forearm.

"Well?" asked the Therengian.

"Not bad," the Dwarf replied, "though I might have to sample some more to make a more definitive answer."

"Is Dwarven wine strong?" asked Natalia.

"Aye," replied Belgast, "though you'd more likely find us drinking ale, or better yet, mead."

"Isn't mead brewed from honey?" said Athgar. "I would think that it would be hard to find in the mountains."

"It is," admitted the Dwarf, "but we trade for it. Elven mead is the best, in my opinion."

"You've never tried Therengian mead," argued Athgar.

"Therengian?" said Belgast in surprise. He leaned forward, looking Athgar directly in the eyes. "I should have noticed," he said, sitting back in his chair in delight. "It's the eyes, you see, gives them away every time."

"I take it you've met one before?" asked Natalia.

"They're common enough in this area of the country," replied the Dwarf. "This all used to be part of Therengia, you know."

"What can you tell me about them?" said Natalia. "Athgar is short on some of the details."

"They were an ancient realm," explained the Dwarf, "covering about a third of the present-day Petty Kingdoms. They fell apart about five hundred years ago, though parts of the old kingdom held on for decades before they, too, were conquered."

"I had no idea," the Water Mage remarked. "Were they powerful?"

Belgast nodded as he took a sip, then put down his tankard to continue. "They were one of the largest empires, though of course they never used that term. They were just 'Therengia'. I bet if they were around today, even Halvaria would see them as a threat."

Natalia's eyes widened, for the Halvarian Empire was immense, occupying most of the western reaches of the Continent. They had grown from a small kingdom into the most powerful military force in the land, and in so doing had become everyone's worst nightmare.

"And now that Therengia's gone, there's no one left to stand up to Halvaria," she said.

"Precisely," agreed Belgast. He took another sip, then raised his hand to get the serving girl's attention, ordering another round. "Tell me," he said at last, "what brings you two to Ostermund?"

"As we indicated earlier," explained Natalia, "we're both mages. We travel the land and hire on where needed."

"That being the case," said Belgast, "why come here? Surely somewhere with more water would have more business?"

"We're taking a break," added Athgar. "It's been a hectic few months for us, and we came here to recover."

"Well, there's talk of war," said the Dwarf. "I suppose once that starts, you'll both be in demand. Dukes love hiring mages in times of conflict."

"Why do you say that?" asked Natalia.

"It's the way of Humans," said Belgast, "always seeking more power. It's been that way ever since the fall of Therengia. Sometimes, I think they're just fighting over the scraps of the old kingdom."

The innkeeper appeared at their table, waiting patiently until they noticed him.

"I apologize for the interruption," he said, "but Master Belgast's room is ready."

"Just in time, too," the Dwarf said, stifling a yawn.

"What of your food?" asked Athgar.

"You have it," said Belgast. "I need a good rest."

"And the extra wine you ordered?" prompted Natalia.

"Ah," he said, "now that, I'll take with me. Lead on, Master Innkeeper, and tell your serving girl to bring the wine."

"Right this way," said Lethrum, leading the Dwarf away.

The two mages watched him disappear through the crowded room.

"An interesting fellow," mused Athgar.

"I agree," said Natalia, "and I doubt that's the last we'll see of him." She tore her eyes from the departing Dwarf and turned back to Athgar. The Therengian was staring at something through the crowd, and she followed his gaze to see the serving girl making her way towards them, three plates in hand.

"Ah," said Athgar, as she placed the food before them, "my favourite, two breakfasts!"

ABOUT TOWN

Winter 1104 SR

Three days later, they were out walking the village, their breath frosting in the cold air. Snow covered the ground, sending a chill into Athgar, but Natalia seemed to like the crispness of the day.

"It's wonderful here," she said. "I wish we could live here forever."

"So do I," he answered, "but we will need to move on soon before the family discovers our whereabouts."

"Where do we go from here?" she asked.

"I've been thinking about that very topic," he answered. "Belgast told us we're in Krieghoff. That means Holstead lies to the east."

"That's where we met," said Natalia, "in Draybourne, the capital, but I have no desire to return there."

"Nor I," he added, "but we have to go somewhere."

"What about the Orcs?" she asked. "They're on the border between the two duchies, aren't they?"

"They are," he replied. "Their land lies on the Holstead side of the Argolian River."

"Maybe we could visit them?" she suggested. "I'd love to meet Kargen and Shaluhk, not to mention baby Agar. I've never seen a baby Orc before."

"That's not surprising," he noted. "Until we got to Corassus, you hadn't seen an Orc at all, let alone an Orc youngling."

"I suppose that's true," she admitted. "So what do you think? Shall we make a trip to Ord-Kurgad in our near future?"

"Certainly," he said, "though maybe we could enjoy another few days here first."

"I'd like that," she responded.

"Something smells good," Athgar remarked as they walked down the street.

"That's a bakery," said Natalia. "Let's go and have a peek, shall we? It's bound to be warm in there, and the smell is making me hungry."

Their noses led them to a little shop that sat halfway down the street. They entered to see a small room with a counter, behind which freshly baked goods sat on the shelves.

The customer in front of them gathered up a few loaves of bread and placed them in a wicker basket, then dropped some coins in the proprietor's hands. Edging past the duo, she opened the door to return to the chilly mountain air outside.

Natalia stepped forward, "It smells good in here."

"As it should," the proprietor answered. "Tell me, what can I get for you today?"

"What would you suggest?" she said.

"We have a variety of loaves," he responded, "along with some more exotic options."

"What's that?" asked Athgar, pointing at a strange pile of darkly coloured biscuits.

"Those," the owner answered, "are Dwarven stonecakes."

"Never heard of them," said Natalia.

"I have," said Athgar, "though I've never seen one."

"They look like lumps of coal," she said, wrinkling her nose.

"You're not far off the mark," explained the owner, "but they're a popular item among hunters."

"Why?" she asked.

"They last forever," he said in reply, "and they don't go bad."

"I'll try one," said Athgar.

The owner handed one over, and the Therengian took a bite, crunching it noisily.

"It's very hard," he complained.

"That's because you're eating it the wrong way," the owner remarked. "You have to put the whole thing in your mouth and then let it absorb your spit. It'll soften, becoming more like a pudding."

Athgar looked at the man, wondering if he was the butt of a joke, but when he saw no malice, he popped the remainder into his mouth, waiting as it softened. Natalia watched, expecting him to spit it out, but much to her surprise, his eyes widened, and he smiled, his mouth still full.

"Surprisingly good," he mumbled.

"You should eat them sparingly," the owner warned. "They're considered a light meal."

Athgar chewed the remainder of the stonecake, revelling in its flavour. When he was done, he looked at Natalia. "Let's get some," he suggested. "We can use them when we finally decide to move on."

"Do you think they'll last that long?" she asked. "I think you'll have them all eaten by dinner time."

"Well," he replied, "they ARE good."

"Fine, we'll take a dozen," she said. "And don't forget to charge us for the one that Athgar just ate."

"Nonsense," replied the owner, "that was a free sample." He grabbed up a handful of the lumps and bundled them into a cloth. "Will there be anything else?"

"No, that's all for now," she replied, dropping some coins onto the table.

They stepped back outside, the sudden change in temperature taking their breath away.

"My, that's cold," said Athgar.

"You're the master of flame," said Natalia. "Why don't you use your magic to warm us up?"

"I have to respect the fire," the Therengian retorted.

"To the point of freezing?" she asked.

"I suppose you do have a point." He gesticulated, uttering words of power in a low voice. Moments later, Natalia felt a warmth flood over her.

"How do you do that?" she asked.

"I'm a Fire Mage, remember?"

"No, I mean how do you cast a spell and remain so quiet about it?"

"It's not about how loudly you cast," he responded, "it's about controlling the magic. Why? Can't you do that?"

"No," she replied. "We were taught to always project the words with as much force as possible."

"Yet another difference in our training," Athgar mused.

"You'll have to teach me that," she said.

"Agreed," he added, "as long as you continue to teach me to read."

She smiled. "I do that because I like it," she said. "One is not dependent on the other."

As they wandered farther down the street, Natalia paused to look into a shop window where a leatherworker was hard at work, making shoes for someone.

Athgar noticed her interest. "Missing shoes?" he asked.

"Boots are much more useful for travelling," she answered, "but I do miss having something on my feet when I'm indoors. I'm not like you, walking around the room in my bare feet."

"I've done that since I was a child," he mused, "but hopefully, one day, we'll be able to settle down, and you can have all the shoes you want."

"I'd like that," she responded, "though I don't think I'd need more than one pair." She continued watching the shoemaker ply his trade.

Athgar, distracted by a sound, looked across the street to see a familiar face, that of Belgast Ridgehand. The Dwarf was standing in the doorway to a warehouse, deep in conversation with a man.

"There's Belgast," said Athgar. "Shall we go and see how he's faring?"

"Yes," said Natalia, "we haven't seen him for days."

They crossed the street, the Dwarf turning away from his conversation with a dour look on his face.

"Greetings," called out the Therengian.

"Athgar, Natalia," the Dwarf called back, "good to see you both."

"Problem?" prompted Athgar.

"As a matter of fact, there is," said Belgast. "It seems my wagon has still not come in."

"What is this place?" asked Natalia.

"A trading post," explained the Dwarf. "It's useful for anyone shipping goods, and it's where my cousins leased their wagon."

"You think something happened to your cousins?" said Natalia.

"I'm beginning to think it's a distinct possibility," said Belgast. "You mentioned that you were both mages for hire. I wonder if I might be able to hire you to accompany me?"

"Accompany you where?" said Athgar.

"To the mine, of course," the Dwarf answered, "though I'm hoping we'll run across my cousins along the way."

"We'd be happy to help," said Athgar.

"Yes," added Natalia, "but you don't have to pay us."

"I'd be much indebted to you," said Belgast.

"When would you like to head out?" asked Athgar.

"Best to start in the morning," said the Dwarf. "We wouldn't get far today before the sun goes down. Do you have horses?"

"We do," answered Natalia, "and you?"

"I have a pony in the local stable."

"Then it's settled," said Athgar. "Let's meet tomorrow morning in front of the Owl."

"Excellent," said the Dwarf, "and when we've recovered my ore, I'll treat you both to a magnificent feast, and pay you back what I owe you for the room, of course."

"You're making me hungry already," said Athgar.

"You're always hungry," teased Natalia.

"Tell us more about this mine," said Athgar. "Where is it, precisely?"

"It's a few days travel from here," explained Belgast, "along a trail that takes you through the Grey Spires."

"There's a pass through the mountains?" asked Athgar.

"Of course," answered the Dwarf, "but we're not going all the way through. The iron mine is on this side of the pass, up a side trail."

"How rough is this terrain?" asked Natalia.

"Not rough at all," said Belgast, "and it's wide enough for a wagon to pass, so the riding shouldn't be a problem at all."

"What am I missing here?" asked Athgar.

"What do you mean?" said Belgast.

"If the trail is so easy, why do you need us?" he asked.

"I don't know what happened to my cousins," explained Belgast. "There could be a wild animal on the loose, or bandits, or maybe they came down sick? I really don't know what we're going to find once we arrive."

"So you've been to this mine before?" asked Athgar.

"I have. When we were first looking at digging there. Of course, it wasn't a mine at that time, just some iron deposits. The big strike didn't come until later."

"Just how many cousins do you have working at the mine?" asked Natalia.

"Only three," said Belgast. "The intention was to hire more once we proved its feasibility, using the profits from the early dig."

"How does one mine iron?" enquired Athgar. "I assume you just dig it out?"

"Not quite," said Belgast. "We dig the raw minerals, but then we have to fire up a furnace and heat iron and coal. The result is called black iron, and that's what we sell to the smiths."

"Is black iron expensive?" asked Natalia.

"Not particularly, but we should still manage to make some profit. Using our own furnace, we save the smith a lot of work, and that's what lets us charge a little more, allowing us to maximize our earnings."

"This furnace you speak of," said Athgar, "did you cart one all the way to the mine?"

"No," said Belgast, "that would have been too difficult. We made one there. That, by the way, was the most expensive part of the operation."

"So if I'm to understand correctly, you don't feel that anyone would, for example, attack the shipment?"

"No, why would they?" answered the Dwarf. "It's not like anyone else would have buyers lined up for it."

"Anything else we should know about?" asked Athgar.

"You should dress warmly," Belgast warned. "The snow can come in quickly that high up, and you don't want to freeze to death."

"We won't freeze," said Athgar, "not while I'm alive, at any rate."

"Why would you say that?" asked the Dwarf.

"Athgar is a Fire Mage, remember?" said Natalia. "He can use magic to keep us warm."

"I wouldn't suggest you put all your faith in magic. It can be dispelled, you know."

"We're both mages," said Athgar, "so of course we're going to have faith in our magic, but your point is still valid. We'll take care to dress warmly."

"Well," said the Dwarf, "if we're to set off tomorrow, I've things to see to. I'll see you in the morning."

Belgast trundled off, leaving Athgar and Natalia standing where they were.

"Strange sort," noted Athgar.

"Indeed," said Natalia, "but you can't really blame him, can you? He has a lot on his mind."

"I suppose he does," agreed Athgar.

INTO THE MOUNTAINS

Winter 1104 SR

The next morning saw them seated in the Owl's common room once
more. Athgar arranged for their horses to be brought round while
Natalia settled the bill. They were soon standing out front, waiting, as
Belgast rode into view.

"I see you made it," the Dwarf called out.

"Of course," said Athgar. "Are you all set?"

"I am."

Athgar climbed into the saddle, looking decidedly uncomfortable.
Natalia, though equally as unskilled, did likewise, but managed to at least
look like she knew what she was doing.

"I take it," said Belgast, "that you don't ride very often?"

"What makes you say that?" asked the Therengian.

"I don't think I've seen anyone look more uncomfortable," said the
Dwarf. "Perhaps we would have been better to rent a wagon?"

"You can do that?" said Athgar, hopefully.

"If you have enough coins," said the Dwarf, "you can rent anything."

Athgar turned to Natalia, but she shook her head. "No, we need to get
going. We can't hang around here all day, not to mention we don't have the
funds to waste on such frivolities."

"Very well," said Athgar, "but my backside will not be happy."

Now that they were properly settled into their saddles, they set off, the

Dwarf leading. The trail they were following took them through the village, then out, eastward, along a meandering path.

"The first part of the way is quite flat," explained Belgast, "but then we turn north and head into the hills. The terrain there will become more uneven, with numerous curves to the road."

"Will we see the mountains?" asked Natalia.

"You can see them now," said Athgar.

"I think she wants to know if we'll be IN the mountains, not just looking at them," said Belgast. "That won't happen until tomorrow afternoon. From that point on, the going gets rougher."

"Rougher, how?" wondered the Therengian. "I thought you told us it should be no problem?"

"The climbs will be a little steeper, that's all," said the Dwarf, "no need to worry yourself. After all, my cousins managed to take a wagon down this path."

Natalia looked skyward. "The clouds look to be moving in," she remarked. "We could be in for some snow."

"Maybe we should seek shelter?" suggested Athgar.

"Nonsense," said the Dwarf, "we've miles to go yet, and the clouds might just blow over."

"And if they don't?" prompted Natalia.

"Then we'll seek shelter at that point," grumbled Belgast.

"Is that wise?" asked Natalia.

"It's only snow," snapped the Dwarf as he rode ahead.

Natalia turned to look at Athgar, who was trotting along behind her, "What do you think?"

"I think our Dwarf friend is in a hurry," he replied. "We'll keep our eyes on the clouds, but if they worsen, I say we build a shelter. Do you have any spells that would help us?"

"I suppose I could use wall of ice," she said, "that should help block the wind."

"Better than that, I would say," said Athgar. "You could cast four of them and make a shelter, couldn't you?"

"I could certainly make four walls," she said, "but I doubt they'd be big enough to protect us AND the horses, and I can't make a roof."

"Why not?" he asked. "Can't you just cast a wall sideways?"

"I'm afraid my magic doesn't work that way," she replied. "What we really need is an actual shelter, maybe something in amongst the trees?"

"If you can make your ice walls, I can see to the roof," said Athgar. "I've got my axe, and there are enough trees around that we can cut boughs off to make a roof if we have to."

"Good idea," she said. "In the meantime, we'll keep our eyes on the look-out. If a storm does brew up, we'll head for the nearest trees."

They rode on in silence. Natalia kept glancing upward, fearful of the coming storm, while Athgar swept his gaze to either side, continually seeking out small clearings where a shelter might be hastily constructed.

Belgast, however, kept up a brisk pace, despite the fact that he was only on a pony. Like him, the beast seemed tireless, and Athgar began to wonder if there wasn't some kind of magic in play. He brought up this very topic with Natalia.

"Does the fellow never tire?" he asked.

"He's a Dwarf," she said. "They have a robust constitution. It's said they can march for days without stopping."

"Really?" said Athgar.

"I doubt it's days," she replied, "but the fact is they can keep marching long after others must rest."

"But shouldn't his pony slow down?" he suggested.

"It's a mountain pony," Natalia replied, "and Dwarves don't weigh as much as us."

"Well, I know I'm growing tired," said Athgar. "Is he going to allow us to rest, or are we to simply collapse from exhaustion?"

"I think I'll suggest a short halt," said Natalia. "My posterior could certainly use a rest."

"I can rub it for you if you wish," he suggested.

Natalia laughed, dispelling, at least for a brief moment, some of her fatigue. She urged her horse forward, coming closer to the Dwarf.

"Belgast," she called out, "can we take a short rest?"

The Dwarf halted, turning his pony sideways to the trail. He stared at her for a moment, a slight look of irritation on his face.

"Very well," he finally answered, "it's about time to eat anyway."

Belgast lowered himself from the saddle, a task made all the more diffi-cult by his short stature. Removing some food from his stores, he then tossed his pack to the ground, using it as a seat.

Athgar dismounted, rummaging around his own sling bag to retrieve the stonecakes.

"Here," he said, handing one to Natalia.

The Water Mage took the offering, tossing it into her mouth and then chewing it as she lowered herself from the saddle. She stretched out her legs, then rubbed her lower back, which was aching from the long hours in the saddle.

"Warm enough?" asked Athgar.

"I'm fine," she replied, "and you?"

"Warmer than I thought I'd be," he confessed. "How about you, Belgast?" The Dwarf popped something into his mouth, crunching it noisily as he talked, "I'm fine."

Athgar was about to say more when he saw a blur of white race past at a tremendous speed, like a galloping horse. One moment they were all chatting amiably, the next, Natalia's horse lay in a pool of blood, turning the snow crimson.

Athgar leaped to his feet and called out, "What was that?"

Natalia stood, her hands ready to cast, her eyes darting around. "I don't see anything," she yelled back.

Belgast ran to his pony and pulled his weapon of choice from the saddle, a pickaxe. They all instinctively moved closer to each other, then turned, forming a small triangle.

Athgar saw it first; an explosion of snow as whatever it was leaped, its white form blending in with the terrain. It crossed the distance to him too quickly for him to adequately react, and when he threw his axe, it missed by a wide margin. The creature rushed past, knocking him from his feet and careening into the Dwarf, who sailed through the air, landing in a drift, still clutching his pickaxe.

Natalia was quicker to react. As it soared past Athgar, she let loose with a spell, sending forth shards of ice to strike the creature in its hindquarters, drawing blood. It fell to the ground, all but disappearing, save for the trail of blood that revealed its most recent location.

"Where did it go?" shouted Athgar, who had wheeled around.

Natalia pointed, "It's hidden somewhere in the snow. It seems to be able to blend into its background."

Athgar's eyes followed the trail of blood. "We need to flush it out into the open."

"Any suggestions?" asked Belgast.

"I'm guessing it's native to this area," said Natalia. "That likely means it's used to the cold environment. Do you think your fire would drive it out of hiding?"

"It's worth a try," replied the Therengian as he began gesticulating while he uttered words of power. Moments later, a streak of fire shot out from his fingertips, lancing across the distance to follow the trail of blood. He had deliberately aimed high, so the flame struck nothing but air, but for just a moment, the heat could be felt, and the snow beneath it melted.

Without warning, a great roar issued forth and the creature rose, turning to face them. It was no taller than a man, but significantly bulkier and covered in coarse white hair. Its head reminded Athgar of the seals they had seen near Corassus, but then its long, sharp teeth dispelled any thoughts of it being timid.

Natalia cast once more, this time sending a solitary spike of ice down-range where it struck the creature solidly, pushing it back, the shard protruding from its chest. Letting out a final bellow, it fell back into the snow where it lay, unmoving.

Athgar trotted forward, picking up his axe. He halted just shy of the body, then advanced more slowly, half expecting the thing to leap back up to its feet. The creature let out a final breath of air, then expired. As soon as the life left its body, the fur turned a yellowish-white colour, standing out in stark contrast to the newly fallen snow that had, until now, hidden its presence.

"What is that thing?" he thought out loud.

"It's an icora," said Belgast, staring at the body.

"Never heard of it," said Athgar.

"They are creatures of legend," the Dwarf declared, "able to turn invisible at will."

"Well," said Natalia, "it definitely didn't turn invisible, but it was hard to see."

"Yes," agreed Belgast, "and very fast. It's a miracle we weren't all killed. Thank the Gods I hired you, or I'd be dead."

"Do you think something like that might have killed your cousins?" suggested Athgar.

"I suppose it's possible," the Dwarf replied, "but my cousins tend to travel in heavy armour. They'd be difficult targets to kill."

"How heavy?" asked Athgar.

"They have chainmail," explained Belgast.

"Let's hope they're solitary creatures," said Natalia. "I'd hate to come across any more."

"How's Natalia's horse?" asked the Therengian.

"I'm afraid it's dead," said the Dwarf. "It looks like you two will be sharing a mount for the rest of our journey."

Natalia looked skyward, "I don't think we're getting any farther today, the sky is getting dark. I suggest we get to building some shelter, and quickly at that."

Belgast looked upward, frowning at the darkened clouds. "I guess you're right," he said. "Do you suppose this thing is edible?"

"I'm sure it is," said Athgar. "Most creatures are, but I wouldn't know where to start with this thing. It might have poison glands or something."

"Are we just to leave it lying there?" asked Natalia. "It might attract wolves."

"Wolves won't trouble us," said Athgar, "they tend not to attack Humans."

"What about Dwarves?" asked Belgast.

"I doubt they're on the wolves' menu either," the Therengian replied.

"And the horse?" added the Dwarf.

"We'll strip the saddle and anything else of value, but other than that, there's little else we can do."

"Where do we start?" asked Natalia.

"I'll look after the horse," suggested Athgar. "You two head to the trees and I'll join you there shortly. With any luck, we'll soon have a nice warm shelter in which to wait out the coming storm."

Belgast trekked back to his pony, leading it eastward towards the distant tree line. Natalia soon followed while Athgar started unbuckling the saddle of the dead horse.

The trees that the Therengian had spotted were clumped together in a tight knot. Natalia cast a wall of ice, creating it as a free-standing structure between two trees.

"How does that help us?" asked the Dwarf.

"Wait and see," she answered. "Now that the first wall is up, there is a small gap between each side of it and the nearest tree. I'm going to use my frozen portal spell to affix either end." Once more, she called forth the words of power, to be rewarded with a now solidly anchored wall.

"That cuts the wind," mused Belgast, "but how long will it last?"

"In this weather, probably until the spring."

She was casting a second wall as Athgar arrived, leading the remaining horse with the extra saddle slung across its back.

"Nice work," he observed.

"They never taught us this at the Volstrum," she admitted.

"Their loss," said Athgar.

He passed the reins to Belgast, then dug out his axe and started cutting branches.

By the time the snow started falling, they had a cozy little shelter, with four ice walls and tree boughs for a roof. Natalia had left a slight gap in one corner as an exit, and Athgar hung a blanket there, effectively forming a door. Now warm and secure, they settled in for the night.

Natalia woke with a start, her breath frosting in the chilly morning air. Looking over at Athgar, she noticed he was still asleep, but his face was drawn and haggard. She realized that he had likely used up all his energy to keep them warm throughout the storm. Now, with the snow squall over, they must continue their journey, but his depleted magic might prove troublesome.

"Athgar," she called out softly.

The Therengian stirred, his eyes opening to take in the form of Natalia.

"Is it morning?" he asked wearily.

"It is," she said, "but you're not looking good. We should have built a fire rather than rely on your magic to keep us warm."

"Nonsense," he said, "a fire would have melted your walls of ice."

"I could have kept them frozen," she objected.

"And then you would be in the same predicament as I am now," he answered. "I will recover my strength in due course. Hand me one of those stonecakes, will you?"

She reached into her bag, extracting one of the coal-like biscuits. Athgar popped it into his mouth, letting it soften to a comfortable, chewy mass.

A grumble sounded, announcing Belgast's awakening. The Dwarf sat up quite suddenly, eyes wide open and alert.

"What time is it?" he asked.

"It's morning," said Natalia. "How did you sleep?"

"With my eyes closed," the Dwarf replied. He winked at Athgar, sharing his mirth.

"I never knew Dwarves had a sense of humour," Natalia mused.

"How many Dwarves have you known?" asked Belgast.

"I have to admit, you're the first," she said.

"Well, don't judge my entire race on me. I'm the exception rather than the rule."

He looked across at Athgar. "What are you eating?"

"A stonecake," the Therengian replied through a full mouth.

"Stonecake?" the Dwarf said in surprise. "You've been holding out on me."

"Would you like one?" offered Natalia.

"I would love one," said Belgast. "After all, what Dwarf doesn't like stonecakes?"

Natalia handed him one, which quickly made its way to the Dwarf's mouth. He chewed it for some time before finally swallowing.

"Delicious," said Belgast, "just like my father used to make."

"Your father baked?" said Athgar.

"Why is that surprising?" asked Belgast. "Didn't yours?"

"Most decidedly not," said Athgar. "He was far too busy plying his trade."

"Which was?"

"A bowyer and fletcher."

"Athgar carries on the tradition," added Natalia.

"Do you now? How interesting. Tell me, is it a lot of work, making a bow?"

"It's challenging," said Athgar, "but the real secret is finding the right wood to begin with."

"Wouldn't any wood do?" suggested Belgast.

"No," replied Athgar. "If you choose the wrong piece, you might find a knot in an inconvenient place or some wood rot. The best bows are made from yew, though birch and ash will work. I made a bow out of oak once, a hard wood to work with, but the finished product was well worth it."

"Fascinating," said Belgast, turning to Natalia. "What about you?"

"What about me?" she replied.

"Did you pick up a trade?"

"Yes," she said, "the trade of magic. Other than that, I have little to offer."

"She's being modest," said Athgar. "She has a wealth of knowledge and not just about magic."

"You Humans continue to fascinate me," said Belgast. "I've travelled fairly extensively, and the one thing that impresses me about your race is the way you rush about."

"Rush about?" said Natalia. "I'm afraid I don't understand."

"Humans always seem to be in a great hurry," the Dwarf explained, "as if everything must be done today. I suppose that's due to your short lifespans."

"Short? Who said we were short-lived?" asked Athgar. "Humans can live to a ripe old age. I remember Skora celebrating the sixtieth anniversary of her birth."

"And you think sixty is old?" asked the Dwarf.

"Yes, why? Don't you?"

"Lad," said the Dwarf, trying to look parental, "Dwarves routinely live well into three hundred years or more. You are but children compared to the elder races."

"Which races are considered the elder races?" asked Athgar.

"That's easy," interrupted Natalia. "Elves, Orcs and Dwarves. They're the races that predate the coming of Humans."

"So all those races live longer lives?"

"No," said Belgast, "though Elves are extremely long-lived, Orcs live more modest life-spans. Shorter than Humans, I think, but that's likely due to their primitive living conditions. I expect that an Orc would live to a similar age as Humans, given decent accommodations."

"I know they age faster," said Athgar. "Shaluhk told me they are fully formed by fourteen."

"And who's Shaluhk?" asked the Dwarf.

"An Orc I know," said Athgar. "A shamaness, to be precise."

"You seem quite well connected," commented Belgast. "You travel with a Water Mage and count a shamaness among your friends. Any other important people you know?"

"None," said Athgar.

"Unless you count Kargen," added Natalia. "He's the Orc chieftain, and then there's Brother Cyric, Temple Knight of the Church of the Saints."

"I suppose we have been rather lucky in our associations," confessed Athgar. "But you're in the same boat, Belgast. You said you knew the King of Kragen-Tor."

"I did," the Dwarf admitted, "and a fine king he was, too. I first met him when I became one of his advisors."

"You mentioned you were a scholar," said Natalia. "What was your area of expertise?"

"Commerce," the Dwarf explained, "specifically, the economics of the Dwarven Kingdom. I had been apprenticed to the trade advisor, but when he died unexpectedly, I was forced to take his place."

"You looked after the kingdom's finances?" asked Natalia.

"Not specifically," Belgast continued. "That was, of course, the king's prerogative. No, I kept track of expenditures and suggested ways to maximize our profits."

"So you're supposed to be good with finances?" said Athgar, grinning. "I only ask because when we first met, you were without means."

Belgast straightened his clothes as if preparing to meet the king. "That was the result of an unfortunate series of events. All my coins were tied up in this enterprise, you see."

"But you're confident it will all work out in the end?" said Natalia.

"Naturally. I wouldn't have invested otherwise. Now, enough of this idle chatter, it's time we were on our way. After all, we still have many miles to go."

Belgast and Natalia packed up their gear and saddled the remaining mounts while Athgar stared down at the spare saddle.

"What do we do with this?" he asked. "It's a lot of weight to carry, and we're down a horse."

"Leave it," said Natalia. "It does little good to us now."

"I suppose you're right," he admitted. "Very well, let's get going, shall we? Will you dispel the walls of ice?"

"I think I shall leave them," she said, "though doubtless they'll melt come spring. It might do someone some good to have use of the shelter. Who knows, we might even use it again ourselves."

"All right," said Athgar, "but I'm taking the blanket, that we'll need."

They left their shelter, making their way across the newly fallen snow.

"Where to, Master Belgast?" asked Athgar. "The trail seems to have disappeared."

"Fear not, my young friend," said the Dwarf, "I have a nose for these things, and yonder hillock tells me all I need to know. Come, we must be off!"

THE DISCOVERY

Winter 1104 SR

They travelled all morning, making decent progress despite the newly fallen snow. Athgar and Natalia took turns walking, letting the other ride. Natalia insisted that Athgar conserve his energy, and so they decided to forego the spell of warmth, relying instead on their warm clothes and physical activity to keep them from growing cold.

By noon, they had topped a rise and chose to rest a moment to give their horse a break. Belgast trotted back to them, his little pony still energetic, despite the morning's brisk pace.

"It's a crisp day," the Dwarf said. "We can only hope this weather continues for the foreseeable future. We've made good time."

"So we have," said Athgar, "and my backside is happy to be walking again."

"What's that up ahead?" interrupted Natalia.

Athgar and Belgast followed her gaze to spot something in the distance, an obstruction of some type on the trail, though the liberal covering of snow hid its true identity.

"I see it," said Athgar, "but I have no idea what it is."

Belgast stared at it a moment, then turned around, trotting towards it.

"What is it you see, Belgast?" called Natalia, but so consumed was the Dwarf with the object of his attention that he paid her no mind.

"Go," said Athgar, "I'll catch up as quickly as I can."

Natalia spurred the horse onward, leaving the Therengian to tread through the snow and catch up to her. Belgast moved closer to it, then halted, dropping slowly from the saddle, his eyes glued to the object before him.

"It's a wagon," he called out, then, realizing the implications, he rushed forward, feverishly brushing aside the snow to reveal the wooden construction beneath.

Natalia pulled up behind him, quickly dismounting. "Is it your cousins?" she asked.

Belgast suddenly stopped all movement, staring at something before him. Natalia's view was blocked, but it was apparent that what he had found affected him deeply.

"My cousin, Dagle," he announced.

Natalia moved closer to see a face staring up at her. Belgast had pushed the snow aside, revealing a body that lay in the back of the wagon.

The Dwarf dug away more snow, and with Natalia helping, they revealed the cause of death, a devastating wound to his stomach.

"Something pierced his mail," said Belgast, his eyes tearing up.

Athgar soon joined them, though he was out of breath from his run. He moved closer, examining the wound in more detail. "This was made by an arrow," he said. "Fired from a very powerful bow, to be sure."

"How do you know that?" asked Natalia.

"It would take a high strength bow to penetrate this armour."

"That makes sense," added Belgast. "Dwarven chainmail is very thick."

"Someone must have ambushed them," said Natalia.

"Yes," said Athgar, now alert to danger, "but who?"

"Bandits?" offered the Dwarf.

"What kind of bandit kills someone, then leaves their mail? Dwarven chain would fetch a high price, I can't see them leaving it behind."

"A valid point," agreed the Dwarf, "but if not bandits, then who?"

"Let's look around some more," the Therengian suggested. "Maybe we can find some evidence of your other cousins' fate?"

"His body looks reasonably fresh," noted Natalia. "I would think the attack was recent, possibly only a few hours ago?"

"No, the wagon is covered in snow," countered Belgast, "so the attack must have been before last night."

"I suspect they were caught napping. Likely, their attackers, whoever they were, took advantage of a chance encounter," suggested Athgar.

"Or it was planned," said Belgast. "I made no secret that they were coming this way. I needlessly put their lives in danger."

"You can't blame yourself for that," said Athgar. "Now, let's see what else we can uncover."

Calling forth his magic, he sent flames across the surface of the snow, melting the top layer. A few more castings revealed two more bodies. Belgast was grief-stricken. He had secretly hoped that his other two cousins had survived, or had not made the journey, but the discovery of their bodies erased all hope from him.

"That's odd," mused Natalia.

"What is?" asked Athgar.

"I just found one of their ingots," she explained. "Whoever did this wasn't interested in loot."

"Maybe they're travelling light?" suggested the Therengian. "After all, an ingot carries some substantial weight."

"Possibly," she replied. "I suggest we widen the search and see if we can find some indication of who attacked, or at the very least, where the attack came from."

"Good idea," said Athgar. "We'll spiral out from the wagon. With any luck, we'll find what we're looking for."

They began searching the ground, but they were hampered by all the new-fallen snow. Iron ingots were spread all over the place, evidence that the wagon had been ransacked.

"I don't see any signs of a horse," Athgar remarked.

"They must have made off with it," said Belgast.

It didn't take long for Athgar to find more evidence.

"Over here," he called out, "I've found something."

"What is it?" asked Natalia.

"A body, I think. There's a slight rise in the snow." He knelt, brushing away the snow to reveal green skin. Abruptly, he rose, backing away, not quite believing his own eyes.

"What is it?" Natalia called out again.

"An Orc!" said Athgar.

"Are you sure?" she asked.

"Yes," he said, crouching back down to continue removing the snow.

Belgast soon joined them. "Likely one of the attackers," he said. "I've heard rumours they've been raiding of late."

"Where did you hear that?" asked Athgar.

"Back in Ostermund," revealed the Dwarf. "When my cousins first set off for the mine, we were warned to beware the Orcs."

"I find that suspicious," Athgar said. "Orcs are not known to raid caravans."

"Nonetheless, here we are," said Belgast. "You're the expert on Orcs. What can you tell us about this fellow here?"

"Help me uncover him," suggested Athgar, "and we'll see what's revealed."

They brushed away the snow, revealing a fur-clad Orc hunter, his bow and quiver laying nearby, along with a knife.

"Athgar, look," said Natalia. She had uncovered the corpse's hand, which was stained red. Athgar stared, taking in every detail.

"The damned Orcs killed my cousins!" Belgast shouted in anger. "They'll pay for this!"

Athgar tried to piece it all together but was unable to see a reasonable explanation for the evidence before him. Belgast, his fury spent, stomped back to the wagon.

"Athgar, why would the Orcs of the Red Hand attack a Dwarven wagon?"

"They didn't," declared the Therengian.

"But the hand," said Natalia, "it's red. Isn't that the mark of the tribe?"

"This hand is stained in blood," said Athgar. "Fitting for a first kill, but not for attacking people."

"But don't they go to war with red hands?"

"Yes, but this fellow's hand has been dipped in blood. The tribe uses dye when they attack. Whoever carried this out wanted us to believe an Orc was responsible."

"Do you recognize the Orc? If he's from the Red Hand Tribe, wouldn't he be from Ord-Kurgad?"

"I don't remember him," Athgar said, "but there are many Orcs in the village, and I didn't know them all. I have a feeling, however, that this Orc is from a different tribe."

"Then what's he doing here?" she asked.

"Someone wants to blame the Orcs for this attack, specifically those of the Red Hand."

"But why?" she asked. "It just doesn't make sense."

"It's a question I can't answer, but I'm going to find out."

"Where do we go from here?" she asked. "I think it fair to say that Belgast's pretty upset."

"And so he should be," said Athgar. "His cousins have been murdered. I would suggest we hook up his pony to the wagon, and he takes the bodies back to Ostermund."

"And us?"

"We're going to follow a trail," he said, somewhat mysteriously.

"What trail? The snow's obliterated everything."

"Not everything," he warned. "Where they've broken a trail before the storm, the new snow lays lower. I can make out where they went, and I'm going to follow."

"I'll come with you," she decided.

He looked at her, first in annoyance, then with understanding, even managing a smile. "A good idea," he said at last, "but I don't think the horse will be any help. It'll only slow us down."

"Why would you say that?" she asked.

"What I can see of the trail leads into some thick brush. The best way to navigate that will be on foot, but we must be aware, lest another one of those icora's attacks. Better to give our horse to the Dwarf."

"It's just as well," noted Natalia, "I don't think Belgast's pony could pull the wagon with three dead bodies anyway, let alone all the iron ingots. How far do you think the trail goes?"

"Not far," said Athgar. "I gather they were caught unawares by the storm, much as we were. That means they've likely taken shelter close by. With any luck, they're no more than half a day ahead of us."

"Then we'd best get to work," said Natalia. "We have some tracking to do."

They helped Belgast place his cousins' bodies within the wagon, along with any scattered ingots they could gather up, and the body of the Orc. Harder work, however, was hooking up the horse to the wagon, for the original beast had disappeared, along with its harness. They solved the problem by rigging up a crude harness from leftover leather straps that were sitting in the back of the wagon.

Once complete, they bid the Dwarf goodbye, calling out to him as the wagon disappeared in the distance, this time heading west, back to Ostermund.

"Will he be all right?" Natalia asked.

"There's little between us and the village," said Athgar. "I'm sure he'll be fine."

"But it'll be two days travel, won't it?"

"I doubt it," said Athgar. "Belgast slowed for us, remember? He'll likely just push the horse until he gets there. He didn't strike me as the type to spare his mount."

"What will they make of it in town?" she asked.

"I have no idea," the Therengian responded, "but I suppose they might send some troops to investigate."

"I didn't see any troops in Ostermund," noted Natalia.

"No," said Athgar, "neither did I, but there must be some around, somewhere. Perhaps they'll send word to Caerhaven, that's the capital, isn't it?"

"You know it is," said Natalia, "but it's more than a week away. There won't be anyone up here any time soon."

"I suppose you're right," said Athgar. "Let's hope we have more success with our tracking."

Proceeding on foot, they followed the faint trail that the Therengian had previously detected. They were helped by the trees, for once they entered the relative shelter offered by the woods, the path became more visible.

"Whoever did this," noted Athgar, "is not an expert in woodcraft."

"Why do you say that?" Natalia asked.

"There's no attempt to cover their tracks, nor avoid obvious markers."

"Such as?"

"Broken twigs, crushed plants underfoot, that sort of thing."

"Can you tell how many there are?" she asked.

"Definitely more than one," he replied, "but I can't be sure of their number. These tracks are quite a few hours old. Once they grow fresher, we'll have to be alert. I shouldn't like to run across them unexpectedly."

"I'll keep my eyes open," she promised.

The day wore on as they made their way through the woods. The ground was very uneven, being in the foothills of the mountains, but at least the woods gave some respite from the howling winds that seemed to echo all around them.

"It'll be getting dark soon," observed Natalia.

"I know," Athgar replied.

"Are we getting any closer?"

"The tracks are fresher if that's any consolation."

Natalia grabbed his arm. "Wait," she said, sniffing the air.

"What is it?" he asked.

"I smell smoke. There's a fire around here somewhere."

"We appear to be closer than I thought," mused Athgar. "The wind is coming from the north. They must have a camp there."

They kept moving, the smell becoming more evident as they travelled. Soon, they reached the edge of a clearing where a small dwelling sat, its chimney pumping out smoke. Natalia eased up beside him.

"It looks like a farmhouse, though I don't see any crops," she said.

"It's too high up for crops," said Athgar. "I suspect it's used by trappers."

A distant neighing caught their attention.

"It seems they have horses," he said.

"They must be over on the other side," remarked Natalia.

"We'll work our way around," said Athgar, "and try to get a better idea of what we're up against."

They moved along the edge of the woods, going slowly and deliberately so as to avoid making any noise. Soon, they found what they sought, seven horses, all tied to a tree in front of the structure.

"What are the odds that this house belongs to whoever attacked the wagon?" asked Natalia.

"It does seem unlikely, doesn't it," mused Athgar. "I think it more likely that they stumbled across this dwelling."

"Meaning?"

"It was abandoned, and they simply took possession of it," he offered.

"It looks inhabited," said Natalia. "What if there's a family inside?"

"We don't know if there is or not," he chided. "In any event, we can't just go barging in, we have no idea who they are or what they're doing here."

"Maybe we should just watch them for a while," she suggested. "Let's try to get closer to the windows."

"They're shuttered," he noted.

"Yes, but we might be able to hear what they're up to."

"I suppose we could," he said hesitantly.

"Do you have a better idea?" she asked.

"No," he confessed, "I guess I don't. Very well, we'll move up to the side of the house."

He rose to move, only to have Natalia grab his arm. Looking at her in surprise, he noticed her pointing at the front door where a trio of men had just exited the building. One, obviously the leader, wore expensive plate armour, while the other two, likely men-at-arms, wore chainmail. They chatted amiably for a while, though Athgar couldn't make out their words, and then they all climbed into their saddles and rode off to the west.

Athgar watched them disappear, then turned his attention back to the remaining horses.

"It seems the odds just got a little better," he said.

"If the horses are any indication, there's four more," warned Natalia.

"Still too many to barge in," he cursed.

"The back might be better," Natalia suggested, "less chance of being surprised by someone coming outside."

"You act like you've done this type of thing before," he noted.

"And you're enjoying this far too much," she accused.

They moved through the woods to the rear of the house, then made ready to cross the open space, listening first to make sure the way was clear.

"Go," whispered Athgar.

Natalia moved forward, her feet crunching on the newly fallen snow. She put her back to the wall, looking behind to Athgar, then waved him forward. Silently, he closed the distance, coming to stand beside her.

"Can you hear anything?" he whispered.

As if in answer, a piercing scream emanated from the house.

THE HUT

Winter 1104 SR

The scream echoed through the clearing, a high-pitched wail that bounced off the trees.

"Leave him alone," a woman's voice begged.

"Time to move," said Athgar, "we can't wait any longer."

"Agreed," Natalia replied.

Rushing around to the front of the building, they immediately made for the door, drawn by the sound of breaking furniture. Athgar paused only long enough to kick the door open.

Inside was a single room with a fireplace along the back wall where a woman and a little girl stood, while two men held a young boy by the arms, a hot poker held before his face. Two more men watched off to the side, their faces lit by the fire.

Athgar took it all in in an instant as he burst through the doorway, sending his axe swinging down savagely into the closest one's shoulder. The bandit shrieked in pain as the blade cleaved its way through the joint, splattering blood everywhere.

Natalia was quick to follow, loosing off a blast of ice shards that struck another in the chest, causing him to fall backward onto the floor where he lay, unmoving.

The final two tormentors dropped the boy, the larger one moving towards

Athgar, swinging at him with the red-hot poker. The Therengian dodged, then thrust out his left hand, sending a shaft of flame towards his opponent. Striking true, it caused the bandit to cry out in pain as his flesh was seared.

Natalia, her first opponent downed, took aim at the last uninjured villain. She opened her hands, ready to cast, but the man ducked behind a table, upending it to provide some cover.

Athgar raised his axe, blocking a sword strike from his burned opponent, a large man with a thick beard, who had managed to pull his weapon free. The Therengian cut again, this time driving the edge of his weapon deep into the man's leg, causing him to scream in agony as he dropped his sword.

Natalia advanced, threatening her foe, but he held his hands up to indicate his unwillingness to fight. As she took a step back, he suddenly heaved the table, sending it across the room, where it struck Athgar on the left shoulder, knocking him to the floor.

Natalia reacted with the quickest spell she could think of. Moments later, frost curled up the man's arms and legs, slowing down his movements.

Athgar regained his feet and advanced towards Natalia's enemy, axe still held firmly in his hand. Their opponent stepped forward, slashing out viciously with a dagger, but the cold had frozen his limbs, causing his attack to falter for a moment. When Athgar's axe struck true, it buried itself in the man's chest, easily penetrating his armour. The man stared down at his wound for a moment, then his eyes rolled up into his head, and he collapsed.

Natalia quickly surveyed the room, noting the other men who lay unmoving, either dead or passed out from their wounds. She turned her attention to the woman, still firmly grasping the young girl's arm, while the young lad clutched her around the waist.

"Are you all right?" she called.

"Yes," the woman stammered. "Thank you, whoever you are."

"Who were these men?" Natalia asked.

"I don't know," the woman replied. "They followed my husband back here this morning."

"Your husband, where is he?" asked Natalia.

"Dead," the woman said, the pain still evident in her eyes. "They killed Hayden. Said he saw too much."

"He likely saw them staging the ambush," said Athgar.

"Do you have any idea who these people are?" asked Natalia.

"No," the woman responded, "I've never seen them before."

Athgar looked over the bodies. "This one's dead," he said, indicating the man with the axe wound in his chest.

"This one's still alive," offered Natalia as she poked the man with the shoulder wound using the tip of her toe, eliciting a painful moan.

The Therengian made his way to the man that had held the poker, but it was clear that he, too, was dead. The last assailant had taken ice shards to the chest. Natalia bent to examine him, noting his wounds. "He'll live," she announced, "though I doubt he'll be fighting anytime soon."

Athgar joined her, watching as the man's eyes fluttered open.

"Who are you?" Athgar demanded. "Who sent you here?"

"Name's Artemis," the man stammered. "I was hired in Caerhaven."

"By who?" the Therengian pressed.

"I don't know," the man choked out, "a knight of some type. He said he wanted to hire some muscle. Higgins did all the negotiating."

"Higgins?" said Athgar.

Artemis nodded in the direction of the dead man with the axe wound to his chest.

"This knight, what was his name?" Athgar demanded.

"I told you, I don't know," Artemis pleaded.

"That must have been the armoured man we saw riding off," said Natalia. "Someone wealthy, if his armour is any indication."

"That doesn't tell us who he works for," cursed the Therengian.

Natalia, who had been staring at Artemis since the beginning of the interrogation, turned to Athgar. "From the look of his clothes, this man is from the city."

"Well," said Athgar, "he did say he came from Caerhaven. What of it?"

"He obviously has a horse. We saw them outside, remember?"

"I do, but I don't see the connection," said Athgar.

"Horses are often branded," said Natalia.

"Branded?"

"Yes, it identifies the owner. Perhaps their horses might reveal who hired them."

"How do you know their employer supplied the horses?" asked Athgar.

"Look at him," she said in reply. "Does he look like someone who could afford a horse?"

"No," he admitted, "I suppose not. What are you proposing we do?"

"I suggest we take the horses back to Ostermund. With any luck, we'll be able to find someone who can identify their owner. Now, what about the wounded here?"

Athgar moved to examine the man with the shoulder wound. "I'm afraid this man has passed into the Afterlife."

"That leaves only one survivor," she said. "What do we do with him?"

"Ask her," he said, pointing to the woman.

"I already know her answer," she said. "They killed her husband, she'll want him dead."

"Would you want anything less if you were in her shoes?" he said.

"No," she replied, "but we need him. He has knowledge that could help us identify this knight he spoke of."

"Then bind his wounds, we'll take him with us."

"To where?" she asked.

"Back to Ostermund. And we'll take their horses."

He turned to the woman. "What's your name?" he asked.

"Mirriam," she replied.

"Will you come with us to Ostermund, Mirriam?" he queried.

"No," she replied, "my place is here."

"Your husband is dead," said Natalia. "Are you sure you wouldn't prefer to leave?"

"This is all I have left," she replied, "and I will not abandon it now."

"Very well," said Athgar. "We'll take care of the bodies in the morning, then set off for Ostermund. The prisoner will come with us."

"Who are you?" the woman finally asked.

"My name's Athgar, and this is Natalia. We came across an ambush back on the pass and followed the trail here. I'm only sorry we didn't arrive in time to save your husband."

"Promise me you'll track down those responsible for my Hayden's death," said Mirriam.

"We will," promised Natalia, "I give you my word."

It took them some time to dispose of the bodies. They had initially intended to bury them, but the frozen ground prevented such an act. In the end, they settled for burning them, a task made all the more time consuming by the need to chop down trees. They built two simple pallets and threw the bandit's bodies all together on one. Hayden's body was recovered but lay on a separate pile, prepared for a trip to the Afterlife. Athgar stood before the pyres, deep in thought.

"Is everything ready?" asked Natalia.

"Yes," he answered, "I thought to say something over her husband's body, but no words will come to me. I know what it is to lose one's family, and yet I cannot speak."

"It's too close to home," she soothed. "The death of this man is too much like your own experience. All we can do is speed him on his way."

"Surely he deserves better," Athgar mused. "Will Mirriam say some words, do you think?"

"No," said Natalia, "she refuses to come out of the house. She is grieving in her own way."

"Very well," said Athgar. He looked at Hayden's pyre, uttering the words of power as he gesticulated. The pile of wood started to smoke, and then flames sprang forth, quickly igniting the wood. The body, soon engulfed in flames, was lost to sight as the inferno took over.

They stood side by side, Athgar and Natalia, holding hands as the fire climbed higher, the crackling of the wood echoing through the trees. It felt like an eternity passed before Natalia looked at Athgar, concerned that he was lost in his own pain, but just as she did, he turned towards the other pyre and cast the spell quickly, letting the flames catch. Finally, he turned to face her.

"We must prepare to leave," he said. "We have already tarried here too long, and Belgast will be waiting for us back in Ostermund."

Natalia glanced up to where the smoke was blanketing the sky. "It looks like more snow is coming," she said. "I think we'll have to delay our departure."

"It's just as well," he replied. "We can't leave the fires unattended. We should wait for them to reduce to ash."

"That could take a while," she remarked.

"Likely till after dark, so it seems we'll be here for some time yet, regardless of the weather."

"We should go inside," she urged, "it's cold out here."

"You go," he said, "I'll be along shortly."

"Dwelling on the past won't help, Athgar."

"I know," he replied, "but we must remember those that came before us."

"You worship your Ancestors now?"

"It is the way the Orcs would mourn their dead. Too many have died these past few days. First that Orc, then the Dwarves, and now this poor trapper."

"What makes you think the Orc was killed first?" Natalia asked.

"They came to the ambush point intent on blaming the Orcs. No Orc would willingly accompany such men. Even finding an Orc outside of their lands is rare."

"And yet we found Tonfer Garul in Corassus," she reminded him.

"Yes, but I believe he is the exception. Kargen once told me that Orcs only travel to hunt and seldom alone."

"Meaning?"

"Meaning that somewhere out there, lie more dead Orcs."

"Wouldn't they be missed?" said Natalia.

"They would," he continued, "but I suspect they weren't Orcs of the Red Hand."

"How can you say that with such certainty?" she asked.

He turned to look at her, a slight smile on his face. "This Orc carried a bow," he said.

"What of it? Don't all their hunters use bows?"

"They do," said Athgar, "but Kargen insists they use their warbows. The dead Orc we found had no such bow."

"What's a warbow?" she asked.

"As you know, I'm a bowyer," he explained. "When I was with the Orcs, I developed a longbow that was made specifically for their physique. It allows them a heavier draw."

"So they can do more damage," she said, "but you said the arrows penetrated the Dwarf's mail, doesn't that indicate a heavy pull?"

"It does, but I believe it was a crossbow that did the damage. The bow we found alongside the body was a simpler construction than the warbows I taught them to make."

"Maybe another tribe, then?" she said.

"It would appear so. Unfortunately, I'm not familiar with the other tribes, or where they might be found."

"Whoever is behind this seems to have planned it out quite well."

"Yes," he replied, "but they hadn't counted on the weather. It might have been spring by the time the bodies were found."

"Maybe they were counting on that very idea?" Natalia suggested.

"The problem is," he continued, "I still can't figure out why someone would do such a thing."

"Maybe they have a grudge against the Orcs?" she suggested.

"But how?" he asked. "They seldom leave their lands."

"Could there be some animosity based on past events?"

"I suppose it's possible, but Orcs haven't been a problem in these parts for, well, forever, as far as I'm aware."

"Could there be something in their land that someone wants?" she asked.

"Like what?" he responded. "They live in the woods between two dukedoms. What could possibly be of value there? Surely, if there was something, one duke or the other would have pushed them off their lands long ago. They certainly have the armies for it."

"We're missing a part of the puzzle," she said.

"The what?" said Athgar.

"The puzzle. Haven't you heard of such things?"

"I've heard of a puzzle, but I don't understand the reference to a missing part. A puzzle is simply something unknown. How can such a thing have parts?"

Natalia laughed, easing some of their tension. "In the Volstrum, we were often presented with mental challenges, the intent being to sharpen our minds. One such task was to assemble a picture made up of many small pieces. You had to place them in the correct order to make sense of the picture."

"An interesting idea," he said, "much like hunting."

"Like hunting? I'm not sure I follow."

"When hunting, one must look at all the clues. Footprints, broken branches, the smell in the wind, everything. Together they paint a complete picture, leading to the prey."

"I suppose that's as close an analogy as I'm going to get," she admitted.

"I like the idea of these puzzles you mentioned, maybe we'll get one someday. Where does one find such a thing?"

"I have no idea," she confessed. "It takes a lot of work to make them, so I suppose, outside of the Volstrum, they'd be catered to the nobility."

"Then we'll have to become nobility," he said, a serious look on his face.

"Athgar, you can't just become nobility. You have to be born to it."

"Do you?" he asked. "Surely anyone can become a king."

"Anyone that can carve out a kingdom," Natalia confirmed. "You make it sound so easy."

He grinned, the smile lighting up his eyes. "I'm just pulling your leg," he said.

Now it was Natalia's turn to be confused. "You didn't touch my leg," she said.

"It's an expression we used back in Athelwald. It means to trick someone or to tell an outrageous lie in jest."

"I'd prefer it if you just touched my leg instead," she said.

"Not in front of the children!" said Athgar, breaking out into laughter.

THE RETURN

Winter 1104 SR

Belgast Ridgehand brought his wagon to a halt, shaking the snow from his beard. He had pushed through the blizzard, travelling all night to enter the village at daybreak. His arrival in Ostermund had created a bit of a stir, and once it was known that he had bodies in the back, the crowds grew as concerned citizens flocked to learn more about what had transpired.

"What happened?" called out Lyman Harrigan, owner of the trading post.

"They were ambushed on the road," replied the Dwarf. "All three of my cousins are dead, along with an Orc."

"An Orc?" said Lyman, obviously intrigued. "What in the name of the Gods was an Orc doing up there, in the mountains?"

"Couldn't tell you," responded Belgast, "but I brought back the body."

"Did you recover the iron?" asked Lyman.

"I did," said Belgast. "Thank Gundar for small miracles."

"Where are your companions?" Lyman asked.

"They followed a trail left behind from the Orcs," said Belgast. "I suspect it'll be some time before they return."

"They're slippery beggars, those greenskins," offered Lyman. "I suppose we'll have to call the guards."

"Why?" asked the Dwarf. "These ingots are mine, fair and square."

"Of that, I have no doubt," said Lyman, "but they'll want to take possession of the Orc's body."

"For Gundar's sake, why would they want that?" asked Belgast. "He's dead. Of what further use would he be?"

The man stared back at him. "Don't you see?" he said. "For months, there have been rumours they were in the area, but now we have proof. If they've travelled this far north, the duke will need to be informed, though I daresay he has trouble enough in the south."

"The south?" said Belgast. "Have you heard something I haven't?"

"Nothing solid," Lyman replied, "but there have been rumours for weeks of trouble down by the capital. They say the Orcs have been getting restless of late."

"How so?" asked the Dwarf.

"Can't say for sure," the Human replied, "and I don't really care, as long as they stay well away from here." He peered into the back of the wagon, "I suppose it's too late for that now, though."

Lyman turned, yelling at a worker to go and fetch some soldiers. Ostermund was a small village on the border of the Duchy of Krieghoff. There was little here of value, but the duke insisted on maintaining a small garrison if only to assist in the collection of taxes.

"What will you do with your kin?" asked Lyman, returning his attention to the Dwarf.

"I'll have to bury them," he said. "It's too long a journey to take them back to Kragen-Tor."

"The ground's frozen solid," Lyman warned.

"True," said Belgast, "I suppose I'll have to burn the bodies instead."

"I thought Dwarves were always buried in stone?"

"We're a very pragmatic people," said Belgast. "Though stone would have been preferred, we must make do with what we have. I'll create a funeral pyre and send them off to the Great Forge in style."

"The Great Forge?" asked Lyman.

"Yes, what you'd call the Afterlife. To us, the body is but a vessel, to be disposed of with reverence, but the manner is not important as long as their spirits can join Gundar and the other Gods."

"Let's get everything unloaded, shall we?" suggested Lyman.

"Yes," agreed the Dwarf. "My customers will be eager to pick up their iron, and I must make arrangements for my cousins."

"What will you do, now that they're gone?"

Belgast stopped short. What would he do?

"I have no idea," he answered. "To be honest, I've been too busy to give it much thought."

"Well, at least the iron should provide you with a decent payout."

"True enough," Belgast agreed.

"Will you start up the mine again, do you think?"

"Not right away," the Dwarf confessed. "I'll likely travel back to Kragen-Tor, I should at least inform everyone of the death of my cousins."

"A sad trip," said Lyman. "I remember having to tell my brother how his son had died."

"I didn't know you had a nephew," said Belgast. "How did he die?"

"From a fever," said Lyman. "He was working as a stable hand here, with me. It took him quite suddenly. I don't think he lasted a day."

The Dwarf shuddered. It was one thing to go down in battle, but to be stricken dead by illness was just horrific.

"I take it there are no healers in Ostermund?"

"No," said Lyman, "more's the pity. Had a Life Mage been present, he could have been easily healed. Still, I suppose that's the price we pay for living in a remote area like we do."

Lyman called on two men to assist, and they began lifting the bodies from the wagon.

"They're stiff," complained one of the workers.

"They're frozen solid," said Lyman. "They're dead Dwarves, they deserve respect. Handle them with care."

The worker grumbled but did as he was bid. A sizable group of observers had gathered by this time, many moving closer to watch as the Dwarves were removed from the wagon.

"I'm not familiar with your customs. Will they be burned in their armour?" asked Lyman.

"No," said Belgast, "only kings and powerful lords are interred in such a manner. I'll sell off their belongings and give the proceeds to their families when I finally return home."

The workers had just lifted the third Dwarf from the back of the wagon when two soldiers finally turned up, both dressed in padded doublets.

"What have we got here?" asked the oldest.

"An Orc, John," replied Lyman. "His body was found at the scene of an ambush."

John moved closer to have a look. "So it is," he remarked.

"And his hand's stained red," offered Lyman.

"Likely to indicate his clan," said the soldier.

"What shall I do with the body?" asked Belgast.

"We'll take it as soon as we can arrange a wagon," replied John.

His companion was examining the back of the wagon in more detail. "What's this?" he asked.

"Iron ingots," said Belgast. "They were bringing them here for resale."

"A hefty burden," the man remarked.

"Never mind Kenson," said John, "he's naturally suspicious."

"Did you manage to recover all the iron?" asked Lyman.

"I don't know," confessed Belgast. "The truth is I don't have any record of how much they were shipping."

"Are there no journals or records you can check?" asked John.

"I'm sure there are some back at the mine, but it's days away. Why? Is it important?"

"Only insofar as it might give a motive for the attack," offered John. "I'd guess those ingots are fairly valuable."

"Only to a smith," said Belgast, "and the weight alone would be a deterrent."

"Likely this was a simple robbery," offered Kenson. "They might have been content with the contents of their purses?"

"A possibility," said John, "but a man would have to be pretty desperate to take on three armoured Dwarves."

"What about the Orc?" asked Kenson.

"I don't think I follow," remarked John.

"I hear that Orcs and Dwarves don't get along. Do you think it's a revenge thing?"

"No," said Belgast, "that's just gossip. The truth is my people have few dealings with the green folk in these parts."

"In any event," said John, "we'll relieve you of the burden. Is this your wagon?"

"No," said Belgast, "we borrowed it from Lyman."

"Borrowed?" asked John.

"Yes," said the Dwarf, "we have a financial arrangement."

"In that case," said John, turning to the owner of the trading post, "the duke's representative would be more than willing to make a similar arrangement. How soon can you have it available?"

"The wagon," said Lyman, "immediately. The horse, on the other hand, will need a rest."

John looked into the man's trading post. "Where do you keep the wagons?" he asked.

"I have a stable out back," the man retorted.

"Can you leave the wagon outside? We don't want the body to decay."

"Certainly," answered Lyman.

"How long for the horse?"

"I'm expecting another pair back later this morning. I can have the wagon ready to go by, let's say, noon?"

"Noon it is, then," said John, turning to the Dwarf. "Oh, and I'll want a written statement of what you found. Can you do that?"

"Of course," said Belgast, "I'll do whatever I can to help."

"Excellent," said John. "Then I suggest you get yourself to bed, Master Dwarf, you look absolutely exhausted."

"I'll help unload the ingots first," he said. "I want an accurate count."

"Are you intimating that I'd skim?" asked Lyman.

"No," said the Dwarf, "but I cannot speak for your men. I think it tempting that such a haul would be readily nearby, wouldn't you?"

"Agreed," said Lyman. "We'll stack and count them, then you can go off for a rest."

Athgar lifted himself into the saddle. "I'll never get used to this," he complained.

Natalia, astride her own mount, smiled. "It was convenient for them to leave us horses," she remarked.

"They're not your horses," said the prisoner, Artemis, sitting on a spare horse, his hands bound securely behind his back, his mount's reins held by the Therengian.

"They are now," Athgar announced. "You forfeited any rights to them the moment you killed this woman's husband."

"That wasn't my fault," the man defended.

"Then whose fault was it?" demanded Athgar. "Give us a name, and possibly the authorities will be more lenient with you."

Artemis sat defiantly in silence.

"He won't talk," said Natalia. She looked back to Mirriam, who stood in the doorway, the two children clutching her hands.

"Are you sure you don't want to come with us?" Natalia asked.

"Quite sure," the woman replied, "but remember your promise."

"We will," Natalia assured the widow, then turned her attention to Athgar. "All set?" she asked.

"Yes," he replied. "Hopefully we can remember the way."

"Just head south," urged Mirriam. "You can't miss the trail, and then it'll lead you back to the village."

Athgar pulled out in front, trailing the prisoner's horse behind him. Natalia soon followed, the spare beast lagging along behind her.

"These horses are well trained," she commented.

"I noticed," the Therengian replied. "If someone doesn't claim this one, I just may want to hang onto it."

"You surprise me," said Natalia. "I thought you hated horses."

"Hate is such a strong word," he said, "and though I do like walking, there's nothing like having a mount to carry all your things."

"And to cost more," said Natalia. "After all, we have to pay for stabling, horseshoeing and a whole host of other things."

"I hadn't considered that," he replied. "Speaking of which, how are our funds doing?"

"We've got a few coins left," she said. "Enough to see us to the end of the month, at the very least."

"Don't forget," he urged, "Belgast still owes us for three nights at the inn."

"Don't worry," said Natalia, "I'm keeping track of everything."

"He should be back in Ostermund by now," mused Athgar.

"Yes," she added, "and with the ingots recovered, he should have been able to sell them to recoup his expenses."

"That means he can pay us back," he replied, "and that gives us a few more days in paradise."

"Paradise? Is that what you're calling Ostermund these days?"

"No," he said, "it's what I'm calling spending time with you."

"Now you're just being ridiculous," she accused.

They rode on in silence for a while, broken occasionally by the sound of snow falling from branches. Halfway through the afternoon, they found the trail. It was covered in snow, but the way through the trees was evident, and so they set off westward, eager to return to civilization, however small it might be.

"You know," Athgar said, "we won't make Ostermund by nightfall, it's still at least half a day's travel away."

"True," said Natalia, "but the shelter we built won't be too much farther. We can camp there again."

"Yes," he said, "but this time, it'll be just the two of us."

"Don't get your hopes up," she said. "We've four horses to contend with, not to mention our prisoner."

"Oh yes," he pouted, "I'd forgotten."

"We'll have plenty of alone time once we're back at the inn," she promised.

"Yes," he replied with a wicked grin, "and maybe we'll have a bath!"

The small shelter they had constructed earlier was mostly intact. With the weather now milder, Natalia cast new walls of ice, creating a small paddock to keep the horses safe. Artemis they kept with them, though his legs were bound as well as his hands.

Athgar built a fire, big enough to keep them from freezing, but not so large as to melt the walls. They spent an uneventful evening in the shelter too tired to even talk, quickly falling into slumber.

Natalia awoke to find herself alone. She had a moment of panic, thinking that the prisoner had escaped, then realized Athgar had likely gone to fetch more wood, taking the captive with him to ensure her safety.

She rose, pulling a cloak around her, and stepped out into the crisp morning air to spot Athgar returning, the prisoner behind him, carrying a bundle of sticks.

"Good morning, beautiful," he said. "Sleep well?"

"I did," she replied, "though I was a little surprised you weren't there when I woke up."

"I thought it best we should warm up before we rode off," he explained. "It's always good to start out that way."

"So it is," she agreed, "but wouldn't your warmth spell have been more effective?"

He looked at her for a moment, his mind trying to grasp her words. "I suppose it would," he said, turning to their prisoner. "You can drop the sticks."

"So all that work for nothing?" Artemis complained.

"You should be more thankful," said Athgar. "We could have killed you like your companions." The man fell silent as Athgar turned back to Natalia. "It would seem we've wasted our time collecting these."

"We'll leave them for the next person that comes across the shelter," she said. "How long do you reckon it will take us to reach Ostermund?"

"No more than half a day, I should think."

"Good. Let's get the horses ready, shall we?"

"By all means," said Athgar.

They were soon on their way, riding west, the sun warming them, despite winter's chill. By noon, the distant smoke of fireplaces could be seen, evidence of Ostermund.

OSTERMUND

Winter 1104 SR

It was almost noon by the time they rode into Ostermund. The little village was quiet, the people going about their business, ignoring the three riders.

"We should drop off Artemis here," suggested Natalia. "There's bound to be a local detachment of troops."

"Agreed," said Athgar, "and then we'll deal with the horses unless our friend here has anything else to suggest?" He glanced over to their prisoner, but the man remained silent, a sullen look on his face.

"It appears he's still hesitant to talk," said Natalia.

"I expect the soldiers will persuade him," replied the Therengian.

They rode farther down the street, finally turning north to discover the local garrison. It was a simple structure consisting of a wooden tower, with an attached building that served as a barracks. The guard was sitting outside was smoking a pipe, but upon seeing them, he rose, moving towards them.

"What have we here?" he asked.

"A prisoner for you," said Athgar.

"Oh, yes?" the guard responded. "And who might you be?"

"My name is Athgar, and this is my travelling companion, Natalia. We came across a group of men attacking a family up in the hills."

"And so you took it upon yourself to make an arrest?" the guard asked.

"It was a bit more complicated than that," said Athgar, "but suffice it to say that we rescued the family from peril."

"This man," added Natalia, "was complicit in a murder."

"Complicit, was he? Well, that's a word I've not heard before. Are you some type of noble?"

"I am a high mage," she bristled. "You would do well to remember that!"

The sudden outburst had the desired effect, for the guard stiffened, then bowed formally. "Sorry, my lady, I meant no disrespect."

"Go and fetch your commander," Natalia demanded.

Athgar stared at her as the man ran inside. "You surprise me," he said, "I thought you were the quiet type."

"We trained for this at the Volstrum," she said. "The family has some fairly practical advice for dealing with inferiors."

"Is that what we all are," he asked, "inferiors?"

"No," she replied, "it was their term, not mine, but it worked."

"I suppose it makes sense," he said. "A soldier must be used to a life of discipline and following orders."

"So it would seem," she agreed.

The guard re-emerged a moment later. "Captain Weimar will see you now," he said.

Athgar dismounted, passing the reins of the prisoner's horse to the guard. "See that this man is detained," he said. "No doubt, your captain will have further orders once we've seen him."

"Yes, my lord," the man answered respectfully.

Athgar moved to Natalia, helping her down from her horse.

"Shall we?" he asked.

"After you," she insisted.

They entered the tower, the base of which was set up as a small office, where a soldier sat at a table, poring over a book while making notes with his quill. Upon their entry, he looked up, taking in their arrival.

"I'm Captain Weimar," he said. "How may I be of service?"

"My name is Athgar, and this is my travelling companion, Natalia. We were riding through the mountain pass when we came across quite a disturbing situation."

"I see," said the captain. "I'm just going to make a few notes if you don't mind. Can you tell me what you saw?"

"Certainly," said Athgar. "We saw a group of ruffians holding a family hostage."

"And this was in the mountains?"

"In the foothills, actually," corrected Natalia.

The captain made a note. "Might I ask how you knew this was a hostage situation?"

"The woman screamed," said Athgar.

"And you took that as proof?"

"Wouldn't you?" asked Natalia.

"Please don't take offense," said Captain Weimar. "My report must be as accurate as possible if we are to see justice done. Now, where was I? Oh yes, this prisoner you spoke of, was he the only one present?"

"No," said Athgar, "there was a group of seven men in total."

"Seven, you say? And you managed to overcome all of them?"

"No," said Natalia, "we saw three ride off before we entered the building."

"Leaving four," mused the captain.

"Obviously," said Natalia, growing irritated.

"And how many of these did you say you captured?"

"We didn't say," noted Natalia, "but we have one."

"What happened to the rest?" asked the captain.

"They were killed in the fight," explained Athgar.

"How unfortunate for them," murmured the captain as he made another note.

"We entered the house to find two of them torturing a child," said Natalia.

"Did you indeed? And I suppose that's when they resisted the attempt to arrest them?"

"They fought us if that's what you mean," said Athgar.

"And you managed to defeat all four men? Just you and your woman?"

"Woman?" said Natalia. "Is that all I am to you? I'll have you know I'm a trained battle mage!"

"A battle mage now, is it? We've no end of people claiming such nonsense."

Natalia made to speak, but Athgar calmed her by placing his hand upon her forearm.

"Allow me to demonstrate," he said.

He held out his hand, palm upward, murmuring the ancient words of power. A small green flame ignited, floating just above his hand. It captivated Captain Weimar's attention for a moment before he swallowed in fear.

"I'm terribly sorry, my lord," the soldier stammered, "but we have many people make such claims."

"You have people pretending to be mages?" asked the Therengian. "I find that hard to believe."

"Well, maybe not mages, specifically," the captain explained, "but visitors often try to overinflate their position in society. It's an effort to be taken more seriously, I suspect. I meant no offense, my lord."

"Then you'll take the prisoner into your care?" asked Athgar.

"I shall," the captain confirmed, "and rest assured we will do everything in our power to deal with the situation."

"Excellent," said Athgar, "now I believe you owe an apology."

"I have already apologized, my lord."

"Not to me, but to Lady Natalia. Or are you in the habit of insulting battle mages? If so, I commend your bravery."

The captain stood, offering up a deep bow. "I apologize most heartily, my lady. I meant no offense."

Natalia was about to bite the man's head off with a stinging rebuke, but something in Athgar's eyes made her reconsider. "Apology accepted," she replied instead.

"If it pleases your lord and ladyship, I'll need a written statement. I can take down your words if you like, or you can write it yourself."

Athgar looked down at the scattered notes of the captain. "Is that not what you've been doing?" he asked.

Captain Weimar looked at his own notes, "These? Gods' sake, no. I've merely taken down some details. We'll need a statement from you for our official records. They'll be used should the accused find himself at trial."

"What do you mean, 'should he find'? Surely there is to be a trial?"

"That would require a magistrate," said the captain, "and their visits are rare, here in Ostermund."

"Then send him elsewhere," suggested Athgar. "Can't he be tried in Caerhaven?"

"It is a distinct possibility," the captain confirmed, "but I will have to conduct an investigation first. We often find, in these cases, that the best punishment is a short jail sentence instead of a trial, providing the prisoner agrees."

"And that's your idea of justice?" said Natalia. "Doesn't the duke himself oversee such things?"

"The duke is a busy man," said Captain Weimar. "Far too busy to deal with petty crime like this."

"But the man was complicit in a murder!" said Athgar.

"Oh, it's murder now, is it?" said the captain. "Why didn't you mention that earlier?"

"Sorry," said Athgar, "I did tell the soldier outside."

"You should have led with that, my lord. It is a far more serious crime. Might I ask who he is accused of murdering?"

"A trapper," replied Natalia. "The husband of the woman we saved."

Captain Weimar looked at them a moment, seeming to gauge their character, then he reached into his desk, withdrawing two blank parchments.

"I shall give you some privacy," he said, "and you can write down everything you remember. I assume you can both write?"

Athgar was about to speak, but Natalia cut him off.

"I shall write for both of us," she said. "Athgar is a Therengian and finds the common tongue difficult."

She noticed a look of disgust cross the captain's face. "You may leave us now," she said.

Captain Wiemar rose, bowing once more to Natalia, but sneered slightly at Athgar as he walked outside, closing the door behind him.

"It seems he doesn't like Therengians," mused Athgar.

"Was it that obvious?" asked Natalia.

"I wonder why?"

"This land was once part of Therengia, wasn't it?" she asked.

"I believe so," said Athgar, "but I fail to see the significance of it."

"Don't you see?" she said. "They're afraid of your people. They believe that one day you'll rise again in a bid to reclaim your land."

"Utter nonsense if you ask me," said Athgar.

"It all makes sense to me," Natalia remarked. "Now, let's get these statements down, shall we?"

It took them the best part of the afternoon to complete their accounts. Athgar found the process laborious, for he had to talk slowly to allow time for Natalia to dip the quill and scratch out his story. Once completed, he then had to wait while she penned her own account. Finally finished, she showed him where to write his own name at the bottom.

"You're getting better," she said.

"I have a good teacher," he commented. "Though I must admit, I'm finding it easier to read than to write."

"You'll get the hang of it," she insisted. "Of course, it would be a lot easier if we had some books."

"We should acquire some," said Athgar, "the next time we're in a city. That is where you get them, isn't it?"

"It is," she replied. "Now, let's get out of here. I don't think I can take much more of Captain Weimar. How about you?"

"I'm in complete agreement," he replied, "and we still have to see to the horses.

They left the local garrison, now without their prisoner, passing by the

Owl as they made their way to the stables, eager to learn more. Natalia stared at the inn as they passed.

"I wonder if Belgast is back?" she mused.

"Of course he's back," he replied, "why wouldn't he be?"

"Any number of things could have delayed him," said Natalia. "We shouldn't take anything for granted."

"Well," said Athgar, "we'll find out soon enough. Let's get this horse business out of the way first, then we'll seek out the Dwarf."

"Agreed," she said.

The stables were just up the street from the local detachment, making it a quick jaunt. They dismounted, leading the animals inside, where a stable hand was quick to intercept them.

"Good day," the woman greeted them.

"And to you," said Natalia. "We've come to see to our horses."

"I would expect no less," the woman replied. "This is a stable, after all. You've had horses here before, haven't you? I recognize you."

"That's correct," said Athgar. "We had two the last time we were here."

"These are not the horses you had then, are they?" she commented.

"Unfortunately, not," said Natalia. "We lost one to a wild animal up in the mountain pass, and the other we lent to a Dwarf of our acquaintance," she looked around the stable, "but I don't see him here."

"There's been no Dwarf here," the woman replied, "but I hear there was one down at the trading post. Maybe he stabled it there?"

"I suppose that's a possibility," mused Natalia as she passed over the reins, then stretched her legs. Athgar waited as the woman led his companion's horse away until she returned a moment later, to take the lead from him.

"I see you've more temple horses," she commented. "They must really like you."

"Pardon?" said Athgar.

"The Church must like you," the woman repeated. "They've given you horses again."

"How do you know that?" he asked.

In answer, she nuzzled the horse, "The tattoo gives them away."

"What tattoo?" asked Natalia.

The woman looked surprised. "Why, the one inside the ear. Haven't you heard of such things?"

"I thought horses were branded?" said Natalia.

"They normally are," said the stable hand, "but the Church prefers to use ink."

"You're sure there's no mistake?" asked Athgar.

"See for yourself," said the woman, gently grasping the horse's ear. Athgar leaned in close and examined the mark. "Fascinating," he said. Natalia soon joined in, taking great interest. "Are those numbers?"

"They are," the stable hand confirmed, "though I can't tell you what they mean, aside from identifying a horse of the Church, that is."

"Does that mean we could find out more about them?" asked Natalia.

"I suppose it does," said the woman, "but you'd have to ask the prioress about it."

"The prioress?" said Athgar.

"Yes, Holy Mother Eugenia. She's the head of the Sisters of Saint Agnes here in Ostermund."

"Is there a Temple of Saint Mathew?" asked Athgar. "We've dealt with them before."

"I'm afraid not. Ostermund is far too small to warrant two orders. Why? Is there a problem with Saint Agnes?"

"No," said Natalia, "not at all. Where would I find this temple?"

"North end of town, but I expect it'll be busy today, what with all the news and such."

"What news is that?" asked Natalia.

"Haven't you heard? There's been an attack on some Dwarves."

"Belgast obviously made it back in one piece," said Athgar.

"That's not the half of it," the woman continued, "they say that Orcs were responsible."

"Orcs?" said Athgar. "I thought we'd disproved that notion."

"Belgast wasn't there when we discussed it, remember?" said Natalia.

"Well, we're back now," offered Athgar. "We need to get this thing straightened out before it gets out of control."

"Our list of things to do is growing longer," said Natalia. "Let's go and visit this temple first, then we'll meet up with Belgast. He must be wondering where we are."

"Very well," said the Therengian, "then we can sort out this whole thing with the Orc body."

"Will you be stabling all four horses?" the woman asked.

"Yes," said Natalia, "for a few days, at least." She pulled forth her purse, counting out some coins. "Will this cover it?"

"That's more than enough," the woman replied.

"Thank you for your help," said Natalia. "What did you say your name was?"

"Matilda," the woman replied, "but I'm just a stable hand."

"Nevertheless, Matilda," said Natalia, "you've been very helpful. Come along, Athgar, it's time we visited the temple."

. . .

It didn't take long to reach their destination, for Ostermund was small enough that any location was but a short walk.

The Temple of Saint Agnes was a small affair. Constructed of wood, it was little more than a large chamber with two smaller rooms behind and a bell tower atop. They entered to see a woman placing candles upon an altar.

"Pardon us," called out Natalia, "are you Mother Eugenia?"

"Saint's sake, no," she replied. "My name's Hannah, I help the Holy Mother out by volunteering my time. What did you need to see her about? Is it something urgent?"

"Our time is limited," said Natalia, "but we can come back later if it's more convenient."

"She's working on her next sermon," Hannah explained. "Give me a moment, and I'll see if she's willing to talk with you."

"That would be much appreciated," said Athgar.

They waited as the woman disappeared through the back door. Athgar looked around, admiring the simplicity of the design. The building had a high, angled roof, the better to ward off the accumulation of snow, and he noticed a balcony above that ran the length of the room. His thoughts were interrupted by Natalia.

"This must be the Holy Mother," she whispered, as an older, plump woman with grey speckles in her hair approached. She carried herself with an air of authority, pausing to take in her new visitors.

"I'm told you came seeking me," Mother Eugenia said. "How may I help you?"

"We were led to believe you might be of some assistance to us," said Athgar. "You see, we've come into possession of some horses that we believe might belong to the Church."

"How interesting," said Eugenia. "Might I enquire as to how they came to you?"

"They were being used by brigands," said Natalia. "We believe they may have been stolen."

"And what leads you to believe they are the property of the Church?"

"They bear tattoos in the ears," offered Athgar. "We've been told this is common within the Church?"

"It is," the Holy Mother replied, "though I must admit to knowing little of such things. It is my understanding that only the Temple Knights use such a method."

"Temple Knights of which order?" asked Natalia.

"Why, all of them, naturally."

"Is there any way to tell which one?" asked Athgar.

"Likely," said the Holy Mother, "but it would take someone with far more expertise than I. You'd probably have to travel to Caerhaven."

"The capital of Krieghoff?" asked Athgar.

"That's right," Mother Eugenia replied. "I can give you a name if you like?"

"If you would be so kind," said Natalia. "I'm afraid we've had little success elsewhere."

"The name you want is Sister Cordelia."

"I assume she's a sister of your order?" asked Athgar.

"She's actually a Temple Knight of Saint Agnes. Their chain of command is outside of my own."

"I thought you were the same order?" said Athgar.

"We both worship Saint Agnes if that's what you mean, but I am a lay sister. My job is to see to the spiritual needs of our flock. Temple Knights, on the other hand, are responsible for protecting the Church. They have their own hierarchy of command separate from us."

"It all sounds so confusing," said Athgar. "Wouldn't it be easier to have the same leaders?"

"We do, at the higher levels," said Eugenia, "but to explain the inner workings of the Church would require far more time than I can spare at the moment."

"So this Sister Cordelia," interrupted Natalia, "will know all about the tattoos?"

"Yes," said the Holy Mother. "She is the equerry of our order."

"What's an equerry?" asked Athgar.

"That's the person in charge of horses for the order in a particular region. As such, she would see to the purchasing and breeding of such animals as the order would require, or at least as far as the Temple Knights are concerned."

"Does she oversee horses for all the orders?" asked Athgar.

"No, just the Sisters of Saint Agnes, but I'm sure she would be able to identify the number you seek, regardless of which order it belongs to."

"Thank you," said Natalia, "you've been most helpful."

"It was my pleasure," the Holy Mother responded. "I only wish that other troubles were as easily solved."

"What vexes you?" asked Natalia. "We might be of assistance, we are mages, after all."

"Mages? How very interesting, we get so few visitors these days. As to your offer, I doubt there's anything you can help us with. My parishioners are complaining about Orcs. They seem to think they're massing in the mountains for an attack."

"I can assure you they're not," said Athgar.

"How can you be so sure?" asked Mother Eugenia.

"I've spent time among them," he explained, "and I promise you they are a peaceful race."

"And yet they attacked a wagon, did they not?" she accused.

"Evidence was certainly created to convince people of that," said Athgar.

"What do you mean?"

"We found proof that someone else was behind the attack," added Natalia, "but we have yet to determine who. You need to reassure your congregation that they are not in danger, and certainly not from Orcs of the Red Hand."

"Thank you," said Mother Eugenia, "that is most reassuring. Now tell me, are these tattoos involved in your investigation?"

"They are," said Athgar, "though we're not sure how."

"Do you think the animals were stolen?" suggested the Holy Mother. "It wouldn't be the first time such a thing has occurred."

"Really?" said Athgar. "I would have thought Temple Knights would be hard to steal from."

"You would think so, wouldn't you," said Mother Eugenia, "but the truth is that many of these orders lack the very discipline they're famous for."

"I take it you don't like the Temple Knights?" said Athgar.

"I have no problem with the Sisters of our order, but many of the others see little value in our role as protectors of women."

"I'm surprised to hear that," said Natalia.

"The Church," the Holy Mother continued, "like any large organization has internal divisions. We have, after all, been around for more than a thousand years, but society has changed. I only wish the orders had changed with it. If you dig deep enough, I think you'll find fractious divisions within the Church."

"I'm surprised you would share your opinions with us," said Natalia. "I imagine your superiors would not be happy with such action."

"They would not," Mother Eugenia agreed, "but then I've always spoken my mind. That's why they sent me here to Ostermund, in the middle of nowhere."

"Well," said Athgar, "we appreciate your honesty and shall say nothing to others."

"Good luck to you both," said the Holy Mother. "Now, if you'll excuse me, I have work to do. The sermon will not write itself!"

They waited until Eugenia returned to her study before speaking again.

"What do you make of that?" asked Natalia.

"I'm not sure," answered Athgar. "On the one hand, we now have a name, although it's quite a distance to find her."

"And on the other hand?" queried Natalia.

"We've learned about internal troubles in the Church."

"We already learned in Corassus that the Church had problems," Natalia reminded him.

"Yes, but we assumed it was just the one situation. Perhaps the Church has larger issues beneath its surface?"

"Only time will tell," said Natalia.

"What do we do now?" said the Therengian. "It appears we've reached an impasse."

"We go back to the Owl," she said, "and find Belgast. Maybe he has more information to share."

"Well," said Athgar, "it will be nice to get some rest."

"Agreed," said Natalia, with a smile, "and I'd love a bath."

BELGAST

Winter 1104 SR

Belgast Ridgehand sat nursing his ale. It had been a trying few days, first the stress of the missing shipment, then the discovery of the death of his cousins. He wondered why Gundar might have allowed such a thing to happen, but he knew, deep down, that the Gods did not meddle in such matters. No, this was the work of the Orcs, Orcs that would pay for the sorrow they had inflicted on him.

He took a swig, drinking deeply, then sat back, a smile coming to his lips. Sooner or later, the truth would come out, he thought, and then he'd take revenge for the death of his cousins.

A gust of cold air alerted him that someone had just entered, and he looked up to see his human companions. He waved to them, and they made their way over, taking a seat opposite him at the table.

"Good to see you made it back safely," he said. "Any luck?"

"You might say that," said Athgar, "but it's not all good news."

"How so?" asked the Dwarf.

"We found the people behind the attack, and it wasn't the Orcs."

"It wasn't?" said an astonished Belgast. "Then who was it?"

"That's the part we're not sure about," explained Athgar. "We even captured someone, but he refused to give up names."

"Yes," added Natalia, in a much lower voice, "and their horses were Church property."

"The Church?" said the Dwarf. "Surely not!"

"I'm afraid it's true," said Athgar. "We don't know who in the Church is involved, nor why, but it seems likely."

"We did see a knight," added Natalia, "and he's involved somehow, but we don't know who he is or where he's from."

"Then it's useless," said Belgast, taking another drink. "It seems my cousins' deaths will go unavenged."

"We have, at least, discovered it's not the Orcs," said Athgar, "though that doesn't help you."

"Oh," said Belgast, "about that."

"What, the Orc?" said Natalia.

"Yes," continued the Dwarf, "the town garrison took the body."

"Where did they take it?" asked Athgar.

"I think they were taking it to Caerhaven. They seemed concerned that the body would deteriorate."

"Boondar's beard," said Athgar, "we must get it back!"

"Why?" asked the Dwarf.

"They're going to blame the Orcs for the attack."

"Surely not, now that you've found the real culprits," said Belgast.

"I'm afraid it's exactly what someone wanted everyone to think," the Therengian continued.

"But why go to all the trouble?" asked the Dwarf.

"I don't know," confessed Athgar.

"We suspect they want to incite a war," said Natalia. "Possibly because the Orcs lie on the border with Holstead?"

"But they'd still have to take on the Holstead army," the Dwarf countered. "Someone would have to be mad to contemplate such a thing."

"We haven't figured out the details yet," said Athgar, "but something suspicious is definitely going on here."

"That reminds me," said Natalia, "we dropped by the stables earlier, but we didn't see our horse."

"Ah, about that," began Belgast.

"What?" asked Athgar. "What did you do?"

"I might have given your horse to the trading post."

"Why would you do that?" Athgar asked.

"Well, you see… when my cousins and I rented the wagon, it came with a horse. When I returned it, I had to make recompense for the missing mare. Don't worry, I've cashed in my ingots and can pay you for it. I've also got what I owe you for the inn. The truth is, I haven't seen this many spare crowns in years."

"I suppose it doesn't matter," said Athgar, "we have the Church's horses anyways."

"Do you know which order they belong to?" asked the Dwarf.

"No," admitted Natalia, "and therein lies the mystery. I expect they belong to one of the fighting orders."

"What makes you say that?" asked Belgast.

"They're large, well-trained," explained Natalia, "and from what we've been told, that's typical of the fighting orders."

"So they belong to Temple Knights? That's a pretty serious accusation," argued the Dwarf.

"It's not the first time we've come across the Church doing strange things," said Natalia. "Last time, it was the Cunars, but there's no guarantee the same is true here. The truth is we don't know which order is involved."

"How many orders are there?" asked Belgast. "I find this whole Church thing quite tedious."

"Six," said Athgar, "and I have to agree with you. Far simpler to worship the old Gods."

"We're not here to debate religion," Natalia reminded him, "but find out who owns those mounts."

"It looks like we have to go to Caerhaven," said Athgar.

"Why would you say that?" asked the Dwarf.

"Sister Cordelia," said Natalia.

"Sister who?" asked Belgast.

"Cordelia," said Athgar. "She's a Temple Knight of Saint Agnes."

"Yes," added Natalia, "and also an equerry for the order. If anyone can identify the owners of the horses, it's her."

"Are you trying to tell me she knows every horse the Church owns?" said Belgast. "I find that hard to believe."

"She doesn't have to," said Athgar. "The Church marks each of their mounts with a tattoo, a series of numbers to be exact."

"And this mark will identify the owner?" asked the Dwarf.

"It will," said Athgar, "but we have to find someone who has access to their records."

"Hence the equerry," added Natalia.

"And I suppose that's why you want to go to Caerhaven, to see this expert?"

"Precisely," agreed Natalia.

"Sounds like it ought to be an interesting trip," said Belgast. "When do we leave?"

"We?" said Athgar.

"Of course," said the Dwarf, "you don't expect me to just sit back and ignore all this, do you? It was my cousins that were killed, I want to see justice done."

Athgar frowned, "If you're hoping for justice, you may be disappointed. Our experience with the Church has not been rewarding."

"Meaning?" asked the Dwarf.

"Well," said Natalia, "the last time we ran into trouble, Athgar ended up burning the Cunar barracks to the ground."

"I can't imagine the Church was too impressed with that," noted the Dwarf.

"All things considered," said Athgar, "they were pretty lenient."

"Although it soon became obvious they wanted us to move on," added Natalia.

"True," said the Therengian, "but they did give us a bag of coins and a pair of horses."

"That was Cyric's influence," noted Natalia. "I'm sure the Archprior would have been happy to have us executed. We did, after all, expose a conspiracy within one of their precious orders."

"It seems you two have quite the past," said Belgast. "Tell me, is this what you do? Travel around exposing plots?"

"No," said Athgar, "that's my fault. My village was burned to the ground, and I was seeking those responsible when I ran into Natalia."

"How long ago was this?" asked Belgast.

"Only a few months," said Natalia.

"You surprise me," said the Dwarf. "I was under the impression you two had been together for some time."

"We're as surprised as you," said Natalia. "Neither one of us was looking for someone to spend our lives with. It just sort of happened."

"Yes," agreed the Therengian, "we just fell in with each other."

"I'm sure there's more to the story than that," said Belgast, "but regardless, it's an interesting tale. You said you met in Draybourne, didn't you? That's not too far from Caerhaven. Think you'll give it a visit?"

Natalia looked at Athgar, but the Therengian was shaking his head.

"No," he said. "I'll always look back on it with fondness simply because it's where I met Natalia, but the city holds nothing for me otherwise. There are other places I'd rather go."

"Really?" said Natalia. "Like where? You've never talked about places you'd like to visit."

"I don't have specific places in mind," said Athgar, "but there's a whole Continent out there."

"Along with your people," Natalia reminded him.

"Yes, but your safety comes first," he replied.

"Is she in danger?" asked Belgast.

"There are those who are seeking her," said Athgar, "people that wish her harm."

"That's one of the reasons we came here to Ostermund," added Natalia.

"Less likely to be found, I'll wager," said Belgast. "Are these people dangerous? I only ask because it sounds like if we go to Caerhaven, we might run across some of them."

"It's definitely something we'll have to be careful of," said Athgar. "We don't want to put you in harm's way."

"Nonsense," said the Dwarf, "I was put in harm's way as soon as someone attacked my cousins. If it's all right with you, I'd like to see this through to the end."

"And if we're attacked?" said Natalia.

"Then we fight," said the Dwarf. "Now, are we going to Caerhaven or not?"

"I see no reason to delay any longer," said Athgar.

"I agree," said Natalia, looking at her companion, "though it is getting late, and I need a bath."

Belgast watched as the Therengian blushed, not sure of the implications.

"Very well," said the Dwarf, "we'll leave first thing in the morning."

Natalia gazed out the window as the sun set, bathing the land in a golden hue.

"I shall miss this place," she admitted.

Athgar came up behind her, wrapping his arms around her stomach. "We don't have to leave, you know. Nothing says we have to pursue this."

"Your friends, the Orcs, are in trouble. We can't sit back and let this pass us by, they need our help."

"I realize that," said Athgar, "but your safety is more important to me. Here in Ostermund, you're free of the influence of the family."

"Yes," she agreed, "but for how long? Don't you see, sooner or later, they'll come here looking for me."

"But until then," he said, "we're safe."

"I can't sit by in safety knowing that others are in peril," she said. "Kargen needs you, he's your family now."

"Does he?" he asked. "Kargen lived for years without me, surely he can look after himself?"

She turned around, leaving them standing face to face. "If one of your people were blamed for an attack, wouldn't you want to know?"

He thought about it for a moment, knitting his brow as he concentrated. "I suppose I would."

"How many Orcs are in Kargen's village?" she asked.

"Ord-Kurgad?" he said. "When I left, there must have been close to three hundred."

"And if an army of knights moves against them?"

"What makes you think it's knights?"

"The man we saw fleeing was wearing heavy armour," said Natalia. "Only knights wear such protection."

"That likely means Temple Knights," he said, "bearing in mind the horses."

"Precisely," she said, "making it imperative that we get to the bottom of this."

"And if it is the Church?" he asked. "We can't take them on again!"

"It depends on whether it's officially sanctioned by those in charge. If we find it is a small group, then yes, we can bring it to their attention."

"We're going to get a reputation as troublemakers," warned Athgar.

"We're past that," Natalia responded. "Those who truly follow the teachings of the Saints know we mean well, people like Brother Cyric."

"Yes," agreed Athgar, "but it's the others I'm more concerned about. Last time it was the Cunars, but only the Gods know who's involved this time."

Natalia laughed, breaking the tension. "Oh, Athgar, only you would invoke the Gods when talking about the Saints."

He grinned back at her, "I suppose there's a certain irony to it, isn't there?"

"That's my Therengian," she said, then kissed him.

"What's that for?" he asked.

"Because I love you," she responded. "Do I need any other reason?"

"I suppose not," he replied, his face still grinning. "Very well, we're in this together to the end, no matter what."

"Spoken like a true warrior," she said.

"No," he corrected, "a master of flame, and perhaps a hunter, but not a warrior. I was never trained as such."

"I thought you were taught how to use weapons back in Athelwald?"

"I was," he said, "but only to stand in a shield wall. I never learned strategy or tactics."

"That's all right," she said, "as a battlemage, I learned both."

"Good," said Athgar, "then if we get into a battle, you'll be the one in charge."

"We have a deal," she said, then smiled.

"I knew there was a reason I love you so much," he said.

"And here I was thinking it was my natural good looks," she countered.

"That too," he agreed. "Now, the sun is down, it's time we were abed."

"Well," she said, "when you put it that way, how can a girl resist? Come along, my love, there are sheets that need warming!"

•

THE JOURNEY BEGINS

Winter 1104 SR

L eaving the next day, the warmth of the sun promised an early spring. The trip to Caerhaven was calculated to take a week, most of it through rough trails and unmarked roads. They set off at a brisk pace, Belgast's pony easily keeping up with the temple horses. The spare mounts proved an advantage, as they could carry their belongings, scant as they were.

It was Belgast that had the most to haul, as he had seen fit to bring the armour and weapons of his dead kin. Athgar wondered at the mindset of the Dwarf, for he could not use the armour himself, being too stout a fellow for the chainmail to fit.

"I'll not be selling it in Ostermund," the Dwarf had said, "there's no one there worthy of it, nor anyone that could afford it. Dwarves are rare enough outside of our own kingdoms. Hopefully, I will find a buyer in Caerhaven, then I can take the proceeds home to my kin."

He had, however, insisted on gifting a shield to Athgar. He had already repaid his debt to them both, and the Therengian felt guilty about taking it, but Belgast had insisted.

"It was passed down from my Ancestors," he had said, "and you are more than worthy to bear it." So it was that Athgar now had a Dwarf shield slung on his horse.

Coming out of the foothills, they entered a thick forest where the going was slow, for the path meandered around, never straight for more than an arrow's flight. At night, they camped under the stars, wrapped in blankets to keep themselves warm.

By the time they finally reached open fields, the temperature had risen significantly, melting the snow and leaving only puddles remaining where days before a blanket of white had enveloped the land. The terrain was now quite flat, with long grass and sporadic trees littering the landscape. For two days, they travelled through this region, then the landscape became more meandering, littered with small clumps of trees and low hills.

Resting beneath the eaves of one of the wooded areas, they watched as the sun slowly sank in the west, casting a crimson glow over the night sky.

"Red sky at night," said Athgar, "hunter's delight."

"What's that supposed to mean?" asked Natalia.

"It means," said Belgast, "that the weather should be clear tomorrow."

Athgar turned to the Dwarf, "I'm surprised you know that."

"I believe the actual phase is 'Red sky at night, Dwarf's delight'," corrected Belgast.

"I must disagree," said Athgar, "it's an old Therengian saying."

"The Dwarves have been on this land longer," argued Belgast.

"Does it really matter?" asked Natalia. "You're both saying the same thing, that we'll have nice weather tomorrow. Leave it at that."

Athgar looked down, abashed. "You're right," he said. "My apologies, Belgast."

The Dwarf hummed and hawed. "I suppose she's right," he finally agreed. "Next thing you know, we'll be arguing about who invented the forge."

"That," said Natalia, quickly, "is something best discussed another time. We need some wood for a fire."

"I'll go and round some up," volunteered the Dwarf.

"Very well," said Natalia, "and while you're doing that, I'll refill the water skins."

"I don't see a stream nearby," said Belgast.

Athgar simply pointed at Natalia, "Water Mage, remember? She'll use magic to refill them. Nice, fresh water, not from some stagnant pond."

"You know," said Natalia, "I can also purify water. I don't have to create it from thin air."

"What's the difference?" he asked.

"Purification takes stagnant or otherwise bad water and makes it drinkable."

"But why do that when you can create it from thin air?" he asked.

"It's all about volume," she explained. "I can purify far more water than I can create."

Belgast wandered off into the woods, searching for kindling as Natalia opened up the first water skin.

"Take this," she instructed as she handed it to Athgar.

He held the container as Natalia started casting. It was an odd sensation when the skin filled itself, slowly growing heavier in the Therengian's hands until water bubbled out the top, causing him to step back to avoid getting splashed.

"This one's full," he said, replacing the stopper.

Natalia handed him the next, repeating her actions until they had filled all three containers, then sat, waiting for the Dwarf's return.

"Where is he?" asked Athgar. "It's getting dark, and I'm hungry."

"He'll be back soon," said Natalia. "Likely, he's having trouble finding suitable sticks."

"I should have gone, I'm the hunter," said Athgar.

Natalia looked at him in surprise. "I thought you said you weren't very good at hunting?"

"I'm not," he admitted, "but still better than a Dwarf, I would imagine."

"How do you know he's not a hunter?" she asked.

"I suppose I don't," he admitted, "but he didn't strike me as the outdoorsy type. Didn't he say he used to work at the Dwarf King's court?"

"He did," she confirmed, "but now that you mention it, he should be back by now."

Off in the distance, they heard a loud rustle as if a single tree was bending in the wind. Moments later, the distinct sound of Dwarf cursing reached their ears. They both stood, instantly alert.

"What do you suppose that was?" asked Natalia.

"I think our Dwarven friend has activated a trap of some sort."

"A trap?" she said. "Who would set a trap way out here? We're literally in the middle of nowhere!"

"Likely a hunter, I would think," he said. "Let's go have a look, shall we?"

"What if there are other traps?"

"Hang on," he said, "I'll light the way." He held out his hands, cupping them, palms upward and uttering words of power. A tiny green flame appeared, enlarging to hover just above his fingers.

"There," he said, "this will float just in front of us. Now keep your eyes open."

"How long will the spell last?" she asked.

"More than enough to find our Dwarven friend," said Athgar.

"Belgast?" called out Natalia.

"Over here," came the Dwarf's strained reply.

They moved towards his voice, stepping slowly and watching for any sign of tripwires. Athgar spotted him first, hanging from a tree, held tight by his ankle, which had somehow become ensnared.

"There he is," said the Therengian.

"What in the Saint's name happened?" asked Natalia.

The Dwarf, in answer, simply crossed his arms, giving him a most comical look, hanging upside down as he was.

"It appears," said the Dwarf, "that I've triggered some kind of snare."

"I'd say that about sums it up nicely," said Athgar, a hint of amusement to his voice. "Now come along, my friend, the time for such games is over, we've got a fire to build!"

"And I'd be mighty pleased to lend you a hand," said Belgast, "but it appears that I am otherwise engaged at present. Now, will you get me down from here before all the blood rushes to my head?"

Athgar looked at the snare, following the rope from the Dwarf's leg to the branch over which it was strung.

"Should be just a moment," said the Therengian as he moved closer to the tree and drew his axe, ready to cut.

"Athgar," called out Belgast.

"Not now, my friend," Athgar replied, "I'm just about to cut the rope."

"But, Athgar!" the Dwarf called out again.

"Not now," said the Therengian, amusement in his voice. "I must do this properly, or you'll fall on your head."

"Athgar!" called out Natalia.

Something in her voice made him look up to see her staring off into the trees, her eyes riveted on something.

"What is it?" he asked.

"We're not alone," she replied.

"What do you mean?" Athgar asked.

"I mean," she explained quietly, "that someone or something is watching us."

"Are you sure?" he asked. "I don't see anyone."

He stepped forward, raising his axe to bring the blade down on the rope. Before he was able to complete his swing, something whizzed by, embedding itself into a nearby tree.

"What was that?" he called out.

He controlled the floating flame, bringing it closer to illuminate the tree. A small indentation marked where something had dug into the bark. Another projectile whizzed past, clipping the arm of his tunic and striking the tree beside its companion.

"Down!" he shouted, unable to see their attackers.

"Behind you!" yelled Belgast.

Natalia quickly turned, letting loose with a blast of magic. Streaks of ice flew, cutting through the trees and sending leaves scattering. Something moved, and she had a brief glimpse of bark-like skin.

"What is it?" she called out.

"I've no idea," said the Dwarf, "but there's more of them."

Just as he spoke, more objects flew towards them. Natalia cast again, conjuring forth a wall of ice in time to protect herself. Small slivers of wood impacted the frozen surface, burying themselves deeply.

"They look like thorns," she called out.

"Thornlings!" called out Athgar. "The Orcs have talked about them."

"How do we defeat them?" asked Natalia.

"Only one way that I'm aware of," said Athgar. He rose from his position and cast, calling forth fire to surge out from his fingers, streaking through the woods to singe trees and startle the birds.

"Get Belgast down," he said, casting again. This time he swept his arms across the small clearing, creating a fan of flames.

Natalia targeted the rope, sending forth a spear of ice to strike the trunk of the tree that Belgast was hanging from. The rope didn't break, but the explosion of splinters was pronounced and a moment later, the tree started moaning as the weakened trunk began to fail.

Belgast looked down in fear, watching as the tree holding him started leaning heavily to one side, no longer able to bear its own weight. This caused the Dwarf to swing just before he struck the ground, and he rolled desperately to get out of the way as the rest of the trunk gave way. Branches crashed all around him, sending leaves flying, but somehow he managed to avoid any damage.

"Belgast!" called out Athgar.

"I'm all right," called back the Dwarf.

"Get back to the camp," commanded Athgar, releasing yet more fire.

"Careful," called out Natalia, "you'll set the whole woods aflame."

Natalia moved towards the Dwarf, freeing him from the rope.

"Come on," she said, lifting him by the arm, "it's time we were clear of here."

Athgar moved towards them, fanning flame left and right.

"Run!" he yelled, then began sprinting.

They crashed through the woods as fast as they could manage. Athgar felt the sting of branches hitting his face as he ran, the grip of undergrowth clutching at them as they fled. He paused once more to send a stream of crimson fire off behind him, then turned, resuming his flight.

Finally, he staggered to a halt, his chest heaving. Natalia and Belgast had stopped just in front of him, both working mightily to recover their own breath.

"What, in the name of the Gods, were those things?" asked Belgast.

"Athgar called them thornlings," said Natalia.

"And so they were," said Athgar.

"What's a thornling?" asked the Dwarf.

"Creatures of legend," the Therengian explained, "or so I was led to believe."

"Will they follow us?" asked Belgast.

"No," said Athgar, "they are said to fear fire above all else."

"But what, exactly, are they?" Natalia asked.

"They are small creatures, with skin like bark. They're about the size of goblins, but are covered in thorns."

"That's what they fired at us," said Natalia.

"Exactly," said Athgar. "The Orcs speak of them to frighten younglings into going to sleep. I assumed they were just creatures of myth."

"Apparently, the myth is based on fact," said Belgast.

"So it would seem," agreed the Therengian.

"What would you suggest we do now?" asked Natalia.

"First, we find our horses, then we move on. There's no sense in trying to camp here, we're likely too close to wherever they call home."

"So we travel in the dark?" asked the Dwarf.

"For now," said Athgar, "but I still have energy left. My magic flame will lead the way."

"All well and good for you," said Belgast, "but that still leaves two of us unable to see."

In answer, Athgar dug around the underbrush, finding a stick that was about the length of his forearm. He uttered some words, and then the end broke into flame, much like a torch.

"Here," he said, handing it to Belgast, "take this. I'll create one for each of us."

"I thought you were going to use the floating flame?" said Natalia.

"I was," he replied, "but this takes much less energy, and it will give us all some protection against the thornlings, should we encounter them again."

"And if we do see them?" asked the Dwarf.

"Then wave the fire at them, it should keep them at bay," Athgar replied.

"Easy for you to say," said Belgast, "you're a Fire Mage."

"Look," said Athgar, "I'm struggling to remember everything the Orcs told me. At least it gives us some sort of protection."

"Come on," insisted Natalia, "let's go find those horses, shall we?"

SOLDIERS

Spring 1104 SR

The woods were thick and the roadway winding, leaving them constantly on the alert, watching for any sign of trouble. It wasn't until they cleared the forest, three days later, that they finally started to relax as they passed by farmland and a small hamlet, their first signs of civilization since leaving Ostermund.

That afternoon they stopped at a local tavern, relishing the warm fire and comfortable surroundings. The brief halt grew longer as they ate, so much so that they decided to stay for the night.

The morning saw them rise early, eager to be on the road. Caerhaven was only a day or two away, and they were keen to get on with their investigation. Mid-morning, they spotted horsemen off in the distance, riding towards them with pennants flying.

"What's this?" called out Belgast in alarm.

"Soldiers," announced Athgar.

"I can see that," replied the Dwarf, "but are they hostile?"

"I doubt it," offered Natalia. "They fly the flag of Duke Leopold. I imagine they're keeping the roads safe."

"There's an awful lot of them for a simple patrol," noted Athgar.

"Perhaps something has them alarmed?" suggested the Dwarf.

Athgar chuckled, "Maybe they're on the lookout for rowdy Dwarves?"

"Not funny," said Belgast, "and if that was the case, they'd need more men."

Athgar looked at his companion in surprise, then the Dwarf broke out into laughter.

"What's so funny?" asked the Therengian.

"You should have seen your face," said Belgast, "it was most amusing."

"Are you two finished mocking each other?" asked Natalia.

"Yes," they both chimed in unison.

The riders drew closer, a full two dozen of them. Their leader wore the plate armour of a knight while the rest were clearly professional soldiers, most in chainmail augmented with some metal plates over their legs and arms.

Athgar moved to the side of the road to allow them to pass, but instead, they halted.

"Greetings," called out the knight.

"Good day, Sir...?" started Natalia.

"Sir Adler," the knight responded, "and to whom do I have the honour of speaking?"

"My name is Natalia," she said. "I am travelling with my husband, Athgar and an acquaintance of ours, Belgast Ridgehand."

"Well met," said the knight, bowing to Athgar and the Dwarf. "Might I ask what finds you on the road this day?"

"We are on our way to Caerhaven," said Natalia. "Why? Is there a problem?"

"There is indeed, Madam," Sir Adler responded. "The duke has increased the strength of our road patrols to protect our countrymen."

"Tell me," said Natalia, "what is it that has the duke so attentive to our safety?"

"There have been reports of Orcs in the area," the knight replied.

"Have there?" said Athgar. "This is the first we've heard."

"They have been raiding of late, greenskins engaged in common banditry. They've troubled us for years, of course, and yet up till now, they've been little more than a nuisance."

"You said 'up till now,'" said Natalia, "I take it something has happened to change that?"

"It has," confirmed the knight. "They have grown bolder for some reason and struck one of the duke's outposts near the village of Tomar."

"Never heard of it," said Athgar.

"It is a small village, little more than a hamlet, really. It lies close to the border with Holstead."

"Isn't that where the Orcs have their lands?" asked the Therengian.

The knight looked at him in surprise. "You know the area?"

"He has a passing familiarity with it," said Natalia.

"When you say they struck," continued Athgar, "I assume you mean they attacked?"

"Raided might be a more applicable term. They burned down some houses and made off with the livestock."

"I didn't know the Orcs raised cows," said Athgar. "My understanding is they are hunters, not farmers."

"The greenskins are a savage race," said Sir Adler, "and you'd be well to remember that."

"Savage?" said Natalia.

"Yes," the knight continued, "a brutal race, unforgiving in battle and ruthless in the extreme. They don't take prisoners, and they refuse to surrender."

"Then how do you deal with them?" asked Belgast.

"The only way we can," said Sir Adler, "we kill them. I wish there was another way, but the safety of our own people must come first, don't you agree?"

"Safety is important," said Athgar, "and yet I wonder what might have started this whole situation? Tell me, have you fought them yourself?"

"No," the knight admitted, "though I yearn to test my steel against them."

"Then how do you know so much about them?" asked Natalia.

Sir Adler looked like he was about to complain, but then he took a deep breath, "My apologies, Lady, if I have been too obtuse in my description. The Orcs are a primitive race, of that, we have no doubt. They have been a constant thorn in the side of the duke for many years. I wouldn't expect you to be knowledgeable about such things."

Natalia was about to lash out with an angry retort, but Athgar spoke first, attempting to defuse the situation.

"We are glad that you have been keeping the roads safe, Sir Alder. I take it the route to Caerhaven is clear?"

The knight nodded in Athgar's direction. "It is, my lord. I trust you will have a pleasant trip."

"I'm sure we shall," said Athgar. "Tell me, have we much farther to travel?"

"No," said the knight. "If the weather holds, you should be there by nightfall. Might I suggest I detach some men to escort you?"

"Did you not just say the road was safe?" interjected Natalia.

"I did," replied Sir Adler, "but I would be pleased to offer the courtesy, especially to one so fair as yourself."

Natalia stared at the man, unsure of how to take his words.

"I think," offered Athgar, "that we will be safe enough. We'd hate to distract you from your duties."

"Not at all," said Sir Adler, "it would be my pleasure."

"But won't you need all your men should the Orcs prove troublesome?"

The knight appeared to wrestle with the problem, his face a mask of turmoil.

"I insist that you keep your men together," said Athgar. "It will assure the locals that the duke is taking his responsibilities seriously."

"Very well," the knight responded. "Lord Athgar, I bid you a good day, and to you too, fair Lady Natalia." He let his eyes linger on her for a moment, then turned his horse back to the road.

They watched them ride off, the men in pairs behind their leader.

"Well, that was... interesting," said Natalia.

"It appears that Sir Adler has taken an interest in you," said Athgar.

"Sir Adler should mind his own business. Did I not tell him we were married?"

"You did," the Therengian replied, "and yet, I don't think that dampened his ardour in the slightest. Not that I can blame him, of course, you are a most enchanting vision."

She looked at Athgar in surprise. "Where in the Continent did you come up with that line? That doesn't sound like you."

"Why? Because I said you were enchanting?" he defended.

"Yes," she said, "you're not usually so eloquent."

"I don't know what that means," said Athgar.

"It simply means well-spoken, my love. Not that I'm complaining, mind you. You just surprised me, that's all."

"What can I say?" he grinned. "You inspire me."

"That's all well and good," interrupted the Dwarf, "but if you two keep chatting away the day, we'll never reach Caerhaven. How about we start riding, and you can talk all you want?"

"He has a point," noted Athgar.

"Very well," agreed Natalia, "we shall be on our way. Would you care to lead, Belgast?"

"I'd be delighted," replied the Dwarf, urging his pony back onto the road.

"Tell me," said Belgast, "do you put much faith in the knight's reports?"

"You mean about the Orcs?" asked Athgar.

"I was thinking more about the village," said the Dwarf. "What was it called again?"

"Tomar," said Natalia.

"That was it," said the Dwarf. "Do you really think the Orcs raided it?"

"No," said Athgar. "Orcs don't raid like that."

"Then how do they raid?" asked Belgast.

"First of all, they don't raid at all, unless they're at war."

"And secondly?" the Dwarf pressed.

"They're hunters," he added. "Why would they steal livestock?"

"Could their woods be low on prey?" offered Belgast.

"No, I can't believe that. Also, Kargen is too smart to attack the duke's lands. He knows what would happen if he did."

"Kargen?" said Belgast. "You said he was their chief, didn't you?"

"I did," Athgar confirmed.

"Could someone else have taken over as their leader?" asked the Dwarf.

"Anything's possible," said Athgar, "but I doubt it. He was almost a unanimous choice when they elected him."

"Elected him?" said the Dwarf in surprise. "You mean it's not a hereditary position?"

"Far from it," explained Athgar. "A chieftain can rule for many years, but if he's unpopular, the tribe can remove him from that position, all they need is a majority vote."

"What a strange way to govern a people," mused Belgast.

"Oh, I don't know," said Natalia, "I kind of like the idea that they get to choose who their ruler is."

"Why in Gundar's name would people want that?" asked Belgast.

"It means all their leaders are popular with their people," said Natalia, "so they're more likely to be able to get things done."

"And how long do these chiefs rule?"

"It varies," said Athgar. "Technically, it's for life, but when an Orc reaches a certain age, they'll usually step down for the wellbeing of the tribe. Of course, they can always be ousted. That's what happened to Kargen's predecessor."

"Oh?" said the Dwarf. "You have me intrigued. Tell me, were you there? What happened?"

"The old leader was an Orc named Gorlag. When I was brought into the village, he objected."

"And?" prompted Belgast.

"And he tried to kill me. Kargen intervened and was injured."

"And he was voted out of his position?" asked the Dwarf.

"Not quite," said the Therengian, "there's a bit more to the story. I woke up to see Kargen and Gorlag fighting in my hut. Kargen went down, a vicious wound to his stomach, so I did the only thing I could, I launched a streak of fire against Gorlag."

"And you killed him?" said Belgast.

"No, I injured him, but he was still the chief. He tried to have me seized so he could banish me, but I challenged him to a duel over Kargen's injury."

"And then you killed him?" the Dwarf said, hopefully.

"No, but I did win the fight. The tribe ruled that Gorlag had violated their most sacred rules, and then he was banished."

"Interesting," noted the Dwarf.

"Say," said Natalia, "do you think that maybe it's Gorlag that's been causing the problems here of late?"

"I hadn't thought of that," said Athgar, "but I suppose it's a possibility. He would certainly want to get revenge on the tribe for banishing him."

"Did anyone leave with him?" asked Belgast.

"Not that I know of," said Athgar. "Few Orcs would willingly leave their homes to live in Human cities."

"Still," commented the Dwarf, "he had to go somewhere."

"Perhaps he's working with someone to discredit the Orcs?" suggested Natalia.

"I can see him hating Kargen, or me for that matter, but I don't think he would seek revenge on the entire tribe. He was much respected while he was chieftain. The entire debacle was really my fault. When Athelwald was destroyed, Kargen and Laruhk brought me back to their village. Gorlag was convinced it would only bring ruin to the Orcs."

"Well," mused the Dwarf, "it looks like he may have been correct, looking at the situation we have now."

"You can't blame that on Athgar," said Natalia. "He had nothing to do with Orc attacks."

"I suppose you're right," said Belgast, "but sometimes it only takes a nudge to send events careening off in another direction. You might have been just the tip of the axe."

"Meaning?" asked the Therengian.

"Suppose you hadn't survived the attack on your village?" mused the Dwarf. "What do you think would have happened?"

"Nothing, other than me being dead, of course. The Orcs would have continued on their lives uninterrupted by Human interaction."

"And Gorlag would still be their chief?" asked Belgast.

"I suppose so," said Athgar. "It's not something I really thought about. After all, it's all in the past now. We can't change things that have already happened."

"True enough," said the Dwarf, "but still a fascinating thing to consider."

"Spoken like a true diplomat," said Natalia.

"Thank you," said Belgast, "I'll take that as a compliment."

"Do you think this Gorlag might have returned to the village and resumed his position?" asked Natalia.

"No," said Athgar. "After our duel, he was banished for life. No Orc would allow him to return."

"Maybe he joined another tribe?" suggested Natalia. "He could have hidden his identity from them."

"That wouldn't work," said Athgar. "The Orc shamans can communicate over long distances, and in any case, there are no other tribes nearby. You'd have to travel clear across three kingdoms to find more."

"I had no idea they were so rare," said Natalia.

"They're like us Therengians," said Athgar, "scattered to the four winds."

"Yes," agreed the Dwarf, "but the Therengians were once a mighty empire."

"So were the Orcs," said Athgar.

"They were?" said Belgast. "I never knew that."

"It's true," defended Athgar, "before the coming of man."

"What happened to them?" asked the Dwarf.

"Their cities were destroyed by the elves," the Therengian explained. "They say there were a number of ancient kingdoms, seven if I'm not mistaken, each ruled by a mighty city."

"I never knew that," said Belgast. "I just assumed they were always primitives."

"They are an ancient culture," said Athgar, "but they've been driven to the ends of the Continent to live out their lives, much like my own people."

"But the Duke of Holstead granted you land?" said Natalia.

"He did," agreed Athgar, "but that was a long time ago. The latest duke is young and thinks only of power and profit. Ethwyn, my sister, tried to tell me that once, but I didn't listen."

"You have a sister?" said Belgast. "You continue to surprise me."

"You find it surprising that I have a sister?" the Therengian replied.

"I have a hard time picturing her," the Dwarf admitted. "Tell me, what is she like?"

"Ethwyn's younger than me by a year," explained Athgar, "and yet she's taller. She has brown hair, like me, and wears it long and braided down her back. Or at least she did."

"Did? You mean she died?" asked Belgast.

"She's either dead or enslaved," he explained. "The last I saw of her, she was staggering through the ruins of Athelwald, bleeding from a head wound. I'm led to believe she was sold as a slave in Corassus. From there, the trail went cold."

"So she could still be alive?" mused the Dwarf.

"We can only hope," said Athgar, "but I can think of no way of finding her."

"And the rest of your people?"

"Some managed to escape and flee east," said Athgar. "I hope one day I'll be able to find them."

"I wish you the best of luck," said Belgast, "and yet I fear our current circumstances might prevent it."

"Whatever do you mean?" asked Natalia.

"It seems clear to me that whoever is behind this plot is powerful. After all, they used resources of the Church and seem to be connected with the duke himself."

"What makes you think the duke's involved?" asked Natalia.

"It was his men that mentioned the attack on the village. I would think the entire debacle was staged, much like the attack on my cousins. It would take some significant resources to pull that off."

"Well," mused Athgar, "we did suspect the Church, but I suppose the duke may have at least been complicit in it. It was his men, after all, that removed the Orc body from Ostermund."

"Hopefully, we'll be able to learn more in Caerhaven," said Natalia. "In the meantime, I suggest we keep all these theories in mind."

That afternoon the road topped a hill to reveal a city spread out before them. From their vantage point, they could easily make out its walls, not as high as those of Corassus, or even Draybourne, but impressive nonetheless. The customary gatehouse beckoned them, and so they rode forward, eager to reach their destination. They were soon riding under the portcullis, their arrival noticed only absently by bored-looking soldiers.

"Welcome to Caerhaven," said Belgast, "city of promise."

CAERHAVEN

Spring 1104 SR

O nce past the gate, Athgar suddenly halted and dismounted.
"That's it," he declared, "I'm officially tired of riding this horse.
My backside needs a rest."

"We need to find lodgings," said Natalia, "not to mention visiting the
Church about these horses."

"First things first," suggested the Dwarf. "We'll find a nice inn and settle
in, and then make some enquiries of the Church."

"Couldn't we split up?" asked Athgar.

"Then how would we find each other afterwards," said Natalia. "Belgast
is right, we need to see to our rooms first."

"Very well," the Therengian capitulated, "have it your way. It's getting
late in the day anyway, shall we leave the horses till morning?"

"It means the expense of stabling them all," said Natalia.

"We can afford it," said Belgast, "and it would be better to start after a
good night's sleep."

"Have you been here before?" asked Athgar.

"I have," admitted the Dwarf, "but not for many years. I think the last
time I visited was back in '81. I'm sure much has changed since then."

"Where did you stay?" asked Natalia.

"At a place called the Golden Spire. It's not too far from here if I
remember correctly, assuming it's still open, of course."

"It's as good a place as any to look," suggested Natalia. "Lead on, Belgast." The Dwarf guided them through the streets. For someone who hadn't been there for more than twenty years, he had a remarkable memory, pointing out places to eat and others to avoid.

"Here we are," he said at last, leading them towards a pleasant-looking building. It was long, similar in length as the great Orc hut in Ord-Kurgad, and yet it was made from wattle and daub, with an ornate wooden entrance and windows that let the sound of laughter and merriment drift out into the street.

"It looks nice," offered Natalia. "You say you stayed here before, do you remember the owner's name?"

"Can't say as I do," admitted the Dwarf. "You Humans all look alike to me, present company excepted, of course."

"I don't suppose it matters," said Athgar, "they'll accept our coins as easily as any other, I suspect."

At their approach, a stable hand ran up to them, offering to take their mounts. As the horses were led away, the group of three entered the structure, letting Belgast lead the way.

Inside, the atmosphere was warm and welcoming. Belgast moved through the crowd to find the owner while Athgar and Natalia secured a table. It didn't take long for a server to find them, a young lad with tousled hair.

"Can I help you, sir, madam?" he said.

"A tankard of ale," said Athgar, who then turned to Natalia, "and you?"

"Wine, if you please," she said.

The young lad nodded and then disappeared back into the crowd.

"This place doesn't look so bad," Athgar mused.

"No, it doesn't," she agreed. "I think it will be a nice base of operations while we look into things. It seems to be located in a safer area of town."

"Good," said Athgar, "I've had my share of staying in run-down lodgings. I was robbed in Draybourne, you know. They took everything they could while I slept."

"Not quite everything," she reminded him. "You kept your axe and your torc if you remember."

"True," he admitted, "and yet whoever it was would have taken those too, if I hadn't woken up. What a place that was!"

She reached across, taking his hand and squeezing it gently. "It's all over now, and we're together."

He smiled back at her, "Yes, and when it comes down to it, that's all that's important." He leaned in closer, dropping his voice slightly, "You don't think the family will have a presence here, do you?"

"I would hope not," she replied, "though I daresay they'd have a tough time recognizing me now. With my shorter hair and more sensible clothes, I blend in quite nicely."

"Good," he added, "but you must be sure to mention it if you notice any unusual attention coming your way. Need I remind you they're still out to get you?"

"No need," she said, "I could hardly forget the family. They likely have connections at the court here, and if we have any interaction with the duke, we'll have to take care."

Belgast soon appeared, a tankard of frothy ale in hand.

"It's all settled," he announced. "Our rooms are next door to each other. I assumed you two were sharing?"

"We are," said Athgar. "Where did you get the ale?"

"Snagged it on my way over," the Dwarf revealed. "Why?"

"I ordered our drinks some time ago, but the young lad seems to have disappeared."

"There he is," said Natalia, pointing.

The youth was struggling to make his way through the crowd, a tankard in one hand, a wine goblet in the other. Finally, he reached them, dropping the drinks to the table with a flourish that caused Athgar's to spill over the edge.

"There you are," the lad declared.

"Thank you," said Natalia. "How much do we owe you?"

"Two pence."

"Is that all?" said Belgast. "Here, take three." He tossed the coins onto the table. The server snapped them up, scuttling off to find other customers.

"He seems enthusiastic," said Athgar.

"Indeed," said the Dwarf, then he took a deep drink, only lowering the tankard to smack his lips.

Natalia burst out laughing. Belgast stared at her with a look of indignation.

"What's so funny?" he demanded.

"Sorry," she said, "but your beard's full of foam."

He used his sleeve to wipe it away, glancing down at his arm afterwards. "So it was," he declared, "but it was worth it. This ale is tremendous."

Athgar sipped his own drink, immediately noticing the heavy aroma. "It's very strong," he said.

"Just the way I like it," said Belgast. "Too many Human ales are weak."

"Do you drink a lot of ale?" asked Natalia.

"I do," the Dwarf confessed, "though it takes a lot to get one of my race drunk. We are a hardy folk, you know."

"I cannot speak for all Humans," said Athgar, "but I've always been a sparse drinker. I prefer to keep my head clear."

"You were a bowyer," noted Natalia. "I shudder to think what your bows would have looked like had you been drunk all the time."

He laughed, releasing the pent-up tension of their trip. "Aye," he said, "so would I. Tell me, what was it like back at the…" he caught himself, then continued, "the place where you grew up? Did you drink much?"

"Only in moderation," she said, "we had to keep our minds sharp to learn our magic. What of the Orcs?"

"Yes," added Belgast, "did they get drunk?"

"Not so much," said Athgar, "they don't brew strong drink like Humans. They prefer a fermented drink made from all sorts of things."

"And how did that taste?" asked Belgast.

"Let's just say you got used to it after a while," said Athgar.

Belgast drained his tankard, then belched quite unexpectedly, covering his mouth in shame.

"Your pardon," he begged, "I don't know what came over me. It must be all this foam."

"We won't hold it against you," promised Natalia.

"Well," the Dwarf said, rising, "I think that's my signal to head off for a nap. How about you two?"

"I wouldn't mind a walk," said Natalia, turning to Athgar. "How about you?"

"A walk it is then, fair lady." He stood, making a show of bowing regally and extending his arm, "Shall we?"

"We shall," she said, rising to the challenge. Taking his arm, she allowed him to lead her outside, where they were surprised by the afternoon bustle as people hurried home from their labours.

"Where would you like to go?" Athgar asked.

"I have no idea," she said, "I simply wish to stretch my legs."

He looked down at her feet, then back to her face. "They seem long enough already, why would you want to stretch them?"

Not missing a beat, she stared back into his eyes, "So that my man can spend more time caressing them, why else?"

"A good answer," he confessed, blushing slightly.

"Let's head down this way," she said, pointing. "It's as good a direction as any other. Perhaps we'll find something interesting?"

"Very well," he replied, guiding her down the street.

They wandered for some time, taking in the sights of the city. Vendors had stalls in the broader streets while the narrower ones contained shops, often with open windows, greeting them with the smell of fresh-baked bread, apples and even leather as a bootmaker plied his trade, sitting outside in the fresh afternoon air.

When they stopped to sample some scones, Athgar looked on in fascination as Natalia dribbled honey over one. She offered it to him, but being unfamiliar with such things, he refused. Natalia polished off the scone, then kissed him, giving him a taste of the honey as their lips met.

After the experience, he was more than willing to try one himself, but there was a sudden burst of activity as someone hastily opened the door, yelling to those inside.

"The father general's going to address the crowd," he announced, then quickly disappeared down the street.

They had no idea who this was, but it was quite apparent that the name was well known amongst the patrons, for they all hurried to pay for their purchases, then rushed from the place, leaving Athgar and Natalia wondering what they had missed.

"Who's the father general?" Athgar asked of the proprietor.

"You must be new to town," said the baker. "He's the head churchman in these parts."

"Does he regularly address the people?" asked Natalia. "It seems such an odd thing to do."

"No," the man admitted, "but these are strange times. I think he's going to address the rumours of those attacks."

"You mean the Orc raids?" asked Athgar.

"Precisely," said the baker.

"And where does this all take place?" asked Natalia.

"Just down the street," the man replied. "Go out and turn right, then two blocks down, you'll see folks gathered under a balcony. That's the Church offices where he'll be speaking."

"Thank you. Can we please have half a dozen of those to take with us?" said Natalia, counting out some coins. The owner passed over a bundle of cloth, six scones nestled snugly inside.

"Glad to be of service," he said, "come again."

"We will," promised Athgar, "and we'll be sure to tell our friend about this place."

Natalia dragged him outside. "Come on," she urged, "we might learn something useful."

They stepped outside only to see people rushing past. Whoever the father general was, he had already started, for his voice echoed down the street, supported by cheers from the crowd. Athgar struggled to make out what he was saying, but the echo from the buildings, combined with the cheering, made it all but impossible.

As they drew closer, the crowd thickened until they could make little headway. Natalia struggled to see the speaker, but with so many people in the way, she couldn't see his face clearly. He was saying something about this being the last straw and how he pledged to drive them from the land. She had to assume he was talking about the Orcs and looked at Athgar, but the Therengian was just staring at the man.

"Athgar," she asked, "what is it?"

"That man," he replied, "he's the one that fled the cabin back in Ostermund."

"Are you sure?" she asked, pushing past a spectator to get a better view. She peered up, and the father general's face came sharply into focus. He was leaning on the balcony railing, his arm raised in the air to give emphasis to his words.

"That IS him!" she agreed. She was about to say more when she chastised herself for not noting earlier that the man was wearing the distinctive garb of the Order of Saint Cunar.

She turned to Athgar in alarm, only to find him staring back at her.

"Do you realize what this means?" he asked.

She nodded, "Indeed, it seems the Cunars are involved yet again."

He grabbed her arm, guiding her back from the crowd. "We don't know if it's the whole order," he said. "Maybe it's just this one individual?"

"Is that what you really think?" asked Natalia. "Come now, Athgar, neither one of us really trusts the Cunars. And did you notice? He's a Temple Knight as well."

"But who is he?" asked the Therengian.

"I heard the name Father General Gilbert mentioned," said Natalia.

"The name means nothing to me," said Athgar.

"Me neither," she admitted, "but his rank means a great deal. He's a father general."

"Meaning?"

"Meaning he commands all the Church forces in this region. That could mean just this dukedom or several, depending on their definition of region."

"How many father generals could there be?" asked Athgar.

"Across the Continent?" she pondered. "Likely dozens."

"So he's got someone above him, then?"

"Only the Grand Master of his order and I doubt we'd find him here in Caerhaven. It's not an important enough city."

"Where does that leave us?" asked Athgar. "Do we go and visit him, perhaps beat the truth out of him?"

"You can't use a strong-arm approach on a high ranking member of the Church," she chided. "We'll have to be more diplomatic."

"What are you suggesting?"

"We'll visit the Church tomorrow. Hopefully, we can arrange a meeting with this Father General Gilbert."

"What good will that accomplish?" he asked.

"It will at least give us some idea of what we're dealing with. As they used to say at the Volstrum, it's always best to know your enemy."

"Very well," said Athgar, "though I don't trust the man."

"You're just feeling threatened," she said.

"Do you blame me after what happened in Corassus? That Cunar was only a commander, while this one is even higher up the chain of command. What if the whole order is corrupt?"

"Then we shall have to rely on the other orders for help," noted Natalia. "What was the name of that Sister of Saint Agnes?"

"Sister Cordelia," offered Athgar.

"Yes, that's it," she agreed. "Tomorrow, we'll see if we can arrange a meeting with the father general. After that, we'll look for Cordelia."

"I wish Cyric was here," said Athgar.

"So do I," Natalia agreed, "so do I."

THE FATHER GENERAL

Spring 1104 SR

As they sat in silence, Athgar shifted his position slightly, trying to stretch his back. Others nearby looked at him in annoyance, as if this simple act had interrupted their private thoughts.

"How long do you think we'll have to wait?" he whispered to Natalia.

"I have no idea," she replied quietly. "It's almost noon, and we've been here since shortly after the sun came up."

"Surely he must see us soon?" he added.

"Look around," she urged, "these people have been waiting as long as we have."

He cast his eyes about, taking in the rest of the room. There were over a dozen people here, all awaiting an audience with the father general.

"I don't think he's here," Athgar noted.

"Why would you say that?" Natalia asked.

"Some of these people have been waiting as long as us," he explained, "and not a single one of them has been taken to see him. Did you tell his assistant that it was important?"

"I did," she insisted, "but that doesn't mean much. I imagine everyone uses that expression."

The door opened, admitting a Temple Knight. He strode across the room, his heavy armour rattling as he passed. Halting at the assistant's desk, he waited for the man to look up.

"Yes?" said the assistant. "Brother Carrington, isn't it?"

"It is," the knight replied.

"What can I do for you, Brother?"

"I have just come from Father General Gilbert," Carrington explained. "He wishes me to convey his sincerest apologies, but he will not be able to see anyone today. His time has been otherwise occupied and is likely to remain so for the foreseeable future."

The assistant let out an audible sigh. "Very well, I shall make a note in my ledger."

Athgar rose, holding out his hand for Natalia. "So much for that," he said.

She stood, taking the proffered hand in hers. "I suppose it was inevitable. Nothing we do ever seems to be easy."

"Hey, now," he said, "I wouldn't say that. We found each other, didn't we?"

She smiled, "We did, but even that was difficult. I almost killed you, remember?"

"True," he said, "but I survived, and now here we are."

The other people in the room were also rising after realizing the futility of their efforts.

"Let's go," Athgar said, "we'll get out of these stuffy surroundings and get some fresh air."

"Good idea," she agreed, "and now we can go and find the Temple of Saint Agnes."

The sun beat down on them as they entered the street, causing Athgar to look up in surprise.

"Hard to believe it's already spring," he mused. "It wasn't that long ago that we were fighting a blizzard.

"We were," she agreed, "but you forget, we were in the mountains. It's always colder up there."

"True enough," he said, "but now we're back down here amongst the civilized folk."

"You sound nervous," she said.

"I am," he said. "I've never trusted big cities."

"How many have you visited?" she asked.

"Only three," he admitted. "The first was Draybourne, where I was robbed and almost killed, then we made it to Corassus."

"Where you were once again almost killed," she added. "But no one's tried to kill you in Caerhaven."

"Not yet, anyway," he grumbled.

"Oh come now, surely you have better memories than that?"

He looked at her and couldn't help but smile. "Of course I do, but being around all these people still makes me nervous."

"What's there to be nervous about?" she asked.

"I don't know," he said, "I just feel as if I don't belong."

"That's just because you were raised in a village."

"What about you?" he asked.

"I was raised in Karslev," she replied. "It's a much larger city than Caerhaven, though, truth be told, I didn't see much of it."

They strolled down the street holding hands, Athgar casting his eyes around nervously while Natalia took in the sights.

"Oh, look," she said, "a playhouse."

"A what?" said the Therengian.

"A playhouse. You know, a theatre."

"What's a theatre?" he asked.

She looked at him in surprise. "Did you not have plays in Athelwald?"

"We played as children," he answered.

"That's not what I meant. Did you have storytellers?"

"Of course," said Athgar, "that's how we handed down our history. There was an old woman, Skora, who was well gifted in that regard. She could mimic people's voices, which made the stories come alive. It was quite entertaining."

"Now imagine if she had help," suggested Natalia. "What if she told the story, and others pretended to play the people she was talking about?"

"Is that what a play is?" he asked. "You make it sound quite interesting."

"It is," she insisted.

"So, you've been to plays before?"

"We weren't allowed to leave the academy," she said, "not until we graduated, at least. No, they brought the actors to us."

"Actors? I assume that's the people that play the parts?"

"Yes," Natalia confirmed. "Perhaps we should go and see a play while we're here in Caerhaven?"

"I'd like that," he answered, "but I think we have more important things to attend to first."

"A good point," she agreed. "Now, let's find this Temple of Saint Agnes, shall we?"

"I think we just did," he said, stopping suddenly.

She turned to face him only to see him staring at the front of a spacious stone building.

"Unless I miss my guess," he said, "that's the temple we're looking for."

Natalia turned to see two guards standing there, both wearing plate armour, covered with scarlet surcoats bearing the image of three waves.

"Those are sister knights, aren't they?" Athgar asked.

"I believe so," she replied, "though, in their armour, they could be anyone."

"Yes, but isn't red their colour?"

"It is," she confirmed. "Shall we enter?"

"Of course," he said, "but are we allowed to? The place IS guarded, after all."

"I believe those knights are ceremonial," said Natalia, "so you can relax now."

"It's hard to relax when a potential foe is encased in steel."

"They're not foes, Athgar. They're Sisters of a Holy Order. We have no reason to fear them."

"Don't we?" he asked. "You heard the father general's speech, or at least a portion of it. Who's to say there aren't other church factions involved."

"Did you trust Brother Cyric in Corassus?" asked Natalia.

"Of course," Athgar replied.

"Then you must trust that others will be as helpful. If we wander around thinking everyone is against us, we'll get nowhere."

"I suppose you're right," he admitted. "Very well, let's get this over with."

Finally, they walked past the two Temple Knights, who stood in silent observation as they passed through a set of double doors that lay wide open, allowing all admittance to the temple grounds. Within, people were already present, some praying before a statue of Saint Agnes, while others simply sat peacefully in the quiet surroundings of the courtyard. They slowly made their way in, to be greeted by an elderly woman.

"Blessings of Saint Agnes upon you this day," the woman intoned.

"And to you," said Natalia.

"I am Sister Adeline. Is there anything I can help you with?"

"Are you a Temple Knight?" asked Athgar.

"Me," said the woman, "Saints, no. I am but a humble lay sister. No, the Sisters of the Temple Knights are found beyond this courtyard. Why do you ask?"

"We are looking for someone," said Natalia.

"Yes," agreed Athgar, "we were sent here by Mother Eugenia, from Ostermund."

"I see," said Sister Adeline. "Is it a particular person you seek, or just a sister knight?"

"Sister Cordelia," said Natalia. "Do you know her?"

"Of course," replied Sister Adeline. "She holds a most important post here, that of our equerry. She came to us from the Ilean coast, you know."

"Did she?" said Athgar. "I'm afraid I'm not familiar with that area."

"It is on the northern edge of the Shimmering Sea," explained the sister, "very close, in fact, to the Holy City of Herani."

"We've been to Corassus," offered Natalia.

"Ah," said Sister Adeline, "that lies to the east. If you were to travel west along the coast, you would reach Ilea, though I'm told the journey would be lengthy."

"Herani," said Athgar, "that's the birthplace of humanity, isn't it?"

"It is," the sister confirmed, "and the place where our order was founded, but where are my manners, you're not here to listen to me prattle on about our saviour. No, you want to meet Sister Cordelia."

"If it wouldn't be an inconvenience," said Natalia.

"Not at all," said Sister Adeline. "Follow me, and I'll lead you to her."

She took them through an archway, then up a flight of stairs where they found themselves on a balcony that stretched around a second courtyard. Athgar looked down to see several women practising with weapons.

"They are constantly drilling," explained Sister Adeline, "the better to protect the temple."

"How many Temple Knights do you have here?" asked Athgar.

"I'm not sure of the exact number here at the moment," replied the lay sister, "as they are often out and about their business, but the full complement is forty."

"And all those just to protect this temple?"

She halted, turning to face Athgar with a smile. "They do more than protect this temple," she said. "They ride around the city, protecting those under Agnes's Grace."

"Meaning?" he asked.

"Meaning," said Natalia, "they protect women."

"Your lady friend is correct," said Sister Adeline, resuming her guiding duties. "Without the sister knights, I'm afraid women would suffer, as they so often do when the Church is not present."

"Do your people not look after their women?" asked Athgar. "I find that hard to believe."

"This is not Therengia," said Sister Adeline. "And yes, before you ask, I noticed your grey eyes."

"What do you know of Therengia?" asked Athgar.

"Amongst my other duties here," she continued, "I have the honour to be the historian. For me, the past is a passion, one which I love to delve into. Therengia, for all its faults, was a very balanced society, with men and women both able to hold high office, and treated as equal by the law. It's a shame that the Petty Kingdoms don't do more to emulate that ancient custom. The world would be a far better place."

She halted before another set of stairs. "Down here," she explained, "is where the main offices of the order are found. It also happens to house the chapel, so I would ask that you remain silent while we cross the inner courtyard. Do you understand?"

They both nodded, and she resumed her steps down the stairs to reveal a third courtyard. At one end stood a solid-looking structure that Athgar took to be the chapel, with the doors wide open and the sounds of voices raised in prayer floating out. He had a brief view of several individuals sitting on benches as they walked past the doors.

Sister Adeline finally reached the other side of the courtyard and halted. "This is the office of the equerry," she announced. "Sister Cordelia should be inside."

"How do you know she's not busy elsewhere?" asked Natalia.

"Simple," the sister replied, "the shutters are open. Sister Cordelia always closes them when she locks up, a force of habit that suits her responsibilities."

"Thank you for your assistance," said Athgar.

"You're quite welcome," said Sister Adeline. "And good luck with whatever it was that brought you here. I'm sure Sister Cordelia will see you out when you're done."

She turned abruptly, once again crossing through the courtyard.

"Well, that was… interesting," said Athgar.

"Indeed," said Natalia, knocking on the door.

"Come in," called out a voice.

Natalia opened the door, revealing a modest office with a woman sitting behind a desk, quill in hand, stray strands of her blonde hair poking out from a series of braids.

"Can I help you?" she asked.

"Sister Cordelia?" said Natalia.

"That's me," she replied. "How may I help you?"

"My name is Athgar, and this is Natalia. We were sent by Mother Eugenia, in Ostermund. She thought you might be able to help us."

"Mother Eugenia? How is she? I haven't seen her in years."

"She is well," said Natalia.

"Tell me," said the knight, lowering her quill, "what is it you need help with?"

"We find ourselves in quite a strange situation," said Natalia. "You see, we have come into possession of a few temple horses."

"I see," said Sister Cordelia. "Might I enquire as to how they came to be in your care?"

"They were used in the commission of a crime," explained Natalia. "The perpetrators have been punished, but we wish to return the horses that were recovered. We were told you were in charge of such things."

"Only concerning the Order of Saint Agnes," said Cordelia. "Do they belong to us?"

"That's what we're here to determine," said Natalia. "We understand that temple horses have tattoos in their ears, and that you might be able to identify which order they belong to."

"That's true," confirmed the temple sister, "though it might require some work."

"You can't just tell from the tattoo?" asked Athgar.

"Horses are generally purchased in lots," Cordelia explained, "and numbered accordingly. I have the records here for all of OUR mounts, but if they're from another order, I will have to try and determine which order purchased them."

"Is that difficult to do?" asked Athgar.

"It can be," she replied. "Luckily, there is only one other order of Temple Knights in Caerhaven, and they are from Saint Cunar. I will have to visit their equerry to see if the horses are theirs. Of course, there's always the possibility that the horses are not from this region at all, but given that you came from Ostermund, I'd say that's very unlikely."

"We appreciate the effort," said Natalia.

"While we have you here," said Athgar, "I wonder if you might answer a question about the Church?"

"That depends on the question," said Cordelia. "I shall certainly give it my best try."

"Is the father general the highest-ranking church member in these parts," asked Athgar.

"Father general is a position, not a rank," clarified the knight.

"What's the difference?" asked Athgar.

"Temple Orders have only three ranks, four if you include the grand master. An initiate to the order starts as a knight. Eventually, if they are given command, they rise to the rank of captain, while a select few achieve the highest rank, that of commander."

"So where does a father general fit in?" he asked.

"Within his own order, he holds the rank of Father Commander, but his position as general places him in charge of all temple forces within the region, regardless of their order."

"So he technically outranks even your own commander?" asked Athgar.

"He does," she continued, "but it's the equerry's office that will have the information you seek."

"And he will have records of these horses?" asked Natalia.

"Not him personally," replied the knight, "the Cunars are far too numerous for only one man to look after it, but his office will, yes. Why? Is that a problem?"

"Not at all," said Natalia, "but due to the circumstances surrounding these horses, we'd prefer it if word of our investigation wasn't made public."

"Yes," agreed Athgar, "we'd hate to embarrass the Church. After all, somehow, these horses ended up in the hands of criminals."

"A point well taken," replied Cordelia. "You may rest assured I will use the utmost discretion. Have you the numbers, or do I have to see the horses?"

"I have the numbers here," said Natalia, withdrawing a folded paper from her purse.

Sister Cordelia took it, unfolding it to examine it in detail.

"Just the four?" she asked.

"Yes," said Athgar.

"Shouldn't be too hard," the knight commented. "They're all from the same lot."

"Meaning?" said Natalia.

"Meaning they likely all went to the same location. These are definitely not horses used by my order, I'd recognize the numbers if they were."

"So you'll look into this?" asked Natalia.

Sister Cordelia rose, extending her arm, "I give you my word."

Natalia shook her hand, "Thank you, it means so much to us."

"Where shall I find you once I have some information for you?" asked the knight.

"We're staying at a local inn," said Natalia, "but we have much to do in Caerhaven. Maybe it's better if we come back in a few days to see how you've fared?"

"Very well," said the knight, "give me three days. I should have an answer for you by then."

"Are you sure that will give you enough time?" Natalia asked.

"If I don't know by then, I likely never will," she responded.

"Let's hope that's not the case," offered Natalia, turning to Athgar. "That gives us time to see a play."

"So it does," he agreed. "It'll be nice to have some time to relax."

"You like the theatre?" asked Sister Cordelia.

"I do," said Natalia, "but Athgar's never seen one. You?"

"Of course," said the knight. "Just because we're Temple Knights, doesn't mean we can't enjoy entertainment from time to time. I'd recommend the Majestic, it has the nicest interior. I think they're running a comedy at the moment, though I can't recall the name of it."

"Thank you," said Natalia, "we'll give it a try."

"Let me show you out," said Sister Cordelia. "The temple grounds can be quite confusing to outsiders. When I first arrived here, it took me weeks to get my bearings."

"Sister Adeline said you were from Ilea," said Natalia.

"I wasn't born there," the knight responded, "but that was my first assignment."

"This is only your second posting, and you're already an equerry?" said Athgar.

"I was raised by horse breeders," said Cordelia, "so you might say it runs in my blood. If you'll follow me, I'll take you through the stables. It's much faster than backtracking to the main entrance."

"Thank you," said Natalia.

Cordelia led them out of the office, taking a moment to secure the shutters and door, then led them across the inner courtyard. The ceremony must have been over, for women were flooding out of the chapel, making their way to scattered destinations.

"Tell me," said Natalia, "you said you were raised by horse breeders. What convinced you to join the Church?"

"A common enough question," said Sister Cordelia, "but if I can offer a word of advice?"

"By all means."

"That's something you should never ask a sister, or a brother for that matter. Their reasons for joining are generally quite private and not meant for discussion."

"I meant no offense," said Natalia.

"And I take none," revealed the sister. "In my own case, it's not so private. My home was destroyed by war."

"I'm sorry to hear that," said Natalia.

"It was a difficult time," noted the knight, "but the sisters were there to help me through it. That's where I first came into contact with the order of Saint Agnes."

"And they recruited you?" asked Athgar.

"No, they simply helped me. I tried to make a living raising horses, but the damage to my family's farm was too great. I ended up selling what few horses I had. With nothing left, I had few options, so I joined the Church."

"And that's how you became a Temple Knight?" asked Natalia.

"Yes," Cordelia admitted. "As you can imagine, I was already an accomplished rider, and the Temple Knights seemed like a perfect fit."

"I take it you already knew how to fight?" said Athgar.

"Not at all," she responded, "but the sisters trained me in everything I needed to know. It's how we do things here. A person is never expected to do something they're not trained to."

"It seems a sensible method," noted Natalia.

Cordelia opened a door. "Beyond this door lies the stables," she said. "I hope you're not afraid of horses."

"Not at all," said Natalia, "though we're not accomplished riders."

They walked past stalls, each one housing a large mount. Athgar was stunned by the sheer number of horses, which appeared much greater than the forty knights they had stationed here.

"You have a very full stables," he commented.

"Yes," she admitted, "though some are for breeding purposes, one of my own innovations."

"Is there an advantage to that?" asked Athgar. "I would have thought it expensive."

"It is, to a certain extent," said Cordelia, "but it gives us more control over the stock. We're breeding larger mounts than we can usually purchase. They're better able to carry a mounted warrior."

"Do you train in battle tactics?" asked Natalia.

"We do," said Sister Cordelia, "both personal combat and formed units."

"I thought the Cunars were the army of the Church?" said Athgar.

"They are," she retorted, "but Cunars are not always able to respond in time. We have learned, over the years, that we cannot always count on the other orders for help."

"You sound bitter," noted Natalia.

"Do I?" Sister Cordelia responded. "I don't mean to be. My last assignment was in a very troubled region. We took it upon ourselves to better the situation."

"I trust you were successful?" said Athgar.

"We were," the knight replied, "though it wasn't through my efforts, rather it was due to a fellow sister, but that's a whole other story." She paused, halting at a door. "And here we are, the exit. This will take you out on Endover Avenue. Are you familiar with Caerhaven?"

"We're staying at the Golden Spire," noted Natalia. "Is that far?"

"No," said the knight, "it's only three blocks north. When you exit, turn right, you'll soon see your inn."

Natalia extended her arm, "Thank you again, Sister Cordelia."

"Thank me later," the knight replied, "when I've found what you're looking for."

"Very well," added Athgar. "We'll see you in three days."

Sister Cordelia opened the door, allowing them egress. Soon, they were back on the street, making their way north.

THE PLAN

Spring 1104 SR

"Well," asked Natalia, "what did you think?"

Athgar rose from the seat where he had watched the play. "Interesting," he said.

"Interesting as in good, or bad?" she asked.

"There were parts of it I found quite fascinating," he mused, "but others I had a hard time following."

"That's likely because of the subject matter," she said. "After all, you're not really familiar with life at court, and this play was all about intrigue."

"Well," he mused, "I've had my fair share of intrigue over the last year. Maybe next time, we can watch something a little more familiar."

"I'll see what I can do," said Natalia. "Likely, there's something different playing elsewhere."

The other theatre patrons began filing out of the building, creating a bottleneck at the doors.

"Are you coming?" asked Natalia.

"Let's wait," said Athgar.

"Whatever for?" she asked. "We've things to do."

"I'm just enjoying the quiet," he responded.

She looked around to see the last few patrons still bunched up around the exit. It was then that it dawned on her.

"You don't like crowds," she said.

Athgar blushed, "I'm just not used to them. All those people crammed together? It's just not natural."

"Yes, but you've been in crowds before."

"Not like this," he said. "They don't bother me outdoors, but inside it feels..." he struggled for the word, "dangerous."

"I suppose it would be if we were in a fight, but this is just a theatre."

"Still," said Athgar, "you never know when one might break out."

She returned her gaze to the door, which by now, stood empty. "They're all gone," she reported. "Now, can we leave?"

"Yes," he said, "and maybe find something to eat."

"Eat? Is that all you ever think about?"

He smiled at her, disarming her complaint.

She blushed at the implication. "Honestly, Athgar, sometimes I can't take you anywhere."

They made their way up the aisle, then stepped into the chilly afternoon air. Spring had decided to delay its arrival, sending a cold snap that came from the north.

"We should have dressed warmer," said Natalia.

"I'll keep you warm," Athgar promised. "Here, take my hand."

She did so, and they walked down the street, their hurried steps taking them south, towards the Temple of Saint Agnes.

"Do you think Sister Cordelia has any news for us?" asked Athgar.

"We'll know soon enough," said Natalia, "though I suppose that means we'll have to return those horses."

Athgar halted, pulling Natalia to a stop. "I hadn't thought of that. Once we turn them in, we'll have no fast means of travel."

"I might remind you we had no horses to get us to Corassus. We didn't need them then, and we don't need them now."

"I suppose you're right," said Athgar, resuming his walk, "though I wonder if there's a reward for returning them?"

"That would be nice," answered Natalia, "but I wouldn't count on it."

"Isn't the Church supposed to be generous?" he asked.

"I don't think that extends to rewards for horses, though I could be wrong."

The temple soon came into view, and Athgar started turning towards it, only to have Natalia pull on his arm, guiding him away.

"I thought we were going to the temple," he said.

"We are," said Natalia, "but we'll go around back by the stables. It'll be much easier than navigating that maze of courtyards."

"That's an excellent idea," he agreed.

"Of course," she retorted, "that's why I thought of it."

"I wonder what a horse goes for?" Athgar mused.

"Warhorses are very expensive," said Natalia. "Each one likely a year's wages to one of these knights."

"It's tempting just to sell them," noted the Therengian.

"It would be foolish," she warned. "Any horse trader in these parts likely knows the penalty for dealing in stolen mounts, especially those belonging to the Church."

"And what punishment is that?"

"I believe it's death," she replied. "It seems to be the common punishment for most crimes these days."

They rounded the corner to see the stables coming into view, a Temple Knight of Saint Agnes standing guard outside.

Natalia walked up to her. "We're here to see Sister Cordelia," she explained.

The knight nodded in her direction. "Go through that door and make your way to the far side of the stables," she said. "Her office is in the courtyard just beyond."

Athgar wanted to reply that there were multiple courtyards but held his tongue. Natalia pushed open the door, and the smell of horses greeted them.

"I'd forgotten how badly they stink," said Athgar.

"Hush now," said Natalia, "these people love their horses. We don't want to go and insult them."

They walked past the stalls, where stable hands brushed down the mounts. Soon, they were on the far side, exiting through an open doorway to see the courtyard beyond.

"It's just over there," said Athgar, pointing.

They angled across the courtyard, to where the office of the equerry waited, the shutters open. Natalia knocked, then waited for a response before opening the door. Inside, sat Sister Cordelia, looking as though she hadn't moved since their last visit.

"Sister?" said Natalia.

"Greetings," she answered. "Good to see you again. How have you been?"

"We've been well," said Natalia, "and you?"

"Very well," Cordelia replied, "and quite busy. Those numbers you had me run down proved difficult to locate."

"So it was a dead end?" said Athgar.

"Oh, no," said the sister, "I found them all right. It just took some extra work." She glanced around her desk, which was littered with papers.

"Sorry," she said, "I've been overwhelmed with paperwork. I've got some notes here somewhere." She finally found what she was searching for, holding it up in triumph. "Here it is," she announced. "It seems those horses were purchased from a local breeder about eighteen months ago. The entire lot went to our brothers at Saint Cunar."

"Under Father General Gilbert?" asked Athgar.

"Yes," said Cordelia, "how did you know?"

"I didn't," he admitted, "though I had my suspicions."

"How do we go about returning the horses?" asked Natalia.

"I can take care of that for you," offered the knight. "Bring them to our stables, and I'll look after the rest."

"We would prefer if our names could be left out of it," added Natalia.

"That shouldn't be a problem," noted Cordelia, "though they'll be eager to pass on the reward."

"There's a reward?" said Natalia.

"I thought there might be," said Athgar, looking at Natalia, "and here you said it was unlikely."

"These are warhorses," explained the knight, "and they're worth a lot to the Church. They'll be glad to have them back, and a reward is much cheaper than buying a replacement."

"What kind of a reward are we talking about?" asked Athgar.

"Likely a nice sum," said Cordelia. "More than enough to purchase two palfreys."

"Palfreys?" said Athgar.

"Riding horses," explained Natalia. "Tell us, Cordelia, was there any record of their theft?"

"No," the sister replied, "and that's what made it so difficult to track down. According to the equerry's office, they weren't missing. I had to convince them to physically check their stables to try and locate them.

"And was that difficult?" said Athgar.

"Let's just say that their equerry was less than cooperative. He seemed eager to get the horses back but was a little reticent to say how he'd lost them in the first place. He seemed quite taken aback that they weren't present."

"It smells a little suspicious to my mind," noted Natalia.

"You and me both," said Cordelia, "but I'm afraid there's little I can do about it. I can, however, arrange the reward. Since you don't want your names mentioned, I'll have them deliver it here to the Temple of Saint Agnes. How soon can you bring us the horses?"

"Later this very afternoon if you like?" offered Natalia.

"That would be perfect," noted the knight. "I'll stable them here tonight. That will give me a chance to look them over and assess their health, then

I'll deliver them to the Cunar stables tomorrow morning. I expect your reward will be here waiting for you by tomorrow night."

"Perfect," said Natalia, "then we'll head back to the inn and retrieve them."

"Glad I could be of assistance," said Cordelia.

"You've been a great help," noted Natalia.

"Tell me," the sister continued, "did you ever get to the theatre?"

"We did," said Natalia, "they were playing 'The Serpent's Coil.'"

"Oh," said Sister Cordelia, "I'm sorry, I thought they were playing a comedy."

"No," Natalia continued, "a tragedy, but I quite liked it."

"And your companion?"

"Athgar was less enthused," said Natalia.

"Yes," agreed Athgar, "I found it lacking something."

"Well, I'm sorry to hear that," Cordelia replied.

"That's all right," Natalia added, "he's promised to try another one at some point in the future."

They turned to leave, but something made Athgar turn back.

"Sister Cordelia," he said, "I wonder if I might ask you a question?"

The knight, who had just picked up some papers, set them down. "Certainly."

"Are you sure about this, Athgar?" asked Natalia.

"We have to trust someone," he replied.

"Trust someone with what?" asked Cordelia.

"We think we may have uncovered a plot of some sort," he said, hesitation colouring his words.

"A plot, you say?" the knight responded. "Could you be more precise?"

"It's a long story," said Natalia.

"I can make time," said Cordelia, "and any excuse to avoid this paperwork would be welcome."

Athgar looked at Natalia, who simply nodded.

"When we were up in Ostermund, we were hired by a Dwarf. His cousins were overdue on a delivery, and he was worried about them."

"I take it something went wrong?"

"Yes," said Athgar, "we helped him find his cousins, but someone had attacked and killed them."

"How tragic," said Cordelia, "and yet, I don't see how that would be of any consequence here in Caerhaven."

"Oh, there's more," said Natalia.

"Yes," agreed Athgar, "you see, someone had staged the attack. They'd planted the body of a dead Orc to make it look like his race was responsible."

"Are you sure they're not?" Cordelia asked. "How do you know it was staged?"

"I lived with the Orcs for a time," said Athgar, "the Orcs of the Red Hand, to be precise. The body we found was painted to look like one of their tribe, right down to a blood-stained hand."

"And?" urged the knight.

"And the Orcs don't use blood to stain their hands, they use dye."

"Are you sure?" pressed Sister Cordelia.

"Positive," said Athgar. "I was inducted into their tribe, and I know their customs in this regard."

"So whoever staged the attack knew nothing of their ways," mused the knight.

"That's not all," said Athgar. "It had recently snowed, and we followed some tracks to find a group of men holding a family hostage."

"How is that related to the attack?" Cordelia asked.

"We think," said Natalia, "that the husband might have witnessed the attack. Whoever was responsible must have tracked him down to ensure his silence."

"This is all quite fascinating," said Sister Cordelia, "but surely it should be brought to the attention of the duke's soldiers, not the temple?"

"I'm afraid I'm not quite done," said Athgar. "When we tracked down the attackers, we saw some riders heading off. One of them was Father General Gilbert."

She stared at them both, obviously having a hard time absorbing it all.

"Are you sure?" she finally asked.

"We didn't know at the time," said Natalia, "but after we arrived here in Caerhaven, we saw him addressing a crowd. There was no doubt it was him."

"These are serious charges," insisted the knight.

"Now you see why we were hesitant to talk of such things," said Athgar.

"Yes," agreed Natalia. "We were hoping you might have some idea as to how we might proceed."

"Those men," said Cordelia, "the ones that attacked the family, they're the ones that had these horses?"

"They were," Natalia responded.

"I can see now why you didn't want your names mentioned," said Cordelia. "Have you taken this to the Archprior?"

"He's a Cunar," said Natalia, "you said so yourself, and we've had some trouble with them in the past."

"You've had trouble with the Church?" asked the knight, her eyebrows rising.

"Just with the Cunars," clarified Athgar. "We recently worked with a Brother of Saint Mathew."

"Yes," added Natalia, "and the Ansgarites."

"The Order of Saint Ansgar only gets involved in internal matters," said Cordelia. "It must have been important for them to take an interest."

"It was," said Natalia, "but the Church made it clear that they don't want it talked about outside of certain circles."

"I can well understand that," the knight remarked, "and yet it might have some bearing on what's happening here. You say it involved the Cunars?"

"Yes," said Athgar, "or a few of them, at least. It wasn't the whole order, you understand."

"I take it this included someone higher up in their chain of command?"

"How did you know that?" asked Athgar.

"The Brothers of Saint Ansgar wouldn't be involved if that hadn't been the case," said Cordelia. "You've given me much to consider."

"Where do you think we should go from here?" asked Natalia.

"Have you considered talking to the duke?" the knight asked.

"We have," said Athgar, "but there's a chance he might be involved."

"Yes," agreed Natalia. "We suspect that this attack was staged to blame the Orcs and give a reason to send in the army."

"To what end?" asked Cordelia. "The Orcs live on the border with the Duchy of Holstead. Any movement of a sizable army would likely lead to an all-out war between the two dukedoms."

"Have you heard of these so-called Orc attacks?" asked Athgar.

"I have," the knight admitted, "though they are sparse on details."

"I believe they are part of the plan. I know the Chieftain of the Orcs, and he would never attack a village in Krieghoff. He knows it would result in the destruction of his people."

"The question still remains," said Cordelia, "why? What possible motive could someone have for blaming the Orcs? And, if what you say is true, what can we do about it?"

"You could investigate, couldn't you?" said Natalia.

"I have to tread carefully here," said Cordelia. "I'm forbidden to interfere in the affairs of another order."

"What about these Brothers of Saint Ansgar?" said Athgar. "Couldn't they be persuaded to investigate?"

"They don't have a chapter here," the knight replied, "and in any case, it would take hard evidence to have them send an inquisitor."

"Surely there is something that can be done?" fumed Athgar.

THE PLAN | 109

"What about Tomar?" asked Natalia.

"The village that was raided?" said Cordelia. "What about it?"

"If the attack in Ostermund was staged, might the attack in Tomar also have been set up?"

"It's possible," said the knight.

"Could you send someone to the village to investigate?"

"It's out of our jurisdiction," said Cordelia, "though I suppose it's quite within our purview to visit and make sure the women are being looked after. I would have to get permission from our local commander."

"Who commands here?" asked Athgar.

"Mother Commander Theresa," said Cordelia. "She is the senior member of our order in these parts, but she's quite reasonable. I think if I approach it correctly, she can be persuaded to look into things."

"And in the meantime?" asked Natalia.

"I would suggest you keep doing whatever it is you're doing," said Cordelia. "You seem to have been quite successful so far. For now, I'll see if we can't send a sister or two out to Tomar to find out more."

"Thank you," said Natalia. "If you discover anything, please let us know."

"Where shall I contact you?" asked the knight.

"We're still at the Golden Spire," said Athgar.

"Now," said Natalia, "we must be on our way if we're to return the horses before nightfall."

"Yes," agreed Sister Cordelia, "and I have to go and see the mother commander."

"Very well," said Athgar, "and thank you again for your help, Sister."

"I'd say it's been a pleasure," said Cordelia, "but I'm not sure that's the right expression in this case. In any event, I'll arrange for things to proceed concerning the reward. Do you need me to show you the way out?"

"No," said Natalia, "we know the way, and you've far too much on your plate at the moment."

They exited, crossing the courtyard yet again and made their way through the stables. It wasn't until they were once more on the streets of Caerhaven that they resumed their conversation.

"What do you think?" asked Athgar. "Can we trust her?"

"We have little choice," said Natalia. "On the one hand, she seems honest."

"And on the other?" asked the Therengian.

"She is a member of the Church. She's likely inclined to brush the whole matter aside."

"Brother Cyric didn't," argued Athgar.

"True," said Natalia, "but we got to know him on a lengthy sea voyage.

We really don't know much about Sister Cordelia, or her order, for that matter."

"Cyric seemed to trust them."

"That was in Corassus," noted Natalia. "I doubt he'd vouch for them here."

"What makes you say that?" he asked.

"The senior church official here is a Cunar," she reminded him.

"Yes," said Athgar, "I find that confusing. How is that even possible?"

"All the orders are united under a single entity," explained Natalia. "Each order has its own hierarchy, but at the highest level, they share the administration. All the orders must supply people to oversee things."

"And this region just happens to be run by a Cunar?" said Athgar. "I find that disturbingly coincidental, considering what we've discovered so far."

She looked at him a moment before resuming the discussion. "I must say, I'm liking this new you. Ever since I started teaching you to read, you've become more expressive."

"What can I say?" he responded. "I've got an excellent teacher."

They strolled down the street, making their way back to the inn.

"So, what's our next step?" Athgar asked.

"We could try meeting with the duke?" Natalia suggested.

"Too risky," said Athgar. "We already tried meeting the father general. If we show up at the duke's estate, we might receive some unwelcome attention."

"First things first," said Natalia, "we'll return the horses and get the reward. Planning is so much easier with coins in your purse."

"I suppose that's true," agreed Athgar, "and I'd be interested to see what Belgast makes of all this. Perhaps he'll have some ideas?"

"I'm sure he will," said Natalia, "but whatever we do, we must tread carefully. We're starting to step on some very big shoes."

Soon the inn was before them, the sounds of merriment within spilling out into the street.

"Sounds like a celebration," said Athgar.

"I wonder what the occasion is?" asked Natalia.

As Athgar stepped closer and opened the door, the noise flooded out, buffeting him with its intensity.

"They're singing," he shouted, desperate to be heard.

Natalia joined him, peering inside to spy Belgast on top of a table, leading the entire establishment in a rowdy drinking song. Servers rushed past, dropping newly filled tankards on tables, then hurriedly ran back to refill the old.

"We're full!" hollered a voice.

Athgar looked at the proprietor to see the man's face change as he identified the Therengian.

"Oh, sorry," the man said, "I didn't recognize you. I can squeeze you in if you like, but the seating's fairly cramped."

"What's the occasion?" called out Natalia.

"Some sort of Dwarven holiday," the owner replied. "Your friend insisted on everyone participating."

Right on cue, Belgast called out from across the room, "Come, my friends, it is time to celebrate the spring thaw, an old Dwarven custom."

As they both moved towards the Dwarf, tankards were thrust into their hands.

"To Gundar," Belgast called out, "the God of the Earth. May the soil always prove bountiful!" He took a deep swig, dribbling some of the dark-hued ale down his beard.

Athgar climbed onto the table, crouching slightly to avoid hitting the ceiling. "Are you sure about this, Belgast?" he asked. "My people worship the old Gods, but I don't remember celebrating the spring thaw."

The Dwarf, already past the tipsy stage, placed a finger to his lips, as if to warn him to lower his voice.

"I made it up," he said, "in order to get some free ale."

"I take it the tactic worked," said Athgar, a smile beginning to crease his lips.

"I'll say, and then some," replied the Dwarf.

Athgar took a swig from his own tankard, then saw Natalia waving him down. He took her hand, letting her guide him to the floor, where she placed her mouth close to his ear and whispered something. The effect was immediate. He quickly downed his ale, then took her hand, leading her from the room.

"To Gundar!" called the Dwarf. The crowd began to chant along with him.

OPPORTUNITY

Spring 1104 SR

Athgar stared down at the plate before him. It was early morning, and the two eggs there appeared to be staring back, daring him to eat them.

"I warned you not to go back down to the common room," said Natalia.

"You did," replied the Therengian, "but then you fell asleep. I was still wide awake, and I didn't want to disturb you."

"So you thought coming back down here was a good idea?"

"It seemed so at the time," he mused, "though I can see now how that might have been the wrong idea."

"A little worse for wear?" she asked.

"I have a headache," he complained. "I know, it's my own fault, I never should have let Belgast talk me into it."

"Speaking of Belgast," said Natalia, "have you seen him this morning?"

"I have not," Athgar replied. "Why? Are we expecting him?"

"We've travelled with him for more than a week," she said, "and he's an early riser. I'm just surprised he's not already down here."

"He did consume a vast quantity of ale last night," said Athgar.

"He's not the only one," said Natalia. "I thought you said earlier that you only drink sparingly?"

"I do, under normal circumstances," he said, "but it's that confounded Dwarf. He's far too persuasive."

"Are you going to eat those eggs," asked Natalia, "or just keep staring at them?"

"They're mocking me," the Therengian complained.

"There's an easy solution to that," she said. She lifted a knife, puncturing the yolk and allowing the yellow liquid to flow.

"They still look like two eyes," said Athgar.

"They already looked like eyes," said Natalia, "there's not much I can do about that."

"Yes," said Athgar, "but now they look like they're crying."

"For Saint's sake," she said, digging in with the knife. This time, she moved the implement around, destroying the pristine condition of the food. "There, now you just have messy eggs."

"Now that," he said, a smile creeping over his face, "I can live with."

He took his own knife, using it to shovel eggs into his mouth.

"You know," said Natalia, "they have this wonderful invention, it's called a fork."

"Never used one," said Athgar, pondering the forked implement that sat by his plate.

"You should try it," she urged, "you never know when such a skill might be needed. One day, we might be dining with a king, and if that happens, you'll need your table manners."

"Table manners? Is that what you call it?" He looked at her, trying to understand the joke. "Oh," he said at last, "you're serious."

"Yes," she said, lifting her own implement. "Let me show you how it works."

Natalia placed her fork on his plate, sliding it beneath some egg. She lifted it carefully, the morsels clinging to the tines. Up went her arm, placing the fork in front of Athgar's face. He opened his mouth, allowing her to deposit the food within.

"There," she said, "that wasn't so hard now, was it?"

He swallowed the egg. "That was remarkable," he said. "Let me try."

He took the fork, trying several times to place food upon it.

"This is harder than it looks," he said.

"Keep trying," she urged, "you'll get the hang of it."

"Well, well, well," came a familiar voice as a cold wind blew past them. They both looked up to see Belgast coming in from outside.

"You're up bright and early today," noted Natalia.

"I am," said the Dwarf, "and it's such a marvellous day, though I daresay the north wind is a bit strong."

Athgar made a face. "How can you be so cheerful?" he asked. "You must have drunk three times what I did last night."

"More like four," beamed Belgast, "but then again, I'm a Dwarf. We don't suffer any after-effects."

"You mean to say you don't get drunk?" asked Athgar.

"Oh, we get drunk," Belgast replied. "It's just that it takes a lot more ale to do so. What we don't get, on the other hand, is what you're experiencing right now."

Athgar groaned, placing his hands to his temple to still the pounding of his head. "I think I'll swear off ale for a while," he declared.

"What were you doing outside?" asked Natalia.

"I went for an early morning walk," said Belgast, "and it's a good thing I did."

"Why?" she asked. "Did you discover something?"

"I did, as a matter of fact, but first, let me ask you a question. How did you make out with Father General Gilbert the other day?"

"We got nowhere," Athgar admitted. "He wouldn't see us."

"He wouldn't see anyone, actually," clarified Natalia.

"Do you still want to meet him?" asked the Dwarf.

"Of course," said Athgar. "Why? Did you meet him?"

"No," said Belgast, "but I might have a way to arrange such things."

"That sounds intriguing," said Natalia. "Tell me, what is this plan you've come up with?"

"Well," mused the Dwarf, "I wouldn't call it a plan so much as an opportunity."

"You're speaking in riddles," complained Athgar. "Get to the point, will you? I've no patience for this today."

"Ah," said Belgast, "I see someone's a little testy. Was it the ale?"

"Yes," admitted Natalia. "Maybe next time you could remember that Athgar is not a Dwarf?"

"Sorry about that," said Belgast. "I often forget how easily Humans feel the effects of strong drink. I promise to look after him in future."

"Apology accepted," said Natalia. "Now, what's this opportunity you were so proud of?"

"Ah, yes," said the Dwarf. "Well, you see, I was down on Fiddler's Green when I overheard something."

"What's Fiddler's Green?" asked Athgar.

"It's a park, you know, a natural area with trees and grass."

"You mean the wilderness?" asked Athgar.

"No," said Natalia, "more like a common. Didn't you have those in Athelwald?"

"Oh, yes," said the Therengian, "the Fyrd used to practise there."

"Well," continued Belgast, "this is similar, except it's frequented by the more prosperous citizens of the town."

"I see," said Athgar, "and?"

"And I heard tell of an interesting development."

"There you go with the fancy words again," complained Athgar. "Get to the point, will you?"

"The long and short of it is," said the Dwarf, "that the duke is hosting a ball, a masquerade ball to be exact."

Athgar looked at Natalia in confusion. "What's a masquerade ball?"

"It's a party," said Belgast.

"Yes," said Natalia, "where the guests all wear disguises."

"Why would guests wear disguises?" Athgar asked. "That makes no sense."

"Not everything a noble does makes sense," said the Dwarf. "But regardless, it gives us an opportunity."

"For what?" asked Athgar.

"I think what Belgast is saying," said Natalia, "is that we could attend the ball."

"I'd stick out like a bear amongst cows," complained Athgar.

"Nonsense," insisted Natalia, "all we'd have to do is walk around and listen in on people's conversations. We might even unravel what's going on around here."

"But we weren't invited," said Athgar. "You do need an invite, don't you?"

"Look," said Belgast, "I know it's reaching, but chances are if you arrive in style and wear an appropriate outfit, no one's going to object. The whole point of one of these things is to remain unknown. You can do that, can't you?"

"I suppose," murmured Athgar, "but what about you? Won't a Dwarf stand out in the crowd?

"Oh, I'm not going," defended Belgast. "I meant that you two would go. I'll finance the costumes and arrange a carriage to take you there."

"To what end?" asked Athgar.

"Look," said the Dwarf, "there's a good chance the duke is involved in this affair, isn't there?"

"We think so," said Natalia.

"Well, the ball's being held at the duke's estate. What better place to nose around? We'll never get another opportunity like this."

"What's the occasion?" asked Athgar.

"It seems it's an annual spring celebration," said the Dwarf.

"All right," said Athgar, "but I'm not drinking. The last time I celebrated spring, I ended up with this massive headache."

"Very well, my friend," said Belgast. "Your objection is duly noted, you don't have to drink."

"So what do we do for costumes?" asked Athgar. "I've never been to one of these things before."

"Don't worry," said Natalia, "I know what to do."

"You do?" the Therengian said in surprise.

"Yes," she admitted, "and I know the perfect place to get outfits, too. Something suitable for a duke's estate."

Now it was Belgast's turn to be surprised, "You do? Where?"

"The Majestic," said Natalia.

"The Majestic?" said the Dwarf. "What's that?"

"A theatre," said Athgar. "A place where they put on plays, but I don't see how that helps."

"Simple," said Natalia. "They have all sorts of costumes. I'm sure if we make a donation, they'll lend us some."

"So we are to become actors?" said Athgar.

"Yes," Natalia agreed. "What do you think? Care to take on a new persona?"

"Why," asked Athgar, "are you tired of the old me?"

"No, of course not," she replied, "but we don't want to identify ourselves to the duke. We're supposed to seek out opportunities to look for information, not tell our life stories to everyone we meet."

"Then who will we be?" he asked.

"I don't know," she confessed, "but this isn't the first time we've acted."

"It isn't?" said Athgar.

"No," she continued, "back in Corassus, you pretended to be a Brother of Saint Mathew, don't you recall?"

"Oh yes," he said, "and you were a Sister of Saint Agnes."

"There you go," she said, "you do remember, after all."

"When is this ball?" asked Athgar.

"In three days," said Belgast.

"Will that be enough time to prepare?" the Therengian asked.

"I should think so," said Natalia, "but we'll need to get to the Majestic soon if we're to be successful."

"There's something else we're supposed to do, isn't there?" asked Athgar.

"Oh, yes," said Natalia, "we forgot to take the horses to the temple."

"Then we'd best take care of that first," he said.

"Are you sure you're up to that?" asked Natalia.

"Yes, why wouldn't I be?" he said.

"Well," she continued, "it was only a few moments ago that you were complaining about the eggs staring at you."

. . .

It didn't take them long to drop off the horses. They were met by the master of the stable, who assured them that Sister Cordelia would be informed. From there, it was only a short distance to the theatre, where they arrived to find someone sweeping out the front doorway.

"Show's not on till this evening," the man said. "I'm afraid you'll have to come back later."

"Actually," said Natalia, "we're looking for the proprietor."

"The owner?" the man said. "That's me." He ceased his sweeping, then rubbed his hand clean on his tunic, offering it in a shake.

"Manfred Morovian, at your service," he declared.

Athgar shook his hand, "Hello, I'm Athgar, and this is my companion, Natalia. I wonder if we might have a moment of your time?"

"Are you trying to sell me something?" asked the owner.

"No, quite the opposite," added Natalia. "We have a business proposition for you."

"Indeed?" said Manfred. "Then you'd best come inside before my competition hears of it."

"You have competition?" asked Athgar.

"Oh, yes," the owner responded. "That damned Covington down at the Escapade's been stealing my ideas."

"The Escapade?" said Natalia. "I take it, that's another theatre?"

"It is," said Manfred, "though I'm loath to call it such. Every time we put on a play, he's copying it within a week. It's all I can do to not storm down there and burn the place to the ground. It's infuriating. Pardon my ill-temper, but he's got me right agitated."

He led them inside, taking them to a small office. The place was overrun with decorations and theatre props, a scene that provided Athgar with no end of amusement.

Manfred pulled a jacket from a chair, tossing it to the floor. "Take a seat," he said, "and make yourselves comfortable." He moved behind his desk, reaching below it to produce a bottle. "Would you like a drink?"

"No, thank you," said Natalia, "though feel free to take one yourself if you wish."

Manfred placed the bottle on the table, unopened, then looked at his new visitors.

"So tell me," he said, "what's this proposition of yours?"

"We recently attended your play, 'The Serpent's Coil'."

"Glad to see someone saw it," the man responded. "You must have seen the last performance. We've moved on to something a little more frivolous."

"I was quite impressed by the costumes," said Natalia. "In fact, we'd like to use some of them, for a suitable fee, of course."

"Why in the Saint's name would you want costumes? You do know they're only meant for the stage, don't you?"

"Actually," said Natalia, "we've been invited to a masquerade. Have you heard of such things?"

"I have," he admitted, "though no one's ever seen fit to invite the likes of me to one."

"Well," continued Natalia, "like I said, we've been invited, but, being from out of town, we have no recourse as to costumes. Having seen your wonderful play, I was struck by the idea that we might borrow two of your outfits, providing we can negotiate a suitable fee, of course."

"I would be amenable to that," the proprietor answered. "How much were you thinking to spend?"

Natalia looked at Athgar, but the Therengian merely shrugged. "A few crowns, I suppose," she said at last.

Manfred leaned forward, resting his elbows on his desk, which was littered with items.

"You have my interest," he said. "Now, which costumes were you after? We have so many."

"I was hoping," she continued, "that we might be able to look through what you have. We'd need to find something in our sizes, after all."

"I'm sure that for a couple of crowns, I can have my people make some adjustments," the owner responded. "When would you need them by?"

"The ball is in three days," said Natalia. "Will that present a problem?"

"Is it at the duke's residence?" asked Manfred.

"It is, why?" Natalia responded.

"Duke Freidrich has seen the play. We'll have to change the costumes a little, or he might recognize them."

"Will that be difficult?" asked Natalia.

"No," the owner responded, "I have a seamstress in my employ. Several, in fact, and for the amount you're offering, I'm sure I can count on them to be quick about their work."

"Excellent," said Natalia, "then we have a deal."

Manfred smiled, slapping the top of his desk in glee. "Perfect," he said. "When would you like to get started?"

"That depends," said Natalia. "How soon can you have your seamstress here?"

"She's here now. She's been working on our next production, but I'm happy to divert her attention. Shall we go and have her take some measurements?"

Natalia stood. "That would be most agreeable," she said. "Come along, Athgar, it's time for us to become nobles."

"How do I look?" asked Natalia.

Athgar looked up from where the seamstress was pinning his cloak. "What's that on your head?" he asked.

"It's a mask," she said. "It's supposed to be a sparrow."

"I can't see your face," he commented.

"You're not supposed to," she replied. "The whole idea is to hide who I really am."

"It seems an odd thing to pretend to be someone else," he mused.

"Come now," urged Natalia, "you need to choose one, too. There's lots to pick from."

He looked down to where the seamstress had been working. She nodded back to him, then rose, taking the cloak from his shoulders.

"Let's take a look, then," he said, moving towards the masks. "What do we have here?"

"All sorts," the seamstress said. "They're mostly carved from wood."

"Aren't they heavy?" he asked.

"A little, but you get used to them fairly quickly."

He examined the collection, finally settling on one that drew his interest. "How about this?" he asked.

"I think that's a raven," Natalia said.

He immediately withdrew his hand, "I'll pass on that, then."

"Why?" she asked. "What's wrong with a raven?"

"They carry souls to the Underworld," said Athgar. "They're a bad omen."

"That's just superstition," said Natalia.

"Do I make fun of your Saints?" he asked.

"I apologize," she said in answer. "I didn't mean to demean your religion."

"This one looks nice," he said, picking up a helmet, then turned it to look at its front, smiling broadly.

"What is it?" she asked.

"A wolf," he said, placing it on his head.

Natalia turned to see Athgar, looking right at her, his face peering out from the wolf's mouth.

"What do you think?" he asked.

"I like it," she responded, "and it does go well with your costume."

"Yes, but does it hide my identity?" he asked.

"I wouldn't know you," she said, "except for your grey eyes, but let's face it, I'm more intimate with you than anyone."

He barked out a laugh, then moved closer. "Come little sparrow," he taunted, "it's time to play."

He reached out with his hands, chasing her around the room. Natalia shrieked as he caught her, then fell into his arms, laughing hysterically.

"Are you two quite finished?" asked the seamstress.

"Sorry, Peg," replied Natalia, "we were just getting into the spirit of it."

"Is that what you call it?" the woman responded. "Now come over here, I've still got some pinning to do. And you, Athgar, take off that helmet. You can't see much with it on, and I don't want you colliding into anything and damaging it."

"Sorry," said Athgar, pulling the helmet from his head and looking down at it. "I must admit, it's rather liberating wearing this thing. I feel like I could get away with anything."

"And chances are you will," said Peg. "I've heard about these costume parties before. They're nothing but an excuse for the nobles to carry on with their excesses."

"Excesses?" said Athgar. "What do they do?"

"Hah," said Peg, "what don't they do? They're all of low moral character," she spat out. "Why, I'd be careful if I were you, it's no place for a proper lady."

"I'll have Athgar to protect me," said Natalia, "and in any case, I'm not interested in anyone else, if that's what you mean."

"It's not about who you're interested in," Peg warned, "but who's interested in you. I hear they use all sorts of concoctions to have their way with others."

Athgar looked at Natalia, worry evident in his features, "We don't have to do this."

"Nonsense," said Natalia, "I can look after myself, remember who I am. No one messes with the family."

"But you'll be in disguise," he warned.

"Yes, but I'll wear my ring. It was given to me by the grand mistress herself."

"Is that wise?" he asked.

"As you said, we'll be in disguise," she explained, "so they won't know who I am. But if members of the family are there, they'll have to bow to me."

"I'm not sure I understand," said Athgar.

Natalia held out the ring, showing it to him. "This ring is made of magerite. It's a mineral that can detect magical potential."

"You mean it shows how powerful you are?" he asked.

"Yes. This is blue magerite, the more powerful the mage, the deeper the colour."

"The stone is almost black," Athgar remarked.

"Yes," admitted Natalia, "and any member of the family must show respect to those of higher power."

"You're hoping that ring will get us close to the duke," he surmised.

"Yes," she agreed, "and likely our best chance of getting information."

"How many people will recognize this magerite?" he asked.

"Any trained mage should. Trust me when I say that no one's going to mess with me."

"Especially when I'm around," noted Athgar. "Which reminds me, what's the approach to weapons?"

"Approach?" said Natalia.

"Yes, do we wear them with our costumes, or is that frowned upon?"

"I suppose it depends on the costume," she replied. "There is the story of the wolf of Adenburg that might fit your outfit quite well."

"Never heard of it, how does it go?" he asked.

"Adenburg is a distant city," she said, "but there once was a man there that turned into a wolf every time the moon was full."

"A shapeshifter? How curious," said Athgar. "When did he live?"

"He didn't," said Natalia, "but it's a well-known folk tale. Everyone's likely heard of it."

"So this wolf-man, did he carry a weapon?"

"He did," admitted Natalia, "though it depends on which version of the character you believe in. He was supposed to be a woodsman that was bitten by wolves."

"So an axe would make perfect sense," completed Athgar. "What about you?"

"I have my magic, that should be more than sufficient."

"You're a mage?" asked Peg.

"We both are," said Athgar, "why? Does that make a difference?"

"No," the woman replied, "but I had no idea I was in such distinguished company."

"Nonsense," said Athgar, "we're just people, like you."

"You harness powers beyond the understanding of common folk like me," the woman replied.

"Well," said Natalia, "you may rest assured we mean you no harm. Tell me, Peg, how did you come to work here at the Majestic?"

"I was always a seamstress," she replied, "but as I got older, it became harder to do the work. It was my nephew that offered me this job."

"Your nephew?" said Natalia. "You mean Manfred?"

"Yes," the woman responded.

"But don't you sew more here than you did in your previous employment?" asked Natalia.

"There's no denying the work here can be strenuous at times, but that's only when we're getting ready for a new show. The rest of the time, I can take it easy."

"Well," said Athgar, "you're a credit to your profession, Peg. You've done an outstanding job."

"Yes," agreed Natalia, "and make sure that nephew of yours isn't short-changing you, we paid a lot for your services."

"You're too kind, Mistress," the old woman replied, "but thank you for saying so."

THE DUKE'S ESTATE

Spring 1104 SR

T he carriage rolled forward, then halted unexpectedly, causing the
occupants to reach out to steady themselves.

"I hate this," muttered Athgar.

"It'll all be over soon," soothed Natalia.

"Tell me again why we have to ride in this thing?"

"We need to arrive in style," she answered. "How better to indicate our
status."

"But we don't have any status," he objected.

"Yes, but they don't know that. Successfully blending in with the nobility
is all about how people see you."

"I suppose you learned that at the Volstrum?" asked Athgar.

"Yes, I did," Natalia replied. "They stressed the importance of court
etiquette."

"That makes sense. Don't they send Stormwinds to all the ruling
houses?"

"Yes," she said, "that's their power base."

The carriage rolled forward yet again, shaking those inside.

"Why in the Afterlife do we have to move like this?" he grumbled.

"We're waiting while the other carriages unload their passengers."

"We could have been there by now if we'd only gone on foot," he said.
"Instead, we're stuck inside this box rolling back and forth."

"Hush now," said Natalia, "there are only a few parties ahead of us. We'll be there soon enough."

Athgar peered out the window, watching everyone making their way up to the duke's manor.

"It's quite a sight," he said. "I had no idea he was so wealthy."

Natalia moved closer, her cheek almost brushing his. "It is quite spectacular, I must admit."

Athgar turned slightly to face her, their lips only a handsbreadth apart. "You smell nice."

"Thank you," she said, kissing him. "Now, are you ready? I see we're up next."

"Oh sure," he said, "get me all excited just before I have to put this helmet on."

"It's not my fault you picked that," she chided. "You could have gone with something lighter."

He placed the ornate device on his head, gazing out through the mouth. "How do I look?"

"Magnificent," she replied. "I'm sure you'll be the toast of the party."

The carriage rolled forth once more, this time only a short distance. As soon as it halted, a servant opened the door and placed a small footstool before them.

"Thank you," Natalia said as she descended from the carriage. She paused as Athgar followed, ducking low to avoid hitting the top of the door with his ornate headgear.

The stately manor was some distance away, up a slight incline that was decorated with stone steps, bordering a carefully preserved pond.

"That looks like a waste of time," said Athgar, nodding his head at the water. "I wonder who has to look after it?"

"Let's take a look, shall we?" she asked.

They moved closer, letting other guests pass them. Natalia stood at the edge of the pond, gazing into it, but all Athgar could see of interest was some fish, flitting around the bottom.

"You know," mused Natalia, "when I was a little girl, I used to think I was cursed."

"Why would you think that?" he asked.

"Because every time I went near the water, fish would come up to me."

"Truly?" he said.

"Yes," said Natalia, "watch." She crouched, placing the tip of her finger in the water. Moments later, the fish, who had been lazily swimming around, migrated towards her, throwing the surface into turmoil with their activity.

"Remarkable," said Athgar, "I've never seen its like. How is it that fish didn't approach us on the ship to Corassus?"

"I'm a fully trained mage now," she retorted. "I've learned to control it, but sometimes I like to remember life before the Volstrum. What about you? When did you first manifest your powers?"

"I didn't," he replied. "As a child, I had no such indication."

"That's unusual, isn't it?"

"When the Orcs took me in," Athgar continued, "Artoch told me that there are two types of shamans, those that are born with magic, and those that only manifest after great trauma. I suppose I must be an example of the second."

"It's good the Orcs found you," she mused, "if not, you might have burned to death. I hear that's common with untrained Fire Mages."

"I suppose it is," said Athgar. "I still remember trying to leave Ord-Kurgad. I wanted to find my people, but Artoch wouldn't let me. He said I was a danger to myself and to others. I didn't understand it at the time, but it all seems so clear to me now."

"I'm thankful you listened," said Natalia, "or I wouldn't have you in my life." She rose, watching the fish return to their previous activity. "Now, it's time we got to work. Are you ready?"

"As ready as I'll ever be," he said, holding out his hand.

She took it as they started moving back up the steps towards the manor. Athgar glanced around, looking at the other guests, marvelling at their costumes. They ranged from simple outfits with plain cloth masks, to elaborate costumes, some with giant plumes or even wings.

"Such a strange custom," he mused.

"It is," she admitted, "but it works to our advantage." She gently squeezed his hand. "Nervous?"

"A little," he said. "After all, I've never done anything like this before."

"Neither have I," she confessed.

"Yes, but at least you're familiar with the concept. This is completely beyond anything I've ever experienced."

"You'll survive," she said, "and that will make you stronger."

"No one else seems to be holding hands," he observed.

"No, they're not," she agreed.

"Should we do the same?"

"No," said Natalia, "I feel safer knowing you're with me. We're a team, remember?"

"To the end," he responded, "whatever that might be."

The crowd grew thicker as they approached the front door. Athgar, too intent on their destination, bumped into someone by accident. The man turned, revealing a mask in the image of a mouse.

"How rude," the man exclaimed. "Mind your manners!"

"Sorry," Athgar mumbled.

"You should be more careful in future," Mouse Face continued, "or you might find yourself in a difficult place."

"And I should think," said Athgar, his voice rising in volume, "that you might watch your tongue when talking to a stranger. Do you have any idea who I am?"

The mouse stared back at him, surprised, no doubt, at the ferocity in his voice.

"I'm terribly sorry," the man said, extending his hand. "Let me offer you the hand of friendship instead."

Athgar wanted to curse the man, but Natalia squeezed his fingers, causing him to consider his words carefully. He paused for a moment, contemplating his next move, then firmly grasped the man's hand.

"Very well," Athgar finally said, shaking the hand, but then he murmured something under his breath. Moments later, the man yanked his hand away, waving it around violently as if to quell a rising heat.

"I'm sorry, Lord Sartellian," the man said. "I didn't realize it was you."

Athgar stared back, the name temporarily paralyzing him. He felt Natalia's hand grow damp with sweat. "Not at all," he finally said, "it was an honest mistake."

"Thank you, my lord," Mouse Face replied.

Athgar turned to Natalia, but she was staring ahead, casting her gaze over the crowd, now alert to the presence of the family. He turned his attention back to the guests before them, only to discover they had moved on.

Athgar led Natalia through a set of double doors, where they were greeted by servants passing out goblets of wine. He took two, passing one to her, then moved forward, guiding her onto the smooth marble floor of a vast room, much larger than he had expected.

The ceiling, at over thirty feet above them, had a balcony beneath it that stretched around its circumference. Up there, guests watched with interest, pointing out extravagant costumes as others arrived. Delightful music drifted through the room, though from their present position, they couldn't see from whence it came.

Natalia pulled him to the side, allowing others to pass them by, and waited till they were out of earshot, then leaned in close to him.

"Where should we start?" she asked.

"I'm not sure," he said, "perhaps we'd best wander around and get the layout of the manor first. I'd hate to be leaving in a hurry and get lost."

"Good idea," she said. "You're thinking tactically."

"Am I?" he commented. "I thought it was just common sense."

"If there's one thing I've learned about sense," said Natalia, "it's that it isn't common. Let's head upstairs first. I'm sure the view from the balcony will be enlightening."

They made their way across the room, then ascended the stairs, taking their time and examining each guest they passed.

"I don't like to think there's a Sartellian here," said Athgar. "The last one we ran into was quite a handful."

"Agreed," said Natalia, "but even if we find him, he's unlikely to cause a problem here, at the duke's estate."

"What if there's more than one?" he asked.

"The family is large," she said, "but stretched thin over the many courts of the Petty Kingdoms. I doubt there'll be more than one."

"So, how do we recognize him?"

"Watch for jewellery," said Natalia. "If he's a Sartellian, he'll be wearing magerite somewhere."

"You mean a ring?" he asked.

"Could be, or a brooch, or necklace even. It'll be somewhere obvious, where other members of the family can recognize it."

"Including us," said Athgar.

"Precisely," said Natalia. "And once I see it, I'll have some idea of his power level. Remember, the deeper the colour, the more powerful he'll be."

"So, we're on the lookout for a dark blue ring?" he asked.

"No," she said, "he's a Fire Mage, his magerite will be red."

"Are all Sartellians Fire Mages?" he asked.

"Yes," she replied, "that's how the family works. Anyone who commands water becomes a Stormwind, while Sartellians all control fire."

"Does that make me a Sartellian?" asked Athgar.

"It would if you were a member of the family," said Natalia, "but then I wouldn't be with you."

"Oh, I don't know," he said, "perhaps I'd win you over?"

She halted, turning to face him, "I never would have met you, Athgar. I refused to have anything to do with them."

"Sorry," he said, "I only meant it in jest."

"No," she replied, "it's me that's sorry, I shouldn't have snapped at you. I know you mean well, but it's a sore spot with me. I love you, Athgar. Please don't jest about such things."

"I won't," he promised. "Now come, we're almost at the balcony."

They made the last few steps quickly, then strolled past a couple dressed as swans. An open section of the balcony beckoned, and they paused, leaning on the railing to observe those below.

"What do you make of it?" he asked.

"There are a lot more guests than I would have expected," she said.

"Good," he replied.

"Good? What makes you say that?"

"The more guests, the easier it will be to move around freely," he said.

"Why would you think that?" she asked.

"It's simple, really. Once the drink gets into them, this crowd will get more difficult to handle. Have you noticed how few servants there are in relation to the guests?"

"Yes," she agreed. "I suppose that means they'll have their hands full."

"And," he continued, "once the party is well underway, it shouldn't be too difficult to make our way into the living quarters."

"And if we're caught?" she asked.

"Then we'll claim we're seeking privacy for some intimate time."

"That sounds like fun," she said, "but shouldn't we wait until we're safely back at the inn?"

He looked at her in surprise, only to see her grinning back.

"Maybe we should leave now," he said, his smile evident, despite the restrictive helmet.

"You'll just have to wait," she said. "In the meantime, I suggest we drink sparingly. We can't afford to be drunk here."

"Precisely my thought," he added.

They watched as the throng below started making their way to the back of the building.

"Something's going on," noted Natalia. "Should we follow?"

"Definitely," he replied. "Let's go."

They descended the stairs and joined the procession, heading outside to a large green area where musicians were playing. Someone dressed as a dragon stood on a chair, drawing everyone's attention.

"Welcome, one and all," the man began, "to the celebration of spring, or, as we like to call it in the fair city of Caerhaven, the Festival of Life. We have decided that since spring has once more embraced us with warmer weather, that we might party beneath the stars this night. So please, eat, drink, and make merry in celebration of the season!"

The crowd honoured their host with a near-deafening cheer as the music grew louder, and then the guests began walking over to the grassy area that had been marked off for just such an occasion. Soon, they were moving around in stately grace, looking, to Athgar's mind, like a strange religious ritual.

"What are they doing?" he asked.

"Dancing," Natalia replied, "what else?"

"It's strange," he said, "certainly not how we danced back in Athelwald."

"I didn't know you danced?" said Natalia.

"I don't," he said, "at least not like that." He nodded towards the costumed guests who were executing their highly practised moves.

"How did you dance in Athewald?" she asked.

"Well," he replied, "you place your hands in each other's and move around."

"Just like that?" she asked. "Don't you run into people?"

"No," he said, "all the dancers move in the same general direction. I'd show you, but I think it would draw unwanted attention."

"Perhaps another time and place," she replied. "In the meantime, let's keep an eye on that dragon costume."

"Yes," he agreed, "he must be the duke."

"You know," she said, "other than getting here, we really didn't plan this out very well. We have no real idea of what we're searching for."

"Agreed," he said, "but at least we now know who to watch. Besides, if we're lucky, he'll lead us to what we need."

"The problem," she added, "is that we don't know what we need."

"Have faith," Athgar replied, "we'll know it when we see it."

They meandered their way around the edge of the dance floor, careful to avoid the crowds until they caught sight of the duke, standing by a statue, deep in conversation with a young lady dressed as a butterfly.

"Akosia," said Athgar.

"What?"

"Akosia," he repeated, "the Goddess of Water."

"I know who Akosia is," she replied, "but what I don't understand is why you said her name."

"That's the statue he's near," he explained.

"So it is," she said. "I was too busy observing the young butterfly."

Natalia felt a hand touch her shoulder. She turned to see a tall man with piercing blue eyes staring down at her.

"Well, well, well," the man said, "it appears that destiny has brought us together again."

She stared at his face, trying to place him. His voice sounded awfully familiar, and yet she couldn't put a name to his countenance.

His expression turned bleak, "Tell me it isn't so. Have you so soon forgotten me?"

"Do I know you?" she asked.

"Oh, how it wounds my heart to hear you speak thus," the man replied.

"Have we met?" asked Athgar, moving closer to the man.

"Of course," the man replied. "We are road companions, are we not? How could I forget the fair Natalia."

"You recognize me?" she said.

"Of course," the man replied, "how could I fail to remember that silky voice and fair skin. It is I, Sir Adler, Knight of the Dragon."

"The Dragon?" said Athgar.

"Yes," Sir Adler replied, "the duke's own personal order. We are small in number but renowned in battle."

"Do you remember me?" asked Athgar. "I'm Natalia's husband."

"Good for you," the man responded. "Now, fair maid, shall I steal you away for a romantic rendezvous?"

"Tell me, Sir Adler," said Natalia, "have I, at any time, given you the impression that I wished to be romantic?"

"Yes," the knight responded, "by your look, if not your deeds."

She looked at him in shock. "Where in the Continent did you get that impression?"

"It's obvious, isn't it?" the man retorted. "We are destined to be together, you and I."

"I think not," said Natalia.

"You need to leave," added Athgar, "before this gets ugly."

"I was not addressing you," Sir Adler responded. "You would do well to remember your place, sir."

"Are you threatening me?" the Therengian demanded.

"If needed," Sir Adler replied. "Now, be off with you and let a cultured man show how a lady should be treated."

Athgar moved forward, his fists clenched, but Natalia stalled him by placing a hand to his chest.

"Let me deal with this," she said quietly, then turned, facing the knight and moving closer, putting her fingers upon his chest.

"Tell me, Sir Adler," she said, "does this approach work on all women, or is it only me you've targeted?"

"You are the one that has stolen my heart," the knight responded.

Natalia uttered the words of command, channelling her energy until her hands turned frosty, then sent a chill into the chest of Sir Adler. The man backed up suddenly, surprised at the sudden turn of events.

"Now," she said, "leave me alone, or I'll freeze your manhood and snap it off."

Sir Adler backed up, knocking into a guest in his bid to put distance between them. He turned, apologizing in his haste as he made his retreat.

"The nerve," she said.

"That was interesting," said Athgar. "I wasn't sure what you were doing at first."

"It was you that gave me the idea," she said.

"I did? How?"

"Yes, earlier, when you shook that man's hand. It worked quite well, don't you think?"

"It did," he said, "though I'm surprised you didn't turn him to ice. You're learning control."

"Yes," she admitted, "you've taught me much." Then she grinned wickedly and added, "In more ways than one."

Athgar, blushing at the compliment, cast his grey eyes around. "Where did the duke go?" he asked.

"We lost him," said Natalia. "That damned knight distracted us."

"Do you think that was planned?" he asked.

"No," she replied, "but if he recognized us, we may have a problem."

"I don't think so," he said. "You managed to humiliate him. I doubt he's eager to share the story."

"Still," she pressed, "we'd best keep our eyes sharp. It might be better if we split up."

"I don't like the sounds of that," he said. "Are you sure?"

"We'll cover more ground that way. If you don't find anything, meet me over by the statue of Akosia."

"And if I do find him?"

"Then see if you can get close enough to hear what he's saying," she said.

"Very well," he agreed, "though it goes against my better judgement."

"I'll move closer to the house," said Natalia, "while you circle around to the other side of the dance area."

Athgar moved off, scanning the crowd for the familiar dragon costume. It was like moving through a nightmarish vision of living animals, each wearing a strange face.

Natalia watched him disappear into the crowd, then turned towards the manor where the guests were more sparse and easier to navigate through.

A door caught her attention, not the main one that led into the grand foyer, but a smaller one, likely leading into the private areas of the estate. She moved towards it, but then two men exited, deep in discussion. Natalia recognized the duke's dragon armour, but his companion, unlike the other guests, was not dressed for the masquerade at all. Instead, he wore the distinctive cassock of a Temple Knight, making him easily distinguishable as the father general himself, Gilbert. Natalia moved closer, turning away from them as they passed, pretending to sip her drink.

"How go the crusades?" asked the duke.

"I hear it goes well," replied the father general. "They say the heathens are being pushed back every day."

"I'm surprised they haven't been decisively defeated," noted the duke. "After all, they're not very well armed, are they?"

"No," replied Father Gilbert, "but they move quickly. They spend so much time running away that we just can't keep up with them." He chuckled at his own remarks.

"I suspect it will all be over soon enough," said the duke. "Tell me, do you miss it?"

"The crusades? No," the father general replied, "I've seen enough battles in my time."

"I hope that doesn't mean you're going soft," said the duke. "I'd hate to think it might put our plans in jeopardy."

"Things are progressing well, my lord, have no fear."

"And your men?" asked the duke.

"Ready to act when needed," the father general responded.

"Good," said the duke, "then let us put this behind us for now and enjoy the festivities."

Natalia watched them turn towards her and quickly noted the location of a nearby guest.

"What a lovely costume," she blurted out. "Did you make it yourself?"

"I did," the woman replied, and then prattled on about things for some time, Natalia nodding her head occasionally as if she was listening. The duke and the father general moved past, ignoring the women's conversation. As soon as they were out of sight, Natalia held up her hands to quiet her companion.

"Excuse me," she said, "but I think I've drunk too much. I must answer a call of nature."

Natalia moved off, heading across the lawn in the direction of the statue, her eyes desperately searching for Athgar. She soon spotted the figure of Akosia, though her Therengian was nowhere in sight.

When the music stopped, the dancers abandoned the dance area, flooding past Athgar, who had to halt his progress to avoid being carried away with them. Once they had safely disbursed, he cut across the open area to the other side, watching for any sign of the duke. He searched for some time, but when he began to see the same costumes, he realized he was walking in circles.

He paused in his route, grabbing a new goblet of wine as a servant walked past. The golden-hued liquid poured down his throat smoothly, filling him with a feeling of warmth.

"It's quite good, isn't it," came a deep voice, so close that he almost spat out the wine.

"It is quite fair," he said, looking at the source.

An elderly man, likely in his fifties, watched the crowd, which was now gathering for another dance. He was immaculately dressed, not in a costume, but in the elegant clothes of someone with wealth and power.

"I'm sorry," said Athgar, "but have we met?"

"I don't believe we have," the man said. "My name is Sartellian, Verineth Sartellian."

"And I'm Gareth," replied Athgar, just in case his real name was known to this man.

"Where do you hail from, Gareth?"

"Down by Corassus," Athgar lied, "and you?"

"I travel about," Verineth replied, "but I call Caerhaven my home these days."

Athgar looked the man up and down as discreetly as possible, searching for any sign of magerite. Finally, he spotted a brooch, the torchlight glinting off the dark crimson centre, pinned to the man's tunic.

"Tell me, my lord," began Athgar, "what brings you to Caerhaven? Are you in service to the duke?"

"I am merely an advisor," the Sartellian said, "nothing more. The duke likes to have someone to consult with on matters of magic."

"Then it would appear he is well advised," said Athgar, "for I hear the Sartellians are the most powerful of mages."

Verineth laughed. "Spoken like a true diplomat. Tell me, Gareth, what brings you to our fair city?"

"I'm a courier," he said, making it up as he went. "I carry messages for the Church."

"The Church? Is that so?" said Verineth. "I would have thought they'd use their own people for that."

"They do, usually," explained Athgar, "but occasionally it serves their interest to pay outsiders."

"You must know the father general," he said.

"Only by reputation, I'm afraid," said Athgar. "I mainly work for the Brothers of Saint Mathew."

"I didn't think they had a chapter here," noted Verineth.

"They don't," said Athgar hastily, "I'm just passing through on my way to Draybourne."

"Ah yes," said the mage, "I've been there. Tell me, are the gatehouses still that terrible white colour?"

"They're grey," said Athgar. "Maybe you're confusing it with another city?"

"That must be it," said Verineth. "Well, I must be off, I've important people to see. Good luck, Gareth, I hope your courier business goes well."

He moved off, leaving Athgar fretting where he stood. Was the mage onto him, he wondered?

THE SECRET

Spring 1104 SR

Athgar, now alerted to the presence of the family, rushed across the dance area, frantically looking for Natalia. He finally spotted her, standing by the statue of Akosia, nervously searching for him.

"We have to leave," he said in greeting.

"Why? What's the matter?" she asked.

"The family is here," he warned.

"Are you sure?"

"Yes, I had a discussion with a man named Verineth Sartellian."

"Verineth?" said Natalia.

"Yes, why, do you know him?"

"I've never met the man, but I certainly know of him, if only by reputation. He's said to be very powerful. Did you get a chance to see his ring?"

"It was a brooch," said Athgar, "and it was a bright crimson colour. Does that tell you anything?"

"It tells me he's likely as powerful as they say," she remarked. "You say he talked to you?"

"Yes," said Athgar, "I told him my name was Gareth."

"What did he talk about?"

"He asked why I was in Caerhaven, so I had to make up something about being a courier of the Church."

"Did he believe you?" she asked.

"I don't know," said Athgar. "He tried to trick me by asking about Draybourne. I have a feeling he knows who I am."

"How?" she asked. "It's not as if he's ever met you, and don't forget your costume."

"They came after you in Corassus," he reminded her, "and it wouldn't surprise me if they knew I was in your company."

"All true," said Natalia, "but no one who's actually seen you has lived to tell the tale."

"Then maybe he recognized me as a Therengian," he said. "Could my eyes have given me away?"

"I suppose that's possible," she said. "There's little we can do about that now in any event, but we can't leave empty-handed."

"There's no alternative," said Athgar. "We haven't found a single shred of information."

"Actually," said Natalia, "we have. I spotted the duke talking to our old friend, the father general."

"What were they discussing?" he asked.

"Something about the crusades, but I'm short on details."

"How is that of any help?" he asked.

"It shows a connection between the Cunars and the duke," she pointed out.

"I guess we could try following them," Athgar suggested. "Hopefully, they'll meet somewhere more secluded, and we can listen in."

"It's worth a try," said Natalia, "but we'll have to be careful, we've got Sir Adler AND a Sartellian onto us now."

"Let's find the duke," suggested Athgar, "but this time, we'll stick together. If things go badly, we may have to fight our way out of this."

"Agreed," she said.

Locating the duke amongst his revellers was problematic, for although his costume was distinctive, it was difficult to spot in amongst the outrageous and gaudy outfits of his guests. In contrast, the father general's sombre dark grey tabard was easy to pick out. They were soon on his trail, watching from a discreet distance as he made his way through the crowd. They developed the habit of carrying a cup, though they were careful to dump out the contents to avoid the temptation to drink and dull their senses.

Finally, as the sun set, the father general made his way over to rejoin the duke. Natalia and Athgar drew closer, trying to make out what they were saying, but the guests, now full of wine and food, had grown more boisterous, making it a near-impossible task.

Natalia placed her mouth to Athgar's ear in an attempt to be heard, "What do we do now?"

"We wait," he replied. "With any luck, they'll head inside, and we can follow."

"But they'll see us!" said Natalia.

"No," he said, "remember the plan. We're just a couple searching to have some private time if anyone asks."

"Look," said Natalia, "they're putting down their drinks, I think this is it. Stay close." She pushed through the crowd, nearing their target.

The duke was heading directly for the house, the father general in tow. They entered the door Natalia had seen them exiting earlier, and disappeared into the manor house.

Natalia counted to ten, then moved towards the door, grasping the handle with determination. Athgar forestalled her, placing his finger to his lips to indicate silence. He then knelt, putting his ear to the door. She watched in silence until he looked back at her and nodded.

Natalia opened the door as quietly as she could to reveal a hallway beyond. Distant voices drifted towards them, and though making out details was difficult, it was clear that they had found their prey, so they moved closer, hoping to hear better.

Silently advancing down the hallway, they came upon the source of the voices, a door off to their right. Natalia pointed to Athgar and then the door, and so he dropped to a crouch, once more pressing his ear to the wood, listening while Natalia stood watch.

The voices were still somewhat muffled, but he distinctly heard the rustle of paper. He strained to decipher more, moving his ear closer to the lock until the words were easier to discern.

"That's too soon," the father general was saying.

"We have the people on our side," declared Lord Freidrich Hartman, Duke of Krieghoff.

"Yes," Gilbert agreed, "but we need time to mobilize our forces. We don't want to upset the Duke of Holstead."

"The Duke of Holstead?" asked Lord Freidrich. "Don't make me laugh. The man's got no balls. As long as we stay in the protected area, he won't lift a finger.

"Very well," said Father Gilbert, "give the command, and I'll start marching."

"I need a little more time," said the duke. "I've some matters to deal with here before we move eastward."

"How long do you think that will take?"

"No more than a day or two," said Lord Freidrich.

"Let's call it three, just to be on the safe side," suggested Father Gilbert.

"Very well," said the duke, "we march in three days."

"That seems to take care of everything," said the father general.

"So it does," said Lord Freidrich, "and in two weeks, we'll celebrate stealing the prize from beneath the very nose of the Duke of Holstead."

A third voice rose, a deep baritone that Athgar recognized as that of Verineth Sartellian, taking him by surprise. "Are you sure everything is in place?"

"I can assure you we've planned down to the smallest detail," said the duke. "The father general has provided us with the appropriate provocation, and the populace believes we are destroying the troublesome Orcs. Now it's just a simple matter of marching."

"Not quite," warned Verineth, "someone's on to you."

"What makes you say that?" asked the father general.

"I ran across one of your guests earlier," the mage continued. "I'm not sure who he was, but he was a Therengian."

"What of it?" sneered the duke. "They are a forgotten race, doomed by history into insignificance."

"And yet," said Verineth, "here we have a low born member of an almost extinct society at a party for nobles. How do you suppose that came about?"

"I think you give him too much credence," said the lord. "Surely he's just trying to see how the wealthy live?"

"I'll remind you of who I am," said Verineth. "I do not entertain flights of fancy. I'm warning you that something unusual is going on here."

"It's not your concern," claimed the father general.

"Not my concern?" Verineth responded. "The family saw fit to support this enterprise, I'll not see its investment put at risk through your stupidity."

"You can't talk to me like that!" admonished Father Gilbert. "I'm a leading member of the Temple of Saint Cunar."

"Listen, you overblown piece of turd," said Verineth, "you made a deal with the family. You'll do as you're told, or suffer the consequences."

"Gentlemen," urged Duke Freidrich, "let us not fight. We all want the same thing here."

"Do we?" challenged the father general. "I'm beginning to doubt that."

"The duke is right," said Verineth, "we must work together, despite our difference of opinion. You say that things are ready to proceed. Is there any chance that word has leaked out?"

"Of our plan?" said the duke. "Doubtful. Only the three of us know all the details. The troops know something's brewing, certainly, but they're all convinced it's retaliation for the Orc raids."

"If you think this Therengian a threat," suggested the father general, "then perhaps you should take care of him."

"That's the first good suggestion I've heard you make," countered Verineth. "Very well, you two continue with our plans, while I see to this interloper."

The room fell silent, and Athgar pressed closer, desperate for more. Finally, he heard the distinctive clang of goblets striking.

"To success," announced the Duke of Kriegoff.

"Success," the other two echoed.

Athgar straightened, looking around desperately.

"What is it?" Natalia whispered.

"Hide," he answered, "they're about to leave."

"Over here," she insisted, indicating another door that she quickly opened. "This looks like a library," she said as she entered the room, moving past a shelf full of books. Athgar followed her in and then closed the door as quietly as possible.

Footsteps were soon heard in the hallway, receding down the corridor. Natalia silently counted to twenty, then opened the door a crack, peering out.

"They're gone," she announced. "Tell me, what did you hear?"

"Verineth Sartellian was there," explained Athgar, "and the family's involved in this somehow, maybe even in charge!"

"The family?" she responded. "By the Saints, what are they up to?"

"I have no idea," said Athgar, "they were short on details. But whatever it is, they're marching in three days."

"Marching where?" she asked.

"I don't know, but the Orcs are just an excuse, they said as much. They mentioned stealing some prize from the Duke of Holstead."

"What prize?" she asked.

"I don't know, they never said," he defended, "but Verineth is searching for me now. He definitely noticed my grey eyes."

"Well," said Natalia, "they are your most striking feature."

"You're not helping," said Athgar.

"We'd best get out of here," she added. "We can't risk you being caught."

"Not until we get into that office," he protested. "There might be something of interest inside."

"Very well," she said, "the way is clear. We'll have a quick look, but then we leave, agreed?"

"Agreed," he said.

She opened the door farther, then poked her head out, confirming their solitude.

"Come on," she urged, moving back into the corridor with Athgar following until they found themselves once more at the duke's office.

"It's locked," said Athgar, trying the handle.

"Can't you pick it?" she asked.

"I'm a hunter, not a thief," said Athgar. "How about you?"

"Do I look like I can pick locks?" she asked. "What about magic? Have you a spell that might be of use?"

Athgar thought through his repertoire. "I could heat the lock, I suppose."

"That won't open it," she noted, "and if we kick the door in, it'll make too much noise."

"And then they'll know we've been here," agreed Athgar.

"They're already onto us," said Natalia. "You said that Verineth was looking for you, didn't you?"

"I did," he admitted, "but if we make a noise, we won't have the time we need to search the room."

"There's likely nothing in there," she said.

"No," he said, "you're wrong. If there was nothing in there, they wouldn't have locked the door."

"What if we work together?" said Natalia.

"How?" he asked.

"What if I freeze the lock, and then you heat it quickly. Might it shatter?"

"Maybe," he replied. "It's at least worth a try."

Natalia lightly touched the doorknob as she uttered words of power. Frost soon appeared, spreading across the door and sending a measurable chill Athgar's way.

She backed up, revealing an ice-encrusted lock. The Therengian moved forward quickly, holding his hand out just short of his target as he closed his eyes, concentrating on his inner spark. Moments later, a small flame leaped across the short distance to strike the ice, causing a sharp cracking sound, then a slight pop as the metal shattered.

"I think it worked," whispered Athgar, reaching for the handle.

"Wait," said Natalia, listening carefully. They stood in silence for a moment, then she nodded. "It's all right," she said, "no one heard."

Athgar pushed the door open into the office, which held a desk to one side and two chairs in front of it, waiting on guests to fill them. He moved behind the desk, searching for anything of interest, but aside from a bottle of wine, little was evident.

"It must be hidden somewhere," said Natalia. "Are there any drawers in the desk?"

"There are," said Athgar, pulling on them, "but this one's locked."

"Easy enough to break," said Natalia. "Use your axe."

"That'll make too much noise," he protested.

"I meant to pry it open with the blade, not chop it into little pieces."

"Oh," said Athgar, "I see what you mean." He pulled forth his axe, jamming it into the gap that topped the drawer. It took only a little strength to force it open.

Inside were several papers, and these he pulled forth, depositing them on the table. "Here," he said, "look through those."

Natalia started scanning them, trying to ascertain their import. "I don't see much of interest," she said.

"I do," said Athgar, staring down at the bottom of the drawer. He reached in, pulling forth a larger paper, which he carefully unfolded. "It appears to be some sort of map."

"How is it," said Natalia, "that you can't read, and yet you know a map?"

"The Orcs have maps," he replied. "They use them to keep track of all the best areas for hunting."

"I'm surprised," said Natalia, "I didn't know they used paper."

"They don't," said Athgar, "they use animal skins, but it's still the same thing. Pictures represent things on a map, that's why they're so easy to read."

They both gazed at their new-found treasure.

"Well," she said, "what do you make of it?"

He stabbed a finger down. "I think this is the borderlands between the two duchies," he said, "and if I'm not mistaken, this area here is the Orc lands."

"You recognize the Orc region?" she asked. "Then what is this mark here?"

Athgar gazed down at the circled area, "I have no idea."

"It looks to be north of the Orc Village," she noted.

"Do you think there's mention of it in one of those letters?" he urged.

Natalia scanned through them one more time, determined to find something, then lifted one up in triumph. "Here," she said, "this might be it."

"What does it say?" he asked.

"It's a letter from someone named Tamrin Schoenbach. He writes that he's awaiting payment for the discovery that he made."

"Maybe that references the area on the map?" Athgar suggested.

"Yes, but without the details, we still don't know what's there."

"At least we have a name," he said, "and that's something. Now, we need to get out of here before we're discovered."

"Yes," she said. "Do we take the map?"

"No, we'll leave it, along with the letters, but grab the wine," he said.

"For what?" she asked.

"Maybe they'll think someone broke in looking for something to drink."

"When they're passing around free drinks outside?" she asked.

"People do strange things when they're drunk," said Athgar, "and even if it only delays them, that gives us a better chance of escape." Athgar stared at the map a moment longer, committing it to memory, then stowed it back in its original place.

"Very well," she said, pushing the letters back into the drawer on top of the map, then grabbing the bottle. "Come on," she urged, "we've no time to waste."

They hurried into the hallway, closing the door behind them. The corridor was, thankfully, still empty, so they made their way to the exit, pausing a moment to listen.

The party was still in full swing, the sound of music coming faintly to Athgar's ear. He could also hear voices, but they were still some way off.

"It's clear," he said, turning the handle.

The door opened just as a group of revellers staggered from the dance floor, heading toward them in a rush. One of them was so intent on his companion's breasts that he bumped into Athgar and Natalia. The man looked up in surprise, then suddenly, recognition crossed his face.

"Ah, Natalia," he said, his boisterous voice easily carrying to the dance floor.

Natalia looked back in shock for a moment until she recognized the now-familiar countenance of Sir Adler. Athgar swore, for even as they recovered, a distant voice called forth from outside.

"There he is!" came the deep voice of Lord Verineth.

Natalia fought back the urge to scream in protest. Sir Adler was blocking her way, his hands still firmly around the other woman's waist.

"Move!" she shouted, trying to push past.

"Nonsense," cried the knight, "come and join us, it's more fun with three."

Athgar's fist struck the knight full in the face, driving him back and sending him tumbling to the ground.

"Run!" the Therengian roared.

They rushed past the fallen knight to spot Verineth Sartellian with the father general, and while the Holy Man began issuing commands, the mage started casting.

"Get down," cried out Athgar, just as a streak of flame shot over their heads to strike the side of the manor, splashing against the stonework.

Natalia was on her feet first. "To the hedge," she yelled, then sprinted, reaching the relative safety of the bushes, only to turn and see Athgar labouring along behind, limping. Beyond him, Verineth was casting yet again, this time sending a spark flying through the air. It struck the dirt, sinking in, and then the field began to tremble. Moments later, the ground erupted, spewing forth a bird made entirely of flames.

Athgar was getting closer, but there could be no doubt he'd fail to make it in time. Natalia loosed her full power, sending a single spike of ice hurtling towards the fiery beast, striking it dead centre to send ice and fire raining down amongst the crowd.

The guests, now alert to the presence of danger, started to panic, running in all directions, blocking Verineth's view. Athgar hobbled to the hedge, where Natalia waited, taking his arm and placing it around her shoulders.

"What happened?" she asked. "You're hurt."

"I twisted my ankle," he complained. "Keep moving, or we're both dead."

They ran as fast as they could, slowed as they were, parallelling the hedge. More bushes came closer, marking the edge of the manor's extensive gardens. Natalia paused, casting her eyes about, desperate to find a way out when the noise of moaning drifted towards them.

"What's that?" she said.

"Sounds like coupling," said Athgar.

"Surely not!"

Athgar listened some more, "I don't think there's any other explanation."

"Here? In the bushes?" she protested.

"Wait," he said, "I have an idea."

"We don't have time," Natalia pleaded, "we have to get out of here."

"No, wait," he repeated, "you don't understand. They're looking for us."

"Yes," she agreed, "I know that."

"But they're seeking a sparrow and a wolf. What if we were wearing different costumes?"

"We don't have any others," she said.

"No," Athgar agreed, "but they likely do." He pointed in the direction of the moaning.

"It's worth a try," she said.

They crept closer, trying to remain unheard. Soon, their targets came into view, a man lying atop his female companion, deep in the throes of passion. They were completely naked, their clothes scattered upon the ground, and Athgar could make out her nails digging into the man's back.

Athgar stooped, grabbing what garments he could, with Natalia doing likewise. Costumes in hand, they ran off, pausing some distance away to examine their haul.

"What have you got?" he asked.

"Looks like a badger mask," she said, "along with a black and white striped outfit. You?"

"A fairy, I think," he said, "but I don't believe it would fit me." He tossed the flimsy garment to Natalia, who looked at it doubtfully.

"I suppose that makes you the badger," she said, passing him the costume. "Hurry up, put this on."

Athgar removed his wolf helmet and costume, tossing them into the bushes nearby. He struggled into the clothes, only to hear the cloth ripping.

"It's too small," he complained.

"It'll have to do for now," she said. "I'm in no better shape."

He looked at Natalia to see her shivering. "Nervous?" he asked.

"No, cold," she countered. "There's next to no clothing here.

"I can take care of that," he said, gesticulating as he called forth words of power.

A warmth settled over her. "Thank you," she said. "Now, let's get out of here."

Distant shouts drifted to their ears, then a streak of flame launched itself into the air, exploding in a cacophony of sound, lighting up the entire area.

Athgar, noticing the approach of soldiers with their swords out, lay down, pulling Natalia on top of him.

"What are you doing?" she cried out as the soldiers drew closer.

"Trust me," he said, placing his arms around her. He pulled her face to his, kissing her fiercely and moaning loudly. Natalia, seeing the wisdom in his actions, did likewise, losing herself in the moment.

The guards moved past, pausing only long enough to nod in appreciation. Natalia kept up the act until they were well out of sight, then fell silent.

"They're gone," she said. "That was close."

"Closer than you think," Athgar countered. "A few more moments and it would have been too late."

She didn't understand what he meant at first, then looked down to note the state of his arousal.

"Later," she said, "I promise."

They stood, taking a moment to straighten their clothes.

"What now?" she asked.

"Now," he said, "we walk out of here like all the other guests."

"They might recognize us," she said.

"I doubt it," he replied. "Tell me, can you see my eyes in this mask?"

"Yes, but I can't make out their colour, it's too dark."

"Good, then let's wander back to the celebration. They'll likely be searching this area for some time."

"What makes you say that?" she asked.

"They'll have found the wolf head by now," he said. "They're bound to think we ditched and ran. The last place they'd expect us to go is back to the party."

THE EXPERT

Spring 1104 SR

B elgast took another swig from his tankard, then placed it back on the table before him as he stared at his companions.

"And that was it? You just walked out?"

"We did," said Natalia.

"I should have liked to see that," the Dwarf mused. "It's quite the story."

"I found it all quite shocking," said Natalia.

"Yes," agreed Athgar, "but luckily, we found that couple. I wonder what happened to them?"

"I shudder to think," said Natalia. "I wonder how long it took them to realize they'd lost all their clothes?"

"Some time, apparently," said Belgast.

"What makes you say that?" asked Athgar.

"Simple," replied the Dwarf. "If they'd realized sooner, they might have gotten the word out, then they would have been looking for a badger and a fairy."

"I hadn't thought of that," admitted Athgar.

"That's what I'm here for," said Belgast. "The big question, of course, is what we do next?"

"We have a name," said Natalia.

"A name?" said the Dwarf. "How does that help us?"

"It appears the duke owed a lot to someone called Tamrin Schoenbach," said Athgar.

"Never heard of him," said Belgast.

"We think he made a discovery in the Orc territory," added Natalia.

"What sort of discovery?" the Dwarf asked.

"That's the big question," said Athgar.

"If we can find him," said Natalia, "he can most likely supply us with the answer."

"It's worth a try," said Belgast. "But where do we find this man?"

"Good question," noted Athgar. "I suppose we'll have to ask around, see if anyone's heard of him."

"Wouldn't that alert them?" asked Natalia.

"Do you have a better idea?" the Therengian responded.

"If this fellow, Schoenbach, discovered something valuable, wouldn't he just sell it?" said Belgast.

"Whatever it was must have been too big to move," suggested Natalia.

"But what could it be?" asked the Dwarf.

"I don't know," said Athgar, "gold, maybe?"

"Gold might be worth a lot, but enough to risk war?" said Belgast. "Didn't you say they'd have it all within a couple of weeks? That hardly sounds like gold."

"What else could it be?" asked Natalia.

"What about something like a magic sword?" suggested Athgar.

"No," said the Dwarf, "he'd just carry it out if that's all it was. It would be valuable, but not enough to risk war. It has to be something else."

"We can speculate all we like," said Natalia, "but our real priority is to find this Schoenbach person. If he does have knowledge of something valuable, might he try selling it off to the highest bidder?"

"That would make sense, I suppose," said Athgar. "But how do we identify other bidders?"

"I might know someone," said Belgast.

"Here? In Caerhaven?" said Athgar. "I thought you'd been away for more than twenty years."

"I have," admitted the Dwarf, "but it's worth a try."

"Who is this fellow you speak of?" asked Natalia.

"An old friend named Lofgrim. If someone's trying to sell something valuable, chances are he's heard of it."

"Lofgrim?" said Athgar. "Is he a Dwarf?"

"He is," admitted Belgast. "Is that a problem?"

"No," said the Therengian, "far from it. In fact, if anything, it's better. Less likely to be aligned with our foes."

"In that case," said the Dwarf, "you two lie low here while I arrange a meeting. And no going outside, they're looking for you, remember?"

Athgar looked at Natalia, smiling.

"What are you grinning at?" she asked.

"We have a lot of time to spend in our room," said Athgar. "I wonder how we might occupy ourselves?"

Natalia smiled knowingly.

Belgast stood, pausing only long enough to down the rest of his ale. "I'll be off then," he announced. "You two try to stay out of trouble."

"We will," Athgar promised.

They watched the Dwarf exit the Golden Spire, then made their way up to their room.

"Do you suppose he'll have any luck?" asked Natalia.

"Can't say for sure," said Athgar, "but twenty years is a long time, even for a Dwarf. I don't know if this Lofgrim fellow will still be alive, let alone here in Caerhaven."

"In any event," said Natalia, "it's all up to Belgast now. We just have to trust that he'll be successful."

"And if he isn't?" pondered the Therengian.

"Then we'll deal with that later," she said. "Now, we have more important things to do."

"I was hoping you'd say that," said Athgar.

"Slow down, my love," she said. "Work first, play comes later."

"Work?" he said. "What work?"

"You're still learning to read, remember?"

"I could hardly forget," he said, "you're a demanding taskmaster."

"Demanding? Is that what you call it? I thought I was being nice."

"You are," he said, "I simply meant that you're good at what you do."

"I am," she admitted. "I tell you what, you give me your best effort, and maybe we'll have a little reward later."

"Let's get started," he insisted.

Belgast stood outside the dilapidated building. The place hadn't changed in decades, still the run-down ruin he remembered. He knocked three times, paused, then knocked twice more, waiting for a count of three between each one. The door opened to reveal a somewhat lanky Dwarf.

"Who's there?" he demanded.

"Belgast Ridgehand, here to see Lofgrim. He's still in charge, isn't he?"

"He is," replied the Dwarf, "but I doubt he'll see the likes of you."

"Tell him," said Belgast, "that I'll forgive him his loan."

The door shut in his face and he chuckled. He could well imagine his old friend's response to such a message. Sure enough, moments later, the door reopened to a familiar face.

"Belgast!" the Dwarf called out. "Well, I'll be an Elf's ear. By Gundar's Forge, how are you?"

"I'm well," he responded. "It's been a long time, old friend."

"So it has," said Lofgrim. "Not like in the old days, eh? We both were so much thinner back then."

"Speak for yourself," said Belgast, "I'm as trim as I've ever been."

Lofgrim looked him up and down, breaking into a grin. "If you say so, old friend, but my eyes haven't gotten that bad yet. I know what I see."

"Are you going to stand there insulting me all day," asked Belgast, "or invite me in?"

"Of course," Lofgrim replied, "come inside and sit down. We'll have a drink and reminisce about old times."

They entered the building, making their way through a rough and unkempt hallway. His host opened the door at the far end, revealing a nicely furnished room filled with very expensive furniture, most seats covered in pillows.

"I see you're doing all right for yourself," said Belgast.

"I do what I can," said Lofgrim. "Tell me, how is that cousin of ours? What was his name again?"

"Dagle," said Belgast. "He was murdered, unfortunately. That's part of the reason I'm here."

"Murdered, you say? By whom?"

"We're still trying to work that out," said Belgast, "but it appears to be some powerful and influential people."

"You say 'we're'? Who's working with you?"

"A mage couple," explained Belgast. "Trustworthy people, I can assure you."

"I'm sorry to hear of your predicament," said Lofgrim. "What can I do to help?"

"We're looking for someone," said Belgast, "a Human, to be exact."

"Good luck with that," noted Lofgrim. "The whole city's overflowing with them, in case you hadn't noticed. What's his name?"

"Tamrin Schoenbach," said Belgast. "We believe he's been trying to sell the location of a discovery he's made."

"Schoenbach?" said Lofgrim. "That name sounds familiar. Do you know his profession?"

"No," said Belgast, "but he discovered something in the Orc lands. We need to know what it was he found."

"Hold on a moment," said Lofgrim, digging into the pillows beside him to extract a somewhat worn-looking notebook. He untied the binding, then flipped through the pages. "Schoenbach," he said, "Scho-En-Bach. Ah, yes, here he is."

"You found him?" asked Belgast.

"I did," replied his host. "I've dealt with him in the past. He's more of an information broker. Reliable, well worth the cost if you're hiring."

"Do you know where we can find this fellow?"

"Well, let's see," said Lofgrim, flipping through yet more pages. He finally paused, reading his discovery. "Do you know the Cuttlefish?"

"That old run-down inn?" said Belgast.

"That's the one, it's across from some stables."

"I know it," said Belgast. "Is that where he lives?"

"No," said Lofgrim, "but he has an office there."

"In the inn?"

"No, beside it," corrected Lofgrim. "He hires out on expeditions. Says he can help find lost ruins and such. I think it's really all a scam, but to each his own."

"I doubt he'd try to scam powerful people, he'd lose his head if he were caught."

"So he would," said Lofgrim, "but what can I say, the man's an opportunist."

"I'll look for him there, then," said Belgast. "Thank you, cousin."

"Hey," said Lofgrim, "what else is family for? Speaking of which, why don't you come and work for me? I could use a trustworthy partner."

"I can't," replied Belgast. "I still have to right this wrong and punish those responsible. Perhaps when I'm done?"

"You're welcome any time. Take care of yourself, Belgast, and let's not wait another twenty years this time, agreed?"

"Agreed," said the Dwarf. He embraced his cousin, and they stood for a moment, patting each other's back.

"Watch out for those Humans," warned Lofgrim, "they're slippery beggars. You never know who can be trusted."

"I will, I promise," said Belgast. "Now, I'd best be going if I'm to find this fellow before darkness sets in."

"This letter," said Athgar, staring at the page, "looks a lot like this other one."

"It does," agreed Natalia, "but it's a 'p' while this other one here is a 'd', though it does look like an upside-down 'p'."

"So it does," mused the Therengian.

"You're picking this up pretty quickly," noted Natalia.

"Well, I did learn the magical alphabet," said Athgar.

"You did," she agreed, "and it's served you well."

"It's not so much the letters that I find hard, it's stringing them together to make words. Here, with you writing them down, it's not so bad, but when I look at signs, they seem all jumbled up."

"That's because people write them differently," she explained. "Unlike the magical letters, these characters can be written in a variety of ways."

"It does make it quite confusing," pondered Athgar.

"You get used to it," said Natalia. "I remember when I first arrived at the Volstrum. I knew nothing of letters in those days."

"How old were you again?" he asked.

"Only ten," she said. "I remember feeling abandoned, but they looked after me."

"Until they wanted something out of you," clarified Athgar.

"There was that," she admitted, "but not everyone was like that. Many of my instructors were just trying to do their best to teach me."

"And you were a quick learner, from what you've told me," he said.

"I was," she replied, "but I was still lonely."

"Surely you had friends," he suggested. "After all, you're such an outgoing person, full of life."

She laughed, and he smiled, enjoying seeing her relax.

"I was very quiet back in those days," she said.

"Oh?" he said. "What changed that?"

"Are you saying I talk a lot?" she asked.

"I would never say such a thing," he said in mock seriousness. "I just find it surprising that you say that."

"I did have one friend," she said, "a girl named Katrin. She actually started as an enemy, but then, somehow, I managed to win her over."

"What happened to her?" he asked.

"I don't know," she admitted. "She was removed from the Volstrum after failing some of her classes. I never heard from her after that."

"Did you look for her?" he asked.

"I did," she said, "or rather, I had someone else look for her. A mage hunter, to be precise."

"A mage hunter?" said Athgar. "I take it that's who took you there in the first place."

"It was," she said, "and I suppose that's another friend I'll never see again. I'm afraid I left in haste. If he's still alive, he's likely living in a dungeon by now, and it's all my fault." Tears came to her eyes.

"Hey, now," said Athgar, "you can't blame yourself. You did what you had to do to survive. No one can fault you for that, and there's no indication that this mage hunter was arrested, is there?"

"He helped me escape," she explained, "to the extent that he fought my guards."

"I'm sorry," he said, "I didn't know. I just assumed you ran away."

"It's much more complicated than that," she said. "I was constantly under the eye of the family."

"You're well away from them now," he promised.

"Am I?" she asked. "We saw one at the party, remember?"

"I could hardly forget," he said, "but it was me he was after, not you."

"You forget," she said, "I destroyed his phoenix."

"And?"

"And he's a powerful mage. Not many Water Mages could do such a thing. It's only a matter of time before he puts two and two together. He's a smart man, he'll figure it out, and when he does, he'll bring his full power to bear on the both of us. What have I done, Athgar? I've put both of us in peril."

"We've been in peril ever since we met," he soothed. "I'd rather face hordes in the Underworld than be without you. We'll get through this, I promise, and one day we'll find a place where we can settle down."

"That would be nice," she said, her voice trailing off.

He moved closer, putting his arms around her and, in response, she laid her head on his shoulder.

Athgar woke to a knock on the door. His arm was in pain, pinned in place by the sleeping form of Natalia, so he gently nudged her with his free hand.

"Natalia, wake up," he whispered.

She stirred, opening her eyes only to realize she had fallen asleep in her chair. She sat upright. "Sorry, I didn't know I was so tired. Why didn't you put me to bed?"

"I didn't want to disturb you," he said, moving his arm and trying to restore circulation.

Again, came a rap on the door.

"Who is it?" Natalia called out.

"Belgast," came the answer.

Athgar rose, crossing the distance to throw the latch back on the door. "Come in," he insisted. "How did you make out with this Lofgrim fellow?"

"I found what we needed," the Dwarf proclaimed. "Schoenbach runs a business down by an inn called the Cuttlefish."

"What kind of business?" asked Natalia, stifling a yawn.

"He sells information," explained Belgast. "He likely maintains a storefront for his more well-to-do clients. They like that sort of thing, and it gives him an air of respectability."

"We should go and see him," said Athgar, waving his arm around.

"By Gundar's Forge, what are you doing?" asked Belgast. "You're flapping your arms around like you're trying to fly."

"My arm is numb," said Athgar.

"You should have a Life Mage look at it," noted the Dwarf.

"No," Athgar replied, "Natalia fell asleep on it."

"Well, that was quite silly of her."

"It wasn't my fault," said Natalia, "he wouldn't put me to bed."

The Dwarf put his hands into the air. "I don't need to know all this," he declared. "You Humans and your sex. Sometimes I think that's all you ever think about."

Athgar turned crimson. "We were talking about sleep, Belgast, nothing more."

"Then why are you blushing?" asked the Dwarf. "Hah! I've got you there."

"Can we return to this person we're looking for," asked Natalia, "or do you need to keep embarrassing Athgar?"

"Sorry," said the Dwarf, shamefaced. "As I was saying, he's down near the Cuttlefish. That's only around ten blocks away if I remember correctly."

"You two go," said Natalia, "I need some sleep."

Athgar turned to her, a worried look on his face. "Are you feeling all right?"

"Just tired, is all," she responded. "It's been a busy few days, and I'd like to get some proper rest."

"We could wait until you've slept?" suggested Athgar.

"No," she insisted, "you must get this information before our enemies decide to silence him permanently. It may already be too late."

"She has a point," said Belgast.

"Very well," said Athgar, "I'll meet you downstairs in a moment. I'm just going to put Natalia to bed first."

"I'm fine," she insisted.

"Nonsense," he said.

"Very well," said the Dwarf, "I'll see you downstairs."

He left, leaving the two mages alone. Athgar walked Natalia to bed, letting her climb in, then pulling the heavy blankets up. Bending over her, he kissed her forehead, then looked at her in worry.

"You feel warm," he said.

"Nonsense, I'm fine," she insisted.

"All right," he said, "but I'm throwing a spell of warmth on you, just in case."

"I'm not cold," she argued.

"The warmth spell will regulate your body heat. It'll keep you at a constant temperature, regardless of how you feel."

"Very well," she replied, "but you need to get going, Belgast is waiting."

Athgar cast the spell, watching her relax as the magic took effect. He briefly wondered if a Brother of Saint Mathew might be found, but then remembered that they had no temple here. Making a mental note to find a Life Mage, he left, closing the door behind him.

SCHOENBACH

Spring 1104 SR

Athgar stood in the stables, gazing across at the building opposite.
"See anything?" asked the Dwarf.

"No one's entered or left if that's what you mean."

"Is anyone there?" asked Belgast.

"Yes," said Athgar, "I saw him open the shutters earlier."

"What's he doing?"

"I have no idea," answered the Therengian, "but I think it's time we went and talked to him."

"Are you sure?" asked the Dwarf.

"We likely won't have a better opportunity," said Athgar. "He's there, and alone as far as we can tell. Let's go."

He set off at a determined pace, Belgast hurrying to catch up. Soon they were at the door, the Therengian pushing it open to reveal a single room where a middle-aged man sat at a small table, quill in hand. He looked up in surprise as they entered.

"Can I help you?" he asked.

"Are you Tamrin Schoenbach?" asked Athgar.

"That depends," the man responded, "who are you?"

"My name is Athgar, and this is Belgast. We've come seeking some information."

"Then you've come to the right place," the man replied, "for I am he that you seek. What kind of information are you interested in?"

"We have heard that you recently did some business with the duke," said Athgar, "and we were wondering if you might be willing to talk about it."

"For a suitable fee, of course," added Belgast.

Tamrin straightened in his chair. "I'm afraid I don't discuss other people's business. You'll have to go elsewhere."

"That's a bit much, isn't it?" said Athgar. "After all, you buy and sell information, don't you?"

"While that's true," the man continued, "I have cultivated many influential clients. I would soon find myself unpopular if I were to discuss their arrangements with others."

"I take it," said Athgar, "that means you won't help us?"

"Not by discussing my business with the duke, but maybe there's something else I might help you with?"

"How do you collect your information?" asked Belgast. "Do you pay others for it, or do you collect it yourself?"

"My methods are my own," replied Schoenbach. "Why? Do you have information to sell?"

"Not at this time," said Belgast.

Schoenbach suddenly leaned forward, placing his elbows on the table. "You know, I might be willing to reconsider your offer. Give me some time to think about it, and I'll let you know. Where can I reach you?"

"At the Golden Spire," said Athgar. "Do you know it?"

"Yes," Schoenbach replied, "I know it well. Tell me, have you been in town long?"

"A few days," said Athgar, "why?"

"Merely curious," the man replied.

"Shouldn't we discuss our offer?" asked Belgast.

"Not at this time," said Schoenbach. "As I said, I've some things to think over. I'll send word to you at the Spire once I've made up my mind."

"Very well," said Athgar, "then we'll bid you a good day."

Schoenbach stood, "It was nice meeting you. I look forward to our next encounter."

Athgar stood, along with Belgast. They exited the building, turning up the road to head back to their own inn.

"Do you think that was wise?" asked the Dwarf.

"What? Contacting him?"

"No, I mean telling him where we were staying."

"How else would he contact us?" said Athgar.

"But now he knows where he can find us," warned the Dwarf.

"Natalia told me I should be more trusting. After all, we trusted you back in Ostermund and look where it got us. Besides, why does it matter that he knows we're at the Spire?" asked the Therengian. "He seemed genuinely interested in our offer."

"Did he now?" mused the Dwarf. "I can't help but feel he was trying to learn more about us."

"You're overthinking things," said Athgar. "We have to trust somebody."

"Yes," said the Dwarf, "I'm just not sure that he was the right person to trust."

The Golden Spire soon came into view, causing Athgar's stomach to rumble.

"Hungry?" asked the Dwarf.

"Famished," admitted the Therengian.

"Well, we might as well eat."

"What about Natalia?" asked Athgar.

"What about her? She's sleeping, isn't she?"

"Yes," Athgar admitted, "but she felt warm. I need to check on her."

"We haven't been gone that long," said Belgast, "she's likely still sleeping."

"What if she's ill?"

"Then we'll find a healer," said the Dwarf. "But first, let's get something to eat. Thinking things through on an empty stomach never leads to good decisions."

"But Natalia..." Athgar objected.

"Look," said Belgast, "we'll order her some food and take it up to her once we're done. Will that suit you?"

"Very well," he surrendered, "but just a quick meal. I don't want to be down here all day."

"No, of course not," said Belgast, "we'll just top up our stomachs."

Natalia tossed and turned, drifting into a fitful slumber, then awakened to see shadows lurking in her room. She fought to focus on them, but when they flitted away, she realized they were nothing but light leaking through the shutters, casting their spell.

She drifted off to sleep once more, her mind struggling to remain focused. Images of the mage, Verineth, came to her. He stood across the grass from her, conjuring forth a phoenix. Natalia desperately tried to focus her spell, but the power wouldn't flow, and she watched in horror as Athgar was consumed by the fiery beast.

She awoke, sweat covering her. Throwing off the blankets, she sat up, casting her eyes around, looking for the reassuring presence of Athgar, but he was nowhere to be seen.

The room was chilly, and she started to shake. The wardrobe sat nearby, so she made her way towards it, intent on finding something to keep her warm. Athgar's warmth spell had helped, but even it had its limitations. Now that it had worn off, she felt the fever gripping her.

Opening the wardrobe, she stared within, then heard some heavy steps outside in the corridor, and something made her pause. They came closer, and then she saw a faint shadow through the gap at the bottom of the door. She had visitors, of that she had no doubt, for if Athgar had returned, he wouldn't wait. Natalia stepped into the wardrobe, closing the door quietly behind her.

Athgar stared down at the bowl before him.

"This looks like Orc porridge," he said.

"You make that sound bad," said Belgast. "What is it?"

"It's a type of gruel made from grains. They make a lot of it in Ord-Kurgad, but they usually put some meat in it."

"Meat? In your porridge?" said the Dwarf. "That sounds disgusting."

"I actually like it," said Athgar.

"Then why aren't you eating it?"

"I said it looks like it," defended the Therengian, "I didn't say it tasted the same."

"You know," said Belgast, "you can always order meat."

"No," said Athgar, "I've lost my appetite. I think I'm going to take this up to Natalia and see if she's feeling any better."

"Do as you like," said the Dwarf, "but I'm staying here till my belly is full."

Athgar rose, lifting the bowl of porridge carefully, lest he spill it as he made his way through the common room and down the hallway that led to their room. He was only halfway through the corridor when he spotted their door partially open, and then he heard noises from within, the sounds of booted feet moving around! He quickly moved closer, edging up to the door. Inside, he heard scuffling as if someone was searching the room.

"Look under the bed," said an unfamiliar voice, "and I'll check the wardrobe. There's bound to be something we can use."

Athgar moved into the doorway, where he spotted two men inside the room, both rough-looking characters. One was crouched low, about to peer under the bed, while the other was just opening the door to the wardrobe when there was an explosion of energy as ice and snow blasted out, sending the villain staggering. Athgar wanted to lash out with flame, but couldn't risk catching Natalia. He moved inside, throwing the bowl of gruel with all the strength he could muster. It struck the icy man on the side of the head, knocking him crashing to the floor.

The other one, who was searching under the bed, had turned as soon as Natalia had fired off her spell. He looked around quickly, then rushed the window, crashing through the shutters and disappearing from sight.

Natalia stumbled out from the wardrobe, clutching its door frame to hold her upright. When the remaining invader rose, Athgar rushed towards him, but at that exact moment, Natalia fell, collapsing to the floor. Athgar immediately changed direction, sprinting to her side, while their enemy pushed past him and ran from the room.

"Natalia!" he cried out.

She looked up at him, trying to focus, her face a mask of sweat, and then her eyes suddenly rolled up into her head as she went limp.

Natalia awoke some time later, lying in a bed, blankets wrapped all around her while someone sat in a chair, watching her. Focusing her gaze, she recognized Athgar, concern written all over his face.

"You're awake," he said, relief flooding his features.

"What happened?" she asked. "Where are we?"

"We're still at the Golden Spire," he replied, "but don't worry, it's a different room."

"We have to get out of here," she said. "Someone was looking for us."

"We can't travel," he warned, "you're too ill."

"Nonsense," she said, sitting up. Her head swam, and she dropped back onto her pillow, "All right, you win."

"I've sent Belgast to find a healer," he said. "I'm hoping there's a Life Mage hereabouts that we can hire."

"Not likely," she replied. "Life Mages typically work for the nobility. You'll not find one willing to come here."

"Let me worry about that," he said, "the first step is finding one."

"And then what?" she asked. "You'll make them heal me? You know that's not going to work."

"Then I'll take you somewhere else. Somewhere where I trust people."

"Where?" asked Natalia.

Athgar thought hard, then an idea cemented in his head. "Ord-Kurgad," he said. "Uhdrig will heal you, and if she doesn't, then Shaluhk certainly will."

"It's too far away, Athgar."

"Then I'll send for her," he promised.

"That would take even longer," she said. "Besides, I can't travel."

He rose, storming around the room in frustration.

"There has to be something we can do," he cursed.

"Did you find out what Schoenbach discovered?" she asked.

"No, the confounded man wouldn't tell us. Said he wouldn't reveal his client's secrets."

"He followed you two back here," she said. "That's likely who broke in."

"Possibly," he replied, "but it won't happen again."

"How can you say that?" she asked.

"I arranged this room under another name, but we're still renting the other one. If anyone comes looking for us now, they'll be in the wrong room."

"You have to get away from here," she warned. "I'm too sick, but you've got a good chance of getting free of this."

"I'm not going anywhere without you," he swore.

"I'm so cold," she said.

He cast his spell, and warmth enveloped her once more. When she appeared to relax, Athgar let out a sigh of relief.

"How does that feel?" he asked.

"Better," she said, "but I still feel weak."

A knock on the door grabbed their attention. After a short pause, there were four more.

"It's Belgast," said Athgar, "that's his signal."

He moved to the door, opening it to reveal the Dwarf.

"Any luck?" asked Athgar.

"I'm afraid not," said Belgast. "There's no Life Mages available."

"Doesn't the duke have one?" said Athgar.

"He does, but the man's away, and only Gundar knows where."

"He's likely with the army that's preparing to march."

"What do we do now?" said the Dwarf.

"We take Natalia to the Orcs," said Athgar, "it's her only chance."

"That's a big risk," said Belgast, "especially if that's where the army's going."

"There's no other choice," he said.

"We'll need a carriage," said the Dwarf, "or at the very least a wagon. She can't ride in her condition."

"Fair enough," the Therengian replied. "You stay here, and I'll go and make arrangements."

"No," said Natalia, drawing both of their attention. "You need to find out what Schoenbach is hiding."

"And how do you propose we do that?" asked Athgar.

"You need to break into his building," she said, "tonight before he has a chance to destroy anything."

"I can't," said Athgar, "I need to look after you."

"Let me contact Lofgrim," said Belgast. "He can watch Natalia and get her ready for travel while we break-in."

"Are you sure you can trust him?" said Athgar.

"With my life," said the Dwarf.

"You must do this," insisted Natalia. "There's no sense in returning to Ord-Kurgad if you can't save them, and to do that, you need to know what's going on."

"Very well," Athgar replied, turning to Belgast. "How much time will it take to get word to Lofgrim?"

In answer, the Dwarf looked out the window, judging the time of day.

"I'll be back before nightfall, I promise."

Verineth Sartellian stood in front of the altar, concentrating on the fire before him. He raised his hands, uttering words of power and the flames grew in intensity, rising to match his own height. He moved his fingers, tracing intricate patterns, and then the centre of the flames cleared, revealing a face.

"Verineth," came the voice of Marakhova Stormwind, "I'm surprised to hear from you. I thought you were in Caerhaven."

"So I am," he replied, "but something has come up here that you might be interested in."

"You have me intrigued," the matron replied. "Tell me, what is it that you have discovered?"

"I believe I've located your rogue Stormwind," he said.

"Natalia? In Caerhaven? I must say that is most unexpected. What makes you think it's her?"

"I encountered a Fire Mage, a Therengian by the looks of it. Wasn't she travelling with one?"

"She was," Marakhova replied. "A man named Athgar. You must be careful, he's said to be powerful."

"I am nothing, if not vigilant," said Verineth. "I shall take all precautions."

"And the girl, Natalia, you've seen her?"

"Not directly," the Fire Mage replied, "but I witnessed the effects of her magic. I conjured a phoenix to finish off her companion, and she was able to destroy it."

"She is quite resourceful," Marakhova replied, "and very, very dangerous. You've likely never encountered one of her power before."

"What do you want me to do with them?" he asked. "Are they to be captured and returned to you?"

"Saints, no," said Marakhova. "You must kill them with all haste. They are far too dangerous to capture. Shall I send you help?"

"No," said Verineth, "that will likely take too long. I have people here I can rely on. I'll take care of this myself."

"You know where they are?" she asked.

"Yes," he acknowledged. "It seems while our Therengian friend was making enquiries to the duke's man, he revealed where they were staying."

"How convenient for us. Tell me, how go our other plans in Caerhaven?"

"They progress slower than I'd like, but we're making progress."

"And the duke?"

"He suspects nothing. Once his men have retrieved our prize, I shall dispatch him, along with anyone else that knows of it. It will be ours, and ours alone."

"Excellent," said Marakhova, "you serve the family well."

"How are things in Karslev?" he asked.

"The matriarch is in ill health," she replied. "It won't be long now, and then the fight for control will begin."

"You have my support," Verineth promised.

"Thank you," she replied, "that means a lot. Now, I have much to do in preparation. I shall leave you to your task."

"Very well," he replied.

He waved his hands, dismissing the flames, then stood in thought for a moment. He must, at all costs, destroy these two mages and yet Markhova's warning gave him pause. He finally left the chamber, determined to avoid a direct confrontation.

BREAK-IN

Spring 1104 SR

A thgar peered through the gloom.
"I can't see anything," he complained.
"Let me look," said Belgast, "I have much better vision at night than you."
Athgar shifted slightly, allowing the Dwarf to move past.

"Is it true that Dwarves can see in the dark?" he asked.

"We see better than you in dim light," replied Belgast, "but we can't see in pitch black if that's what you mean."

"Any sign of activity?"

The Dwarf stared across the street. Finally, a light appeared as Tamrin Schoenbach, holding a lantern, left the building, pausing only to turn and lock the door. They watched him as he disappeared up the street.

"Shall we?" said the Dwarf.

"No," warned Athgar, "we'll wait a while longer, just to be sure. Can you tell if anyone is watching the place?"

"You mean other than us?" said Belgast. "None that I can see."

Athgar waited, counting to one hundred. He wondered, briefly, if he was being too cautious, but then remembered how much was at stake here. Finally, his tally finished, he looked at his companion.

"Let's go," he said, leading them across the street. They moved quickly, halting in front of Schoenbach's door which was made of oak, and boasted a large padlock.

"I don't suppose you can pick a lock?" Athgar asked.

"No," replied the Dwarf, "you?"

"No such luck, though I'm beginning to think I should learn how."

"We'll have to use a more direct approach," said Belgast. "I'll smash it with my pickaxe." He hefted the tool, but Athgar held up his hand.

"No, wait," he urged. "Someone might hear it."

"I'm open to other suggestions," said the Dwarf.

"We'll try around back. There has to be another way in, one that's not so out in the open."

Athgar moved to the south side of the building and looked down the alley. On his left was the Cuttlefish Inn, while to his right lay the information broker's building.

"Any windows?" asked Belgast.

"No," he said, moving down the alley, "but maybe there's something around back."

The Dwarf looked up and down the street to assure himself that they weren't being watched, then followed Athgar as he made his way to the back.

Athgar paused at the sound of voices, peering around the corner to spy a group of men chatting out back of the inn. Moments later, he heard the soft footfalls of Belgast coming down the alleyway. Athgar placed his finger to his lips, and the Dwarf nodded. They watched and listened, hoping the group would move on, but it appeared the interlopers had much to discuss.

"For the Gods' sake," whispered Belgast, "are they to talk all night?"

"It seems so," said the Therengian.

"What do we do?"

"There's little we CAN do," said Athgar. "We'll just have to wait."

The evening wore on as they stood in the shadows, lingering in the alleyway in anticipation of the chance they needed. It came when a voice from inside the inn called out, indistinct to the pair of them, but obviously understood by the small crowd who filed back inside, leaving the back alley deserted.

Athgar breathed a sigh of relief, "Finally."

He led Belgast around to the rear of the building and examined the door. It was of simple construction, nothing like the oaken door out front.

"I see no sign of a lock," said Belgast. "That's good, isn't it?"

"It is," the Therengian agreed, "though I rather imagine there's a bolt on the other side holding it closed."

Athgar tried the door, only to find it resisting his efforts. "Just as I thought," he swore.

"Allow me," said Belgast.

Athgar moved aside, then watched in fascination as the Dwarf threw his full weight against it. The door groaned under the assault but resisted his efforts.

"Now what?" asked Athgar.

Belgast smiled, "Don't worry, this will work. It just takes a few tries."

He shouldered once more, and this time the door moved slightly while a groaning noise escaped.

The Dwarf smiled, "There, you see? The bolt is starting to bend. One more push ought to take care of it."

He attacked it again, to be rewarded with a splintering sound as wood was ripped from its place. Belgast disappeared into the gloomy interior, falling to the floor with a grunt.

"Are you all right?" called out Athgar.

"I'm fine," replied Belgast. "Just had the wind knocked out of me."

Athgar stepped through the doorway into the darkness and then paused, extending his right hand, palm upward, while speaking a few words of magic. A green flame flickered to life, illuminating the narrow hallway.

He let his eyes adjust and then took in his surroundings. The corridor couldn't have been more than half the building's depth with a door at the end, likely leading to Schoenbach's office, while another was to his immediate left.

"Which way?" asked Athgar.

Belgast, who had now risen, scanned both before reaching his decision. "This one," he said, picking the door to his side.

"Why that one?" asked Athgar.

"We visited his office," said the Dwarf, "and I didn't see anywhere he might store information. I'm guessing it's hidden back here somewhere."

"How do we know he doesn't keep it at home?" asked Athgar.

"We don't know for sure," said the Dwarf, "but he'd need to have it close in case one of his clients showed up. He wouldn't want to lug it back and forth every day, that would be too risky."

"You think he has that much information?"

"Well," said Belgast, pausing to gather his thoughts, "he has enough to operate out of an office. That would seem to indicate he knows a lot of things about a lot of people."

"A valid point," said Athgar. "Is the door locked?"

Belgast pushed the door, and it swung into the room. "It appears not," the Dwarf remarked.

Something skittered across the floor, and the Dwarf made a face of disgust. "Rats," he murmured.

Athgar stepped forward, holding out the flame to bathe the room in its greenish glow. It appeared to be a storeroom of sorts, with shelves lined with boxes, jars and urns.

"What's all this?" asked Athgar.

"Likely from the previous tenant," said Belgast.

"You'd think he'd get rid of it."

"I beg to differ," said the Dwarf. "It's perfect for him. It makes it much easier to hide things." He began rooting through the boxes.

"What are you doing?" Athgar asked.

"Looking for information," said Belgast. "He won't have left it out in the open."

"Wouldn't he lock it up somewhere?"

"Tell me," said the Dwarf, "if you broke into this place and saw a locked box, wouldn't that be the first place you'd look?"

"Of course," said Athgar.

"That's why it won't be in plain sight. Now, start searching that other shelf. We're looking for any sort of papers, they could be loose sheets or even a journal."

Athgar pulled a box from the shelf and dropped it to the floor. He used the head of his axe to pry it open, only to see straw within. Digging down farther, he found some old clay pots.

"What in the Gods' name is this?"

"That's packing," said Belgast. "The straw cushions the pots, helps prevent breakage."

"Breakage?" said Athgar. "You mean someone truly sends their pots elsewhere?"

"Yes, why?" asked the Dwarf. "Does that surprise you? Surely you've heard of commerce?"

"I wouldn't know of such things," noted the Therengian. "In Athelwald, everything was made locally."

"You traded with the Orcs, didn't you?" asked Belgast.

"We did," he admitted, "but we never had to transport anything. The Orcs would trade with us and then take their new belongings home."

The Dwarf looked at him in disbelief. "I had no idea your people were so primitive."

Athgar bristled, "We can't all be masters of... what did you call it, commerce?"

"Yes," said Belgast. "Sorry, I meant no offense. I've just never met someone quite like you before, my friend."

"What do you mean?" asked Athgar.

"Well," mused the Dwarf, "on the one hand, you're very powerful, but you're also not..."

"Not what?" said Athgar, growing defensive.

"Worldly," explained Belgast. "You're an intelligent person, Athgar, and you learn quickly, but in matters of the world at large, your knowledge is surprisingly lacking. I suppose that's only natural considering your background."

Athgar wasn't sure how to take the Dwarf's words, so he hefted another box onto the floor, prying it open to peer inside.

"Now you've grown quiet," said Belgast. "I've said too much."

"No," said Athgar, "it's not that. It's just that this box seems strangely heavy for one so small."

"Oh?" said Belgast. "Let's have a look, shall we?" He moved closer, watching as the Therengian dug through the straw.

"What's this?" said Athgar, pulling forth a book.

"That must be what we're looking for," said Belgast. "What does it say?"

Athgar looked at the letters embossed on its cover but struggled to understand their meaning. "Here," he said, handing it off to his companion, "you look through it, I'll search for more." He resumed his work.

Belgast took the tome, opening it to examine the elegant handwriting within.

"This looks to be a record of payments," he said. "Interesting, but not what we're after."

Athgar stared down at the box. "What are these?" he asked, pulling forth a sheaf of papers and showing them to Belgast.

"Let me see that," said the Dwarf. He placed the journal down, taking the papers from Athgar. Someone had stitched together half a dozen of them, making an impromptu journal.

"What do you make of it?" said Athgar.

"Reports of an unfaithful wife," revealed Belgast. "I suspect it's for black-mail purposes as it lists witnesses. We're definitely getting closer. Are there any more like this?"

"I'd say about a dozen," said Athgar.

"We're looking for something that mentions the duke," said Belgast.

"I can't be sure," said Athgar, "but I think this has something about the father general."

"That could be it," said the Dwarf. "Let me see."

Athgar handed them over, then waited while his companion read through the notes.

"This is it!" exclaimed the Dwarf.

"What does it say?" asked Athgar.

"It appears," said Belgast, "that someone discovered Godstone in the Orc lands."

"Godstone," said Athgar, "what's that?"

"It's metal that falls from the sky," said the Dwarf. "You may have heard it called sky metal or sky stone, both terms are equally as accurate."

"And what is this Godstone used for?" asked Athgar. "Does it have magical powers?"

"No, not by itself," said the Dwarf, "but in the hands of a master smith, it can be used to forge weapons of great power."

"Like magical swords?" asked Athgar.

"Oh, yes," said Belgast, "swords, axes, even armour if there was enough of it."

"A master smith you say," said Athgar. "I take it Godstone is hard to work with?"

"I'll say," said the Dwarf. "I doubt there's more than a handful of smiths that could create the kind of heat needed to smelt that stuff."

"What about magical fire?" said Athgar.

"What about it?"

"Could magic be used to melt the stone?"

"I suppose it could," said Belgast. "Why do you ask?"

"We discovered a Sartellian working with the duke. Natalia knew of him by reputation and said he was quite powerful. How valuable is this stone?"

"It's worth a king's ransom," said the Dwarf, "possibly even more. It really depends on how much there is."

"The duke seemed to think they'd be able to cart it all off within a week or so. How much does that sound like to you?"

"I have no idea," said Belgast. "Sky stone, or Godstone as they call it, falls from the sky. It typically buries itself into the ground, requiring a lot of digging. On top of that, you have to separate it from all the dirt and rocks that are in the area. All that takes a lot of people."

"So it's rare?" said Athgar.

"Oh, yes," admitted Belgast, "but highly sought after, and very powerful when enchanted. All the famous weapons of history are said to be made of the stuff. Kings have bankrupted their realms to obtain even small amounts. I think we've found what we're looking for."

"Yes," agreed Athgar, "and now it's time to leave."

Belgast began scooping up all the papers he could lay his hands on, stuffing them into his belt.

"What are you doing?" asked Athgar.

"Gathering information," he replied. "Lofgrim will be interested in this." He handed a pile to Athgar, "Here, carry these."

Moments later, they were stumbling from the building, their arms full.

· · ·

As they made their way through the town, they drew strange looks from those they passed.

"What's everyone staring at?" asked Athgar.

"I suppose it's not every day you see someone walking down the street with so many papers," noted the Dwarf. "I think we should conceal them."

"How do you suggest we do that?" asked Athgar.

"Tuck them into your tunic," suggested Belgast. "Hold still for a moment, I'll give you a hand."

Athgar waited as the Dwarf started rolling up the papers, stuffing them in Athgar's clothes. His task complete, Belgast stood back, examining the Therengian with a critical eye.

"There," he said, "that should do. Now, let's get moving."

As they headed farther up the street, they soon noticed an increase in foot traffic, somewhat unusual for the middle of the night. Streams of people were heading north, many in their nightshirts.

"What's happening?" asked the Dwarf. "Did we miss something?"

"No one's panicking," noted Athgar.

He tried to flag a person down, but the townsman ignored him, heading north at a brisk pace. Another half block up, and Athgar noticed a glow coming from behind some buildings.

"That's a fire," he said and then a moment later, panic started to settle over him. "That's in the direction of the Spire!"

"Hurry," urged Belgast, "before it's too late!"

They rounded a curve in the road, and the inn came into sight, smoke billowing from its windows while fire climbed higher and higher. A feeling of dread fell over Athgar, and he pushed through the crowd, emerging to a full view of the conflagration. He watched, helpless, as the fire consumed the structure, sparks flying into the air as the roof collapsed.

Athgar fell to his knees, watching in horror as the flames grew higher. He wanted to rush in, to find Natalia, and prayed to the Gods to spare her but knew it would do no good. Another great spray of sparks rushed up as more timbers fell. Athgar was gutted by sorrow.

Time appeared to stand still as people rushed past him carrying buckets, tossing them onto the raging fire in a vain attempt to stop it from spreading. Finally, someone stepped forward, calling them back. Athgar watched as the man raised his hands, and the flames began to slacken.

Witnessing the entire process, Athgar was numb beyond imagining and yet somehow entranced by the flames. It was only as the man turned to talk to someone that the Therengian recognized Verineth Sartellian. At that moment he knew, beyond doubt, that the Fire Mage had burned the Golden Spire down to little more than embers.

Athgar was consumed by an immense wave of grief at the thought of poor Natalia, burned to death in the flames, for there was no way she could have escaped, Verineth would have seen to that.

He gripped his axe, ready to attack his enemy, to bring vengeance down upon the man that had deprived him of his heart, but as he did so, he felt a hand pulling him and looked to see a Dwarf beside him.

"Come with me," he requested. "Quickly now, before they see you."

Athgar followed, stumbling through the streets, his eyes stung by ashes and tears. Tripping on some cobblestones he fell to the ground. Arms pulled him to his feet, and he somehow got moving again. He was in a daze now, his mind confused by the conflicting emotions. On the one hand, he felt immense loss, even greater than that of his village, but on the other, he felt rage, a thirst for vengeance on those that had inflicted this horrible death on Natalia.

Someone pushed him through a doorway, and he made his way down the corridor of a filthy and disgusting boarding house. Moments later, he was led into a well-appointed room, crowded with people. He tried to focus through his smoke-filled eyes, and then she appeared in front of him, Natalia!

His heart nearly stopped as he fell to the floor, his tears flowing freely again. He felt her arms wrap around him and wondered if he had died and gone to the Afterlife, but the sound of Dwarves speaking soon brought him back to his senses.

He stared into Natalia's eyes as he wept with joy.

"I'm safe," she assured him.

He looked her over and noted her still pallid features. "I thought you were dead," he said. "What happened?"

Natalia simply held him, as if he were a newborn babe.

"We brought her here," came the strange Dwarf's voice.

"This is Lofgrim," said Belgast, "my cousin."

"Thank you, Lofgrim," said Athgar. "You'll never know what it means to me, to both of us."

"Yes, we're thankful," said Belgast, "but I still don't understand why she's here."

"You asked us to arrange transportation," said Lofgrim. "I couldn't very well leave her to her own devices while I did that, so I brought her here."

"And the fire?" asked Athgar.

"That was long after we left," said Lofgrim, "but I had someone watching for your return to let you know we had moved Natalia. The fire was a complete surprise to us. I have no idea how it started."

"I do," said Athgar. "I saw Verineth there."

"Who is this Verineth character," asked Lofgrim, "and why would he set fire to the Spire?"

"He tried to kill us," said Athgar. "He likely thought we were still inside."

"What kind of a man burns down an entire inn to kill two people?" asked Belgast.

"A member of the family," came the weak voice of Natalia. "They're ruthless."

"What will you do now?" asked Lofgrim.

"I'll take Natalia to the Orcs and hope I get there in time," said Athgar.

"I have something that might help," offered Lofgrim as he rummaged around some pillows, producing a small wooden box.

"Do you keep everything in there, cousin?" asked Belgast.

"Pretty much," answered Lofgrim. He opened the box, revealing a small vial within. "I was saving this for an emergency, but I think she needs this more than I do."

"What is it?" asked Athgar.

"A potion," Lofgrim replied. "It won't cure her, but it should help her last a little longer."

"Long enough to get to the Orcs?" asked Athgar.

"If you're lucky," the Dwarf answered.

He passed it to Athgar, who unstoppered it. "Are you sure about this?"

"Oh, aye," said Lofgrim, "it's an old family recipe. It'll help revitalize her, give her some energy for the short term."

Athgar poured the milky liquid into Natalia's mouth, watching as her eyes went wide. She sputtered and coughed, but the medicine went down.

"Oh, yes," said Lofgrim, "I forgot to mention, it tastes like donkey droppings."

"Donkey droppings?" said Belgast. "That's a strange expression for you to use, cousin."

"Well," said Lofgrim, "there is a lady present, after all."

"What now?" asked Athgar.

"Ordinarily, she'd need to rest for a while," said Lofgrim, "but that's not really an option in this case. I'd suggest you get underway as quickly as possible. I have a cart standing by."

"Thank you," said Athgar. "I don't know how we'll ever repay you."

"Don't thank me," said Lofgrim, "I'm doing this for Belgast. He spoke quite highly of you."

"When do we leave?" asked Belgast.

"Actually," said Athgar, "I have another mission for you if you'd be willing?"

"What is it?" asked the Dwarf.

"I'd like you to take word to Sister Cordelia, at the Temple of Saint Agnes."

"I'd be happy to," said Belgast, "but that won't take long."

"True," said Athgar, "but then again, you know where the Godstone is. They'll need you to guide them."

"You want the Church to have it?" said Belgast in surprise.

"Better the sisters than the Cunars," said Athgar. He dug into his belt, pulling forth the papers that indicated the location. "Here, take this with you."

"Won't you need it?" asked his Dwarven friend.

"No, I know the area, and in any case, I'll be far too busy helping the Orcs prepare."

"Prepare for what?" asked Lofgrim.

"Invasion," the Therengian replied.

"Or flight," said Natalia. "They might decide it's safer to leave."

"True," said Athgar, "the tribe will have to make that decision, but whatever they do, I'll help."

"We'll help," corrected Natalia. "I'm still here, remember? I might be weak, but I can still cast."

Athgar smiled. Her strength appeared to have returned for the moment, but he knew it was only a result of the Dwarf's potion.

"You'll need to exit the city before daybreak," warned Lofgrim. "We've friends on the gates that can see to that, but they only work the night shift."

"Very well," said Athgar, "let's be on our way."

ESCAPE

Spring 1104 SR

Athgar sat in the cart, holding the donkey's reins while the wagon in front moved on, finally allowing him room to advance to where the guards waited.

"State your business," said a soldier with a long beard.

"I'm heading out to the Stendon farm," Athgar said, "to pick up some hay."

"Bit late at night for that, isn't it?" asked the guard.

His companion, an older, clean-shaven individual, moved closer. "Stendon, you say?"

"That's right," said Athgar.

"Did Lofgrim send you?"

"He did. He wanted it delivered before sunup."

"Send him on his way," the older man ordered.

"What?" the bearded guard complained. "Surely not, Halloway?"

"Look," said the clean-shaven guard, "you're new here, Carver, so I'll forgive you this, but you need to let this man go."

"We haven't even searched his cart," complained Carver.

"Fine," said Halloway, "I'll see to it."

Athgar was about to complain, but Halloway moved quickly around to the back, pushing aside the straw to reveal the sleeping form of Natalia. Athgar made a fist, feeling the heat of his magic begin to warm his hand.

"Nothing here," proclaimed Halloway as he looked up at Athgar, nodding slightly, then covered Natalia with the displaced straw.

"All right," said Carver, "on your way, and make it quick, others are waiting."

Athgar opened his hand, letting the magic dissipate, then clenched his fist a few times to release the tension, finally snapping the reins. The donkey trotted forward, and they passed beneath the gates of the city and onto the road beyond.

The sun rose just as the city disappeared from view. Athgar finally relaxed, settling into the rhythm of the cart. It had been a tense few days, and he looked over his shoulder to see Natalia stirring.

"Athgar?" she called out.

"I'm here," he replied.

"Where are we?" she asked. "Did we make it out of Caerhaven?"

"We did," he said, "early this morning. We've nothing but clear roads ahead."

She sat up, looking around. He pulled on the reins, halting their progress and turned to face her.

"You need to rest," he urged.

"Nonsense," she said, "I'm coming up there with you."

"You've been ill," he reminded her.

"Yes," she admitted, "but I'm feeling better, at least for now. I'm just a little weak."

"It's not the most comfortable seat up here," he warned.

"That may be," she replied, "but at least it's with you."

Natalia struggled forward, dropping onto the bench beside him and leaned her head on his shoulder, using her arm around his waist to steady herself. Athgar tried to put his arm around her as well but realized he needed both hands for the reins.

"Never mind," she said, "I'm content to be here with you. Just ignore me."

"As if I could do that," said Athgar. He snapped the reins once more, and the donkey resumed its trotting.

"How long, do you think, before we arrive?" asked Natalia.

"Several days yet," said Athgar. "I don't know the exact distance, but I suspect it's a week or more by foot."

"We're not moving much faster than that now," she said. "What if you take the donkey and ride on?"

"I'm not leaving you again," he replied. "I don't care how much danger there is."

"My hero," she said, stifling a yawn.

"I might remind you that you're more powerful than I am," he said.

"Perhaps," she replied, "but you'll always be my hero."

"That's nice to hear," he said, wondering if it was the potion talking.

"Tell me about Ord-Kurgad," she said. "What's it like?"

"I don't know that there's much to tell," said Athgar. "It's a small village, with a palisade around it. The Orcs live in huts made of sticks and bark."

"That must be cold in winter," said Natalia.

"You'd be surprised how warm they can be," he noted, "but then again, Orcs don't feel the cold like we do."

"And you lived with them, didn't you?" she said.

"I did," he admitted, "though they gave me my own hut."

"Is that normal?" she asked.

"In Orc society, most live in communal huts. Families, those with younglings, at least, get their own huts, as do the shamans."

"Shamans?" said Natalia. "You mean their mages?"

"Yes, though they don't use that term."

"How many shamans do they have in Ord-Kurgad?" she asked.

"When I left, there were only three," said Athgar. "Uhdrig is the most powerful, she's their healer."

"Is that what they call a Life Mage?" she asked.

"Yes, though they prefer the term 'Shamaness'. It's a distinction they think important."

"Why?" she asked. "Are females seen as inferior?"

"Quite the contrary, actually," he noted. "Female shamans tend to be more powerful, at least the healers do. Shaluhk is a shamaness as well, though technically she's still being trained."

"That's Kargen's wife, isn't it?" she asked.

"Yes, though bondmate is the term they use."

"Yes, that's right, bondmate," she repeated. "I quite like that. Can I be your bondmate?"

He tried to look at her, to judge if she were joking, but with her head on his shoulder, he couldn't quite manage it.

"Whenever you wish," he said. He was getting ready to say more when Natalia spoke again.

"And the Fire Mage, what was his name again?"

"Artoch," said Athgar. "They call him master of flame."

"I like that," she said. "I think that's what I'll call you, the master of flame. Can I be the mistress of water?"

"You can be whatever you want," he said. It was becoming clear to him now that whatever was in that potion was having an inebriating effect on her. Maybe it was for the best, he thought, at least she had energy.

His thoughts were interrupted by Natalia. She had shifted slightly, adjusting her seating.

"Agar," she said, "that's the baby's name, isn't it?"

"It is," said Athgar, "the youngling of Kargen and Shaluhk."

"I like that name," she said. "What does it mean?"

"It means 'he who is strong' in the Orc tongue," he replied.

"I'd like a baby one day," she said.

"You would?"

"Yes," she replied, "but only with you."

He smiled at the thought. "Really?" he asked.

"Yes, why?" Natalia said. "Does that surprise you?"

"We've only been together for a short while," he said, "and we've never really talked about it."

She sat up straight, turning to look him in the eyes. "Well," she said, "now we are. What do you think?"

"I'd love a child," he said, "though not at this precise moment. I'd like for us to settle down first."

Natalia smiled. "Naturally," she said, "I wasn't suggesting we get started right away. We've years before we can seriously consider such a thing."

They rode on in silence for a while, Athgar's head full of images of running through a field, a child between them.

"What about a name?" she asked.

"Pardon?" he said. "I'm sorry, I was deep in thought."

"I was wondering what you thought about for a name?" she pressed.

"I suppose it depends if we had a boy or a girl," he finally replied.

"Do you have a preference?" she asked. "I always assumed a man wanted a son."

"I'm a Therengian," said Athgar, "both are a blessing."

She smiled, looking at him with love in her eyes. He snapped the reins, urging the donkey to increase its speed, then looked back at her, still watching him closely.

"What?" he asked.

"Nothing," Natalia said. "Can't I look at the man I love?" She let out a yawn.

He chuckled, "It appears that you've exhausted what little energy you had. I think it's time you returned to the back of the cart.

"Nonsense," she replied. She leaned into him, placing her head once more onto his shoulder. Moments later, he heard gentle snoring.

· · ·

By late afternoon, they were well clear of the cultivated land surrounding Caerhaven. Now, the vista offered fields of long grass with the occasional clump of trees.

Athgar had been looking around, searching for a suitable place to make camp, for food must be cooked, and a shelter prepared, all things that took time. The road here was winding, with straight stretches of more than an arrow's flight rare in appearance.

The cart rolled between two hills, the donkey keeping a relatively brisk pace, and Athgar gave some thought to how he might go about preparing their camp for the evening. All that flew from his head as soon as the soldiers came into view. Two of them were on the road, watching his approach, while others moved about their camp, set up to their north.

Athgar cursed his luck, for there was little he could do now. Had he been more alert, he would have noticed them earlier and could have turned off before the camp, but now such action would only serve to put them on alert. He gently shook Natalia, causing her to stir.

"What is it?" she asked.

"Company," he said, slowing the cart.

"Halt!" cried out a soldier.

Athgar did as he was bid, watching the warrior with great interest.

"State your name," the soldier ordered.

"My name is Gunther," he lied, "and this is my wife, Hildegard."

The soldier eyed them warily as his partner, leaning on his spear, stood watching.

"Where are you going, Gunther?" the man asked.

"To visit relatives," said Athgar, "in the Duchy of Holstead. This is the road to Draybourne, isn't it?"

"It is," the guard admitted, "but I'm afraid we've had some trouble on the road of late. I'll have to ask you and your wife to come with me."

"Very well," said Athgar, "but my wife is ill. She has a fever."

At the mere mention of her condition, the soldier's face changed from surly guard to fearful man.

"A fever, you say?" he asked.

"Yes," Athgar continued, "though I, myself, have no sign of it."

"Wait here," the soldier ordered. He backed up, consulting a moment with his companion, then marched off into the nearby camp.

"What do you suppose he's up to?" said Natalia.

"He doesn't know what to do with us," said Athgar, "that much is clear. I think he was going to detain us, but he doesn't like the sound of your fever."

"I'm surprised he didn't check me himself," she declared. "After all, he only has your word for it."

He looked at her in surprise. "You've never seen a plague before, have you?"

"No, why?" she asked.

"People are scared. Plague doesn't care how young or old you are. It kills indiscriminately."

"But can't Life Mages cure such a curse?"

"They can," said Athgar, "but I'm guessing there are none here."

"But I have a fever, not the plague," she replied.

"True, but to them, the two are one and the same. They don't want to take the chance it's something else."

They sat for some time, the sun sinking lower on the horizon, throwing long shadows before them. Finally, another individual arrived, this one a member of the Church, a lay brother from the look of him, wearing the simple black cassock of the Cunars, not the fighting armour of a Temple Knight.

"I'm sorry for the delay," the man said. "I'm Brother Rupert."

"Greetings, Brother Rupert," said Athgar. "My wife and I are on the way to Draybourne."

"Yes," the brother replied, "the guard said as much. I understand your wife is ill?"

"She is," he admitted. "She's got a fever."

"Might I enquire how long this has been going on?"

Athgar thought back, deciding honesty was the best policy. "Only since yesterday," he said.

"And have there been any other symptoms?" Brother Rupert asked, keeping his distance.

"Some dizziness," Athgar admitted, "and she's been sleeping the day away."

"Any signs of retching, skin irritation or pustules?"

"None whatsoever," he replied.

"May I examine her?" the brother asked.

Athgar was caught, but the concern for her health soon overcame his fear of capture. "By all means," he finally said.

Brother Rupert came forward, standing to the right side of the cart, where Natalia sat. He leaned in, placing his hand to her forehead.

"She is warm," he confirmed.

"As I told you," said Athgar.

"Please do not be offended," said Brother Rupert, "but fevers can take many forms. Though she is warm, she is not burning up. Do you have any symptoms yourself?"

"None whatsoever," the Therengian replied.

The lay brother looked back at his camp, then returned his attention to the newcomers. "I must insist that you come with me," he said. "I'll take you to the medicinal tent."

"What's a medicinal tent?" asked Athgar.

"It is where the army keeps its healers," Brother Rupert replied.

"You have Life Mages here?" said Athgar, betraying his surprise.

"Alas," the brother admitted, "I wish it were so. We do have those skilled in the healing arts, but none that have mastered the arcane arts. However, I have treated those that lie with fever before."

"How successfully?" pressed Athgar.

"Half have survived," confessed the Holy Brother, "but you must realize that many do not report such conditions until it is too late."

"And you think you can heal her?" asked Athgar.

"I do," said Brother Rupert, "but it might take a few days."

Athgar paused. He knew the army was due to march in three days. No, he corrected himself, it was only two days now, and if the father general arrived early, he was sure his presence would be noticed.

"Might I ask," he finally said, "how you would treat her condition?"

"With rest," replied the brother, "along with a cordial of my own devising."

"A cordial?" said Athgar.

"Yes, a mixture of herbs, drunk in a liquid form."

"You mean a potion?"

"Of sorts," replied Brother Rupert, "though there is no magic involved."

"Might I suggest you give her this cordial and send us on our way?" said Athgar. "I would hate to risk the fever spreading among the troops."

Brother Rupert looked back to the camp before resuming the discussion. "I suppose there is that concern. Very well, let me gather a few things and then we'll send you on your way."

"Thank you," said Athgar, breathing a sigh of relief. He watched the lay brother return to the camp.

"I think we dodged an arrow on that one," he said.

He looked at Natalia, expecting a reply, but her eyes were closed once again. With her sitting there, consumed by a fever, and the enemy so close, he was in a fretful state. He was almost ready to admit to their identities if only to save her, but reason told him that the confession would likely condemn them to death.

Brother Rupert soon returned, a satchel bag slung over his shoulder. He was digging through it as he approached, producing a small stoppered bottle.

"Have her drink this," he said, "but not all at once. She'll need a sip or two in the morning and the same just before bed. It may not cure her, but it should keep her fever down."

"Thank you again," said Athgar.

"Not at all," said Brother Rupert, "I only wish there were more I could do."

"Do you know what the terrain is like around here," asked the Therengian, "for it's getting late, and we'll soon have to camp for the night?"

"As a matter of fact, I do," said Brother Rupert. "If you keep heading in this direction, you'll cross a small stream. A little beyond that, you'll see an open field to your right. It's nice and flat, with plenty of fresh water. Good luck to you both."

"And to you," said Athgar, snapping the reins.

The donkey started moving, dragging the little cart along behind, both wheels groaning in protest. Athgar kept his eyes on the army as they trotted past, counting tents and watching the troops as they walked around.

By evening, they had found the indicated field. Athgar saw to Natalia first, nestling her into the cart and surrounding her with straw and a blanket. He gave her the cordial then shivered, feeling a chill. Was he sick now? The little bottle stared at him, inviting him to partake of its healing effects, but he knew that Natalia needed it more. He placed it back into his pack and settled in for the evening.

The night dragged on interminably as Athgar tossed and turned. He kept seeing Natalia's face, her eyes sunken and her skin sallow. To make it even worse, he woke feeling a chill descending. He cast his spell of warmth several times, but even his fire magic appeared to have little effect.

By morning he was chilled to the bone. Convinced that he now carried the fever that had wreaked so much damage on Natalia, he climbed into the seat, praying silently to the Gods that they give him the strength to see her safely to Ord-Kurgad.

THE DWARF

Spring 1104 SR

S ister Cordelia had just dipped the quill in the inkpot and was holding
her hand over the ledger when a knock at the door drew her attention.
"Who's there?" she called out.

"Sister Adeline," came the reply.

"Come in," said Cordelia, waiting patiently until the lay sister had
entered. "What can I do for you, Sister?"

"You have a visitor, Sister Cordelia," the older woman said.

"Send them in," said Cordelia.

"But…"

"But what, Sister?"

"It's a Dwarf," declared Sister Adeline.

"What of it?" asked Sister Cordelia. "Do you suppose he's here to attack
me? If so, I can assure you I'm quite capable of defending myself."

"No, of course not," said Adeline, "it's just that… well, you know."

Sister Cordelia looked at her, trying to ascertain her meaning. "I'm
afraid I don't, Sister. You'll have to explain."

"They're a rough folk, the Dwarves," Adeline persisted.

"Rough?"

"Yes, full of foul words and ill-humour."

"Are you trying to tell me all Dwarves are rude?" asked Cordelia.

The lay sister merely nodded in agreement.

"Where is this visitor?" asked Sister Cordelia.

"In the outer courtyard. Shall I go and fetch him?"

"Yes," said Cordelia, then, as Adeline turned to go, she changed her mind. "On second thought, I'll go and meet him."

"Shall I escort you?"

"I hardly think that's necessary," said Cordelia, "unless there's more than one Dwarf out there?"

Adeline shook her head.

"Good," said Sister Cordelia, "then I'll go alone. Thank you for informing me."

"You're welcome, Sister," Adeline replied.

Cordelia waited until her visitor had left before closing up her office. With the shutters securely in place, she walked through the temple, greeting those she met along the way. It was a pleasant enough place, a far cry from the fighting she had seen on the Ilean coast, and yet somehow, she found it lacking. Was it conflict that drove her, Cordelia wondered, or was she just surrounded by dull and unconcerned people.

She soon found herself in the outer courtyard. As she thought, there was only a single Dwarf present, sitting on one of the benches. He spied her as soon as she entered, rising to his feet.

"Sister Cordelia?" he enquired.

"That's my name," she replied, "though I'm afraid you have the advantage of me."

"Pardon my rudeness," her guest replied, "my name's Belgast, Belgast Ridgehand."

"I'm afraid I don't recognize the name," said Cordelia.

"There's no reason you should," said the Dwarf, "but I've been sent by some mutual acquaintances." He looked around the courtyard, then lowered his voice, "Athgar and Natalia, you remember them?"

"Yes, of course," said Cordelia. "Tell me, what can I do for you?"

"They've come across some important information," said Belgast. "Information that has put their lives in danger."

"Are they all right?" asked the Temple Knight.

"They're fine, for now," said the Dwarf, "but I cannot say for how much longer that will be the case."

"Go on," urged the sister, "you can speak plainly here."

"It seems they uncovered a plot of sorts," said Belgast.

"They mentioned something to me earlier," Cordelia replied. "I take it they need help?"

"They do," agreed Belgast. "You see, they've discovered a plot to invade the Orc lands. Have you heard of Godstone?"

"Of course," she replied, "why? Is that what the father general was after?"

"Not just him," said the Dwarf. "It appears he's working with the duke, not to mention someone named Verineth Sartellian."

"Should I know that name?" she asked.

"I'd be surprised if you did," said Belgast, "but he represents a powerful and influential family."

"Family has little sway here," noted Sister Cordelia.

"Be that as it may," continued the Dwarf, "their actions could well trigger a war."

"That would be disastrous," said Cordelia. "There's a whole system of alliances set up around the Petty Kingdoms. If war comes here to Krieghoff, it'll soon spread across the entire Continent."

"Is it truly that dire?" asked Belgast.

"If anything," said Cordelia, "I've understated it. Tell me what's happening."

"A large army is due to move towards the eastern border," said Belgast. "If they cross the river, it'll mean war with Holstead."

"Surely they must know that?" said Cordelia.

"They likely think it worth the risk," noted Belgast. "Godstone is the most valuable mineral known to the five races."

"When are they marching?" she asked.

"In less than two days, if our information is accurate."

"Then I'll go and talk to the father general," she declared. "Perhaps I can talk some sense into him."

"I doubt that will work," said Belgast. "They tell me he's determined to destroy the Orcs and take the ore for himself."

"Then I must hurry," said Sister Cordelia. "Do you know where this Godstone lies?"

"Aye," said the Dwarf, reaching into his tunic. "I have a map here that shows it's location." He handed her the neatly folded paper.

"Very well," said Cordelia, "saddle up your horse and meet us outside of the temple. We've some riding ahead of us."

"We do?" said Belgast. "I just gave you the map, surely that's enough to deal with this, and what do you mean by us? Are you taking other sisters?"

"Of course," she replied, "I'm mustering the entirety of the temple forces here."

"You have that authority?" he asked.

"No, but the mother commander does. I'm sure once she sees this, she'll be in complete agreement. If not, I'll take what knights I can. Either way, you need to be ready to ride."

"Very well," said Belgast, "I'll get my pony and meet you out front."

He rose, bowing slightly, "I thank you for listening. It's not every knight that would pay heed to such things."

Sister Cordelia looked down at the Dwarf. "Let's just hope we can talk some sense into Father General Gilbert."

Belgast returned later to find the Temple Knights already assembled. They were thirty strong, each armoured in the heavy plate armour synonymous with their order.

Belgast looked up to their leader, dwarfed by their massive chargers. "Is this everyone?" he asked.

"It is all that we can spare," replied Sister Cordelia. "And now we must ride."

"Where to?" he asked.

"Our reports indicate the duke's army is camped to the east of here. If what you've said is true, they'll be massing there in preparation for their attack. It takes time to organize a march with that many people. That's likely where we'll find the father general."

"If the army is as big as you say, won't it be dangerous?" he asked.

"There's always an inherent danger when dealing with warriors," said Sister Cordelia, "but these are Temple Knights, sworn to keep the peace. The duke's men wouldn't dare attack them."

"It wasn't the duke's men I was worried about," noted Belgast. "What about the Cunars?"

"They are brother churchmen, there is no conflict with them."

"And if they don't back down?" said the Dwarf.

"Then we shall have to improvise," she replied.

"This could result in conflict," warned Belgast. "Once we start on this journey, we might have no control where it will take us."

"I'm willing to take that chance," said Cordelia. "We cannot sit by and let others suffer."

"In that case," asked the Dwarf, "what are we waiting for?"

In answer, Sister Cordelia spurred her horse forward, the rest of the Temple Knights falling in behind. They rode through the city, their mere presence causing quite a stir. It was one thing to see a Temple Knight ride through the streets, quite another to see twenty.

Word of their journey spread quickly, and by the time they arrived at the eastern gate, the doors were already flung open, allowing them to pass without interference. They were soon riding across the countryside in search of the duke's army.

. . .

Just after noon, the army came into sight. The first sign was a pair of soldiers watching the road. At the approach of the horses, one of them ran off, no doubt to inform his superiors.

Sister Cordelia slowed their pace, giving the army ample time to prepare for their arrival. She soon spotted a group of men walking towards the road, the distinctive garb of the Temple Knights of Saint Cunar easily visible among their number. She stopped, waiting as the knights drew closer.

The men halted by the road and one of them, taller than the rest, stepped forward. He was clean-shaven with closely cropped hair, a look common enough among the fighting orders. His dark grey tunic hung over a battle-tested suit of plate armour, as evidenced by the numerous dents and scratches, a mark of honour among the brethren of his order.

"I'm surprised to see you here, Sister," he said. "I am Father Commander Andreas. To whom do I have the pleasure of addressing?"

"Sister Cordelia," she replied, "Temple Knight of Saint Agnes."

He glanced quickly at Belgast, displaying a brief annoyance at his presence, then returned his attention to Cordelia. "And what brings you here, Sister? For I can think of nothing that requires your presence."

"There is an army massing here, is there not?" she asked.

"There is," admitted the commander, "but only for training purposes."

"You say it's for training," she pressed, "and yet the Church is here as well. Is it not strange that both should be present?"

"The Church prides itself on the way it cooperates with our hosts."

"And yet," said Cordelia, "church doctrine forbids it. Church forces are to augment local rulers only in times of war, the Holy Commandments are very clear on this matter."

"Do you mean to lecture me on church doctrine?" Andreas snarled. "I might remind you that I am a Father Commander of the Temple Knights of Saint Cunar. You, on the other hand, are merely a Sister of Saint Agnes. I think it is clear enough who has jurisdiction here."

"I am here at the behest of the Sister Commander of my Order, and it is my duty, as a Temple Knight, to investigate matters of consequence to the Church," she said. "Who commands here?"

"That is none of your concern," Father Andreas replied.

"I demand you take me to the father general," said Cordelia. "He is the ranking church member here, is he not?"

Belgast noted the look of surprise on the man's face.

"Father General Gilbert is here, isn't he?" insisted the Dwarf.

Father Andreas stared at them both, his face wracked with indecision.

"You can take me to the father general," said Cordelia, "or I can go and summon the mother commander and alert the rest of the Church hierarchy. The choice is yours."

The Cunar commander wore a look of resignation. "Very well," he finally said, "leave your horses and follow me. I'll take you to him."

Sister Cordelia dismounted, passing the reins to another knight. Belgast followed suit, climbing down off his pony. She looked at him a moment as if to say something, but his words forestalled her.

"I'm going," he declared. "I'm the one that brought word of this. I'll not stand by and let others make decisions without my input."

"Very well," said the sister.

Father Commander Andreas led them through the camp. Soldiers were here in numbers, some sharpening swords while others made arrows. A large group of Cunar Temple Knights rode past, their armour glinting in the afternoon sun.

Belgast watched them pass, taking stock of their heavy plate. It was very similar to that of the Sisters, but somehow, with dark grey tabards draping them, they looked far more sinister. Sister Cordelia largely ignored them, her concentration on the direction of travel.

The Cunar commander finally halted at a tent. "Wait here," he said, then disappeared inside.

"Well," said Sister Cordelia, "what do you make of all this?"

"It's a large army," noted the Dwarf. "Far larger, I would say, than is warranted, wouldn't you?"

"I would," agreed the knight, "but we'd best talk of this later, when we are away from this place. In the meantime, keep your eyes sharp, it will do us well to know what forces they have here."

"A good point," said Belgast. "I had been thinking along similar lines."

The tent flap opened, revealing an unknown Temple Knight, who bid them enter. Sister Cordelia led Belgast inside, where the place was surprisingly roomy, with rugs spread on the ground and some camp chairs sitting around a rough-hewn table where the father general was sitting, cup in hand. Beside him stood the commander, having just informed Gilbert of the visitors.

"You wanted to see me, Sister?" asked the father general.

Sister Cordelia bowed, "I did, Your Grace."

"Your Grace?" he said. "So formal? My commander tells me you weren't so when talking to him."

"He was not in charge," she replied, "and you are a father general, after all."

"So I am," he said. "Which makes me wonder why a lowly sister wishes to speak to me. Can't someone in your own order take confession?" He chuckled at his own remarks, a reaction that was taken up by his aide.

"I have come to you on a matter of great importance," said Sister Cordelia.

"Then speak," the father general commanded.

"It has come to my attention that this army is about to cross the border into Holstead, Your Grace."

"Politics are no concern of yours, Sister."

"In this case, they are, Your Grace. Intervention in secular matters is beyond your purview. Only the Council of Peers can make that decision, or the Primus, in emergencies."

"And what makes you think we are preparing to invade Holstead?"

"I know about the Godstone," she revealed.

The father general's face gave the barest flicker of annoyance.

"Then you know what's at stake," he said.

"So you admit it?" she accused.

"Of course," he replied, "but you don't understand the importance."

"Then enlighten us," said Sister Cordelia.

"War is coming," Father General Gilbert began, "everybody knows it. The Petty Kingdoms are preparing for a major conflict, and the Church will be caught in the middle. With Godstone in our possession, our armies will be invincible."

"That is not your decision to make," argued Cordelia.

"Sometimes, we must make the hard choices ourselves," said the father general, "and act decisively to seize what is rightfully ours."

"Rightfully ours?" said Sister Cordelia. "Why would you say that? It's not even in Krieghoff. You have to invade another duchy just to retrieve it."

"But the Saints have seen fit to tell us of its location," said the father general. "Do you not see? It is their divine will."

"The Saints were Humans, not gods," she said.

"Yes," he agreed, "but divine all the same. It is our destiny, as the Church, to lead the Continent to victory against the Halvarians. Doing so will be so much easier with Godstone in our possession."

"I think you overestimate the value of it," said Belgast.

The father general looked at the Dwarf, surprised by his comment. "What would you know of such things?" he demanded.

"I'll not deny that weapons of great power can be made from it," he said, "but a few weapons will not guarantee victory against the empire. Only a united people can do that."

"Precisely," said Father General Gilbert, "and we can use the Godstone to unite the Petty Kingdoms."

"By invading Holstead?" said Cordelia.

"We are not invading Holstead," said the father general, "merely the Orc lands which lie on its border. Do you really think the duke will raise arms against us to defend the greenskins?"

"The Orcs will resist," said Belgast, "and people will die."

"I'm sure they will," said the father general, "but many more will survive. They are warriors, that is their lot in life."

"Where is the Duke of Krieghoff?" asked Cordelia. "Is he aware of your plans?"

"Of course," said the father general. "After all, most of the army here is his. The Church is only supplying the cavalry."

"Can't you see how dangerous this is?" she insisted.

"It is a risk, to be sure, but what's needed here is a firm hand."

"The Grand Master of your order would not be so inclined," she warned.

"The grand master? He is old and will soon be replaced. Stay out of our stable, Sister. It is none of your concern."

"I cannot condone your actions, and will protest, directly to the Primus if need be."

"Go ahead," he suggested. "By the time the message even reaches his Holiness, everything will be over and done with."

"I will prevent you from carrying out your plans," she warned.

"How? By stopping us with less than three dozen of your knights. Come now, be serious. The Sisters of Saint Agnes have never been a real fighting order, THAT is the job of the Cunars. You are vastly outnumbered here, leave us in peace and return to Caerhaven. From there, you may make whatever complaint you wish to the Church."

He paused, looking her in the eye, triumph written on his face.

"My people will not forget this," warned Belgast.

The father general turned to him in a fury, "Your people? The ones that skulk back into their mountain caves whenever conflict arises? Don't make me laugh. Your people haven't been a threat for centuries. Go back to your home, Dwarf, and leave the affairs of the world to men."

Belgast wanted to lash out, even moved his fist to his belt where his pickaxe stood ready, but the guards placed their hands on sword hilts, causing him to back down.

"Come, Master Belgast," said Cordelia, "there is nothing more we can do here."

"Escort them away from here, Commander Andreas," ordered the father commander, "and make sure they don't return."

The tent flap opened, and they made their way outside. Cordelia paused only long enough to quickly scan the area, then made her way back to the horses, Belgast following.

They climbed into their saddles, taking the reins to turn their mounts around. It was a long ride back to Caerhaven, and it would be dark before they reached their destination.

ORD-KURGAD

Spring 1104 SR

As Laruhk drew back the bow, he felt the strain of his shoulder muscles stretching with the effort. Holding the arrow by his ear, he waited a moment, then let loose, watching as it flew through the air to impact a tree trunk. He moved up, satisfaction written on his Orcish features.

"A good shot," said Durgash.

"Easy enough to hit a tree," replied Laruhk, *"but I am curious to see how deep it went."*

Durgash jogged forward, watching intently as his companion tried to pull the arrow from the bark. Orc muscles tensed, and then he heard Laruhk cursing.

Durgash chuckled. *"Having trouble?"* he asked. *"Maybe next time you should not draw back so far."*

Laruhk turned to face his companion. *"The whole point of this is to see if we can penetrate Human armour."*

"How?" asked Durgash. *"By shooting at trees?"*

Laruhk pulled a knife from his belt and began digging at the trunk. *"I will get this arrow back if it takes all day,"* he grumbled.

Durgash was about to say something when a distant noise echoed through the woods.

"What was that?" asked Laruhk.

In answer, Durgash put a finger to his lips. They both stood motionless, listening eagerly for any repetition.

Once more, a noise drifted towards them, this time closer, and slowly growing more distinct, like that of an animal walking with a regular gait, but accompanying it was a sound as if something was being dragged.

"Come," said Durgash, *"forget the arrow. Let us investigate this. I fear something strange is afoot in our forest."*

"You fear too much," said Laruhk.

"And you are not afraid?" asked Durgash.

"I fear nothing," said Laruhk, *"but I am curious."*

"Then come, let us seek out this strange sound and see what it is."

"Very well, then," said Laruhk, *"lead on."*

"Oh, no," said Durgash, *"I would not want to steal the surprise from your inquisitive mind. I must insist that you go first."*

Laruhk made a face at his companion, then shrugged his shoulders, *"Very well, Durgash, follow me and try to keep up."*

They moved quickly, traversing the forest at a run, leaping over fallen branches and splashing through a stream. Laruhk finally paused, signalling Durgash to do likewise, then pointed south. From this point on, they moved with quiet deliberation. As the sounds grew louder, Laruhk notched an arrow while Durgash held his axe at the ready.

Slowly they moved, dodging from cover to cover, drawing inexorably closer to their prey. Laruhk finally crouched behind a bush, then pushed the branches aside to look beyond. Durgash watched as he did so, then his companion turned to him, a look of confusion on his face.

"It is a female," said Laruhk.

"A female?" said Durgash. *"Are you sure?"*

"Yes," said Laruhk, *"a Human woman. She is riding in a cart."*

"There are no more Humans in this land," said Durgash, *"not since Athelwald was destroyed."*

"And yet here I see one."

"So you say," said Durgash.

"Look for yourself," said Laruhk.

Durgash moved up, parting the branch to gaze at their quarry. It was a small wagon being pulled by a donkey with a Human woman sitting at the front, reins held firmly in her hands. Laruhk stood, revealing himself.

"Halt," he cried, in the Human tongue.

"Who are you?" added Durgash.

"My name is Natalia," the woman replied. "Are you from Ord-Kurgad?"

Laruhk stepped out from behind the bush, lowering his bow. "How do you know of such things?"

"I'm a friend of Athgar's," she said. "I need your help."

"Athgar?" said Laruhk. "How is it that you know him?"

"It's a long story," she replied, "but he's sick, and he needs a shaman."

"We can not take her to the village," said Durgash, *"it is forbidden."*

Laruhk smacked his companion on the chest. *"Do not be stupid, Durgash. Athgar is a member of the tribe."*

"But this woman is not," Durgash replied.

In answer, Laruhk moved closer, spotting Athgar lying in the back of the cart.

"Come," he said, "I will take you."

Durgash approached the wagon, also reverting to the Human tongue. "Athgar may go, but this woman must remain here."

Laruhk returned his attention to Natalia. "How are you connected to Athgar?" he asked.

"He is my bondmate," she replied.

Laruhk roared with laughter. "My sister was right," he said at last. "Athgar has returned with a mate."

"Then she must be made welcome," said Durgash.

"Come," said Laruhk, "follow us, and we shall take you to safety. My sister will be happy to look at him."

"Your sister?" asked Natalia.

"Yes, Shaluhk, bondmate to Kargen, our chief."

"And shamaness in her own right," added Durgash.

"Yes," agreed Laruhk, "that too. You would never have believed it, she was so puny when she was birthed."

Laruhk took the reins from Natalia's hands, leading her along the forest path.

"Tell me, Nat-Alia, how did you come to meet Athgar, Master of Flame."

"It's a long story," replied Natalia.

"That is fitting," said Laruhk, "for it is some distance to Ord-Kurgad."

"I met him in the city of Draybourne," said Natalia. "Do you know it?"

"I have never been there," Laruhk admitted, "but I have heard of the great city."

"He tried to rescue me from men that were trying to kill me."

"He tried?" said Laruhk. "I take it, that means that he failed?"

"I'm afraid I didn't really need his help," she said.

"Why? Are you a warrior?"

"No, a mage," she explained. "A Water Mage, to be exact."

"A Water Mage? We have no such shamans in our tribe. Have you come to settle down with Athgar and make Human younglings?"

Natalia blushed. "No," she said, "at least, not yet. We came to warn you of danger. An army is marching to destroy you."

"You must wait to tell us the details," said Laruhk, "such things should be brought to the tribe."

"Will Shaluhk be able to save Athgar?" she asked.

"What is wrong with him?" asked Laruhk.

"He has a fever," said Natalia. "I had it myself, but I seem to have recovered.

"Do not worry, Nat-Alia," said Laruhk, "I can not think that the Ancestors have returned him to us, only to have him die."

He turned to his companion, *"Durgash, run ahead and tell Kargen that we are coming. Uhdrig and Shaluhk will both be needed."*

"Very well," said Durgash. He rushed off down the trail, soon disappearing from sight.

"You are lucky we were out hunting," said Laruhk. "You might have been wandering these woods for days searching for us. Ord-Kurgad is not an easy place to find."

"Perhaps your Ancestors were looking over us?" suggested Natalia.

"Possibly," said the Orc. "Tell me, are you a Therengian, like Athgar?"

"No," she replied, "I hail from Karslev."

"I have never heard of it," said Laruhk. "Where does it lay?"

"It is a great city," said Natalia, "much bigger than Draybourne. It lies far to the north, where the weather is always cold."

"A place where the snow never leaves?" asked Laruhk.

"No," admitted Natalia, "but it certainly seems like it sometimes. I was trained there."

"There must be many water shamans there," he replied. "Is it by the sea?"

"You know of the oceans?" asked Natalia. "You surprise me."

"We know of many foreign lands," said Laruhk. "In fact, we are even allied with Humans across the Sea of Storms."

"Allied?" said Natalia. "Does that mean they can help you?"

"I am afraid not," said Laruhk, "for they are too far away to be of assistance, and we are but one tribe."

"How many tribes are there?" she asked.

"Across the Continent? Dozens," said Laruhk. "Uhdrig would know more for she is the one that can communicate over great distances."

"Athgar told me of her," said Natalia.

"You will meet her soon enough, the village is just ahead."

"I thought you said it was some distance," she said.

"And so it was," said Laruhk, showing his teeth in a grin. "Some distance is not the same as a long distance."

He halted, bringing the cart to a stop, then moved to the back, lifting Athgar into his arms with little effort.

"We must proceed on foot from here," he explained. "Do not worry about the cart and donkey. I will send others to get them. Come Nat-Alia, let me show you our village."

He pushed through the underbrush as she struggled to keep up. She soon saw the palisaded walls of Ord-Kurgad and the welcoming sign of smoke drifting up from inside.

As they drew closer, a group of Orcs came out, rushing towards them. One of them, a female, stopped to examine Athgar even as Laruhk held him.

Natalia could see her muttering something and then the Orc's hands began to glow as she placed them on the sleeping Therengian, the light transferring to him, then dissipating.

"*Take him inside,*" said Shaluhk, "*and Uhdrig will examine him more.*"

She turned her attention to Natalia, resorting to the Human tongue.

"Who do we have here, Laruhk?" she asked.

"This is Nat-Alia," replied her brother, "she is bondmate to Athgar."

"Welcome, Nat-Alia," said the shamaness, "I am Shaluhk, bondmate to Kargen, the leader of our tribe. Welcome to Ord-Kurgad."

"Thank you," said Natalia.

"She is a water shaman," announced Laruhk.

"Hush now, my brother," said Shaluhk. "I am sure she has travelled a long way to get here. She needs rest." She turned her attention back to Natalia, "Are you hungry?"

"Famished," said Natalia. "I was in such a hurry to bring Athgar here that I haven't eaten in quite some time."

"Then, come," Shaluhk beckoned, "and I shall feed you. I feel we have much to discuss, you and I."

"We do?" said Natalia.

"Of course," said Shaluhk. "Athgar and Kargen are like brothers and, as their bondmates, that makes us sisters."

"I've never had a sister before," said Natalia, "not that I know of, at least."

"That makes two of us," the Orc replied.

"I'd like to see to Athgar first," said Natalia.

"Of course," said Shaluhk. "It is only fitting that you be by his side. I will take you to him and then fetch food."

Shaluhk offered her hand, and Natalia accepted. The Orc shaman led her into the village, passing through the palisade where an opening lay.

"You don't have a gate?" asked Natalia.

"No," answered Shaluhk, "there is no reason. The palisade itself is only to keep out animals."

"We'll have to change that," noted Natalia.

"I sense you have much to share," said Shaluhk, "but we must see to Athgar first."

Athgar opened his eyes to see a familiar green face looking down at him.

"Kargen?" he asked.

"It is me, old friend," said the Orc. "You are in Ord-Kurgad."

"Natalia?" Athgar asked.

"I'm here," said her reassuring voice. He felt her hand grasp his, holding it to her face, fresh tears dripping onto him.

"I take it you've recovered?" he asked.

"She is still weak," came Uhdrig's voice, "as are you, but you will both be well in time."

"How much time?" asked Athgar. "Danger is coming."

"A few days, at most," said the healer.

"Natalia has told us there is an army coming," said Kargen. "What more can you share?"

"They come seeking Godstone," said Athgar. "A rare metal used to make weapons of power."

"Sky stone?" said Kargen.

"Yes, you know of it?"

"We have heard tell of its properties. It is said that our allies in the west forged a weapon of great magic from such metal."

"Then they must have a master smith," said Athgar, "for only such a person could do it."

"And a mighty mage," added Natalia, "to empower it."

"Powerful enough to come to your aid?" asked the Therengian.

"No," said Kargen. "We must rely on our Ancestors to guide us. Tell me what you remember? How many are coming?"

"Judging by what I saw of the camp, a large force," said Athgar, "maybe as many as a thousand, though I can't be sure."

"Do they wear metal?" asked the Orc.

"They do," said Athgar, "at least some of them. They have Temple Knights, the same type of warriors that burned Athelwald."

"This is bad news," said Kargen. "And the others?"

"Mostly footmen and archers in service to the Duke of Krieghoff," he replied. "They wear lighter armour, and their archers won't have the range of your warbows."

"And yet," said Kargen, "the range will not matter once they reach the clearing for even a regular bow would suffice. Who leads them?"

"A man named Father General Gilbert. He's a Temple Knight himself, and quite experienced I would gather."

"You know of him?" asked Kargen.

"As I said, he's a father general," explained Athgar. "I'm led to believe only the experienced warriors are promoted within the Temple Knights."

"I see," said Kargen. He looked around the room, seeking the faces of the other Orcs.

"We shall have to consult the tribe," he said at last. "Only they can decide on fight or flight."

"You would abandon your homes?" asked Natalia.

"Only if the tribe wills it," said Kargen. "This is too important a decision for me to make alone. Lives will be lost if we choose to resist, they must have a say."

"Very well," said Uhdrig, "I shall have Artoch call a meeting immediately."

"And if they should decide to fight, what will you do, Athgar?" asked Shaluhk.

In response, the Therengian looked at Natalia, who simply nodded.

"I'll fight with you," he said.

"As will I," added Natalia.

A wave of heat hit Athgar as he entered the great hut, Natalia at his side. The fire pit, which ran almost the full length of the place, was lit, illuminating all the Orcs gathered within. Athgar and Natalia were guided to seats near the end of the great fire, close to Kargen and Shaluhk.

"Where's Agar?" asked Natalia.

"He's sleeping," answered Shaluhk, "but I will wake him later so he can meet his aunt. That is the correct term in your language, is it not?"

"It is," said Natalia, smiling at the compliment.

"Good," said Shaluhk. "You are family now, that means you are a member of the tribe. Your vote will be counted like the rest."

"My vote?" said Natalia. "How does that work?"

"Kargen will address the tribe," Shaluhk explained. "Do not worry, I shall translate his words for you. When he is done, a pot will be passed around. If you vote in favour, you place this stone into the pot," she held one up to demonstrate. "When the pot is returned to Artoch, he will count the stones and inform Uhdrig of the results. If the count is greater than half our number, the motion will carry."

"And if not?" asked Natalia.

"Then we leave our home, never to return."

Kargen stood, bringing the room to silence.

"Fellow Orcs," he began, *"our brother, Athgar, has returned to us with his bondmate, Nat-Alia, a sure sign from our Ancestors that we are blessed."*

The assembled Orcs began thumping the ground, leading Natalia to look to Shaluhk for an explanation.

"They are applauding his words," the shamaness explained.

Kargen waited for the noise to die down before continuing, *"But with his return comes dire news, word of an imminent attack."*

The room grew silent as they all looked at their chieftain. *"A group of Humans is coming, intent on destroying our home."*

An Orc held up his hand.

"Yes, Khorsune?" said Kargen.

"Gorlag predicted that the Human, Athgar, would bring us ruin. Do you not now see the error of your ways?"

It was Uhdrig that answered. *"That name was stricken from the tribe when he disgraced us,"* she said. *"How dare you mention him now!"*

Kargen held up his hand for silence. *"Athgar did not bring this trouble, but his arrival has given us the chance to react. We have two choices, to flee our homes or fight to preserve what we have. The choice is yours."*

Another hand shot up.

"Yes, Kragor?" said Kargen.

"What is arrayed against us?" the Orc asked.

"A good question," said Kargen, *"and one which is better answered by Athgar himself."*

Athgar stood, then, as custom dictated, waited for Kargen to sit, yielding him the floor.

"I will not lie to you," the Therengian started, *"the enemy has a large force, hundreds more than Ord-Kurgad itself. Chief among them are the Temple Knights, heavily armoured horsemen similar to those that wiped out my village, Athelwald."*

Khurlak, a renowned hunter, stood. *"Tell us, Athgar. If we choose to fight, will you stand with us?"*

"I shall," said Athgar.

Natalia, who was listening to Shaluhk's translation, suddenly stood, unsure of the correct protocol.

"I shall fight with you, too" she said in the Human tongue.

Athgar translated her words into Orc, causing the tribe to look on in confusion.

"She is a water shamaness," he declared.

Floor pounding resumed, and he waited for it to die down.

"I see the look of contempt on your face, Korsune," said Athgar. *"Say what you wish. All are free to speak here."*

"How do we know your bondmate is powerful," the Orc said. *"She looks weak to me."*

Athgar turned to Natalia, "He wants proof of your magic, do you think you're up to it?"

In answer, she turned to Kargen, who nodded his approval. Natalia looked upward, clearing her mind and deciding what spell to cast, then lowered her eyes once more to face the crowd. At first, she started weaving her hands in the air, tracing intricate patterns before her, then words of power began to issue from her mouth.

A sense of calm fell over her as she pointed at the entrance to the hut, then a small chunk of ice flew from her fingers, landing just before the exit. It appeared to sink into the ground, and then spikes of ice emerged, blocking all movement. She twisted her wrist slightly, and the spikes began to wheel around, forming a wall of icy blades, each razor-sharp. Next, she stooped to the floor, where the food lay, selecting a melon and tossing it to Athgar.

"Throw it," she said.

He did as she bid, tossing it towards the whirling blades of ice. It struck them, exploding in a fury, sending bits of food flying everywhere. The crowd watched in fascination, entranced by the display. Natalia uttered another phrase and the wall of ice dissolved, leaving only water in its wake.

The ground-pounding commenced again, drowning out all other remarks. Kargen nodded to Athgar and Natalia, who sat down.

"Now," said Kargen, rising to his feet, *"are there any other questions, or are you satisfied with the demonstration of her power?"*

Nods all around gave Kargen the information he needed. *"Very well,"* he said at last, *"it now falls to Uhdrig to take the vote."*

The great shamaness rose, all eyes on her. *"Let us cast our votes,"* she said. *"Stones represent the desire to fight, while the lack thereof represents flight. As is our custom, the tribe will abide by the decision."*

Shaluhk stood, taking the entire assembly by surprise.

"You have something to add, Shaluhk?" said Uhdrig.

"Yes," she replied. *"Our very existence is at stake here, and no matter the vote, lives will be lost. There are many younglings within our tribe, and any Orc that wishes to leave may do so with no shame attached."*

Uhdrig turned to Kargen, *"You agree with this provision?"*

"I do," the chief replied. *"Shaluhk and I speak with one voice."*

"Very well," said Uhdrig, *"then a vote for flight will allow those who wish, to seek shelter elsewhere. Artoch, you may now take the vote."*

The master of flame moved forward, passing around the earthenware pot. Natalia watched in fascination, dropping her stone in as it went by.

Artoch, having completed his task, moved to the side, emptying the contents onto the ground to take their tally. He tossed the stones back into the pot as he counted, then moved to whisper to Uhdrig.

"The tribe has spoken," the *shamaness* announced. *"It is the decision of the Red Hand that we fight our enemies."*

The pounding resumed, growing in intensity, and then the Orcs started chanting something, leading Natalia to look at Shaluhk.

"What are they saying?" she asked, trying to be heard over the roar.

Shaluhk smiled. "They are calling on the both of you," the Orc explained. "They are calling out 'Fire and Ice!'"

DEFENCE

Spring 1104 SR

"Tell me, my friend," said Kargen, "how much time do you think we have?"

"A week," answered Athgar, "maybe a few days more."

They were sitting around a fire pit, eating venison. It was a small group, with Kargen and Shaluhk there, along with Athgar and Natalia. Uhdrig and Artoch were also present, as was little Agar, tottering around the hut.

"I'm surprised he's walking already," said Natalia.

"He is almost six months old," said Shaluhk, "and growing quickly."

"Orcs mature much faster than Humans," said Kargen. "I imagine Agar will be running around with a wooden axe in a month or two."

"Tell me," said Artoch, "this army that is approaching, does it boast any mages?"

"Yes," said Natalia, "a very powerful Fire Mage by the name of Verineth Sartellian."

"More powerful than Artoch?" asked Kargen.

"He's likely more powerful than any of us," said Natalia. "He's been practising magic for decades."

"Have they any others?" asked Shaluhk.

"I'm afraid we don't know," said Athgar. "I only got a brief glimpse of their camp, and we only know about Verineth because we had an encounter with him."

"You fought him?" said Kargen.

"Natalia did," replied Athgar. "She managed to destroy a bird of flame that he conjured."

"A phoenix?" asked Artoch.

"Yes," Natalia confirmed, "I used an ice shard to destroy it."

"Then you are powerful indeed," said Artoch. "To kill such a manifestation is no small feat."

"Interesting," said Kargen, "but I fear we must concentrate on our defences. I have already sent out hunters to watch for their approach. We shall have word when they reach the river. In the meantime, we must prepare ourselves as best we may." He turned to Athgar, "I would be interested in your thoughts, my friend."

Athgar took a sip from his gourd, letting the drink soothe his throat before beginning. "I'd say there are a number of things we need to do. You have a palisade, and though it gives some protection, there are improvements we could make to it."

"Like adding a gatehouse," suggested Natalia.

"Precisely, though I think a gatehouse is a little ambitious, but certainly a nice sturdy gate that we can barricade from within would work."

"Easy enough to accomplish," said Kargen, "I can have hunters out chopping wood immediately. What else?"

"The palisade is a simple wall, but if we were to put a small platform near its top, it would allow us to return fire from above. That would enable our warbows to keep the enemy archers at range."

Kargen nodded his head.

Athgar continued, "I'd also suggest a ditch around the outside of the palisade. It would make it even harder to assault."

"A wise precaution," noted Artoch, "and if we filled it with flammables, we could ignite it should they attack, an easy enough task for a master of flame."

"Excellent ideas," said Kargen.

"You mentioned you sent out hunters," said Athgar. "What else have you been up to?"

Kargen grinned, revealing his sharp teeth. "You know me well, my friend. We have set up traps along the most likely route."

"What kind of traps?" asked Natalia.

"Tripwires, snares and such. They will not inflict much damage, but it will force our enemy to advance cautiously, securing us more time. Once they enter the woods, my hunters will begin using hit and run tactics, the warbows will be excellent for such work."

"We could help," offered Natalia. "I'm sure a nice blast of ice would do some damage."

"I would rather keep your magic in reserve," said Kargen, "so that it is a surprise for them when you finally strike."

"I suppose that makes sense," said Natalia.

"I would, however, like Athgar to accompany me when they finally cross the river. It will allow us to scout their strength and determine the composition of their army."

"Of course," said Athgar.

"I could help with that," said Natalia.

"Are you a hunter?" asked Kargen.

"No," she replied, "but I'm a battle mage, and very familiar with troop types, likely more so than Athgar."

"She has a point," added the Therengian.

"Very well," said Kargen, "then you shall both go."

Shaluhk looked at Natalia, "Can you use an axe, or maybe a spear?"

"No," the mage replied, "we were trained to rely on our magic."

"Then come," said Shaluhk, rising from her seat on the ground, "it is time you learned."

Natalia rose, following the shamaness as she left the hut. Little Agar, noticing his mother leaving, ran after them, curious to see what they were up to.

Athgar watched them go. "He has a lot of energy," he said.

"He takes after his mother," said Kargen. "It wouldn't surprise me if he becomes a shaman one day."

"You make that sound like a bad thing," said Uhdrig.

"I suspect," said Athgar, "that your son will choose his own way. Perhaps he'll be both hunter and shaman?"

Kargen laughed, a deep-throated growling noise that rumbled in his chest. "Maybe he will, my friend."

"The archers and footmen we can fight," said Artoch, "but tell me about these armoured warriors. We must find a way to defeat them."

"They wear metal from head to foot," began Athgar, "and ride large horses. I fought one such man in Athelwald, and I was unable to injure him. My arrows simply bounced off his armour."

"Surely the warbows can penetrate this metal?" asked Kargen.

"I'm sure they would," said Athgar, "but you'd have to be close to guarantee it. The metal's also angled so you would have to hit it squarely, or your arrow would be deflected."

"How do you fight that?" wondered Uhdrig.

"You target the horses," said Kargen.

"NO!" said Artoch. "It is not our way to kill animals outside of the hunt."

"We have little choice," said Kargen. "The very existence of our people is at stake."

"And if we lose this fight?" asked Uhdrig.

"Then we shall all die," said Athgar. "I doubt this army is interested in taking prisoners."

"Why do you say that?" asked Artoch. "Is it not the Human way?"

"Normally, yes," said Athgar, "but the true nature of this campaign has been kept secret. They can't very well turn around and produce prisoners without a lot of questions being asked. Bodies, on the other hand, would simply support the stories of Orc raiding."

"Raiding?" said Kargen.

"Yes," the Therengian continued, "they've been claiming that Orcs raided an outlying village, a place called Tomar."

"We have never left our territory!" declared Kargen.

"I know," said Athgar. "That's how we knew something big was happening."

"Who commands this army," asked Kargen, "the duke?"

"I can't say for sure, but I would think it's being directed by Father General Gilbert. I doubt the Duke of Krieghoff is with the army, though he's likely sent someone to watch over things."

"Why would you say that?" asked Kargen. "Surely the duke would want to be in charge."

"By staying away, he gives himself the ability to distance himself politically. He can deny knowledge or even punish underlings if things go badly."

"Then we shall endeavour to do just that," said Kargen.

"You make it sound so easy," said Athgar.

"No," said Kargen, "it will be quite difficult, but we must persevere, the survival of our clan depends on it. Let it not be said that the Orcs of the Red Hand disappeared from history without a fight."

"You shall not disappear," swore Athgar, "I promise you that."

Kargen stared into Athgar's face. "Two years ago, when I brought you here to Ord-Kurgad, I knew the tribe would never be the same."

"Are you saying that I brought disaster?"

"No," said Kargen, "but you signified a great change. For generations, the Orcs have been a diminished people, our territory shrinking in size as we decrease in numbers. We have, as a race, been driven to the far reaches of the Continent, but something has changed of late. For the first time in centuries, we count Humans among our allies, both here and to the west. Great change is coming, I know, but with great change comes great sacrifice. Orcs will die, of this, I have no doubt. The real question, in the end, will be whether or not it is worth the price we must pay."

"How can it not be worth it?" asked Athgar. "It means your survival."

"For the Orcish race, yes," said Kargen, "but I was referring to the long term survival of THIS tribe."

"I'm afraid I don't understand."

"Let us suppose that we are victorious," said Kargen. "What would be the result of that?"

"Ord-Kurgad would be safe," said Athgar.

"Yes, but word would quickly spread that a force of Orcs defeated a Human army. How long do you suppose it would be before another army comes to defeat us?"

"They're after the Godstone," said Athgar. "If we were to remove it, there'd be no reason to attack in the future."

Kargen sighed, an action that Athgar had never seen him do before. "You are an optimist," said Kargen. "It is one of the things I like about you, but I, as the chief, must look to the longer picture. The Human realms are constantly at odds with each other, can you tell me it is not so?"

"I hate to admit it," said Athgar, "but you're right. What of it?"

"Humans like to portray strength. If the Duke of Krieghoff is defeated by us, how long until his neighbours learn of it?"

"Not long, I suppose."

"Exactly," said Kargen, "and that means that he will have no choice but to attack again. He can not be defeated and remain in power, those who covet his land will not stand for it."

"If that's the way you feel," said Athgar, "then why fight? Why not take the tribe and move east?"

"To where?" asked Kargen. "We would have to march clear across the kingdom."

"But if what you're saying is true, you'll still have to do that."

"Yes," said Kargen, "but we would have a reputation as fierce fighters. The Duke of Holstead would be hesitant to fight us."

"I suppose that's true," said Athgar, "but I can't help feeling it's a mistake."

"What do you know of our ancient history?"

"Only what you've told me over the years," admitted Athgar. "I know the Orcs are one of the Elder Folk. You were around a long time before Humans showed up. You had great cities at one time, did you not?"

"We did," said Kargen. "In the time of our Ancestors, there were many great cities of Orcs. Our culture flourished, much as the Therengians did many generations later."

"I remember something else," said Athgar. "Orcs were driven to the edge of extinction by the Elves in a war that lasted for centuries, weren't you?"

"We were," Kargen agreed, "and we never truly recovered our numbers. Deprived of our cities, we regressed as a people, and now we live in small tribal villages, a shadow of our former selves."

"It is a sad tale," said Athgar.

"There is more," said Kargen, "for ever since the ascendance of man, we have been pushed farther and farther away from our ancestral lands, and always eastward. One day there will be no more land in that direction, and then it will be too late."

"And it has always been so?" said Athgar.

"There was a brief time where the Orcs thrived under the rule of Therengia, but that, too, has ended."

"Orcs worked with Therengia?" said Athgar. "I didn't know that?"

"It is true," said Kargen, "or so our Ancestors say. At the height of Therengia's power, Orcs lived throughout their kingdom. We traded with them, much as we traded with you, in Athelwald."

Athgar sat up suddenly, a thought crossing his mind.

"What is it?" asked Kargen. "Is something wrong?"

"No," he replied, "but I just remembered, there are Therengians out there, to the east, I believe."

"What of it?"

"You said that Therengians and Orcs worked together," said Athgar. "Could it be so again?"

"An interesting idea," noted Kargen, "but how would we find these Therengians? And who is to say that they would be willing?"

"They are persecuted, just as you are," said Athgar. "It would make sense to band together for common protection, would it not?"

"Possibly," said Kargen, "but that depends on the people themselves."

"Still," persisted Athgar, "it's worth considering."

"I shall give it some thought," promised Kargen, "but for now, we had best concentrate on defeating this army."

Three days later, Athgar stood watch while Orcs dug the ditch. They had started out well enough, using picks to break the soil, but it was Natalia's suggestion of creating wooden spades that increased their pace dramatically. The Orcs had never seen such implements, but took to them quickly, moving vast amounts of dirt swiftly and efficiently.

More Orcs cut down trees and hauled the timber back to Ord-Kurgad to build the walkways while others created two great doors that could be closed off, protecting the entrance. Natalia had shown them how a drop bar could be implemented, holding it tightly closed, and the Orcs proved to be enthusiastic in their efforts.

Their time here had been pleasant, and if it hadn't been for the impending attack, Athgar would have considered settling down, for never would the family think of looking for Natalia in such a place.

It was this very thought that was on his mind as he saw her approaching, her dress covered in dirt and wood chips, evidence of her work with the Orcs.

"How are things progressing here?" she asked.

"Well," he said, "they'll have the ditch complete by nightfall tomorrow."

"Any sign of the enemy?"

"Not that I've heard," he said.

She stood beside him, watching the Orcs work, their backs bent to the task.

"I wish we had an Earth Mage," she said. "It would make this so much quicker."

"An Earth Mage?"

"Yes, they can move large amounts of dirt using magic."

"That WOULD be nice."

"Not only that," she continued, "but if they're powerful enough, they can turn dirt into rock."

"How do you know all this?" he asked. "You're a Water Mage."

"I'm a battle mage, remember? We learned all about the capabilities of the other magical disciplines."

"What I'd like to know," said Athgar, "is what Verineth is likely to do. My only experience with fighting a Fire Mage comes from Corassus."

"Well," mused Natalia, "let's see. Once he knows the Orcs have a wooden palisade, he'll likely try to burn it down."

"Yes," said Athgar, "we thought of that. Artoch and I will be inside, ready to extinguish any fires. I only hope we're powerful enough."

"Combined, you will be," she assured him, "but that will only be one of his tactics."

"And the others?"

"He can use smoke to blind us, allowing the soldiers to get closer."

"I hadn't thought of that," Athgar confessed.

"I believe that he'll target the shamans, once he knows they exist. He'll want to eliminate any rivalry."

"Rivalry? You make it sound like a slight disagreement."

"Sorry," she said, "what I meant was he'll want to eliminate any source of power that might rival his own. I doubt he knows we're here, but if he sees his flames being extinguished, he'll figure out there's magic involved."

"So how do we fight him?" he asked.

"We don't," she said, "at least not directly. We concentrate on the soldiers. It doesn't matter how powerful he is, without the army to back him up, he can't destroy us."

"But as a mage, he can call down a rain of fire," said Athgar.

"Can you?" she asked.

"No, it's not among the spells I know," he confessed.

"Every spell has its limits," Natalia explained. "I'm considered a powerful caster, but even I can't destroy more than a single target at a time. Mages are meant to augment an army, not be their major strength. Don't get me wrong, in a one on one battle, a mage can be devastating, but magic is not very effective against large numbers."

"Good to know," said Athgar. "I wonder why Artoch never mentioned this?"

"He isn't a battle mage," she answered. "He can only talk from his own experiences."

"Or those of their Ancestors," Athgar reminded her.

"True," she said, "but how many actual battles have these Orcs been in? I doubt it's very many."

"That's true," said Athgar. "My understanding is that Ord-Kurgad has never been attacked."

They stood in silence for a moment, listening as spades dug into the dirt.

"I'm glad you're here," he said at last.

"I'm just taking a break," she explained. "We're waiting on some more timber for the door."

"No, I mean here, in Ord-Kurgad," he corrected.

"It's where I belong," Natalia said, "with you."

"I feel the same way," he confessed.

"I'm only sorry I had to lie to them," she said.

"Lie to them? What do you mean?"

"I told them we were bondmates," she said.

"And so we are," he said.

"But we've never been bonded."

"We can take care of that once we settle down somewhere safe."

"I can't wait that long," said Natalia. "I'd ask the Orcs to do it, but they already think we're bonded."

Athgar chuckled, "I suppose they do. Wait, are you saying you want to marry me?"

Natalia blushed slightly. "Of course," she said, "isn't it obvious?"

Athgar felt his pulse quicken. "I feel the same way," he said, staring into her eyes, his smile growing bigger by the moment. The Orc workers around them started chanting in their own language, thumping the ground with their spades.

"Fire and Ice. Fire and Ice."

"It seems," he said, with a chuckle, "that they like the thought of us together." He kissed her, to the cheers of the Orcs, lingering in her embrace until Natalia pulled back slightly. "Save it for later, my love, we've work to do."

Laruhk crouched low, peering through the foliage. He had topped a rise and now, looking down at the distant fields to the west of the great river, he noticed some movement. At first, it was just a dust cloud, raised by a half dozen horses, but soon it grew, as hundreds of soldiers made their way across the plain.

"Durgash," he said, turning to his companion, *"return to Ord-Kurgad. Tell Kargen we have sighted the invaders."*

"What numbers have they?" asked Durgash.

In answer, Laruhk raised his hand, forming a V shape with between his thumb and finger. He held it before him, using it to estimate numbers, then counted out the enemy.

"I estimate more than four hundred foot, probably closer to five. There is an equal number of archers that I can see, and a large group of horsemen."

"Those must be the Temple Knights Athgar spoke of," said Durgash.

"Yes," Laruhk confirmed, *"I can see the sun glinting off their armour."*

"Will they cross the river tonight, do you think?"

Laruhk looked skyward, judging the position of the sun. *"No, it will be dark soon, they will have to make camp. They will likely cross in the morning."*

"And then the fighting will begin," said Durgash.

"Yes," said Laruhk. *"Now be off with you, Kargen needs to know they are here."*

"Very well," said Durgash. *"Will you remain here?"*

"For now," said Laruhk, *"but I shall keep my distance."*

OUTRIDERS

Spring 1104 SR

A thgar looked out over the fields below. From their vantage point on the hill, the enemy camp was easy to spot for it stretched across acres of land beyond the river. The early morning sun was just rising, bathing their enemy in a golden hue.

"What do you make of it?" asked Kargen.

"It is just as I suspected," answered the Therengian. "The army appears to be mainly footmen and archers."

"And the Temple Knights?"

"Over there," pointed Natalia. "You can see their standard by those tents. There'll be a paddock behind that holds their horses."

"Paddock?" said Kargen.

"Yes," Natalia explained, "a field where their horses will be kept."

"And what of their numbers?" asked the Orc.

"I can't tell," said Athgar. "Maybe when there's a little more light."

"I estimate close to one hundred knights," said Natalia, causing Athgar to look at her in surprise.

"What makes you say that?"

"Caerhaven is a fair-sized city, and they have a father general in command. That indicates a significant detachment. One hundred such men would form two companies, though they'll likely be deployed in smaller contingents."

"Two companies," mused Athgar, "you make it sound like so few."

"In a sense, it is," said Natalia, "but you must remember they're shock troops, the most elite warriors, trained to deliver the decisive blow. They won't be committed until they're sure of victory."

"Great," said Athgar, "so when we're at our weakest, that's when they'll attack?"

"Precisely," she replied.

"These other warriors," said Kargen, "the footmen and the archers, what is their quality?"

"Unknown," said Athgar.

"Agreed," said Natalia. "Krieghoff was considered too insignificant to be of interest to the Volstrum, and I heard nothing in Caerhaven to indicate how well trained they are."

"We might be able to tell something from their equipment," offered Athgar, "providing we can get close enough to see."

"What do you mean?" asked the Orc.

"Better trained troops are likely to have better armour and weapons," said Athgar.

"Yes," agreed Natalia, warming to the task. "If they're a local militia, they'll have rudimentary weapons, like spears but no armour. Regular troops might have leather jerkins, but what we're really looking for is anyone in chainmail. They'll be the ones to worry about."

"So we should target armoured opponents first," said Kargen. "Good to know."

"On the other hand," continued Natalia, "sometimes it's more effective to target the weaker troops first. It's easier to break their morale."

"Also good advice," pondered the Orc, "but I must make a decision."

"I think that will likely depend on what the enemy does," said Natalia. "In any event, your warriors should know what to expect."

"Hunters," corrected Athgar.

"Pardon?" Natalia replied.

"The Orcs aren't warriors, they're hunters."

"My mistake," she said. "We learned so little of your people in training."

"What did you learn?" asked Athgar.

"Why does that matter?" she responded.

"I was just thinking," he said, "that our enemy's knowledge of the Orcs might be similar to your own. Perhaps we can use that to our advantage?"

"I suppose that makes sense," she said. "Let's see now, Mistress Dominique always told us that Orcs were not very effective, no offense Kargen."

"None taken, Nat-Alia. Please continue."

She closed her eyes, thinking back to her time at the Volstrum. "They tend to operate in small groups with little cohesion or discipline. Main weapons include axes and spears with a small number being proficient in small bows."

"Small bows?" said Kargen. "What are those?"

"The same weapons used by that army down there," said Athgar. "They've never seen a warbow before."

Kargen grinned, "I can not wait to show them how they work."

"What else?" urged Athgar.

"They were described as irregular skirmish troops, meaning they don't stand in a line of battle. Skirmish troops typically let loose with a volley of spears or axes and then withdraw. If our enemy's training follows standard Human principles, then we can expect them to deploy troops to counter us."

"Meaning?" said Athgar.

"They'll likely send bowmen up ahead to scour us out, and light cavalry, if they have it."

"I don't see any other horses down there," said Athgar, "other than what must be the leaders', I mean."

"Thank the Saints for small miracles," said Natalia.

"And the Ancestors," added Kargen.

"And let's not forget the Gods," said Athgar. "We need all the luck we can muster."

The Therengian returned his attention to the army below.

"Any sign of siege weapons?" asked Natalia.

"Not that I can see," said Athgar, "just lots and lots of men scurrying around. It looks like they're getting ready for something."

"The sun has risen," said Kargen. "They are getting ready to cross the river."

"And will they do so, unopposed?" asked Athgar.

"My hunters have orders to let a few across before they begin their... what did you call it Nat-Alia?"

"Skirmishing," she replied.

"Yes, skirmishing," said Kargen, rolling the strange word over in his mouth. "We will wait here and judge the effectiveness of our tactics."

"Might they not spot us?" asked Athgar.

"And what if they do?" asked Kargen. "We are too far away for them to attack us. Even that Fire Mage could not hit us all the way up here."

"I suppose you're right," said Athgar. "I just feel like I should be down there, helping."

"Your time will come," said Kargen. "For now, we are better served by watching. How our enemy reacts to our tactics will tell us how well trained they are."

"You surprise me," said Athgar. "I had no idea you were so well versed in such things."

Kargen laughed, letting out a low rumble, "That is because Uhdrig spent the evening communing with our Ancestors. It is their wisdom that I speak this day."

"It must be nice to be able to get advice from Ancestors," said Natalia. "That's something they definitely didn't teach at the Volstrum."

"Look," said Athgar, pointing, "they're beginning to move."

They watched as a small group of archers advanced to the edge of the water. There, the river was shallower, and the army had selected a suitable ford for their crossing.

A small group, no more than a dozen, began wading across, their bows held above their heads to keep the strings dry. They soon emerged on the other side, moving farther up the bank and taking cover. Once they were in place, the next group began moving, this time footmen armed with shields and spears.

They were midstream when the first arrow flew. It struck a footman in the neck, causing him to cry out briefly in pain before sinking into the water. Moments later, more arrows followed, taking out two more. The remainder, struggling as they were against the current, held their shields before them in a desperate attempt to protect themselves.

Athgar saw one man endeavouring to hold his shield upright. It had three arrows in it, and from the Therengian's point of view, the shafts had deeply penetrated the thin wooden construction, for the man was bleeding from his arm.

"Powerful bow," said Athgar.

Kargen grinned again, "You should know, my friend. You showed us how to make them."

"I've never seen archers in action," said Natalia, "though we learned all about them, of course."

They watched as the first enemy archers started peppering the tree line with arrows.

"There is no sign of coordination," said Kargen. "I had expected them to use volleys, is that not the normal Human custom?"

"It is," said Natalia, "but I imagine they have no officer with them, either that or whoever is in charge is inexperienced."

"Good for us," said Athgar, "not so good for them."

The men in the river started advancing once more, only to be met with more arrows. Two more invaders fell, then the group started backing up, crouching low in the water, their shields still held out in front.

Suddenly, a roar erupted from the edge of the woods, and then a dozen Orcs burst from cover. Two of them threw spears, one hitting an archer in the chest, the other narrowly missing another. The rest kept running, closing the distance rapidly. Arrows trickled out from the enemy archers, and then they broke, running as fast as they could back to the river.

Athgar watched as the first Orc swung his axe, sinking the blade into a bowman's back. His victim fell, shuddering a little as the Orc stood over him, then lay still. The hunter pulled the axe free and then plunged into the water.

The footmen, no longer concerned about holding their formation, turned and fled, several dropping their shields and swords in their haste to get away from danger. Only half the bowmen made it to the river, two more getting cut down as they waded across to the western bank.

The Orcs, content with their victory, turned back towards their own bank, disappearing, once more, into the safety of the tree line.

Kargen slapped Athgar on the back, almost knocking him over. "Success!" he said.

"A small victory," said Athgar, "but they'll be back."

"Of course," said Kargen, "but did you see the effects of those bows? The arrows went right through their shields."

"It was impressive, I'll grant you that," said the Therengian, "but there are plenty more troops where those came from."

"We have won some time," said Kargen, "and hopefully dulled their enthusiasm a little."

"What now?" said Natalia.

"Now," said Kargen, "we wait and see what develops."

It was noon before the enemy tried again. This time, they moved up some heavier footmen, men with chainmail and metal shields. They advanced towards the river in a tight group, their shields almost touching. Behind them came a second group, though Athgar couldn't make out what they were doing.

It was only as the footmen started entering the water that it became apparent the second group were crossbowmen. They lined the bank to either side, sending bolts whizzing into the trees beyond.

"What is this?" asked Kargen.

"Crossbows," said Natalia. "They'll have a range similar to your own."

"Surely they are not as powerful as our warbows?" asked the Orc.

"Oh, yes, they are," said Natalia, "but they're slow to reload. They have to use a special lever to crank them."

"Crank?" said Kargen. "Not a term I am familiar with."

"They use a lever to force the bow into the ready position," she explained.

"It seems a strange way to fire a bow," noted Kargen.

"It is," agreed Natalia, "but it means that even someone with little experience can use one. They are capable of penetrating plate armour, with a bit of luck."

"Something worth remembering," said Kargen. "The Ancestors did not warn me of this."

"Your Ancestors likely never encountered them," said Athgar. "They are, I understand, a relatively new invention."

"You Humans," said Kargen, "always trying to change the world with new ideas."

The footmen, by now halfway across the river, kept up a slow but deliberate pace. Their swords were out, their shields held ready, eager to take the fight to their opponents.

The Orcs began sending arrows forth, but this time the soldiers kept their formation. Arrows that had punctured the wooden shields so easily before, now found the metal shields more resistant to their attacks.

It didn't take long for the crossbowmen to home in on the location of the Orc archers. Bolts sailed across the river, sinking into the green flesh of the defenders. Kargen watched, helpless to intervene as his hunters fell back from the onslaught.

"It appears they have the advantage of us," he cursed.

"It is the inevitable ebb and flow of battle," said Natalia, "as each side tries to out-think the other. Don't worry, it's still early in the campaign."

"It is more troubling than that," said Kargen. "I can accept that they will attempt to counter our moves, but this shows they can adapt quickly. Someone in their army is well versed in tactics."

"Likely the mage, Verineth," said Natalia. "He would have had the same training as me."

"And," added Athgar, "likely more experience. Do you know if he's seen battle?"

"He has," she replied. "We learned about him in class. He's very accomplished in that regard."

"I wish I hadn't heard that," said Athgar, "now I'm worried."

"He is one man, my friend," said Kargen, "and we are many. We know he is coming, but he does not know that you two are here. We can defeat this enemy, I know it."

"How can you be so sure," said Athgar.

"The Ancestors brought you two here, did they not?" said Kargen. "I can not believe they would do so to let us suffer defeat."

"You put a lot of faith into your Ancestors," said Athgar.

"Do you not trust your own gods?" countered the Orc.

"The Gods don't interfere in the lives of mortals," said the Therengian.

"The Ancestors do not interfere," said Kargen, "they only advise. It is us, the living, that make the decisions."

"I suppose that's as good an arrangement as any," said Athgar.

Natalia cast her eyes towards the river where the footmen had now completed their crossing and were forming up into a line, pressing towards the trees.

"I think it time we withdraw," she said, "before they cut off our path to the village."

Kargen tore his attention from Athgar to note the enemy's progress. "Nat-Alia is correct," he announced. "Come, we must be gone from this place."

They began to make their way down the hill when Athgar tripped, sending him sprawling into the underbrush.

"Are you all right?" asked Natalia.

"I'm fine," Athgar replied, but he remained in place, staring at the ground before him.

"What's wrong?" she asked.

"I just had a thought," he said, rising to his feet. "Kargen, I need some of your hunters."

"Of course," said the Orc, "how many would you like?"

"I should think two dozen will do," the Therengian replied.

Kargen grinned, showing his teeth, "Your mind is working again."

"It is," he said, "but we'll have to hurry to make use of it."

Captain Wagner watched as the men marched past. The advance was moving at a fair pace, despite the early morning fiasco at the river. Now, with the obstacle behind them, they marched briskly, confident of brushing aside any resistance they might encounter.

The bowmen took the lead, fanning out in front and to the sides, while the crossbowmen followed the foot, ready to step in should the greenskins prove troublesome. They had tried to warn him of the power of the Orc bows, but the captain was inclined to ignore the advice, blaming it on little more than panic among ill-disciplined troops. His troops, he knew, would stand and fight, as they had at the river when they finally made the crossing. No Orc was going to scare HIS men!

The trail took them steadily eastward, and the archers struggled to hold their positions among the thick foliage to either side. Captain Wagner looked at them with derision, for in his mind, the bowmen were little more than trained militia, not the hardened soldiers under his command.

A shuffling off to the north drew his interest, and then someone called out in dismay, only to fall into silence. The captain halted the men, turning them to face this new potential threat. The footmen stood ready, their weapons drawn, waiting as sweat dripped down their necks. The day was growing hotter, despite it still being spring, and the closeness of the woods only added to the sense of foreboding.

Captain Wagner absently brushed away an insect, then peered into the woods. There was a slight movement of a branch, and he realized that the Orcs were nearby.

"Over here!" he shouted, pointing with his sword. His men stood ready, his own arm itching for a fight, and then the woods fell quiet.

"Skirmish order!" he roared, and the men began to move to either side, spreading out their line. Soon they were two arms lengths apart, and he gave the order to advance. "We'll show these greenskins how a Human fights," he called out.

They had progressed no more than twenty paces when the forest appeared to erupt around them. One moment, there was just the crunching of leaves and sticks as the men advanced, the next the very ground appeared to come alive as Orcs rose from the forest floor.

He tried to issue orders, but it was too late. They were now fighting for their lives.

Athgar rose, throwing the leaves and sticks from his back. Off to his right, Laruhk was already standing, hefting a spear that sailed past him to dig into a soldier's leg. The enemy warrior fell with a scream, his voice echoing off the trees.

All around him, Orcs took up the challenge, hurling axes and spears at their surprised enemy. Athgar, axe in hand, made his way towards the enemy captain. Mistaking his intention, the officer called out, "Over here, man, form a circle, it's our only hope!"

In answer, Athgar raised his axe, bringing it crashing down onto his opponent's head, the blade digging deeply into the man's helmet. Captain Wagner fell, tearing the weapon from the Therengian's grip. Athgar stood over the body, leaning down to grasp the axe handle. He placed a foot on the captain's chest, giving it a tug, and then the blade came free. An Orc ran past him, black blood spilling from his left arm, spear still held firmly in his right.

The enemy, now bereft of their leader, attempted to form a defensive line, with a group of no more than twenty standing back to back in a rough circle, their swords stained black. The Orcs began to encircle their opponents, daring them to come out from behind their defence, but the enemy's discipline held.

Athgar knew they didn't have much time. The sound of fighting would have echoed down the line, and he couldn't risk enemy reinforcements finding them here, exposed as they were, the surprise now gone.

"Fall back," he called, using the Orcish tongue.

The Orcs launched a final volley of axes at the enemy, then turned and ran, disappearing into the woods once more. Athgar watched for just a moment longer, then, content no one was following, joined his adoptive people.

Natalia waited a short distance away, Kargen beside her, along with Shaluhk. Athgar arrived just in time to see the shamaness healing a wounded Orc. He watched, fascinated, as the skin knitted itself back together at her touch.

"We did well," said the Therengian. "We killed about a dozen and injured just as many. What are our losses?"

Kargen looked at Shaluhk, who had finished healing the wounded Orc.

"Only a minor wound," she said. "It seems our surprise was total."

"They will not fall for that a second time," said Kargen.

"No," said Athgar, "they won't, but they'll be more cautious in their advance."

"We will pull back farther," said Kargen, "the traps are nearby. Let them get snagged up, and then we will launch another attack. By nightfall, they will be too nervous to sleep."

"Yes," agreed Athgar, "and then we'll have some fun."

INFILTRATION

Spring 1104 SR

"You seem to be enjoying this," said Natalia, smearing more of the green ointment onto Athgar's face. The Therengian stared back at her, unused to the green colour of her skin.

"I don't see why this is necessary," he said.

"It will help hide us," she said. "After all, we don't want to stick out in the dark."

"I suppose it's a valid point."

"Now remember," urged Shaluhk, "your job is to get behind their lines and disrupt things, nothing more."

"I'll remember," said Athgar. "We're to scare off horses, torch tents, and do whatever we can to create mayhem."

"Mayhem," said Shaluhk, "what strange terms you Humans have."

"Remind me again," said Natalia, "whose idea was this?"

"Yours," said Shaluhk, "though I argued against it. You are not a trained warrior, Nat-Alia."

"Agreed," the Water Mage responded, "but Athgar and I are the only two that can pass as enemy soldiers."

"Yes," said Athgar, "and Natalia is better able to understand the enemy forces than I, her training saw to that."

Shaluhk looked at Athgar, whose face was covered in green grease. "That is enough Nat-Alia, any more, and he will be ready to baste."

"By the Saints, Shaluhk," said Natalia, "you made a joke."

The shamaness grinned, "I learned from my sister. Now be careful you two, your path is dangerous."

"We will," promised Natalia. She stepped forward, hugging the Orc.

"Here," said Shaluhk, handing her an axe, "take it. This has served my Ancestors well."

"I couldn't," said Natalia.

"Of course you can," said Shaluhk, grinning. "Now remember, the sharp part goes into the enemy."

"I'm not likely to forget that," she replied, looking at Athgar. "All set?"

"Now is as good a time as any," the Therengian replied. "Follow me."

He led her into the woods. The enemy encampment lay some distance off, but to get there, they would have to pass through the enemy lines. Rather than head in a straight line, Athgar led them farther north, the idea being to loop around and approach from the rear where they were less likely to be discovered. The woods were thick, but the full moon gave them ample light to guide them to their destination.

"You seem to know your way around here," Natalia noted.

"I spent nearly two years with the Orcs," Athgar replied, "that's a lot of hunting. I think I know this area better than the woods of Athelwald."

"Did you not hunt at home?" she asked.

"Let's just say my gifts lay elsewhere."

"And yet here you are, using those hunter skills."

"That," said Athgar, "was mainly Kargen's doing. He and Laruhk taught me to hunt the Orc way."

"Is that different than the way Therengians hunt?" she asked.

"Yes," said Athgar. "Orcs prefer to hunt with the bow, though they use spears from time to time. In Athelwald, we hunted by forming a long line of spears and then driving the prey towards them."

"That sounds very dangerous," said Natalia.

"It is," he agreed, "and you have to be brave to stand up against a wall of animals charging you, but the Orc's way is much more effective."

"And," said Natalia, "requires you to learn more things, like moving silently and tracking, for example."

"Yes," he admitted, "not to mention knowing all about the plants that grow in the forest."

"I'm not sure I understand," she said. "Why would that matter?"

"In order to hunt animals, you need to understand what they eat. Foxes, for example, like to eat greenberries while bears are known to be partial to parchberries. Find one of those two and your prey is likely close by."

"You seem so alive in the wilderness," she noted.

"It's how I spent most of my life," he said, "but you're no different. You're the one who's at home in the city."

"I suppose that's true," said Natalia.

Athgar suddenly halted, holding up his hand to stop her.

"Be careful," he said, "there's a snare up here. Likely one of the ones set by the Orcs."

Athgar guided her around the obstacle, then they resumed their trek. They were well north of their starting point now, and he emerged into a clearing, looking up at the stars to get his bearings.

"This way," he continued, "we can start heading west."

"How much longer?" she asked.

"A while yet," he replied. "We still have plenty of time to talk."

"Very well," she said, "what do you want to talk about?"

"You said some things while you were feverish," he began.

"I did?" she replied. "I hope it wasn't anything embarrassing."

"Something about children," he offered.

"I don't recall anything," she said. "Why don't you refresh my memory."

"We were talking about the Orcs," Athgar continued, "and you said you wanted to have a baby, then you asked me whether I wanted a boy or a girl."

"Did I?" she said. "Now you have me intrigued, what was your answer?"

"I said I didn't care," said Athgar, "and by that, I mean that I would love either."

"Did I lay out a time frame for this," she said, "because I can't imagine settling down long enough for any of this to occur?"

"We both agreed on that," he said, "but you can't always predict when a pregnancy might happen."

"Fair enough," she said, "but I assume I was clear on who the father would be?"

"Yes," he said, smiling, "you were most insistent that it be me."

"Good," she said, "because I definitely don't want it to be anyone else. They tried to force me into breeding back at the Volstrum, and that's what made me decide it was time to leave."

"That's barbaric," said Athgar. "Why would they do that?"

"The family has been breeding mages for many generations. They think that by selectively matching spellcasters, they can produce more powerful mages."

"And did that work for them?" he asked.

"It seems to have," she remarked, "but I have no proof. There were certainly a lot of high born mages at the Volstrum. A high born can trace their lineage back down the family line. Of course, it didn't work for everyone."

"No?"

"No, remember my friend Katrin? Both her parents were powerful, but she failed out of the program, and I never saw her again after that."

"So she's still out there somewhere?" he asked.

"I would like to think so," said Natalia, "but my gut tells me she's dead. The family doesn't like failure."

"Why is that?" he asked. "Everyone fails from time to time."

"Not the family. They're determined to be the most powerful mages on the Continent, both magically and politically."

"You really think so?" he asked.

"I knew they were powerful mages," she explained, "but the political part I've only just come to realize. They're in all the major courts of the Petty Kingdoms, yet until recently, I don't think I really knew how influential they were."

"What tipped you off?" he asked.

"Discovering a Sartellian in Corassus was a start," she said, "then finding Verineth here, in this small duchy, was a real eye-opener."

"How so?"

"You have to understand," she said, "Verineth is not just a mage, he's a legend within the family. The man's done more to advance the cause than anyone."

"When you say the cause, do you mean the breeding or the influence?"

She chuckled, "Possibly both, but certainly the influence side of things."

"Hopefully, we won't run across him in the camp," said Athgar, "I'd hate for him to recognize us."

"Maybe," she said, "if we're lucky, we'll find him asleep, then we can finish him off quickly."

"You'd do that?" he said. "Kill a man in his sleep?"

"To save the Orcs? Of course, they're my family now!"

"You seem to have blended in well, much better than I did when they first took me in."

"That's because I'm your bondmate," she teased.

"And now Shaluhk's sister," he added.

"Yes," agreed Natalia, "I finally have a family again. I hope when this is all over, we can settle down here."

"I'm afraid we can't," said Athgar. "The Orcs won't be staying."

"What? Why would you say that?"

"These are hard times," said Athgar, "and the Petty Kingdoms are at each other's throats. Any ruler that is seen as weak will be carved up by his enemies."

"And you think if the Duke of Krieghoff fails here, that will be his fate?"

"He'll be eager to be seen as a victor. If this army loses, another will follow, Kargen is sure of it."

"Does anyone else suspect?" she asked.

"Perhaps Shaluhk," he said, "and maybe her brother, but I doubt anyone else does."

"Even Uhdrig or Artoch?"

"I can't really say," said Athgar. "Kargen keeps things very close."

"When will he tell the tribe, do you think?" she asked.

"I suspect he'll wait until the fighting is over," he said, "assuming we win, of course."

"All this fighting," she mused, "and for what? So they can all leave anyway?"

"The Orcs need this victory," said Athgar. "In order to leave, they have to cross Holstead, and they don't want the duke there interfering with them along the way."

"There's no guarantee they wouldn't be attacked," said Natalia.

"True," he agreed, "but anyone would hesitate at attacking a group that just won a battle against such odds, and if they tell him they're just passing through the duchy, then so much the better."

"I can see his reasoning," said Natalia. "If I were in the duke's shoes, I'd leave the Orcs alone too."

Athgar halted, listening carefully.

"We're getting close to their lines now," he said. "From here on, we'll have to keep as quiet as possible."

Athgar led them west, though Natalia had no clue as to what direction they were travelling. It was only when they turned to the south that she realized they were closer than expected. Athgar crouched, using a finger to indicate she should come closer.

"Do you hear that?" he whispered.

She strained to listen but heard nothing save the wind in the trees.

"What is it?" she asked.

"Horses," he said. "We must be near the paddock. Follow me closely."

He moved forward slowly, keeping his eyes to the ground and watching for anything that might give them away. Natalia followed his lead, her footsteps seemingly loud compared to the soft footfalls of the Therengian.

She noticed him crouch once more and moved closer, lowering her stance. He pointed to the east, then parted some branches revealing a series of tents beyond.

"It's the command tents," she whispered.

"How can you be sure?" he asked.

"Common soldiers will be sleeping under the stars. Only the wealthy can afford pavilions."

"Pavilions?" he said.

"A fancy word for tents," she remarked, "though the term sometimes refers to those that are a little more ornate in their design."

"Let's go and have a look, shall we?" said Athgar. "With any luck, we'll find something useful inside."

He was about to move ahead when Natalia caught his arm.

"No, wait," she urged, "there are guards nearby."

Athgar looked to where she was pointing. Sure enough, a group of warriors were moving past, Temple Knights by the look of them.

"We won't be able to get close to those tents," she said.

"Well," he added, "not without a disguise, at least."

"A disguise? How do you expect to manage that?"

"There's a whole army here," he said, "I thought we might borrow some clothes."

"You mean steal some," she clarified. "Don't you think someone would notice if we were to make off with their clothing?"

"I was actually thinking of killing a soldier and taking his armour. All we'd need is a coat and helmet."

"We're green," she said.

"Yes, but we'll steer clear of the torches. Anyone seeing us from a distance will assume we're part of the army."

"Then why a helmet?" she asked.

"To hide that pretty face of yours," he said. "I'm sure that without one, you'd be noticed."

"What about you?" she asked.

"I look just like most of them," he replied.

"Except for your grey eyes," she reminded him.

"All the more reason to stay clear of those torches."

"All right, where do we find a victim?" she asked.

Athgar peered into the gloom wishing, not for the first time, that he had the Dwarf's excellent night vision.

"I'm not sure," he finally admitted.

"If you were a soldier," asked Natalia, "where would you go to relieve yourself?"

"You mean if I had to take a piss?" he asked. "I suppose I'd find a tree somewhere. Ah, I see what you're getting at."

"Urine has a distinct smell," she said. "I think if we get close enough, we'd be able to detect its presence?"

"But soldiers will go anywhere," he replied.

"You forget," said Natalia, "this army is under the command of the father general. The Church is emphatic about some things, chief among them being the use of a designated area for Human waste."

"Why would they care?" he asked.

"They like to minimize the smells," she explained, "and they believe it can lead to sickness."

"The Church has some very strange ideas," he said.

"Be that as it may," she continued, "it means there is likely an area marked off for such things. If we can locate it, we might have better luck finding a victim."

"Very well," he said, "I'll keep my eyes... or rather, my nose open."

They skirted the edge of the camp, sticking to the tree line. It was quite late, and only a few soldiers wandered around, likely heading to or from guard duty. Reasoning that the camp would probably be upwind of the privy, they headed north.

Finally, after what seemed like an interminable search, they found what they were looking for. Someone had dug a small trench, into which Human waste and urine had been tossed. They settled down to wait for the inevitable visitor to arrive.

Athgar had no idea how long they sat there, but his legs began to cramp from his crouched position. He was about to stand and stretch when Natalia pointed out their target. A soldier had wandered over, carrying a spear along with a hooded lantern, which he placed on the ground before he raised his tunic and squatted.

Athgar was ready to release a torrent of fire, but Natalia halted him. He wanted to argue, then realized his spell would draw attention, so instead, he nodded for her to proceed.

She cast her spell, weaving an intricate pattern in the air before her. He could barely hear the words flowing from her mouth, but a moment later, the squatting man frosted up, as if winter had just caught up with him, and then fell to the side.

Athgar rushed forward, dragging the soldier back from the pit while Natalia took the lantern.

"He's dead," the Therengian declared.

"I would suspect no less," she replied, "but the real question is whether or not the clothes will fit me."

"Let's find out, shall we?" asked Athgar. He removed the man's helmet, then watched as Natalia fit it over her head.

"It's a little large," she said, "but I can make do."

Next, he examined the soldier's clothes. The man was wearing a padded overcoat, something with which Athgar was not familiar, but he managed to ascertain how it unfastened and then passed it to Natalia.

"It's a gambeson," she said, threading her arms into the sleeves. "It's a bit large for my size, care to join me?"

In answer, he merely handed her the spear, then took up the lantern, using the hood to direct the light from it away from their faces.

"Come on," he said, "it's time we patrolled this camp."

They walked into the field as bold as brass.

"The trick to this," Natalia said quietly, "is to act like we belong."

Another guard came towards them, and Athgar avoided making direct eye contact. Closer they came, until they drew parallel to each other, and Athgar started to sweat. The soldier, however, merely nodded a greeting and went on his way, leaving the Therengian to draw a breath, unaware that he had been holding it.

"That was close," he mused.

They wandered past a large fire pit, around which soldiers struggled to sleep. Some had bedrolls, but the vast majority were simply laid out on the ground, a thin blanket all they had to keep the chill of the night from their bones.

"Strange to think we're here," he whispered, "walking among our enemies."

Natalia waited till they were out of earshot before replying, "I don't see any worthwhile targets."

"Let's head over to those pavilions," he suggested.

They continued on their way, making a wide turn to avoid an abrupt change of direction. The pavilions came into view, the largest one lit by lanterns that hung inside.

Athgar led them past the two Temple Knights that stood watch at the door, and they circled around to the back. Here, they cast about, looking for any observers and, having found none, crouched by the tent and listened as inside, two men discussed something.

"It'll be over soon enough," said a voice Athgar instantly recognized as Father General Gibert's.

"That's easy for you to say," said the other, slightly younger voice. "It wasn't your soldiers that took casualties."

"Still," soothed the father general, "once we reach the Orc village, we'll quickly brush aside any opposition."

"I don't know why we need to involve the Orcs," said the younger. "Isn't our target north of here?"

"It is," the Holy Man replied, "but we cannot afford to leave witnesses. They say the Orcs know everything that happens in their forest."

"Perhaps," offered the younger man, "we could reason with them?"

"For Saint's Sake," said Gilbert, "grow some balls, will you? These are Orcs, nothing more."

"They've been quite effective so far," the younger man complained.

"A resistance that will soon fade," said the father general.

"And their shamans?"

"That's what Master Verineth is here for. You worry about getting us there, my men will take care of the rest."

"Your men?" asked the warrior. "You mean the duke's men, don't you?"

"Let us not argue over semantics," said the father general.

"Does that mean you'll be committing the Temple Knights?"

"Not unless it's absolutely necessary."

"Then what is this all about?" asked the younger man.

There was a noticeable delay as Athgar watched a shadow tip the contents of a tankard down its throat.

"This is the duke's operation," Gilbert finally answered. "The Church is merely here to supervise and offer support where it may."

"We both know that's not true," said the younger voice. "You intend to keep the Godstone for yourself, don't you!"

"And why not?" said the father general. "After all, who better than the Church to wield such power? If the duke took possession, all the neighbouring kingdoms would covet it. Don't worry, your duke will be properly compensated."

"And where does the mage fit in?"

"His family is a benefactor of the Church," Gilbert explained.

"How do we know he can be trusted?" asked the younger voice.

"I have worked with him before," the father general revealed, "in the crusades."

"To the north?"

"Yes, past the Grey Spires. I have seen Verineth use his powers before, at the Battle of Umrault."

"I take it that was a victory."

"Yes, the Therengians fled like rats from a sinking ship."

Athgar looked at Natalia, his eyes wide with the revelation. She pointed to the distant trees then pointed upward, to where the sky was starting to lighten. Dawn would soon be upon them, and they must be on their way.

They made their way back through the camp, the lantern swinging as they ambled onward. When they finally reached the edge of the trees, Athgar placed it on the ground while Natalia tossed the spear aside and removed her helmet. He helped her out of the coat and then they made their way through the dense underbrush until they were far from the sounds of a camp rousing from slumber.

"Therengians," said Athgar, "I thought we were the last."

"Could it be your companions, from Athelwald?" Natalia asked.

"No," he replied. "They fled eastward, but Father General Gilbert referred to events north of the mountains."

"We shall have to investigate further," said Natalia.

"Yes," he agreed, "but first, we must help the Orcs."

"I'm afraid our infiltration didn't work," she said. "We didn't do any damage at all."

"True," he admitted, "but now we have confirmation that the family is wrapped up in all of this."

"We knew that already," she said, "as soon as we saw Verineth."

"Yes, but we didn't know to what extent. Now we know the family is involved with the crusades. What I don't understand is why?"

"More questions for the future," she said.

They cut north, then after some time, turned eastward, well clear of the enemy lines.

"What do you know of the crusades?" asked Athgar.

"Not much," said Natalia. "We were told that worshippers of an old cult lived there. The Church is trying to convert them."

"Convert?" he said. "Into what?"

"Followers of the Saints," she said.

"Why? Just because they worship the old Gods? I thought the Church was all about living in harmony with other religions?"

"It is," she said, "but the heathens, as the father general called them, were said to be cult worshippers. That term is usually reserved for practitioners of Death Magic."

"But they're Therengians," he said, "you heard him say so."

"Yes," she agreed, "but I doubt that knowledge is public. If it were, it would create a huge outcry."

"Would it?" said Athgar. "I have my doubts. My people have been blamed for many things over the generations, much like the Orcs."

"Let's concentrate on the here and now," she said. "We're far too distant to do anything about it at this precise moment."

They continued their trek eastward, towards Ord-Kurgad.

PREPARATION

Spring 1104 SR

K argen stamped his foot on the walkway, peering out over the palisade.

"*It is a sturdy construction,*" he said.

"*Yes,*" agreed Laruhk, "*and it will give our warbows a clear view of their targets, once they arrive. Athgar was wise to suggest it.*"

"*How close are they?*" asked the chieftain.

"*They shall likely be here at first light tomorrow,*" replied Laruhk.

"*That close? I had hoped our traps would have had a greater delaying effect.*"

"*We caught several with snares and pits,*" said Laruhk, "*but these Humans learn quickly.*"

"*Have the younglings left?*" asked Kargen.

"*Yes, along with the elders. Only hunters remain now, along with our shamans.*"

Kargen stared at the distant edge of the clearing.

"*Is something wrong?*" asked Laruhk.

"*I remember running through that field as a youngling,*" Kargen mused. "*My mother would always take me with her when she picked berries.*"

"*As did mine,*" said Laruhk, "*but I remember your mother as a hunter, not a gatherer.*"

"*It is true,*" said Kargen, "*she was one of the best hunters in the entire village, and yet she always found time to pick berries with me.*"

"*With you?*" said Laruhk. "*I somehow think you spent more time eating them than gathering. Your memory is very selective."*

Kargen grinned, *"So it is."* The Orc Chieftan fell silent a moment, deep in his thoughts.

Laruhk moved up beside his friend, *"We have been through a lot, you and I."*

"So we have," Kargen agreed.

"I even let you bond with my sister."

"You let me?" said Kargen. *"I do not think that is the way that Shaluhk would see it."*

"Doubtless," agreed Laruhk, *"but she is younger than I and less likely to know of such things."*

Kargen looked at his comrade then returned to gazing out over the wall.

"I am going to miss this place," said Kargen. *"No longer will we be able to hunt these trails."*

"No," Laruhk agreed, *"but hopefully, our new home, wherever that ends up being, will prove abundant in game."*

"If the Ancestors will it. I suppose the worst part will be starting all over again. We will have no huts, no well, and no palisade."

"Then we shall build a new home, finer than this," declared Laruhk.

"Finer?"

"Yes, bigger and better, and we will have a walkway like this. I like it."

"It is quite useful," noted Kargen, *"but we have to get our people there first. That is the most difficult task of all."*

"No," said Laruhk, *"first we must defeat our enemy, or there will be no one to find this new home of ours."*

"You speak with wisdom."

Laruhk looked at the chief in surprise, *"And here I thought you were the great speaker."*

"No," said Kargen, *"I am merely the guardian of the tribe."*

"Well then, guardian," said Laruhk, *"we had best cease this maudlin discussion and get back to work."*

"Maudlin?" Kargen replied.

"It is a word I heard Nat-Alia use. I quite like it."

"At this rate," said Kargen, *"we will ALL end up speaking the Human tongue."*

"Hold your hand up higher, Nat-Alia," said Shaluhk, "you need to block."

"It feels so awkward," the mage replied.

"That is because your body has not spent a lifetime learning it. Do you find your own spells difficult?"

"No," said Natalia, "I could almost cast them in my sleep."

"Let us hope not," said Shaluhk, "or you might wake up to a frozen bondmate."

Natalia laughed, Shaluhk quickly joining in.

"Now," the Orc continued, "let us try once more. I shall slowly strike at you with my axe, you try to block my attack."

"Go ahead," said Natalia.

Shaluhk stepped forward, bringing her hatchet down in slow motion. Natalia moved her own axe to block the attack, causing the heads to strike one another, eliciting a shriek from the mage.

"I wonder if a spear would be a better weapon for you," said the Orc. "You seem to lack the strength for an axe."

"How strong should I be?" asked Natalia, lowering her weapon.

"Well," said Shaluhk, moving closer, "let us see." She pinched Natalia's arm, feeling the muscle. "Hmmm," she said.

"What does 'hmmm' mean?" asked the mage.

"On second thought, I think you should avoid the spear."

"But you just said-"

"I know what I said, but you are weak. Do not take it personally, all of your race is weak."

"Even Athgar?" asked Natalia.

"Oh, yes," agreed Shaluhk, "it is like having an underfed younger brother. Do you Humans not eat properly?"

"We manage to get by," said Natalia.

"How Humans dominated the land is beyond me," the shamaness confessed.

"We procreate rapidly," said Natalia.

"Procreate?" the Orc replied. "That is not an expression I am familiar with."

"It means we have children quickly," said Natalia.

"Ah," said Shaluhk, "then maybe that is the problem, you need to have a youngling. Will that make you stronger?"

Natalia blushed, "I've only known Athgar for a few months. Give us some time, won't you?"

"Why?" asked the shamaness. "Does it take a long time for Humans to engage in the act of... what did you call it?"

"Procreation," the mage replied, "and to answer your question, no, it does not take a long time, but not every act results in a birth."

"Ah, I see now," said Shaluhk, "you are not in heat."

"Pardon me?"

"Your body is not ready to receive his seed. Do not worry, it will catch up in time."

"Catch up?" said Natalia.

"Yes, to your heart. It is obvious that you and Athgar love one another, but you must wait for your body to be ready before you can bear a youngling."

"I'm not sure this is a subject we need to talk about at this time," said Natalia. "Can we get back to learning how to fight?"

"I think," said Shaluhk, "that there is little more I can teach you in the time we have left. I think it best if you rely on your magic. You are, after all, quite powerful."

"Now that," said Natalia, "is the first sensible thing I've heard you say all morning."

"Tell me," asked the shamaness, "other than to create swirling knives of ice, what can you do?"

"Many things," said Natalia. "For example, I can purify water, removing things like poison or disease."

"A useful thing, but I doubt it will come up in the impending fight."

"No," agreed Natalia, "I suppose not. My usual spell for a battle is ice shards."

"That sounds interesting," noted Shaluhk.

"It is my signature spell."

"Meaning?"

"Meaning that I am very familiar with it due to casting it so often.

"From the sounds of it," said Shaluhk, "I assume it allows you to throw shards of ice towards the enemy?"

"It does," admitted the mage. "It can be quite effective against an individual, but not so much against a massed army. Perhaps a wall of ice might be more useful."

"Now that sounds more like it," said Shaluhk. "You could use it to reinforce a wall, could you not?"

"I could," Natalia agreed, "or even to funnel the invaders."

"How long would such a wall last?"

The Water Mage looked skyward. "In this weather? Likely only long enough for one assault, and Verineth would be able to destroy it easily enough."

"How?" asked Shaluhk. "Is he capable of dispelling your magic?"

"No," said Natalia, "but the wall of ice can be destroyed by damaging it, or applying excessive heat. I'm afraid it's not very useful against a Fire Mage."

"My Ancestors tell of a spell that can conjure the spirits of ancient warriors," said Shaluhk, "though neither I nor Uhdrig can cast that spell. Do you have anything similar?"

Natalia thought back to her days at the Volstrum. Was there something she was forgetting?

"I seem to recall something about conjuring an ice golem," said Natalia at last, "but I don't remember the details."

"What is an ice golem?" asked Shaluhk.

"It is a creature made entirely of ice."

"And is it a living creature?" the Orc asked.

"No," said Natalia, "it is what we call a construct. It is animated by the will of the caster, but it has no mind of its own."

"I take it they are dangerous?"

"Very," said Natalia, "but such things were considered too powerful for mere students."

"What if we could help you remember the spell?" offered Shaluhk.

"How would you do that?" said the mage. "You weren't there at the Volstrum."

"No," agreed Shaluhk, "but we have access to the collective wisdom of our Ancestors. Maybe one of them can help you unlock this memory."

"But you practise Life Magic," said Natalia, "and Artoch the magic of fire. To the best of my knowledge, neither one of those can create a construct."

"While it is true that Life Mages can only call on Ancestors, practitioners of the flame can conjure fire snakes and phoenixes, not too different from your idea of a golem."

"I suppose that's true," said Natalia, "and yet the magic of water is very different from that of fire."

"That is all true," noted the Orc, "but not all our Ancestors were masters of flame."

"Are you saying that some of them might have been Water Mages?" asked Natalia.

"It is possible," said Shaluhk, "but I can not say for certain. My training as a shamaness is incomplete, but Uhdrig knows more of such things. She might be able to call on our Ancestors to help you unlock that which is buried within your memories."

"It's worth a try," said Natalia.

Father General Gilbert knelt before the altar.

"Most venerable Saint Cunar," he prayed, "guide me in this trying time. Give me the strength to carry out your will and bring blessed clarity to the unbelievers. Heed me this day, and I will bring glory to your most Holy Order."

He rose, his bones creaking as he stood. Gilbert had been a warrior his entire life, devoted to his one true calling, that of the Church. He had spent a lifetime honing his skills, skills which had been tested on the battlefield again and again. Deep down, he knew that what he was doing here was wrong, but he consoled himself that this minor transgression would, inevitably, bring greater glory to the Church and lead to its eventual victory over the Halvarian Empire, which stood ready to engulf the Petty Kingdoms. He exited the tent, emerging into the bright morning light, his two guards presenting their swords in salute. Ignoring them, he made his way to the command tent, where the Duke of Krieghoff's commander, Berkath Thuleman, waited, along with the mage, Verineth Sartellian.

He found them, as expected, gathered around a small table, upon which lay a hastily drawn map of the area. They both looked up at his entrance, their discussion interrupted by his arrival.

"Good morning, gentlemen," Father General Gilbert began, "I trust you both slept well?"

"We did indeed," said Commander Thuleman, "and we are eager to see what you have planned this day."

Gilbert smiled, moving to stare down at the map. "I see your scouts have been busy, Commander. Can you vouch for the veracity of this map?"

"It is as good as we are likely to have," Thuleman responded, "but I fear the woods plays havoc with any degree of accuracy."

"Have they managed to locate the enemy encampment?"

"They have," the commander agreed.

"What can you tell us of its defences?" asked the father general.

Commander Thuleman pulled forth a folded paper from his belt, consulting his notes. "They have a ditch and palisade," he said at last, "though it is a bit crude in construction, with no sign of towers."

"And the entrance?"

"A simple opening," said the commander, "which they've seen to block up with a makeshift gate. Nothing that would prove too much of an obstacle for determined men."

"This is all good news," said Gilbert. "Tell me, Verineth, have you anything to add?"

"Little, I'm afraid," replied the mage, "though Orcs are known to employ spellcasters of their own. They call them shamans, but they are typically quite weak compared to Human users of magic."

"What type of magic can we expect?" asked the father general.

"Life Mages, mostly," said Verineth, "though my understanding is that this tribe, the Orcs of the Red Hand, is known to employ Fire Mages."

"Fire mages?" said Gilbert. "That surprises me."

"Don't let it affect your judgement," said Verineth, "I can easily handle whatever they throw at us. I shall eliminate the threat, do not fear."

"How do you intend to do that?" asked the commander. "They will be behind their walls!"

"I shall lure them out," said Verineth.

"Can't you just lob fire into their huts?" asked the father general.

"I'm afraid you have no concept of how magic works," said the mage. "I have to be able to see an individual to target my spell, and fire does not 'lob' over walls, it requires a direct line of sight."

"Very well," said the father general, "then I shall leave that in your very capable hands."

"Might I ask how you plan to begin, Your Grace?" asked the commander.

"Our first job will be to encircle them," explained Gilbert, "thus cutting off any possibility of retreat. While this is underway, we shall send archers forward to keep the enemy busy."

"How long will that take?" asked Verineth. "I'm eager to come to grips with them."

"You must be patient," explained the father general. "The encirclement will take some time, and once it is done, we must prepare our own defences, lest the Orcs sortie out."

"I see," said Commander Thuleman. "Is that when the assault will commence?"

"No," said Gilbert. "Once darkness falls, we will begin loosing off flaming arrows. That was Verineth's idea."

"Yes," agreed the mage, "that should keep their fire shaman busy trying to extinguish any flames that may catch."

"It will also have the added effect of keeping their people up all night," added Father Gilbert, "making them exhausted by morning when we finally commence the assault."

"And how will we assault?" asked Commander Thuleman.

"I have men already working on ladders," said the father general, "in addition to a battering ram. We shall assault the walls at the same time we attack the main gate. That will keep the defenders stretched to the limit."

"You seem to have thought of everything," noted Thuleman, "and yet I see no mention of our Fire Mage, or your Temple Knights, for that matter. Are the duke's men to take the brunt of the fighting, then?"

"Only for the first part of the assault," said Gilbert. "When your men manage to open the gate, my Temple Knights will reinforce the attack. Once they are through the gates, there will be little effective resistance. You may rest assured, we shall have this place in our hands by nightfall tomorrow."

"And then?" asked Verineth.

"Then," continued Father General Gilbert, "we shall dispatch the remaining Orcs with all haste and march to the dig site which lies only a short distance away."

"And you're convinced this plan will result in victory?" asked Commander Thuleman.

"Of course, aren't you?" said Gilbert. "These are Orcs, little more than savages. They wear no armour and carry only crude weapons. They are no match for Temple Knights."

"This dig site," said Verineth, "you're confident we can extract the Godstone before the Duke of Holstead gets wind of it?"

"Based on Schoenbach's report," noted the father general, "the ore is near the surface and mostly intact. Extraction should take little more than a few days. We will be well on our way back to Caerhaven before Holstead's Duke is even aware of our presence."

"Have you specific orders?" asked Commander Thuleman.

"I have," confirmed Gilbert, reaching into his glove to extract a folded paper. "This details out the numbers required for each stage of the operation. I'll leave it in your hands to assign individual companies to the tasks."

Commander Thuleman took the note, examining the writing carefully. "You don't want the crossbowmen moving up with the archers?" he asked.

"No," said Father Gilbert, "they will support the attack on the gate, once it commences. I'll need them to keep the Orcs busy while the battering ram is moved into place."

"And what will you require of me?" asked Verineth.

"I hadn't counted on the necessity of your magic," admitted the father general, "but should the Orc shamans make themselves known, I'll leave it to you to handle them."

"Of course," the mage replied. "Now, if you'll excuse me, I must prepare myself. I'd like to go over my arsenal of spells and contemplate how I might best use them."

"You need to memorize spells?" asked Commander Thuleman.

"Memorize? Don't be absurd. I can cast spells whenever I wish, I merely like to think over how they might best be employed. Do you not think of tactics when your troops attack?"

"Naturally," the commander responded.

"Well," continued Verineth, "the same is true for me. I have learned much from my long and distinguished career, including many ways to employ my spells to greater effect."

"Then we shall let you be about your business," said Gilbert. "I will let you know if your services are required later."

Verineth bowed politely, then fled the tent, hurrying back to his own pavilion where he paused, taking a moment to examine the two guards at his door. They were sworn men of the family, and utterly trustworthy, having served him for years.

"Let none enter," he ordered, making his way inside. He moved directly to the chest that lay at the foot of his bed. Opening it, Verineth retrieved a small bowl, filling it with a green powder that he poured from a bottle. His actions complete, he carried it to his bed, placing it down carefully, then knelt before it.

Verineth closed his eyes, digging deep to bring forth words of power. As they trickled off his tongue, he felt the hairs on the back of his neck begin to rise as his power grew. Moments later, he uttered a final phrase and a flame leaped to life in the bowl, producing a green light that lit the confines of the tent. He sat staring at the magical fire, waiting patiently until a face appeared within it.

"Yes?" spoke a woman's voice.

"It is Verineth," the mage declared, "contacting you to report to Marakhova."

"One moment," the woman replied, "and I shall fetch her."

The face disappeared while the Fire Mage waited, framing his report in his mind. Finally, the familiar countenance of Marakhova Stormwind appeared before him.

"Mistress," said Verineth, "I am happy to report that we have arrived."

"Excellent," said Marakhova, "and the attack?"

"It will commence in full tomorrow morning," replied the mage, "and the father general expects it to be over by nightfall."

"And Natalia?"

"I have heard nothing," said the Fire Mage.

"You must be careful," warned Marakhova, "her companion is a Therengian, and may have contact with the Orcs."

"You suspect they may be here?" said Verineth. "I find that hard to believe."

"They have already cost us one Sartellian in Corassus," she warned him. "Make sure you do not provide them with another."

"This changes things considerably," said the Fire Mage.

"I'm sure you're more than equal to the task," said Marakhova. "And I needn't remind you what's at stake here. Secure the Godstone, and I'll see to it you are elevated to the senior ranks of the family."

"I shall do as you bid," said Verineth.

"Good," added Marakhova Stormwind. "Contact me again when this whole affair is over with."

Her face disappeared, leaving Verineth staring into the verdant flame.

SURROUNDED

Spring 1104 SR

Laruhk turned for a moment, hefting a spear at an archer who was following too closely. It struck the man in the thigh, causing him to fall to the ground, his cry echoing through the clearing. The Orc looked to either side, where his companions were falling back towards Ord-Kurgad.

Durgash took an arrow to the bicep, causing him to grunt in pain and drop his axe. Clutching his wounded arm with his other hand, he kept running.

The enemy was pressing in now, their bowmen stretched out in a long line. Laruhk wasn't sure how many there were, but their constant rain of arrows was peppering the ground. He resumed his run, sprinting for the gate. Before him went the others, making their best speed possible under the circumstances. Kragor and Khurlak were dragging a wounded Orc between them, but then an arrow took the poor fellow in the back, silencing him forever. They dropped their burden, rushing to the open gate.

Laruhk was in the rear, urging the others forward. He spotted Athgar and Kargen waiting in the open doorway, bows held ready and aimed directly at him. He dropped to the ground and arrows sailed over him, their impact clearly heard as his pursuer went down.

He instantly rose, pushing his body to its limits, and crossed the remaining distance, rushing through the gate just before it was closed by four massive Orcs who held it while a fifth dropped the crossbar.

"That was close, my friend," said Kargen, speaking the common tongue for Natalia's benefit.

Shaluhk, who was tending to Durgash's injured arm, looked over to her brother.

"That was reckless," she chided. "You could have gotten yourself killed."

"Nonsense," Laruhk replied, "I can look after myself. I am the firstborn, remember?"

"I could hardly forget," said Shaluhk, "you remind me so often."

"I hope," said Natalia, "that all this argument is not for my sake."

"No," said Athgar, "these two always fight. It's their way."

"So it is," agreed Kargen. He finally lowered his bow, turning to Laruhk. "Report," he commanded.

"We lost six," said Laruhk, "and five more wounded, though my sister is healing them even as we speak."

"And the enemy?" asked Kargen.

"It is hard to be certain, but I believe we killed or injured at least twelve."

"I was hoping for better," said Kargen.

Laruhk bristled, "We killed two for every one of ours that was lost!"

"So you did," said Kargen, "but they outnumber us. At such a rate of exchange, we will run out of hunters long before they do."

"There is only so much we can do," defended Laruhk.

"I know," said Kargen, "and you bear no blame, but we must improve our odds."

Kragor stepped forward, "Let me take my warbows to the wall, my chieftain. I shall drive the enemy archers back to the edge of the trees."

"Very well," said Kargen, "but be careful, even though our bows are powerful, they are many, and we are few."

Kragor bowed his head, then turned and ran off, yelling out orders in Orcish.

"Get some rest, Laruhk," ordered Kargen, "I shall need you at your strongest. You must assume command while I sleep later."

"Who can sleep with all this going on?" asked Laruhk.

"We must all rest while we can," said Kargen. "Is this not true, Nat-Alia?"

"It is," she responded. "The enemy will try to wear us down. They'll keep us busy all night long, then, when we're all tired and not thinking at our best, they'll attack."

"Very well," said Laruhk, "I shall try to get some sleep, but you must promise to wake me the moment the Humans attack."

"I will," said Kargen, "but you must think of the enemy not as Human, but simply as the force we must destroy. It does an injustice to Athgar and Nat-Alia."

"Nonsense," defended Laruhk, "they are both members of this tribe now and as such are considered Orcs. There is no harm in calling the enemy Humans."

"That's fine with me," said Athgar.

"Yes," agreed Natalia, "and we take no offense."

"Very well," Kargen surrendered, "it shall be so."

"Have you given any more thought to our suggestion?" asked Shaluhk.

"To call on the Ancestors?" said Kargen. "That will depend on the recommendation of Uhdrig. She is the only one that knows if such a thing is even possible."

"Then you will not stop her?" asked Natalia.

"Stop her?" said Kargen. "It is not for me to dictate what she does or does not do. That decision is hers alone. In any event, even if Uhdrig does support the endeavour, it will likely be some time before the ritual could be performed. Shaluhk has expended much of her energy in healing the wounded. I suspect she would have to be at full power to attempt such a perilous task."

"You think it dangerous?" asked Athgar.

"I think it has never before been attempted," said Kargen, "and that alone tells me it is likely done at great risk."

"I still don't understand it," said Athgar.

"My understanding," said Kargen, "is that they will call on an Ancestor to possess Shaluhk's body, allowing them to cast a spell to recover Nat-Alia's memory."

"I'm not sure I like the sound of that," noted Athgar.

"Nor I," admitted Kargen, "but it is not our choice to make. Only Shaluhk and Nat-Alia can make that determination."

A slight swishing noise echoed off the wall, followed by a thud as an arrow struck a distant target. They all looked up at the palisade wall, where Kragor and his Orcs were loosing arrows.

One or two enemy arrows flew past in response, but the mighty warbows, fired by expert hunters, soon forced them back out of range. The area fell silent as the Orcs peered over the edge of the palisade, seeking targets in vain.

"I suspect that will hold them till nightfall," called out Kragor.

"Yes," agreed Kargen, "but they will use the cover of darkness to return."

"We have bought some time," said Athgar, "but Kragor will have to stay vigilant in case they try advancing again."

Kargen looked at the wall. "What do you have to say to that, Kragor?"

"I am ready for them," the Orc archer replied.

"I didn't know so many of you spoke common," said Natalia.

"Only a handful," said Kargen, "those that trade with Humans. Laruhk and I were the first, along with Durgash. Of course, once Athgar came to stay with us, more grew interested. There are now nearly a dozen of us, all told." He leaned closer to Natalia, lowering his voice, "It also allows us to talk among ourselves without other Orcs listening in. I suppose that is why Shaluhk insisted I teach her."

"You've done well," said Natalia, "you're all quite easy to understand."

"It is an easy language to learn," said Kargen, "though names can be difficult, yours in particular, Nat-Alia."

"Athgar has taught me some Orcish," she replied, "but I'm afraid I'm not nearly as fluent as he is."

"You shall learn it in due course," said Shaluhk. "After all, you are a member of the tribe now."

"Yes," said Kargen, "as long as the tribe still exists. We may all be dead in a week, in which case it won't matter."

"Yes," said Shaluhk, "but then we will all join our Ancestors and be together again."

"Our children will remember us," said Kargen, "and that is all we can ask."

"Where is little Agar?" asked Natalia.

"With the rest of the younglings. We have sent them deep into the woods for their own safety. Do not worry, they are protected by a small group of hunters. If we should fail here, they will take them northward into the mountains."

"Let's hope it doesn't come to that," said Athgar.

"It has grown strangely quiet," called out Kragor.

They all strained to listen, but the only sound that came to their ears was the gentle rustling of leaves.

"It is eerie," said Shaluhk.

"And far too quiet," noted Natalia.

A flurry of birds exploded into the air some distance off, eliciting a shout of alarm from one of the hunters on the wall. They flew off to the north like some great portend, and then a distant thud echoed through the forest.

"Axes," said Kargen, "they must be cutting down trees."

"That makes sense," noted Natalia. "They're going to need a ram to batter down the gate."

"Yes," agreed Athgar, "but I wouldn't put it past them to build ladders."

"You think they mean to climb the walls?" asked Laruhk.

"Only a fool would count on one method of attack," noted Natalia, "and

I would say this confirms that the father general has some experience where battles are concerned."

"Don't forget Verineth," added Athgar. "He has also seen many battles, you said so yourself."

"Yes," agreed Natalia, "and I'm afraid that the two of them, combined, are far more experienced in this sort of thing than any of us."

"Then how do we out-think them?" asked Shaluhk.

"We do the one thing they can not," said Kargen, "we think like Orcs."

"That's worked well so far," said Athgar, "but our enemy adapts quickly."

"And so shall we," Kargen assured him.

Athgar was woken by the firm grip of Laruhk.

"It has started," the Orc said. "We need you to come and assist Artoch."

"Why?" asked Athgar. "What's happening?"

"As soon as darkness fell, the enemy started firing flaming arrows into the village in an attempt to set the huts ablaze. Artoch is doing what he can to extinguish the fires, but another master of flame would ease his burden."

"Very well," replied Athgar, "I'll be there in a moment."

Laruhk left him to rise from his slumber. He doused his head in a bowl of water, using the chill of it to clear his sleep-addled mind.

"Shall I come, too?" asked Natalia.

"No," said Athgar, "conserve your energy for later. This is only the beginning." He instinctively grabbed his axe, then left the hut.

Natalia tried to go back to sleep, but the thought of Athgar labouring away to stop the fires kept her mind fully occupied. Finally, unable to halt her worrying, she rose, making her way outside to witness many Orcs running back and forth, carrying leather buckets of water to put out the smaller fires while Artoch and Athgar managed the larger ones.

Natalia sized things up quickly, noting the length of time that it took the Orcs to pull water from the well. She picked an open spot in the centre of the village and called out to Athgar.

"Tell them to bring the buckets to me," she yelled.

Athgar translated her words to Orcish, and the buckets were carried and laid before her. She traced an intricate design in the air, calling on arcane forces, and when she pointed downward, the buckets began filling up with water. The Orcs quickly picked up their speed, carrying them away to replace them with empty buckets. Soon they reached a comfortable pace, Natalia filling the buckets as they appeared, and the Orcs carting them off.

Athgar stood before Uhdrig's hut, where a flaming arrow had struck the very top, quickly setting the thatching alight and gushing thick smoke upward. He cast a spell, dampening the flames, as one last puff of smoke rose into the sky.

The arrows appeared to slacken and then, finally, halt altogether. Everyone stood still, waiting for the next assault to begin, but nothing came. Instead, a distant thumping sound echoed through the trees.

Natalia looked at Athgar.

"Drums, I think," he said.

"Likely to keep us awake," she offered.

"It's effective," said Athgar, "I'll give them that. I don't think I could sleep with that racket going on."

"That's precisely what they want," she said.

"What about their own troops?" he asked. "Won't they have the same problem?"

"Possibly," she said, "but they might have moved their camp farther back, out of earshot."

"What can we do about it?"

"Nothing really," she mused. "It's too bad we didn't have an Air Mage, or we could have dampened the sound."

"Yes," Athgar agreed, "or an Earth Mage to help with our defences. Actually, any kind of mage would have been helpful or even just soldiers. It seems like we're all alone here, and hopelessly outnumbered."

"You forget," said Natalia, "I'm a Stormwind."

"And Verineth is a Sartellian," added Athgar.

"True," she admitted, "but if I could conjure an ice golem, it would make a huge difference."

"Just how powerful would this golem of yours be?" he asked.

"I can't say for certain. Mistress Nina, who told us of it, said it was one of the most powerful spells a Water Mage could use."

"How does it work?" he asked. "Does it just rampage around, killing everything in sight? Does it use a weapon, or bite things?"

"It's vaguely humanoid in shape," she said, "but the end of its arms are spikes of ice that can impale, much like spears. It's said that their attacks will penetrate even the toughest of armour."

"Even plate armour?" he asked.

"So I've been told," she replied, "but the cost of casting the spell is high."

"Meaning?"

"Meaning it would likely use up a good portion of my energy. You'd also have to make sure I stay conscious."

"Why," he asked, "what happens if you get knocked out?"

"The golem will just keep attacking and won't be able to distinguish friend from foe."

"Can it be dispelled?" asked Athgar.

"Only by me, or a more powerful Water Mage. Of course, it can be destroyed through damage. My understanding is that it can take quite a beating, but being made of ice, it's particularly susceptible to fire damage."

"So we have to keep it away from Verineth," said Athgar.

"Precisely."

"What does Uhdrig think of this plan?" he asked.

"I don't know," Natalia replied. "I believe Shaluhk was going to speak to her about it, but I haven't heard anything back yet."

"Perhaps you'd best go and seek her out. She likely has an answer, and things have grown quiet here, at least for now. You may not get a chance later."

She cast her eyes around the village, taking in the Orcs that had collapsed to the ground, exhausted by their efforts. "I suppose you're right," she admitted.

Natalia found them in Uhdrig's hut. The old shamaness sat before the fire, across from Shaluhk, both waiting while the Human took a seat.

"So," she said, "what have you decided?"

It was Uhdrig who spoke first. "Shaluhk and I have discussed this at length. Such a thing has not been attempted in living history."

"But it is possible?" asked Natalia.

"It is," the old shamaness replied, "but it is not without risk."

"What type of risk?"

"In order for this to work," continued Uhdrig, "we have to allow an Ancestor to enter Shaluhk's body. This will cause great distress to her, and the longer she remains possessed, the greater the damage will be."

"When you say damage, what do you mean, exactly?"

"Her physical form will begin to bruise, the skin rupture, and there may even be bleeding."

"Nothing beyond your ability to heal, I hope?" asked Natalia.

"We honestly do not know," said Shaluhk.

"No," agreed Uhdrig, "and we have no idea how long it would need her body to carry out the casting."

"The spell to retrieve my memories?"

"Yes," confirmed Uhdrig. "I have heard of this spell, of course, but I have never mastered it myself. My understanding is that it is a ritual, a spell cast over a longer period of time compared to a spell of battle. The length of time would likely depend on how deeply the memory is buried."

"But it can work?" pressed Natalia.

"Yes," said Uhdrig, "but it will be up to Shaluhk as to whether or not she will attempt it."

"I shall," declared Shaluhk. "The tribe needs all the help it can muster."

"I can't risk hurting you," said Natalia, "There has to be another way."

"None that I can see," said Uhdrig, "unless you know another, equally powerful spell?"

"We can't even be sure this would work," noted Natalia.

"I have communed with our Ancestors," said Uhdrig, "and they assured me that such a thing is not beyond the possible. I even have the name of she that we must summon, Khurlig."

"Khurlak's Ancestor?" asked Shaluhk.

"Indeed," said Uhdrig.

"I don't understand," said Natalia, "who is Khurlig?"

"One of our greatest shamans," said Uhdrig. "She lived more than two centuries ago. It is said that she had power over life and death itself."

"You mean she could bring people back from the dead?" asked Natalia. "I thought that was impossible."

"If the rumours are true, yes," said Uhdrig, "but stories are often shrouded by time. Only Khurlig herself could tell us if such things were true."

"And you think you can contact this Khurlig?" asked Natalia.

"Contacting her is not the problem," said Uhdrig, "whether or not she will agree to help us is the issue."

"Why wouldn't she?" asked Shaluhk. "Is not the safety of the tribe at stake?"

"It is," said Uhdrig, "but the spirits of our Ancestors often work in mysterious ways. Things that seem important to us hold little sway over them."

"And do the Ancestors have any advice for us?" asked Natalia.

"As a matter of fact, they do," said Uhdrig. "If we should decide to proceed with this ritual, we can do it only once, so we should choose the timing carefully."

"Only once?" said Natalia. "Why is that?"

"As I mentioned earlier, it will be hard on Shaluhk, as the recipient of the host Ancestor, but it will also be hard on you, Nat-Alia. Probing someone's memories can be difficult. If something goes wrong, your mind might end up permanently damaged. It should only be considered as a last resort."

"I am willing to give it a try if Shaluhk is," said Natalia.

"As am I," added Shaluhk.

"Very well," said Uhdrig. "I shall prepare everything that is needed for the ritual. When the time comes, you must seek me out here, and we will proceed. In the meantime, you should see to your other duties. The enemy will, no doubt, keep us on our toes, and we must be prepared."

ASSAULT

Spring 1104 SR

F ather General Gilbert peered into the early morning mist.
"Send them forward, Commander," he ordered.

"Aye, Your Grace," said Commander Thuleman, who rode off, issuing orders as he made his way through the camp. The sound of men rising to their feet along with the clatter of armour and weapons soon drifted back to them.

"I don't like this mist," said Verineth.

"It will hide our advance," declared the father general. "We'll be at the gate before they realize it."

"It will be barred," warned the mage.

"I'm counting on it," Gilbert replied. "That's why they'll be taking the ram forward. And as soon as that starts its business, we'll be assaulting the wall clear over on the other side of their palisade."

"A sound plan," noted Verineth. "My compliments, Your Grace. It seems you have outdone yourself this day. I trust I shall be remembered in this great victory of yours?"

"Of course," said Father General Gilbert, "I always give credit where it's due. I am fully aware of your influence, Lord Sartellian, and we welcome the chance to work with the family. They've been so good to the order in the past."

The mage nodded his head. "It is a mutually beneficial relationship," he admitted, "and one that I look forward to continuing."

Kragor let fly with an arrow, watching as it sank into a warrior's chest. Dozens of Humans were surging forward, struggling through the ditch with crude ladders held above them. Beyond, their archers had moved up, sending volley after volley towards the palisade, forcing the Orcs there to duck to avoid taking a hit.

Kragor knelt, nocked another arrow, then waited. The clatter of arrow-heads striking the wall was quite pronounced, and then the inevitable delay as they waited for the order to loose another round. The Orc popped up, taking only a moment to pick his target, and then let fly before he ducked back down, his ears listening to hear the distinctive thud as his aim struck true.

Suddenly, a roar came to Kragor's ears, followed by a series of solid thumps as ladders were laid against the palisade. The storm of arrows halted, and Kragor knew this was the moment when the true fight would begin. He tossed his warbow onto the walkway, and retrieved his axe, holding it two-handed, the better to sweep the wall. A hand appeared before him as someone struggled up the ladder. He struck out, severing three fingers and digging into the upright of the ladder. The enemy soldier let out a bellow of pain and fell backward, clutching his injured hand. The Orc struck the man climbing behind him, also knocking him from his perch.

Kragor used his axe to push on the rung of the ladder, but the weight of so many men made it impossible to budge. He looked down to see three more surging up, the first carrying a sword. The man's advance was awkward as he climbed one-handed, his weapon waving around menacingly before him.

The Orc waited, allowing the Human to reach the top of the ladder before he struck. Kragor lifted his axe high in the air and brought it crashing down onto the man's skull, splitting his helmet and sending a shower of blood and brains upon those below.

An arrow sailed past the Orc, but he ignored it, concentrating instead on the steady stream of warriors climbing up only to feel the bite of his axe.

Athgar heard the yelling and raced towards the wall, where he saw men and Orcs fighting. Somehow, the enemy had managed to scale the palisade already! He spotted Kragor only a moment before he fell beneath the onslaught, a man moving to stand over him, ready to deliver a death blow.

Athgar's hands went up as he called on his inner spark. Flames leaped from his fingers, streaming across the intervening space to splash onto the man's face. A scream erupted from the invader's mouth as his hands made a futile gesture to brush aside the magical flame.

The Orc rolled, striking out with his axe and driving it into his opponent's leg. The man fell to the ground with a scream, his blood spilling across the walkway.

Athgar rushed to the steps, ascending them two at a time, to come face to face with a burly soldier wielding a warhammer. The Therengian ducked as the man struck out, then thrust his hands out in front of him, sending a stream of fire forth that pushed his opponent back and ignited his crude armour. This, he followed with a kick to the chest, sending the man tumbling back over the palisade.

Athgar peered over the wall, examining the mass of soldiers below as they tried to climb the ladders. Pulling on his inner fire once more, he uttered words of magic. A small spark appeared in his hand, and he tossed it below, where it sank into the ground. Moments later, it erupted in flames, sending soldiers scattering in fear and igniting the ladder.

Artoch, Master of Flame, watched from the east wall. The fight to the west was dire, but Athgar had appeared, and the old Orc knew the invader's attack would fail. He turned his attention to the east, watching as men moved up. They had ladders, much like their companions to the west, and were advancing, ready to navigate the ditch.

He waited till they were crammed in tight, struggling to place their ladders against the wooden palisade. Calling on his inner spark, he pointed, using a controlled release to simply ignite a fire. It roared to life, fed by the animal fat and oil that had been strewn around the ditch.

Men screamed, abandoning their ladders and fleeing for the safety of their own lines. Artoch watched them dispassionately, wishing only that they had enough combustibles for the entire ditch, but the Ancestors were fickle in their gifts. This would have to do.

He spotted a group of soldiers rallying for another attack and let loose with a stream of fire. It fell short, sizzling the ground before them, but it was enough to dissuade them from advancing. They turned and ran, fearful of the fire that still burned fiercely.

Artoch returned his gaze to the palisade, but the fire below was contained and in no danger of spreading to the wooden walls. He reached into his satchel, withdrawing an apple and took a bite, relishing the taste as the juice dribbled down his face. This was only the beginning, he knew, and he must conserve his strength.

Natalia was running towards the gate, where the Orcs stood ready when she heard a massive thump as the great ram struck. It echoed through the village, lending a sense of doom to the battle.

A splintered cracking announced the door had broken, and she increased her pace, finally rounding a hut to see a group of Orcs pushing against the remains of the door, the end of a massive timber poking through. Natalia heard the grunt as the soldiers began pulling the ram back, readying for the blow that would finally break through.

She halted, taking a deep breath and calming herself. Magic required concentration, and she closed her eyes to clear her mind. She spoke the spell, and as her eyes snapped open and she pointed, the ram broke through again. This time it splintered more wood, forcing the centre of the doors to buckle, but then her spell took effect. It started simply enough, a frost that appeared on the end of the mighty ram, but it spread quickly, turning to ice, then crawling across the door, thickening as it went. The soldiers behind the gate tried to pull back the timber, but it was held fast in the spell's icy grip.

Natalia could feel the strain as the magic continued to pour through her, causing the ice to thicken even more. Outside, men's cheers quickly turned to dismay. Orders were barked out, and then the sounds of fleeing feet came to her ears, leaving the ram where it was frozen solid.

The soldiers ran past, eager to be free of the slaughter. Commander Thuleman, watching them retreat, grabbed one by the arm as he came closer.

"What happened?" Thuleman demanded.

"It was magic fire, sir, exploding all around us. They were tossing it from the walls."

"The Orcs must have had their shamans nearby," mused the commander.

"It was no Orc," the man swore, "but a Human."

"Are you sure?" pressed Commander Thuleman.

"I know an Orc when I see one," the man said, "and their Fire Mage was definitely no greenskin, he was a man, like us."

Thuleman released his grip. "Very well," he said, "get back to the camp and have someone see to your wounds."

"Yes, sir," the man replied, hobbling off.

The commander surveyed the area. The men were slowing down now that they were clear of the enemy bows, but this development troubled him deeply. Who was this Human that was helping their enemy, and why had he not been informed of his presence? Was the father general hiding something? Thuleman resolved to seek out the man immediately and so turned, heading for the command tent.

Father General Gilbert looked up as the duke's commander entered, a brief flicker of annoyance the only indication that he was aware of the intrusion.

"Your Grace," said Commander Thuleman.

"How goes the battle, Commander? Have we taken the wall?"

"No," the commander replied, "we most certainly have not. It appears the defenders have a Fire Mage among them, a Human, to be precise."

The father general met the commander's gaze. "Are you sure? We had no reports of such."

"I can assure you my men are not making this up. Who is this individual, and why were we not warned of his presence?"

"I'm not sure," confessed the father general. "We had best summon Lord Sartellian. Hopefully, he can provide the answers we seek." He turned to one of his guards, "Brother Terrence, go and find the mage. Tell him I would value his counsel."

The Temple Knight bowed, "Aye, Your Grace." He left quickly, and Father Gilbert returned his attention to the commander.

"Have you any word of the gate?"

"Not yet," the commander replied, "but I expect news shortly."

"Unless I miss my guess," continued the father general, "I think you'll find the gate attack failed."

"How could you know that?" asked the commander.

"I believe we are looking at outside interference. The truth is we've had some difficulties of late. There was some trouble at the duke's estate about a week ago. Are you familiar with it?"

"I recall something about an intruder," said Commander Thuleman. "Your Fire Mage had to use a spell, did he not?"

"He did," Gilbert confirmed. "In fact, there were two intruders, a man and a woman. At least one of them was a mage, she used a spell to destroy Verineth's phoenix."

"A Water Mage?" said Thuleman.

"Yes, how did you know?"

"I heard the stories, Your Grace. Do you think this Fire Mage is the other intruder?"

"You tell me," said the father general. "You are privy to the duke's investigation, are you not?"

"I am," said Thuleman.

"And what did he surmise?"

"Someone tried to impersonate Lord Verineth," the commander revealed. "At least one guest noted he was given a handshake that heated his hand. We didn't put much faith in the report at the time, but it appears obvious in retrospect. The big question is, who are these people?"

The sound of approaching footsteps announced the arrival of Verineth.

"Perhaps," noted the father general, "our distinguished colleague can shed some light on that."

The tent flap parted to reveal the Fire Mage. "You wished to see me, Your Grace?"

"Yes," said Gilbert, "it appears that a mage is working with the Orcs, a Human to be precise. I'd be interested in your thoughts as to who it might be?"

"Let me guess," said Verineth, "she used ice?"

"No," said the father general, "but you've now confirmed your knowledge of them. No, this defence was conducted by a man, a Fire Mage, to be exact. It would have been nice to have been informed of this before the attack."

Lord Verineth bowed his head slightly, "My apologies, Your Grace. The truth is there were some rumours, but I hadn't put much faith into them."

"Who are these individuals?" demanded the father general.

"The Fire Mage goes by the name of Athgar," said Verineth. "He is a Therengian, and, as you mentioned, a Fire Mage, though we don't know who trained him."

"And the woman?"

Verineth paused before answering, trying to be diplomatic. "A fairly powerful individual that goes by the name Natalia."

"And where is she from?" asked the commander.

"She is from Karslev," the mage replied.

"Karslev?" said Commander Thuleman. "That's where the great academy is located, isn't it?"

"Yes," agreed the father general, "the Volstrum. They train Water Mages there, don't they?"

"They do," admitted Verineth. "The truth is the woman's full name is Natalia Stormwind."

"Stormwind?" said Gilbert. "Surely not! Are you telling me we're facing off against the family?"

"I can assure you, Your Grace, that her actions are not sanctioned by the family. The woman has gone rogue."

"What do you mean 'rogue'?" demanded Commander Thuleman. "I thought the family kept tight control over their mages."

Verineth bristled. "We do, but I'm told she proved to be most resourceful in her escape."

The father general exploded into a tirade, "Then how did she end up with this Therengian? By the Saints, their very presence here jeopardizes the entire operation!"

"It is a minor inconvenience," soothed Verineth. "I can assure you I am more than capable of dealing with them, now that I know they're here."

"I should hope you are," said Gilbert. "This is much more than just a minor inconvenience, it's a major disaster."

"Come, come, Your Grace, it is not as bad as you surmise," said the Fire Mage. "I shall kill them both, and the matter will be settled."

"You'd best be successful," said the father general. "If they should survive and word gets out about this, it'll mean our heads." He looked around the room. "All of our heads."

"I shall be most vigilant," said Verineth.

"Oh, you'll be much more than vigilant," fumed Father Gilbert. "You're going to accompany the next assault, I insist on it."

Verineth's first impulse was to put the father general in his rightful place, but sombre reflection convinced him to adopt a different tactic.

"Of course," he said instead, "I would insist on nothing less."

"When will we next attack?" asked Commander Thuleman.

"This very afternoon," said the father general. "That will give our troops a chance to rest up after this morning's debacle."

A Temple Knight arrived, passing a note to the father general. The Holy Father scanned its contents carefully, then looked to his companions.

"It's confirmed," he said. "The attack on the gate has failed, and there are reports of magic."

Verineth smiled, this was good news indeed. With Natalia firmly within his grasp, he could secure his position within the family.

"Have you nothing to say?" asked the father general.

"It merely confirms what we already discussed, Your Grace. Fear not, I shall counter this rogue Water Mage with magic of my own. She will not last long against the onslaught of my full power."

"And what of this Fire Mage?" asked Commander Thuleman. "How do we deal with him?"

"I will deal with him in time," answered Verineth. "But if your men should encounter him again, send word to me, and I shall make it my priority to assist."

"An easy promise," grumbled the commander, "since it's my men, not yours that will be facing his magic."

"You seem to have an overinflated opinion of this man's abilities," said Verineth. "Magic is powerful, that I'll grant you, but it seldom affects more than one person at a time."

"He was tossing some kind of exploding flames," said Commander Thuleman. "Tell me how that only affects one person!"

The Fire Mage stared at him in surprise. "Are you sure?" he said. "That's not a spell they teach in Korascajan."

"Are you suggesting this Fire Mage was also trained by the family?" asked the father general.

"No," Verineth replied, "we know that for certain. A Therengian has never graced those hallowed halls."

"Why is that?" asked Commander Thuleman.

Verineth turned to the duke's man, forming his answer carefully. "The truth is that the Therengian mages were all destroyed centuries ago."

"And yet we have one fighting against us," said the father general. "I think you have seriously underestimated their resilience."

"Tell me," added the commander, "if one has survived, could there not be more?"

Verineth was about to say something, but the shock of the statement left him suddenly speechless. Could this be a resurgence of the Therengian mages? The family had eradicated them centuries ago, none could have survived, and yet here was this anomaly.

"Let us not get ahead of ourselves," said Verineth, finding his tongue. "If there are more Therengian mages, they certainly wouldn't be here. This lone man must be a remnant, nothing more than a freak of nature."

"And yet he's obviously trained," Commander Thuleman added. "Unless you think he's a wild mage?"

"Put such things from your mind," said Verineth. "Wild mages are the stuff of legend. In the real world, they amount to little more than curiosities, unable to properly harness their power."

"Did Korascajan teach you that?" asked the father general.

"Yes," said Verineth, "and the instructors there are the most knowledgeable scholars of magic on the entire Continent. It takes great discipline to learn to control the power of the elements, and fire is the most difficult of all to master. This Therengian you speak of likely has a few tricks he's learned, nothing more. Make your men aware of that, Commander Thuleman, and they will no longer fear him."

"I shall tell them," the commander promised, "but I cannot guarantee they will believe me."

"It will matter little," said the father general. "I only want them to carry out a feint when we next attack."

"You don't mean to take the wall?" asked Commander Thuleman.

"You can certainly try," the father general acknowledged, "but they are only to draw off defenders, the main attack will be on the gate. That's where I'll commit the Temple Knights."

"And if they should use their Water Mage to freeze the gate again?" asked the commander.

"Then I shall brush her aside," promised Verineth.

"Very well," Commander Thuleman responded, "I shall go and speak to my men. Let's hope we can still secure victory by nightfall."

"You can count on it," promised the father general.

Commander Thuleman departed, followed by the guards. This left Verineth alone with Gilbert, a fact not missed by His Grace.

"He can be a bit headstrong," the father general said, "but we need the duke's forces. I cannot capture the place with just my Temple Knights."

"Understood," said Verineth, "but I fear that if we push him too hard, he will break and go screaming back to his master. We cannot lose the support of the duke at this time."

"Don't you worry about the duke. I'm confident that he will see the wisdom in all of this. Rather, you should concentrate your efforts on defeating these two mages."

"It will be an absolute pleasure," said Verineth.

CORDELIA

Spring 1104 SR

"**M**y arse is sore," grumbled Belgast.

They had been riding for days, an endless journey that seemed, to the Dwarf at least, to pass nothing but a repetitive landscape.

"Are you sure we're not going in circles?" he said. "This land looks so familiar, I'm positive we've seen it before."

"Krieghoff lies on the plains of Amberly," said Sister Cordelia. "It is only to the north where hills can be seen."

"There are hills here," said the Dwarf.

"Yes," she agreed, "but they're small, nothing more than slight rises. You came from the north, did you not?"

"I did," he confessed, "my companions and I travelled south from Ostermund."

"Then you would be more familiar with the foothills than I," she said.

"How much farther, do you think, before we reach the army?"

"It shouldn't be long now," she said. "The tracks here are quite fresh, and I can see where they camped before they crossed the river."

Belgast slowed his pony, "River, you say?"

"Yes," Sister Cordelia confirmed, "it forms the border with Holstead. Why? Is that a problem?"

"I know this might sound a bit typical for a Dwarf," he said, "but I really don't like water."

"Don't worry," she soothed, "the army will have crossed at a ford, it should be quite shallow."

"How shallow?" he asked.

"Shallow enough for footmen to wade across, so you will be fine on your mount."

"Hmph," Belgast grunted.

The whole column slowed as the lead riders entered the water. They were soon wading across, the water rising to their horse's underbellies.

Belgast looked on with fear as the water rose. Soon it was lapping at his boots, and he had to fight the impulse to gallop to safety.

"Aha!" said Cordelia, exiting the river. "There was some sort of skirmish here."

"You think the Orcs were opposing the crossing?" asked Belgast, momentarily forgetting his peril.

"I do," she replied, "but likely only their scouts. If there had been a bigger battle, the ground would be more trampled."

She halted while the other riders cleared the ford and formed back up. Off in the distance, the echo of axes doing their work drifted towards them.

"That's them," said Belgast. "We're very close."

Sister Cordelia looked skyward, judging the sun's position. "It's almost noon. We should reach their camp with plenty of daylight remaining."

"What kind of reception do you expect?" he asked.

"Not a pleasant one, if that's what you're asking. The father general made it quite plain on our first visit that we were not welcome."

"And yet we return?" said Belgast.

"We will try one more time," said Sister Cordelia. "We must try to avoid bloodshed if at all possible."

"And if he doesn't listen?"

"Then we shall have to fight him," she said. "I pray it doesn't come to that, but we must be prepared to take whatever action is necessary to prevent this from escalating."

"Even taking up arms against the Cunars?" he asked.

"If necessary," she replied, urging her horse forward once more.

The path they followed was plain for everyone to see, for you cannot march an army through the woods and not leave a trail. It appeared to Belgast that they had only been in the woods for a short space of time when they finally found the army's pickets.

There was a brief exchange between the guards and Sister Cordelia, and then they were on their way once more, heading towards the main camp itself.

They soon found it, a large clearing littered with small campfires and, most importantly, the pavilions that housed its leaders. They rode into the paddock, where the Temple Knights of Saint Cunar watched them with interest.

Sister Cordelia dismounted, passing her reins to a fellow knight. "Wait here, Sister Evania," she said. "You're in charge while I go and implore the father general to halt this madness."

"Yes, Sister," the knight replied.

"Hold on," said Belgast, lowering himself from the saddle, "I'm coming with you."

Sister Cordelia waited till the Dwarf dismounted, then walked towards the command tent, easily identified by the guards that stood before it. She moved slowly, allowing the Dwarf to easily keep pace, then halted as she reached the guards.

"Sister Cordelia to see Father General Gilbert," she announced.

A guard nodded his head, then turned, entering the tent, while his companions eyed the newcomers uneasily. Moments later, the guard re-emerged.

"His Grace will see you now," he announced.

They stepped inside, instantly recognizing the father general.

"Your Grace," said Sister Cordelia in greeting.

"Sister Cordelia, isn't it?" said the father general.

"It is," she replied, "and this is Master Belgast Ridgehand."

Gilbert's eyes bored into the Dwarf, leaving Belgast with a feeling of dread.

"If you've come here to lecture me again," said Gilbert, "then you've wasted your time."

"I implore you to reconsider," she said. "This endeavour you have embarked on will do great damage to peace in this area, and may well result in a wider war."

"I think you have overestimated my influence," he said. "This is merely a small punitive expedition, designed to teach the greenskins not to raid our land."

"You and I both know that's not the truth," said Cordelia. "As you admitted when we last spoke, you're here after the Godstone."

"Yes," the father general said, "but to the average man, we are merely righting a wrong. Nobody will shed a tear for the Orcs. They have been seen as a pestilence for generations."

"And so you seek to kill them all?" said Cordelia. "I'm afraid I cannot permit it."

"You cannot permit it? Who do you think you are? I am a Father General of the Holy Order of Saint Cunar. That makes me the military leader for the Church in this region. Cross me, and it will have far-ranging consequences, both for you and for your precious order!"

"Nevertheless," said Sister Cordelia, "you have given me no choice."

"You make an empty threat," Father General Gilbert declared. "You cannot act against me, for to do so would violate your own sacred oath to serve the Church."

"I am sworn to Saint Agnes," she said, "and that oath takes precedence."

"Begone from here," commanded the father general, "or I shall have you arrested, Temple Knight or not, and take that Dwarf with you. He has no business being here with the army."

Sister Cordelia bowed her head. "So be it," she said, "but know that by your actions, you have set into motion a series of events that you will not be able to control."

She turned, leaving the tent quite abruptly. The action caught Belgast off guard, and he struggled to catch up, finally doing so as she made her way across the open field to where the horses waited.

"That was short," he said. "What do we do now?"

"We ride," she said, "and pray that the Saints will forgive us."

Athgar stared at the bodies before him. The fighting on the walls had been dire, and many Orcs had fallen. The shamans had done their best, but even magic has its limits, and now their forces were significantly depleted. Hearing footsteps, he turned to see Kargen coming towards him.

"How many?" asked the chieftain.

"Our losses were high," said Athgar, "but we inflicted much more damage on our attackers."

"Yes," the Orc agreed, "but was it enough? We can not afford to trade losses like this. Their numbers will soon tell. We barely have enough to repel another wall attack, let alone hold the gate. Next time they come, they will break through. Of that, I have no doubt."

"And we shall fight them to the bitter end," declared Athgar.

"It appears we have little choice," added Kargen. "They have us surrounded with no hope of escape."

"Have they tried to parley with us?" asked Athgar.

"No," Kargen replied, "nor would I expect them to. They are not intent on taking prisoners. I think the only negotiating they would be interested in would be our unconditional surrender."

"We still have our magic," offered Athgar.

"And they have still not used theirs," said the Orc. "Another assault is brewing, I can almost smell it, and this time they will come in much greater numbers."

"How do you know that?" asked Athgar.

"Simple, our enemy learns fast. We have revealed our secret weapons, you and Nat-Alia. When next they come, their mage will be among them, you can count on that."

"The big question is where they will attack," replied the Therengian.

"They have little choice," said Kargen. "I think they will assault the gate again, but this time they will be prepared. I suspect they will use those Holy Knights of theirs. If what you say about them is true, then they will not back down, nor will we be able to force them to retreat. The only way to defeat them will be to kill them all."

"A hard task, given their armour," said Athgar.

"Still, we must do our best. Perhaps, if we do well, we shall join our Ancestors in the hallowed halls of the Afterlife."

Uhdrig looked across the fire to where Natalia and Shaluhk both sat.

"Are you ready?" the elder shamaness asked them.

Natalia quickly glanced at Shaluhk, then returned her gaze once more to Uhdrig, "As ready as we can be."

"Very well," said Uhdrig. "When I begin communing with the Ancestors, I will pass into what looks like a trance. You will hear me speaking to them, but you will not be able to hear their replies. Should I succeed in convincing them of our dire situation, then I will ask Khurlig to occupy Shaluhk's body. At that point, what will happen is unknown, for this spell, to the best of my knowledge, has never been attempted."

The old shamaness closed her eyes and began speaking the ancient words of power. The entire hut seemed to close in as the shadows danced around them, the flames sputtering higher and higher. The chanting stopped, and Uhdrig's voice rose, though they could not make out the other end of the conversation.

"*Mighty Ancestors,*" Uhdrig began, "*help us in our moment of despair.*"

When Natalia felt the hairs on her arms stand up on end, she knew something was happening.

"*I call on the great Shaman Khurlig to heed my words,*" Uhdrig continued.

Natalia watched in fascination as the ritual continued. A cold breath of air appeared to hover before her, and then a slight mist appeared over the fire. Was she imagining things, or could she make out a ghostly face? She shook her head, trying to clear her mind and experience the magic that was flowing around her.

Uhdrig's words flowed forth in an endless drone, all in the Orc tongue. Natalia wondered if languages mattered to the spirits of the deceased, but then chided herself for the distraction. The spell seemed to go on and on until she found herself itching to stretch her legs.

Shaluhk suddenly sat up straight, as if someone had pushed her against a wall. The Orc's head rolled to the side, and then her eyes opened, revealing nothing but white orbs. Her mouth opened up, spilling out words in the Orcish tongue. Natalia had no idea what she was saying, but the voice was lower in pitch than Shaluhk's, and it quickly became apparent that a struggle was going on within the young shamaness's body as it began to twitch.

Uhdrig was talking to Khurlig now, the Orcs both speaking rapidly, the air buzzing with energy as they conversed. Suddenly, Shaluhk/Khurlig turned to face Natalia, her hands reaching out.

"She is about to begin," warned Uhdrig, "prepare yourself."

When the green hands were placed on either side of Natalia's head, she felt a warmth flow through them, and then a searing pain as if a red-hot spike had been driven into her head. She screamed in agony, but the Orc held her immobile, probing her mind with new threads of magic, each one more tortuous than its predecessors.

Time lost all context. Natalia witnessed fleeting images of the Volstrum flash by and then she was sitting in a classroom while Mistress Nina spoke of spells.

"It is, perhaps," said Nina, "the most difficult of all Water Magic spells."

"Why is that?" asked Tatiana.

"The mage that conjures it must also control it, requiring intense concentration. Failure to do so would result in sending it on a rampage."

"How powerful is it?" asked Tatiana, always the inquisitive one.

"Powerful enough to penetrate the toughest armour," replied Mistress Nina. "Now, who can tell me who invented this spell?" She looked around the room, singling out Katrin.

"Astigar Stormwind," the young woman replied.

"Very good, Katrin," praised the mistress. "Now, let's look at how the spell is cast."

Natalia raised her hand.

"What is it, Natalia?"

"If it is so difficult," the girl asked, "why are you showing it to us?"

"To give you an appreciation for the spell," the mistress explained. *"None of you here are capable of casting it, of course, but one day, if you continue with your studies, you might be."*

The image shifted, making Natalia cry out in anguish. She opened her eyes to see the glowing face of Shaluhk/Khurlig staring back at her. The Orc appeared to be lit like a beacon, and Natalia watched as sores began to manifest on the young shaman's skin. Even as she stared, blood trickled from Shaluhk's ears.

"No!" called out Natalia, "you're hurting her. Make her stop, Uhdrig!"

"It is too late for that," roared the voice in her head. "I am Khurlig, Shamaness of the Red Hand. For too long have I wandered in the Afterlife."

Natalia stared in shock at the face of Shaluhk as it hung before her eyes, motionless.

"You must stop this madness," called out Natalia.

"No," said the voice of Khurlig, "this body is mine now. Only I can save my people, the Ancestors will it."

"Cease," came Uhdrig's voice, once more echoing in Natalia's mind. "This shell is not for you."

"You brought me here," said Khurlig, "and gave me this body to inhabit. Did you really think that such a gift could be refused? I am Khurlig, greatest of all shamans, and I shall live again!"

"No," said Uhdrig, "you are damaging the very body you inhabit. Release Shaluhk now, or I shall be forced to destroy you."

Khurlig laughed, her voice echoing through Natalia's mind. Wracked with pain, there was nothing the Water Mage could do but listen and watch as the events unfolded before her.

She saw glowing figures, and then Uhdrig appeared to step out from her body. Khurlig turned away from Natalia, seeking out this new threat, and when Shaluhk's body fell to the floor, it left the misty form of Khurlig in its place.

Uhdrig stepped forward, grasping the ghostly figure by the neck. In answer, the ancient shaman fought back. Natalia felt a titanic surge of energy that knocked her backward to sprawl on the dirt floor, her head spinning, and then everything went black.

ATTACK

Spring 1104 SR

Athgar looked out to see the enemy troops massing to the west. "They're getting ready," he declared.

"Indeed," said Kargen. "You have the logs ready?"

Athgar looked at his feet. All along the walkway, logs had been placed, ready for action.

"They're ready," he said. "If they attack the wall, I'll ignite them, and then we can send them tumbling into the ditch. Artoch is doing likewise on the east wall, in case they come that way."

"How is the arrow count?"

"It's not good news, I'm afraid," said Athgar. "We've barely six arrows left apiece."

"Then it will be hand to hand," noted Kargen. "I must be off to the gate. Take care, my friend, and if we should both die this day, I will look for you in the Afterlife."

"Let's hope it doesn't come to that," said Athgar.

Kargen climbed down the ladder, making his way south, to where the gate stood waiting.

Laruhk was already there, up on the small platform that bridged the door.

"Did you manage to repair it?" asked Kargen, nodding his head at the entrance.

"No," said Laruhk, *"but we have reinforced what remains with extra timber. I hope it is enough."*

"It will have to be," said Kargen.

"Where is our Water Shaman, Nat-Alia?" asked Laruhk.

"I do not know," said Kargen. *"The last I saw of her, she was with Shaluhk. I believe they were going to visit Uhdrig. Do not worry, my friend, they will be here when we need them."*

"How can you know that, Kargen? Are you controlling their destinies?"

Kargen let out a low rumbling laugh. *"No,"* he said, *"Shaluhk has a mind of her own. She is more than capable of knowing when she is needed. We, on the other hand, must concentrate on the task at hand."*

A noise drew Laruhk's attention, and he looked towards the distant tree line that was out of Kargen's view.

"Here they come," Laruhk reported, *"and it looks like they are sending in their armoured knights."*

Just then, the Orc ducked as a bolt flew over his head.

"They have crossbows," he announced.

"So they do," agreed Kargen. *"Now, get down from there and stand ready to hold the door."* He moved to the gate, peering through the hole left by the ram. Off in the distance, he could see the Temple Knights beginning their advance. They were stirrup to stirrup, their ranks packed so tightly that they blocked the view of those behind. Only the thunder of hooves gave away their true numbers.

Laruhk, who had descended from his position atop the wall, came closer, peering through the hole alongside his old friend.

"What are they doing?" he asked. *"Do they intend to knock down the door with their horses?"*

The two Orcs watched in fascination as the knights drew closer. It looked like they were getting ready to speed up, but then the men in the front rank peeled off to either side, revealing their own secret weapon. Temple Knights were riding two abreast, holding onto ropes on which a small ram was suspended.

"Do they really think that will work?" asked Laruhk.

"I doubt it," said Kargen, *"they must have something else in mind, though what it might be, is beyond me."*

The answer came soon enough. As the ram drew closer, another individual on horseback appeared just behind the ram, and as it neared its target, he began to gesticulate. Moments later, a streak of flame shot forth from his fingers.

Kargen pushed Laruhk aside, landing next to him as the fire struck the door. Wood exploded into splinters, and a wave of heat rushed over their heads. They had barely enough time to stand when the ram hit the door. The flimsy wooden construction, weakened by the previous attack and now further damaged by the mage's spell, flew apart, sending fragments flying everywhere.

Smoke filled the entrance to the Orc's village, and then the thundering of hooves shook the very ground as Temple Knights poured in.

Kargen swung his axe, striking a rider on the thigh, but the steel leggings deflected the blow, rendering it useless. The rider turned in the saddle, striking out with an overhead blow, but the mighty Orc ducked low, then swung again. This time, he remembered to aim for the horse, striking the animal's hind legs, causing it to collapse. It rolled as it fell, pinning the Temple Knight beneath its bulk, and Kargen seized the opportunity to ram the back of his axe into the front of the man's helmet, the armour collapsing under the great force, crushing the knight beneath it.

More Temple Knights thundered through the gates, driving the Orcs back. Kargen watched as two hunters were trampled to death beneath the hooves of their massive horses, helpless to intervene.

Laruhk twisted, avoiding a blade, then reached out, grabbing the knight's sword arm and pulling him from the saddle. There was a moment of resistance as the man's feet caught in the stirrups, and then he was on the ground, the Orc severing the knight's head with his axe.

Laruhk turned to attack another target, but the bulk of a horse struck him, sending him sprawling. Moments later, he was crushed beneath the hooves of dozens of horses as they rushed past.

"Fall back!" yelled Kargen, desperate to mount an organized defence. All around him, the ground was stained black with Orc blood, a testament to the ferocity of their defence, but it was to little effect for they were pushed inexorably backward until there was nowhere left to go.

Suddenly, a streak of fire shot past Kargen, striking a Temple Knight in the chest. The rider appeared stunned for a moment, then turned slowly to face this new threat. Athgar stood on the walkway, readying another spell, but while the knights had been busy driving the Orcs back, their crossbowmen had advanced. A volley of bolts sailed forth, and the Therengian had to duck down to avoid being hit.

When a horn sounded somewhere off in the distance, Kargen knew their fate was sealed. The Orcs of the Red Hand would perish this day, to join the ranks of their Ancestors. He parried a sword strike and swung with his axe, cutting into a horse's saddle. The knight kicked out with his boot, driving the Orc back, then swivelled his horse, rearing it up to lash out at Kargen.

More knights poured through the gates, swelling their numbers. Kargen saw Khurlak go down beneath their blades, his face contorted in pain. Driven back by the hooves of his enemy, the chieftain felt his back bump into a hut. The horse reared again and the Orc dove, rolling to the side to come up in one quick motion. As the horse landed, Kargen sprang into the air, jumping behind the surprised knight and lifting him bodily from the horse, only to toss him to the side, then leap into the saddle himself. Having never ridden a horse, Kargen was confused by how to control the beast. The mount, not used to its new rider, started running, fearful of the strange creature which now sat atop its saddle. Kargen hung on for dear life as the beast ran around the village in a panic.

Artoch saw the charge coming. This time, the men were armed with fascines, large bundles of sticks tied together to provide filler. As they approached the earthworks, they tossed them inside, attempting to fill the ditch.

To the master of flame, it was a gift. He pointed, calling forth his power and smoke began billowing from the fascines. The enemy soldiers, intent on gaining the advantage, moved up their archers and arrows began to rain down on the wall.

In answer, Artoch conjured thick black smoke. It billowed out of the fires, stinging eyes and blocking the archer's field of view. Thanks to the prevailing winds, it drifted eastward, directly into the enemy lines.

He watched as they fell back. The sound of fighting was growing closer, no doubt the knights were now within the village, and yet he must hold here. He ordered the other hunters to reinforce the village and gripped the top of the palisade, leaning out to peer through the smoke.

Amid the yelling, he saw them, a group of soldiers, cloths around their mouths, advancing with a ladder. He watched them, fascinated by their perseverance. How brave these Humans were, and how stupid.

He thought back to Natalia's story and decided to give it a try. Pointing his finger, he called forth his power. A small flame leaped from his hand, dropping to the outside base of the palisade. He watched it disappear into the dirt, then fire erupted, growing into a phoenix. It was small, he knew, but as the fiery creature flew into the air, the attacking soldiers spotted it. Overwhelmed by the magical opposition, they dropped their ladder and fled, the phoenix chasing after them.

Father General Gilbert struck out with a sword, a clean, efficient jab that took the greenskin in the face. His enemy collapsed, and the Holy Man moved his mount forward, finishing off the job with the iron-shod hooves of his horse.

He glimpsed an Orc to the side, an axe descending, but a quick twist in the saddle brought his shield to bear. The blade caught on the edge, pulling it downward. The swing had been strong, but now, its energy expended, the attacker was left defenceless.

The father general smiled in grim satisfaction as he struck out once more, his blade digging into the neck of the Orc, spraying black blood in a wide arc.

With the fighting was dying down, he flipped open his visor, the better to take stock of the situation. The Orcs were fleeing, trying to take refuge in their flimsy huts. He saw one greenskin on the back of a horse, tearing its way through the village in a mad gallop, and he wondered, absently, what had happened to the Temple Knight that had been its original rider.

Gilbert barked out commands, and some of the knights began dismounting. Now would come the house to house search that would eliminate all opposition. Unexpectedly, a streak of fire shot past him, and he looked up in surprise to see a man on the walkway.

"The Therengian!" he called. "Get him."

"No!" yelled the distinctive voice of Verineth. "He's mine!"

Athgar had missed the father general and was about to recast when the voice of the Fire Mage, Verineth Sartellian, echoed across the open space. He turned to re-target, only to see Verineth already in the midst of casting.

Athgar quickly fired off a streak of fire, flames shooting from his hands, but the enemy mage had been just as fast. The two flames struck one another, exploding into a fiery ball where they met. The Therengian concentrated on pouring all his energy into his attack, but he could feel his flames receding. The fiery ball drew closer, pushed towards him by the unrelenting strength of Verineth's attack.

It was too much for Athgar, and he halted his spell, diving from the walkway just as flames struck his perch. He felt the blast of heat explode behind him as he fell, landing among stacked firewood with a thump.

The enemy mage advanced, the knights making way for this duel of flame wielders. Verineth cast again, this time producing an immense ball of flame. It rolled across the ground, igniting all in its path, leaving a trail of smoke and destruction in its wake.

Thinking quickly, Athgar rose and stepped to the side, casting once more. This time, a small spark sailed across the ground, burying itself in the enemy mage's path. Verineth, too intent on his target, began casting once more, this time a flaming phoenix, but before the spell was complete, he tripped the fire trap and flames shot up, searing the mage's legs and disrupting his concentration.

"You fool," he called out, "do you think that will stop me?"

Verineth again called on his power, and Athgar felt the heat as a wall of flame appeared behind him, cutting off all retreat. The Therengian looked skyward and closed his eyes, muttering words of power. Small hailstones fell, igniting as they struck surfaces. Horses ran around in fear, and the Temple Knights, searching the huts on foot, stayed well clear of the area.

Verineth Sartellian waved his hands and uttered a single word of command. The hailstones immediately ceased their downpour, and Athgar finally realized just how powerful a mage could be.

Brother Carrington kicked open the door. Inside, stood an Orc warrior, his spear ready to strike out. The Cunar waited as the inevitable lunge came at him, easily knocking the clumsy attack aside. He stomped forward, stabbing out to be rewarded with resistance as his sword dug into the Orc's chest. The greenskin let out a dying breath and fell to the floor, lifeless.

A low rumble outside drew his attention, and he turned, expecting some reinforcements, but instead, the side of one of the huts exploded outward, sending sticks and fragments of bark flying. The courtyard echoed with the sound and then fell silent. Drawn by the unexpected explosion, all stood motionless, not knowing what to expect next.

The answer came soon enough as an enormous creature stepped through the opening. It was taller than a mounted man and had vaguely humanoid features, standing upright on two legs with a noticeable head and two arms, but there the similarities ended. The face was featureless, and the arms ended in spikes that looked like spears of ice. It lumbered from the opening, moving towards the nearest enemy.

A Temple Knight, still mounted, took his horse closer, raising his sword for a strike, but this was his undoing. The creature struck out with an arm, punching clean through the plate armour that protected the knight's chest. Withdrawing its arm, it pulled the dead man from the saddle and tossed it aside while the horse ran away in panic.

More knights rushed in to fight, this time on foot, swords raining down on the creature but to little avail. While small pieces of ice flaked off, each punch the golem dealt was a dead knight, their armour doing little to protect them.

The horse, having expended its energy in its mad dash, finally slowed. Kargen slid from the saddle and was casting his eyes about, trying to get his bearings when he spotted the great hut nearby. Across from it sat Uhdrig's dwelling, and he suddenly thought of Shaluhk. He rushed to the door, entering the structure just in time to see an enormous creature punch a hole through the wall in its mad dash to escape.

Off to the side, Uhdrig lay motionless, her body strangely twisted and contorted. He spotted Nat-Alia, standing behind the creature, concentrating on controlling it. He was about to rush forward to lend assistance when he noticed Shaluhk, lying near the fire, blood streaming from her nose and ears.

He rushed to her, kneeling by her side and feeling for a pulse, but to no avail. Kargen raised his head upward and let out a wail of grief loud enough to rouse the dead from the Afterlife.

The ice golem moved forward, sweeping aside a Temple Knight and sending him sailing through the air to strike hard against the side of a hut, where he fell to the ground, motionless.

The Temple Knights tried encircling the construct, striking out, but to little effect. Six knights were quickly felled, with many more falling back, bleeding from wounds. The creature was unstoppable, and so they began withdrawing as they fought, trying to lead it out into the open.

One horseman came too close, and the golem's arm struck out, slicing down through the knight's leg to draw blood from the horse beneath. The mount reared up, and the Temple Knight struggled to maintain control. It looked like he was about to succeed, but then he toppled from the saddle, falling to the ground and bleeding out from his wound.

The golem stepped forward, sweeping both arms in a wide arc to send three more knights to the ground, their armour ripped and torn.

Natalia, now free of the hut, concentrated all of her energy on controlling the construct. Her ears were ringing with the effort, her head pounding, but still, she drove it on, her will controlling its every move.

Verineth stooped, picking up a small stone from where it lay. Uttering an incantation, he hurled the pebble towards Athgar, and as it hit him, it exploded into flames, throwing him backward.

With the Therengian down, the mighty Fire Mage turned his attention to the ice golem that was now rampaging through the Temple Knights. He paused long enough to identify the creature's weakness, then began casting. Small flames leaped from his fingers, racing across the intervening space to strike the monstrosity in the chest. Hearing the distinctive sound of ice cracking, he noted his success as a large chunk slid from its torso.

The Temple Knights, taking advantage of the situation, renewed their attacks, bringing swords to bear on the new wound. In answer, the creature lashed out, smashing one warrior into the ground with a vicious overhead attack that split the man's helmet as if it were made of butter.

Verineth watched for a moment, appreciating the skill required to create such a construct. Another Temple Knight went down beneath the behemoth's onslaught before the mage had readied his next spell. The creature was made of ice, and he knew that only the direct application of heat would defeat it. He pulled forth all the power he could muster and then directed it at the golem, a solid stream of fire that seared the very air around it.

It struck dead centre, sending pieces of ice flying in every direction. Knights raced to get out of the way as a tremendous cracking sound reverberated off the nearby huts. There was a moment of stillness, where everyone held their breath, and then the golem exploded into thousands of tiny ice shards that flew far and wide.

Two knights staggered back, the force of the explosion pushing them like a gust of wind. It was then that Verineth spotted the woman. She had collapsed as the creature was destroyed and now lay on the ground, attempting to rise.

"Well, well, well," he mocked, "if it isn't Natalia Stormwind."

She looked up at him, her pale face drawn and haggard.

"I must commend you on your spell," he said, "few have the power to attempt such a casting, let alone succeed, but I fear it was too little and too late." He stepped closer until he was but a horse's length from her. "And now," he announced, "it is time for you to die."

As he raised his arms, tiny flames began to dance along his fingers.

DEATH

Spring 1104 SR

Athgar rose, shaking his head to try to clear his vision. His chest ached, and he knew it was soaked in blood, but Verineth was still out there somewhere.

Out of nowhere, a massive cracking sound drew his attention, but before he could find where it was coming from, an explosion sent ice shards flying through the air. He moved towards the blast only to see a sight that nearly stopped his heart.

Natalia lay prone, trying to lift herself from the ground, but appeared to lack the strength to do so while Verineth stood before her, chatting away as he raised his hands to cast.

Athgar halted, bracing himself for what he was about to do. He closed his eyes, digging deep to find his inner spark. Time seemed to stand still as he fed the fire within, building it into a great inferno. He felt his skin turn hot, his fingernails begin to burn, then he opened his eyes, locking them onto his target.

Speaking the words of power released the fire within, and it leaped forth, striking his enemy and knocking him from his feet. Still, the flames poured forth, but Verineth, despite his pain, managed to cast a globe of fire that enveloped him, temporarily holding the Therengian's spell at bay.

Athgar released all control and allowed the flames to flow freely. His skin started to crackle, and his vision blurred as fire began to eat away at him. This was the moment where it would consume him, and still, he poured forth all the power he could muster.

Natalia watched in horror as Athgar's eyes burned with fire. When small cracks began to appear on his body and flames leaped forth, she realized it would be mere moments before his entire body was consumed.

She reached out, calling on all her reserves to cast one final spell. The flames on Athgar suddenly went out as frost engulfed him. He fell to the ground, lying motionless, but she feared she had been too late.

Verineth watched the Therengian fall, then felt the fire of his attack vanish. The Sartellian returned his attention to Natalia in surprise. No one had ever stopped an immolation before!

"How did you do that?" he snapped. "Once a Fire Mage immolates, there is no stopping it!"

In answer, she raised a single digit, her final act of defiance.

"I suppose it doesn't matter," said Verineth. "I will kill you and then allow the Temple Knights to finish off your green friends."

He moved slightly closer, the better to watch her die, but her eyes were staring past him. Sensing some new development, he turned to see more knights rushing through the gates, but rather than wearing the grey tabards of Saint Cunar, they were wearing scarlet.

"What's this?" he called out.

Father General Gilbert, now on foot, knelt by an Orc. He had been badly trampled, a wound that would have killed a man, and yet when the Temple Knight turned him over, his eyes opened.

"You will never win," the Orc said in the common tongue.

"Oh, but I already have," declared the father general.

He drew his dagger, ready to finish the greenskin off when the thunder of hooves grabbed his attention. He looked up to see scarlet-clad knights riding through the gate. Standing, the Orc now forgotten, he watched in shock as the Temple Knights of Saint Agnes made their entrance.

Even more annoying was the presence of the Dwarf, who, having halted his pony, was pointing at the father general himself.

Sister Cordelia watched as her knights spread throughout the village. The Cunars were rushing to a rallying point, eager to make a stand against this new threat. She let them continue, waiting for them to gather in one spot.

"There he is," called Belgast, pointing to the leader of the Cunars.

"Father General Gilbert," called out Sister Cordelia, "I am placing you under arrest in the name of Saint Agnes."

"On what charge?" the man asked.

"You have violated the basic tenets of the Church," she said.

"I do not recognize your authority," he declared.

"It matters not," she replied. "You will come with us or be taken by force."

In answer, Gilbert drew his sword, moving into a cleared area. Behind him, his knights stood ready, watching events unfold before them, even as they formed into a defensive circle.

Sister Cordelia dismounted, drawing her own blade. It was a strange sensation, taking the fight to a member of the Church, and she prayed to Saint Agnes to guide her hand. She stepped forward, her sword held two-handed.

In answer, the father general did likewise. This would be a test of endurance, for swords did not typically penetrate plate armour, relying, instead, on the concussive abilities of the blade, rather than the point. This fight would consist of two knights, battering each other until one fell, making them vulnerable to a final strike.

Sister Cordelia started circling the father general, watching his feet for any sign of bracing that might indicate an attack.

Gilbert, on the other hand, was a seasoned warrior, and as such, was confident he could easily overpower an under-trained Sister of Saint Agnes. He watched, waiting for the moment she would launch her attack.

Kargen staggered from the hut, his heart full of rage. Shaluhk was dead, and these Humans must pay!

He spotted Athgar, lying motionless nearby, his clothes frosted with ice. From there, his eyes travelled to Nat-Alia, who lay unconscious on the ground, her arms still extended towards her bondmate. It was Verineth, however, that finally locked eyes with him.

"What is this now?" said the mage. "Yet another greenskin to distract me from my purpose?"

"Your people have killed my bondmate," Kargen yelled, "and for that, you will die!"

Verineth laughed, "And let me guess, you are to be the instrument of my defeat? I think not. Come closer, and I shall promise you a quick death. Your people have interfered enough for my tastes."

Kargen broke into a run, pouring all the strength he could muster into closing the distance as quickly as possible. In answer, Verineth raised his hands, sending flames gushing forth to strike the mighty Orc Chieftain squarely in the chest, blistering his skin, but the determined hunter kept advancing.

"Die!" screamed Verineth as his flames continued to engulf the Orc.

Kargen felt his hair catch fire, his muscles strain with the effort, but his mind stayed locked on his target. Closer he drew, his skin erupting into flames. Soon, he was a pillar of fire, and he let out a bellow of rage that seemed to shake the whole village.

Everyone stopped what they were doing to watch in morbid fascination as the flaming Orc closed the distance. Verineth kept feeding the fire, but the damned greenskin wouldn't fall. The mage backed up a step, but then the Orc was upon him, knocking him to the ground, embracing him with his fiery arms.

Verineth called out in agony as his clothes caught fire. He tried to push the great beast away, but the strong arms held him in a death grip. The mage felt his skin catching fire, and then his flesh melted from his face, the magical flame intent on claiming them both.

Father General Gilbert watched in horror as Verineth Sartellian, the most powerful mage he had ever met, burned to death in a fiery column.

He turned back to look at Sister Cordelia, then at the sisters who were, even now, securing the village. This was a fight he could not win. He realized he must live to fight another day.

He tossed his sword to the ground. "I surrender," he said, "and place myself at the mercy of the Church."

Sister Cordelia advanced, placing the tip of her sword in the man's face. "Order your knights to surrender," she commanded.

He turned to face the Brothers of Saint Cunar, words forming as he readied himself to speak. They were the elite of the elite, the finest warriors on the Continent, and to admit defeat here, in this place, seemed so dishonourable. He fought with the urge to order a last stand, but it would accomplish nothing.

"Surrender yourselves," he finally ordered, "and live to fight another day."

The look of confusion on their faces betrayed their dishonour. They gripped their weapons, ready to sell their lives in one last stand.

"Stand down, I say!" bellowed Gilbert. "I am your general. Would you disobey a direct order?"

Scowling, they lowered their weapons, and the sisters moved in among them, relieving them of their swords.

Belgast ran across to Natalia. She was lying still, and he feared she had travelled to the Great Forge, but as he drew close, she raised her head.

"Athgar?" she called out.

"He fell over there," the Dwarf replied, "though I'm not sure if he still lives. Let's get you up now, shall we?"

He lent her his arm, and she staggered to her feet, grateful for the aid.

"Where is he?"

"I'll take you to him," said Belgast,

She shuffled towards Athgar, her feet stumbling as she walked. She knelt by her love, feeling for a pulse.

"He lives," she said, relief flooding her voice.

Belgast leaned over the Therengian, noting a distinct odour. "Burned flesh," he said. "Look, Natalia, he's badly wounded, I'm afraid he won't live long."

Natalia scanned the area, then looked back at Athgar, grief finally overcoming her calm demeanour.

"Is there a healer here?" asked Belgast.

"Not anymore," said Natalia, "they're both dead, and it's all my fault. I'm afraid this has all been in vain. I have saved him from immolation only to see him die a lingering death from his wounds."

"I don't understand," said Belgast. "How did he catch fire? I didn't see Verineth cast a spell."

"It is the curse of Fire Mages," explained Natalia, through tears. "When they use up their energy, it begins to draw on their physical bodies, using it to power their spells, but if they draw too much, they will be consumed by it."

"And you stopped it?" said the Dwarf in surprise. "How is that even possible?"

"I don't know," she said, between sobs. "I just acted. I didn't think about it, but I was too late."

Shaluhk staggered from the hut. With Khurlig gone, she had wandered in the spirit realm, trying desperately to regain her physical form. It had been a most distressing situation, made all the worse by seeing Kargen find her. He had presumed she was dead, for while the spirit wanders, the body does not breath. Now free of her imprisonment, she cast her eyes around, seeking her bondmate.

"Kargen!" she called out. "Where are you?"

"Over here," called a voice.

She looked to see a strange warrior woman, dressed in the full plate armour of her order. Questions went unanswered as her eyes followed the pointing fingers to a group of Orcs standing around the charred body of Kargen.

Everything else became a blur as she ran to his side. She cradled his head, watching in surprise as his eyes opened.

"Shaluhk," he said, through blackened lips.

"You are alive!" she called out. "Hold still while I use my magic."

She dug deep, calling upon the power within her. Her hands turned a brilliant yellow, and she placed them on her bondmate's face, watching as the burned flesh slewed away.

"I thought you were dead," said Kargen.

"I am here," she replied. "Did you think you could be rid of me so easily?"

"And Uhdrig?"

"She has joined our Ancestors, killed by the spirit of Khurlig."

"But I saw you," said Kargen, "you had no breath."

"I was trapped in the spirit realm," said Shaluhk, "trying to find my way back. I will tell you all in due time, but you must rest now."

"Athgar," said Kargen, "does he live?"

Shaluhk looked across the clearing to where the Dwarf and Natalia cradled the unlucky Therengian.

"He is injured," she said, "I must see to him. Wait here, and I shall return." She lowered his head.

"Very well," said Kargen, "it is not like I am going anywhere."

Shaluhk rushed to Athgar, calling forth her arcane powers even as she ran. Kneeling, she placed her hands to his chest, watching as the energy flowed into him.

"He will live," she said, "yet, like Kargen, he will have to rest for some time."

"He is so badly burned," said Natalia.

"Yes," said Shaluhk, "but I can regenerate the flesh. It is a slower process than weapon damage though, and takes much longer to heal. They will both be in pain for some time yet, but will make a full recovery."

"Thank you," said Natalia, hugging the Orc shaman tightly.

AFTERMATH

Spring 1104 SR

Athgar looked up from his bed, to where Natalia and Shaluhk stood over him.

"Well?" he said.

"Well, what?" said Natalia.

"When can I be out of this bed?" he asked.

"When I say so," said Shaluhk, "and not a moment sooner. You were very badly burned, you are lucky to be alive."

"That's what I told him," said Natalia.

"He is stubborn," noted Shaluhk.

"Yes," Natalia agreed, "but I still love him."

"What about me?" came a voice.

They both turned to see Kargen, lying on another bed, close at hand, sitting up, despite his condition.

"I suppose you want to know the same thing," said Shaluhk.

"I do," the mighty Orc replied. "I am the chief, after all, I have things to do."

"And you will do them when I say you can," said Shaluhk. "Or do you seek to argue with the tribe's shaman?"

"I would never do that," said Kargen, lying back down. He turned his head to gaze at Athgar. "I can see we are outranked here, my friend."

"So we are," agreed the Therengian.

Footsteps drew closer and then the face of Laruhk peered down at the two patients.

"How are they doing?" asked the new visitor.

"As well as can be expected," said Shaluhk.

"How is it," said Kargen, "that Laruhk is up and about while I am still here, lying in bed."

"He only suffered from broken bones and torn flesh," said Shaluhk, "while you were half-burned to death."

"You should enjoy the rest while you can," said Laruhk, "our new shamaness is a hard taskmaster."

"How so?" asked Kargen.

"While you have been resting," continued Laruhk, "we have been locating the Godstone.

"Just how much time has passed?" asked Athgar.

"You've both been out of it for nearly a week," said Natalia, "and I daresay it will still be three or four more days before you'll be up and about."

She knelt by Athgar, feeling his forehead, a look of concern knitting her brow. "How's the pain?"

"Tolerable," he said, "but not nearly so bad as it was."

"What have we here?" came the voice of Artoch. The master of flame came into Athgar's view, his pale green face standing out against the darker shade of Laruhk's.

"You are lucky to be alive," he said.

"So I've been told," said Athgar.

"You two," continued Artoch, pausing for a moment, "you seem to have a connection."

"They are bondmates," said Laruhk.

"That is not what I meant," said the shaman. "What I mean is, there is some type of magical connection between you. You should not have been able to quench his fire, Nat-Alia. Such a thing has never been done before."

He turned his attention to Athgar. "And you, what did you think you were doing? Did I not tell you to control your spark? Why, if Nat-Alia had not been there, there would be nothing left of you but embers."

"I had no choice," defended Athgar, "Verineth was about to kill Natalia!"

The wise old Orc nodded his head, "It seems the Ancestors watched over you."

"Do not talk to me of Ancestors," said Shaluhk. "I have had enough of them for the time being."

"So I have heard," offered Artoch, "and yet, as our new shamaness, you must consult with them on occasion, if only for naming ceremonies."

"Yes," said Shaluhk, "of course, but I shall try to avoid any mention of possession."

"What of Khurlig?" asked Natalia. "What will happen to her spirit?"

"She will be shunned by our other Ancestors," said Shaluhk, "and I will contact the other tribes to warn them of her duplicity. She will never again be allowed to tread the realm of mortals."

"And Father General Gilbert?" asked Athgar. "Did he survive?"

"He did," said Shaluhk, "but he was taken into custody by Sister Cordelia. How strange it was to see Human women in armour. I never thought to see such a thing. I always thought of Human women as weak. Not including my sister, Nat-Alia, of course."

"I'm sure the Sisters of Saint Agnes take their devotions seriously," said Athgar. "I certainly wouldn't want to be on the receiving end of their wrath."

"What will happen to him?" asked Shaluhk.

"Belgast seems to think he'll get away with everything," said Natalia. "He doesn't have much faith in the Church."

"At the very least," said Athgar, "I suspect he may be reduced in rank."

"Yes," agreed Natalia, "but he'll likely rise again. I have a feeling it's not the last we'll see of him."

"Where is Belgast?" asked Athgar.

"He has returned to his people," explained Natalia, "to bring back word of the death of his cousins. He wanted to say farewell, but you were sleeping."

"How was he doing?" he asked.

"He was happy to see Verineth killed and the father general arrested, but was disappointed that the Duke of Krieghoff went unpunished."

"His army suffered a major defeat," said Athgar, "and there'll be ramifications of that. I wouldn't be surprised if someone tried to take advantage." He was overcome with a coughing fit, sending his body into spasms of pain.

"I think we have disturbed our patients for long enough," said Shaluhk. "It is time they had a rest. Come along, Nat-Alia. You too, Laruhk, we have things to discuss."

They left the hut, leaving Athgar and Kargen alone.

"Well," said Athgar, "what do you make of things?"

"It is strange to think that it was only two years ago when you first came to us," said Kargen. "So much has happened since then."

"You think I'm a curse?" said Athgar. "You've certainly suffered in that time."

"But," added Kargen, "if you had not come to us, we never would have been aware of this attack. We would have been murdered and lost to history. Instead, thanks mainly to you and Nat-Alia, we are a free people once more."

"Even though you have to abandon your home?"

"We have earned a respite, nothing more," reflected Kargen. "The Duke will not stand for this loss, and now he has a reason to return."

"You think so?" said Athgar. "Even though it could lead to war with Holstead?"

"I think," said Kargen, "that the ways of men are consistent. There are very few like you, Athgar. Most men of power seek to grow their influence."

"I'm not a man of power," said Athgar.

"That is where you are wrong," said Kargen. "You are powerful, as is Nat-Alia, but neither of you realizes that together you are more powerful still."

"Like you and Shaluhk?" asked Athgar.

The Orc grinned at the compliment. "Yes, and now I must face another problem."

"Which is?"

"It is unheard of for a shaman to be bondmate to a chieftain."

"I don't see how that's a problem," said Athgar.

"Shamans are supposed to be neutral in disputes," said Kargen. "How can a bondmate remain neutral?"

"Come now," said Athgar, "shamans are never neutral. After all, it was Artoch who told me I could use my magic in a duel."

"He was merely informing you of the rules," said Kargen.

"If you say so," said Athgar, "but I think you'll find the tribe behind you. Besides, Shaluhk is the least of your problems. You need to start thinking about the trek eastward."

"Indeed," said Kargen, "but not this day, for my head is weary, and I am in need of sleep."

Shaluhk stepped into the daylight, followed by the others.

"They seem in good spirits," said Natalia.

"And well they should," said Shaluhk. "I have brought them back from the brink of death. It took all the power I had to save them." She turned to face her tribe-sister, her voice breaking, "For a moment, Nat-Alia, I thought I had lost Kargen. My heart broke."

"I know exactly how you feel, Shaluhk. I, too, thought I'd lost my love."

Shaluhk stepped forward, embracing Natalia. They clung to each other, then Laruhk placed his arms around them.

"What are you doing, brother?" said Shaluhk.

"I am hugging my sister," he replied, "and her sister. I suppose that makes Nat-Alia my sister as well."

"You can not have her for a sister," said Shaluhk, "I claimed that honour first."

"I am the older sibling," said Laruhk, "if anything, she should be my sister."

"Enough, you two. I can be a sister to you both. Would that be acceptable?"

"Very well," said Shaluhk, "but you will be my favourite sibling."

"Typical," said Laruhk, "to claim such an honour. Well, if it must be so, then Nat-Alia will be my favourite sister as well."

Natalia rolled her eyes, an action that was noticed by both Orcs.

"What are you doing?" asked Laruhk, trying to emulate her.

"Nothing that needs concern you," said Shaluhk, recognizing the behaviour. She suddenly halted, causing the rest to slow.

"Laruhk," she said, "what are you doing here?"

"I am talking to you and Nat-Alia," he said.

"Is there not somewhere else you are supposed to be?"

"Not that I recall," said Laruhk.

"Where is Agar?"

"I..." Laruhk's voice trailed off, and he flushed, turning a darker shade of green.

Shaluhk whispered to Natalia, "He was supposed to be watching Agar."

"I shall leave you two sisters to continue your discussion," Laruhk said, then ran off, giving them their privacy.

"He means well," said Natalia.

"He does," agreed Shaluhk, "but in some ways, he has never grown up. Maybe he needs a bondmate."

They both chuckled and resumed their walk.

"What will you do now?" asked Shaluhk.

"I haven't discussed it with Athgar yet," said Natalia, "but I imagine we'll accompany the tribe as it moves east."

"I would suggest otherwise," said Shaluhk.

"Oh? Why would you say that?"

"Despite what I said back there," she said, "I have already consulted the Ancestors. They believe your way lies north, beyond the Grey Spire mountains."

"The crusades?" said Natalia.

"People are suffering there," said Shaluhk, "both Human and Orc."

"We can't save the world," said Natalia. "It's hard enough just keeping ourselves alive."

"I know that," said Shaluhk, "and yet Athgar's destiny is to find his people."

"And what is my destiny?" asked Natalia.

Shaluhk smiled, "The Ancestors have something special in mind for you, Nat-Alia. You will grow in magical power even as Athgar gains more influence."

"You speak in riddles."

"As do the Ancestors," said Shaluhk. "I do not claim to know their ways, but they have offered this advice without my asking. They seem to think it important you travel north, to a place called Ebenstadt."

"I've never heard of it," said Natalia.

"No," agreed Shaluhk, "nor have I."

EPILOGUE

Summer 1104 SR

Mage Hunter Akael stepped into the marble-floored atrium as the guards eyed him warily. Beside him strode his companion, Rogar, a mage of some repute.

"I still don't understand why I'm here," said Rogar, wiping the sweat from his bald head. "Surely you could have done this without me."

"These people are Kurathians," said Akael. "They don't talk to outsiders. How am I to ascertain the truth of the matter if no one will talk?"

"And so you brought me," said the mage.

"Yes," said the mage hunter. "After all, you're the one that can detect magical auras."

"It must have been important to bring me here, to Kouras," said Rogar. "I didn't know the family had connections among the Kurathians."

"The family is always interested in extending its reach," Akael replied, "and we have been given a golden opportunity here."

"I don't understand," said the Life Mage.

"The Kurathians trade far and wide. Once news travels that we are in the court of one of their princes, everyone will want a member of the family in their retinue."

"But first," said Rogar, "we have to assess this apprentice. What if he has no potential?"

"Better to inform the prince now, than to have his court mage waste further time in training."

"So you're not taking him back to Korascajan?"

"No, not this time," said Akael. "We are only here to assess his dormant powers."

They arrived at an ornate set of double doors where two more guards stood, resplendent in their silver and gold armour.

"Mage Hunter Akael, and Master Rogar to see His Highness, Prince Tarak," announced the mage hunter.

They must have been expected, for the doors swung open, as if by magic, into a room that was large beyond belief. Built of sandstone, beautiful frescoes decorated the walls, while the ceiling was arched, reaching three full stories above them, supported by squared-off columns. The floor, still marbled, was inset with precious metals which acted as seams between the slabs.

Akael and Rogar advanced, feeling intimidated by the sheer splendour of the place. To either side of the room stood nobles and their retinues, many having servants or slaves who stood by waving fans in a vain attempt to keep the heat at bay. At the far end sat Prince Tarak himself, magnificent on his throne of gold. To his side stood his consort, the legendary beauty, Olani, who was said to be the perfect example of womanhood, surrounded by only the most alluring slaves that one could buy. After seeing her, the mage hunter was forced to agree with the legends.

The hall was masked in silence as they advanced, save for their footfalls. They approached the throne, then halted, a horse's length away, and bowed deeply.

"Most glorious Highness," Akael began in Kurathian, *"it is with great honour that I answer your summons."*

The prince leaned forward, setting his elbows on the arms of his throne. "You have come from Korascajan, yes?"

Akael, surprised by the prince's command of the common tongue, paused for a moment, then replied.

"I have, Your Highness, and I bring greetings from those sacred halls."

The prince looked to his left, where an opulently garbed man waited, his black beard standing in stark contrast to his white clothes.

"This is Nedune, my court mage," said the prince.

"Pleased to meet you," said Akael, bowing once more.

"You honour us with your presence," said Nedune, returning the bow.

They stood staring at each other for a moment, the mage hunter at a loss for words.

"I understand you can assess people's magical potential," said Nedune, after some delay.

"Yes," said Akael, "I have brought this man, Rogar, for that express purpose. I understand you have an apprentice you wanted us to examine?"

"Indeed," said Nedune.

The Kurathian mage turned, beckoning someone forward. A young man, likely in his early twenties, shuffled forward, bowing his head respectfully.

"This," continued the court mage, "is Rasim. It is hoped that he could be taught to control fire. I shouldn't like to invest the time and effort necessary to train him if he were to prove unequal to the task."

"I understand entirely," said Akael, "but in order to make that determination, Rogar will have to cast a spell." He looked at Prince Tarak, who nodded his head in approval.

Akael continued, "He will cast a spell that will enable him to see Rasim's magical aura. This has been proven quite effective in the past in determining magical potential."

"Will we be able to see the effects of this magic?" asked the prince.

"I'm afraid not, Your Highness, nor will I. Only Rogar, as the caster, will be able to view his aura."

"And, I suppose," said Nedune, "we must trust this man's word?"

"I can assure you the family has complete trust in his abilities," defended Akael.

"Proceed," said the prince, "and let us see what this man finds."

Rogar moved back two steps, shaking out his arms to loosen them up for the casting. As a Life Mage, he was used to performing healing, the results of which were readily apparent to all those who bore witness, but this spell was different. It was said by the wise that each potential practitioner of magic contained an inner power that allowed them to develop their abilities. Someone, long ago, had discovered that under the right circumstances, a Life Mage could view this energy, which manifested itself as an aura. He had used the spell before, of course, and yet here, among these wealthy and influential people, he felt nervous.

He closed his eyes to begin the incantation. Soon, the power was flowing through him, and he opened his eyes to gaze upon the apprentice before him. Sure enough, a red haze appeared to engulf the young man, indicating, as thought, the potential to harness fire magic.

Rogar turned to Akael, intending to report his findings, only to see a brightly glowing red aura among the queen's retinue. He moved slightly, giving himself another view. A young woman sat at the queen's feet, her fine features highlighted with make-up, and her brown hair styled in a most decorative manner.

He moved towards her, ignoring those around him. The guards sprang to attention, placing themselves between the Life Mage and the queen, whom they thought the target, but Prince Tarak waved them off. Rogar halted, kneeling down to look at the young woman, whose aura was almost blinding him.

"What is your name?" he asked.

She looked up, her grey eyes boring into him. "I am Ethwyn," she declared, her voice defiant, "Ethwyn of Athelwald."

CONTINUE THE SERIES WITH FLAMES: BOOK THREE

REVIEW EMBERS

If you liked *Embers,* then *Temple Knight,* the first book in the *Power Ascending* series awaits.

START TEMPLE KNIGHT

A FEW WORDS FROM PAUL

The Frozen Flame series is set in the world of Eiddenwerthe, which is the same as Heir to the Crown, but in a different geographical region. The two series exist in tandem, each telling their own story, and yet events in one affect the other. Embers occurs in the year 1104 SR (Saints Reckoning), which corresponds to the date of 962 MC (Mercerian Calendar), meaning the story happens during the same time period as the ending of Fate of the Crown. As the two series progress, this will become clearer, and the observant reader will find several references throughout both series showing the connected world. (Orc Warbows ring a bell?)

Embers also introduces another important character that you will see more of in the future, Sister Cordelia. She has already hinted about events in her past, events that will unfold through the eyes of another Sister of the Order of Saint Agnes in the first book of the Power Ascending series due out this spring.

In this, the second book of The Frozen Flame series, the Church once again takes centre stage, and we learn that there are internal divisions between the different orders. The Church is not inherently evil, but there are those within it that seek to gain power for the coming war, just as there are those that fight to preserve all it stands for. The Holy Crusades are also mentioned in Embers, military campaigns led by the Church to subjugate the eastern lands. This religious war will take on new meaning as our two mages journey north to Ebenstadt, a great city on the eastern border of the Petty Kingdoms, in book three, Flames.

This book has taken a lot of effort, and I couldn't have done it without the support of a great number of people. Once again, I must thank Christie Kramburger for her cover art, and special thanks to Stephanie Sandrock and Amanda Bennett for their encouragement and support.

Thank you as well to the following people for their valuable input: Brad Aitken, Jeffrey Parker, Stephen Brown, Rachel Deibler, Tim James, Phyllis Simpson, Don Hinkley, James McGinnis, Stuart Rae, Michael Rhew, Shelly Heddings, and Mark Tracy. Also, a big shoutout to Dianna-Lynn (Dee) Lundgren and Cody Anne Arko-Omori for being fantastic proofreaders!

As always, I must thank Carol Bennett for her tireless efforts in the preparation of this story. I couldn't have done this without you.

Finally, I thank you, my readers, for responding to these tales with such enthusiasm. Reading your reviews inspires me to continue this journey!

FLAMES - THE FROZEN FLAME: BOOK THREE

CHAPTER ONE - AROUND THE FIRE

Summer 1104 SR*
(Saints Reckoning)

Athgar stared into the flames, his mind deep in thought.
"A copper for your thoughts?" said Natalia.
He gazed across at her, taking in her black hair and pale features. He had met her less than a year ago, and yet somehow, he felt as though they had known each other their entire lives. He smiled, feeling a warmth at the thought of her embrace.

"Well?" she asked. "Are you going to keep staring, or are you going to come over here and tell me your deepest thoughts?"

"I was thinking of Kargen and Shaluhk," he confessed, "though I will take you up on the offer." He rose, moving closer while she took the blanket from her shoulders, spreading it to encompass them both as he sat beside her on the log.

"They must be well on their way by now," she mused.

"I'm not so sure about that. It's not easy convincing an entire tribe to leave their home."

"They have little choice. You know the Duke of Krieghoff won't take his defeat very well. He'll retaliate. I only hope the Orcs escape in time."

"They will," said Athgar. "The Ancestors watch over them."

"Would that be the same Ancestors who sent us here?" She looked around the forest.

"They work in mysterious ways. We're on our way to Ebenstadt, remember?"

"We spent weeks crossing the mountains. Of course I didn't forget, but why? What do they have in mind for us?"

He shrugged. "I have no idea. Maybe it's better that way? What we don't know can't worry us."

"Do you believe they control us?"

"No, the Orcs are quite clear in their beliefs. The Ancestors guide them, not control them."

"With some exceptions," Natalia added.

"True. I doubt either of us will ever forget the treachery of Khurlig. Her spirit was almost the end of us all."

Natalia nodded her head thoughtfully. It wasn't so long ago that she had, with Shaluhk's help, tried to contact one of the Orc Ancestors with somewhat disastrous results. If it hadn't been for the timely intervention of Uhdrig, they both might have ended up dead, or even worse, trapped in the spirit realm forever.

Athgar saw her shudder and put his arm around her shoulder. "It's all right he soothed. "It's all over now."

She glanced around the small clearing, turning skyward to where the majestic pines gazed down on them. "I've never been one for the outdoors, but you make it quite bearable."

A spark from the fire drew their attention. "It appears the hare is almost done," he said as he reached forward, withdrawing the makeshift spear from the ground and examining its slightly burned offering. "I think I cooked it too long."

Natalia laughed, the sound echoing through the trees. "My hero, the mighty hunter. Did no one ever teach you how to cook?"

He offered her the spear. "You're welcome to give it a try?"

"I'm the city girl, remember? I spent my life at the Volstrum." She smiled, lessening the blow. "Don't worry, I'm sure there's enough unburned meat for us to survive."

He pulled forth a knife and began cutting off a thin strip.

Natalia took the tender morsel, popping it into her mouth and chewing. "Not bad," she said, "but it could use some spice."

"I'll give you spice," he said, lowering the spear. He leaned in close, kissing her even as she tried to chew. They both fell back from their makeshift perch into the leaves and pine needles that blanketed the forest floor.

Natalia shrieked out with laughter, Athgar soon joining in the merriment. Eventually, they fell silent, each looking into the other's eyes.

"I would rather be here with you than anywhere else in the world," she said.

"I feel the same." He was about to say more, but when he felt the prick of a metal point at the back of his neck, he froze.

Natalia turned her head slightly to see the tip of a spear only a finger's breadth from her face. Her eyes drifted up the wooden shaft to where strong, green hands gripped the weapon. A massive Orc stood staring down at them while his two companions held the spears. He knelt, bringing his face close to Athgar's.

"*He has the grey eyes of the Torkul,*" the Orc announced in the guttural speech of his race.

"*Greetings,*" said Athgar, using the same language. "*I am Athgar, of the Orcs of the Red Hand.*"

A look of surprise erupted on the Orc's face. "*You speak our language! What manner of magic is this?*"

"*It's not magic,*" insisted Athgar. "*I am a member of the tribe. Move your spears, and I shall prove it.*"

The Orc looked at one of his companions. "*This is most unexpected.*"

"*It is a trick, Urughar,*" insisted his comrade. "*A trap set by the Torkul. Do not trust him.*"

The Orc turned his attention to Natalia. "*And what of this female?*" asked Urughar. "*She is not of the Torkul.*"

"*Is she his prisoner?*"

"*No,*" said Athgar, "*she is my bondmate.*"

Urughar turned his attention back to the Therengian. "*You know our culture, I will grant you that, but give me a good reason why I should not kill you both here, right now.*"

"*I know the way of your people,*" the Human replied. "*It is not the Orc custom to kill uninjured prisoners. Take us to your chieftain, and let the tribe decide our fate.*"

The Orc stood, stretching his back while looking around the pine forest. He glanced at the third Orc, a somewhat rotund fellow. "*What think you, Ogda?*"

"*Let Kirak decide,*" he replied. "*It is not for us to make that decision.*"

Urughar looked back at Athgar. "*It seems my companions wish to take you back to Ord-Ghadrak. If you give us any problems, I shall have you killed on the spot. Is that clear?*"

Athgar turned to Natalia. "They want to take us to a place called Ord-Ghadrak. I'm assuming it's the name of their village."

"And then?" she asked.

"I imagine we'll meet their chieftain."

"Will your torc keep us safe?"

He instinctively put a hand to his neck where the golden necklace lay beneath his clothes. It had been a gift from Kargen to symbolize his close ties with the Orcs of the Red Hand, a sure sign he was held in high esteem. But now, amongst these new Orcs, he wondered if they would recognize it. He and Natalia had been expecting to arrive in a Human city, not an Orc village. So he had hidden it, for such open displays of Orc culture might be seen as provocation amongst Humans.

"Orc tribes have many differences," he announced. "I can't guarantee we'll see the same sort of reception as we had in Ord-Kurgad."

"I wish Kargen and Shaluhk were here," said Natalia. "They'd know what to do."

A spear pressed close, eliciting a wince from Athgar as the point drew blood.

"*Silence!*" the Orc roared. "*Now, get to your feet. We have a long way to travel, and darkness will soon be upon us.*"

ABOUT THE AUTHOR

Paul J Bennett (b. 1961) emigrated from England to Canada in 1967. His father served in the British Royal Navy, and his mother worked for the BBC in London. As a young man, Paul followed in his father's footsteps, joining the Canadian Armed Forces in 1983. He is married to Carol Bennett and has three daughters who are all creative in their own right.

Paul's interest in writing started in his teen years when he discovered the roleplaying game, Dungeons & Dragons (D & D). What attracted him to this new hobby was the creativity it required; the need to create realms, worlds and adventures that pulled the gamers into his stories.

In his 30's, Paul started to dabble in designing his own roleplaying system, using the Peninsular War in Portugal as his backdrop. His regular gaming group were willing victims, er, participants in helping to playtest this new system. A few years later, he added additional settings to his game, including Science Fiction, Post-Apocalyptic, World War II, and the all-important Fantasy Realm where his stories take place.

The beginnings of his first book 'Servant to the Crown' originated over five years ago when he began a new fantasy campaign. For the world that the Kingdom of Merceria is in, he ran his adventures like a TV show, with seasons that each had twelve episodes, and an overarching plot. When the campaign ended, he knew all the characters, what they had to accomplish, what needed to happen to move the plot along, and it was this that inspired to sit down to write his first novel.

Paul now has four series based in his fantasy world of Eiddenwerthe and is looking forward to sharing many more books with his readers over the coming years.

Printed in Great Britain
by Amazon

22945795R00171